Blood Will Have Its Season

Joseph S. Pulver, Sr.

Blood Will Have Its Season

Hippocampus Press

New York

"A Line of Questions"—in *Tales of Lovecraftian Horror* No. 11 (Eastertide 1999); in French as "Une File de questions," translated by C. Thill in *En compaignie du Roi en jaune* (August 1999); in *Rehearsals for Oblivion* (Dimensions Books, 2006); in *Terror Tales* No. 1 (February 2000), online zine.

"I, Like the Coyote"—in *dreams and nightmares* No. 58 (January 2001).

"Orchard Fruit"—in *Tales of Lovecraftian Horror* No. 11 (Eastertide 1999).

"The Night Music of Oakdeene"—in *Al-Azif* No. 3 (May/June 1998); in *Nightscapes* No. 12 (January 2000), online zine; in *Cthulhu Creatues* (JnJ Publications/Rainfall Books, 2007).

"Chasing Shadows"—in *Nightscapes* No. 8 (July 2, 1998), online zine; in *Al-Azif* No. 2 (March/April 1998).

"The Black Litany of Nug and Yeb"—in *Nightscapes* No. 2 (April 10, 1998), online zine; as read by Bob Price for the *Strange Aeons* CD by Stormclouds (August 2000); in *The Book of Eibon* (Chaosium, 2002).

"An Engagement of Hearts"—in French as "A mon bien-aimé," translated by C. Thill in *En compaignie du Roi en jaune* (August 1999).

"W a t e r   l i li e s"—in *frission* No. 18 (Summer 2000).

"Lovecraft's Sentence"—in *Midnight Shambler* No. 5 (Eastertide 1997).

"The Faces of She"—in *Al-Azif* No. 4 (February 1999); in French as "Les Visages d'Elle"—translated by C. Thill in *En compaignie du Roi en jaune* (August 1999).

"A Spider in the Distance"—in *Studies in the Fantastic* No. 1 (July 2008).

Published by Hippocampus Press
P.O. Box 641, New York, NY 10156.
http://www.hippocampuspress.com

Cover art by Thomas S. Brown. Interior illustration by Stanley S. Sargent.
Cover design by Barbara Briggs Silbert.
Hippocampus Press logo designed by Anastasia Damianakos.

First Edition

1 3 5 7 9 8 6 4 2

ISBN 978-0-9814888-8-2

contents

To my friend—*Brother!*—Bob Price!!

Who has stood by my side in the fields where the plagues burn
and nEvEr stopped believing in me.

Hail beelzeBOB!! !

"in starless cities of insanity, and their slums . . . my awe-struck little deer and I have gone frolicking."

—Thomas Ligotti, "The Frolic"

Foreword

I first met Joe Pulver at the H. P. Lovecraft Film Festival in Portland, Oregon, in early October 2007. In all honesty, I was a bit apprehensive at the meeting: some years ago, I had written a far from charitable review of his Cthulhu Mythos novel, *Nightmare's Disciple* (1999), and so I would not have been surprised if Joe had greeted me with a swift right hook to the chin—as, indeed, I perhaps deserved. Instead, the gracious Mr. Pulver wanted nothing more than to sit down over some beers and shoot the bull about matters weird, Lovecraftian, and so forth.

At that festival, Joe took the opportunity to give a public reading of some of his newer work: he had recently turned to short fiction of a sort very different from his novel, and I for one was interested to see how he would work in this new medium. The story he read was, I believe, a version of "Carl Lee and Cassilda."

I was—in the parlance of the streets—blown away.

Joe Pulver had found his voice. Not only does his imagination work best in the short form, but his prose is also perfectly suited to the kind of grippingly intense, take-no-prisoners pungency that he displays throughout this book. The subject matter of his stories may be at times almost unbearably grim—the shattered lives of crack whores; the hard-bitten anomie of serial killers; the hate-fueled relentlessness of those who seek to avenge, and avenge with extreme prejudice, the grisly murders of their loved ones—but Joe has a remarkable talent for lacing his cheerless scenarios with an unexpected flash of poignant metaphor or prose-poetry that suddenly infuses a scintillating beauty into what would otherwise be merely depressing. Every single work in this volume—whether it be an orthodox narrative, an avant-garde experiment, or a delicately ephemeral vignette—is endowed with this kind of prose-poetry, and it is this that provides the thread of unity to what might seem a bewilderingly diverse array of themes, subjects, and approaches.

Lovecraft remains a key source of inspiration for Joe Pulver, but the alert reader will also observe another literary figure lurking in the background of many of these tales—the Robert W. Chambers of *The King in*

Yellow. And yet, Joe's tales of Cassilda, Cordelia, and the other characters whom Chambers invented for the mythical play that structures his 1895 collection are very far from the originals, and the tales themselves are anything but mechanical homages: Joe seems to have penetrated to the heart of the inscrutable mystery that Chambers has created in this deliberately mysterious play, so that every mention or allusion carries a wealth of implication that spreads far beyond the overt narrative. (The second time I met Joe Pulver, at the World Fantasy Convention in Saratoga Springs, N.Y., in early November 2007, I was granted the high privilege of being led by him to Chambers's grave in the nearby town of Broadalbin.)

This volume comprises a kind of re-introduction of Joseph S. Pulver, Sr., to the fantasy and horror community, and it shows what great results can be achieved by a sensitive writer who draws not only upon the inspiration of his literary predecessors but upon his own experiences in the hardscrabble world of our day and transmutes them by the alchemy of his imagination into something transcendently beautiful in spite—or, paradoxically, perhaps even because—of its chilling subject matter. The prose of Joe Pulver can take its place with that of the masters of our genre—Poe, Lovecraft, Campbell, Ligotti—while his imaginative reach is something uniquely his own.

—S. T. Joshi

Blood Will Have Its Season

Choosing

for A. V. and R. L. T.

We are a simple, broken people. We live like frightened animals in caves
and tunnels. Above us lie the great mountains of rubble left in the wake of
the Storm: the great city where our forefathers once lived; crowded together, but believing they were their own masters.

On the third day of each cycle, the High-Priest, Uhuot, comes from
the hills beyond the ruined city to claim a new bride for his master, Assatur. And we the Conquered, freely—for what can we do?—give him one
of our own. The day after he has come, we utter silent curses against the
horde of Terrible-Beings he serves; Uagio Tsotho, Shupnikkurat, Kas-
Ogthqa, and the other titans who it is said descended from the stars and
rose from seas on the day the New World was born.

❉

The time of the Giving drew near and so the Council came together to
begin the Choosing again. The women were gathered together. Numbers
were painted on their foreheads. Then each council member walked among
them and selected three. Afterward the members of the council sat by a fire
and decided who would be Assatur's new bride.

On this day, my Lily was chosen. Fear and rage took my thoughts.
My Lily cast into that midnight of pain. Had I been a bolder man like my
father . . .

I stood there for an hour as the men of the council compared each
woman. Once or twice I heard a council member comment on one of the
women. I dared to hope; I hoped they would select the blonde, number
fourteen, or the scarred redhead who bore the number forty-one on her
brow. But in my heart I knew none of these women compared to my Lily.
Even in rags she was something brilliant.

Like the season of death moving among us, they rose and walked to
the women. Langer, senior among them, with tears in his eyes—he always
cried; he'd given both his wife and daughter—spoke. "She, who the Coun-

cil has numbered twelve, will be Assatur's bride." Never a name after the Choosing, just She.

I was scared. For her. For me. More for me. How much darkness can a man breathe in before he suffocates? What light would I now find in this dungeon?

I thought to cry out, but Lily looked at me and I was silent. She had accepted it. So must I, her eyes said.

To keep me from taking her, or to keep her from running, she was held—guarded night and day—near the spot Langer lived on. I told Langer I would stay with her. He nodded. I could see the remembering in his eyes.

Food and water were brought to us. The days of waiting began.

✤

"You will not come to the Giving. You must promise me. . . . I could not bear to see you." There were tears in her dark eyes.

"I—"

"Promise me."

"But we could run."

"Where would we go?" she asked.

I lied to her. "We'll find a place."

"Where? Outside? And how would we survive in the wilds Outside?"

I had no answer. She put her hand on my cheek as if I were the one who needed comforting.

"Promise me."

And I did. But I knew in my mind I would watch the Giving from a distance. I think she knew it too.

Our conversations on leaving ended—

Huddled in our bed of rags, we spent our last night together. With our eyes closed we took pleasure in each other.

As the voices of morning rose around me, I was instructed to leave her. She cried as we embraced. Then I was gone. Too frightened to look back, I never saw her last look.

An hour or two must have passed, but I did not notice. I stood just inside the entrance of a tunnel. Waiting.

Then came the procession. I could see the priest and his men. As fearless as a disease moving through children, they walked among the clans.

There stood Langer. With no ceremony he gave Lily to the beasts. She made no sound I could hear. She never looked up. Hands tied before her with a rope, Lily followed where they led.

I ran down the tunnel. My fear stayed closer than my shadow. My rage was silent.

✸

I have lived for twenty-five days with the pain of losing my cherished, Lily. She was the only light, the only tenderness, I had ever known. Now, as the Council of our necropolis comes together to pick another woman for the Giving, I cannot bear the thought of one more of our wives, or daughters, or sisters, being taken for the evil frolics of the Red Circus. Often as Uhuot looks over our women with his hungry eyes, my people have heard his guards and retainers speak of the cruel horrors our women undergo. We know we can do nothing, for even the great armies of our fathers' fathers were meaningless on the day when the Storm came. But we dream. The members of our Council whisper, "Oppression is a forge." Perhaps? But the steel it makes is weak. Flawed.

Tomorrow I will leave here and, with this hard black hate in my heart, travel into the foothills to find the city Uhuot calls Karakossa. And there, like a rat, rushing through alleys and squirming through cracks and walls, find a way to plunge the blade of my knife into the priest's heart.

In a world of insanity made flesh, I sit in the dark and cry. I hope Lily, now and forever, rests in a land of peace. I know I will not.

Carl Lee & Cassilda

Scissors telling Mama the Truth . . . A white court house in a small white town; hard men in dark suits with cold ugly eyes behind unsightly horn-rimmed eyeglasses, and a host of questions . . . The bells of a church—a white church with a white cross—ringing . . . Then Inside Dr. Archer's asylum; brutes in starched whites with cold ugly blue eyes, and bitchy, skinny-ass nurses with pills, and later, after the attack on fat, bouncy Nurse Barbara, needles. A lifetime commitment; Violent Ward, Room 1.

Shut away for eleven years in Dr. Archers' asylum . . . AND—

Fourteen days in The Room (this last time). White room, glaring light overhead; false light, blinding light. Night and day the artificial white light blazed, unless he closed his eyes. Fourteen days, lying on the white floor, back to the white door. Beyond the white door, beyond the sterile white halls and the crowded wards, and Dr. Archer's office, and the caretaker's bungalow, the highway, and the desert with its good-for-nothing little towns of tattered no-names. The great painted desert; hungry lizards slash-ing across shimmering, shamanic sands; rebel cactus under siege; road-houses; hombres; the survival games of bugs and scorpions and birds and mice and rattlesnakes; and the line in the sand, on the other side, winter in Mexico. Fourteen days under the glare of Dr. Archer's cold dark eyes be-hind unsightly horn-rimmed eyeglasses. Fourteen days in doubt's icy shadow, pressed by endless questions about The Book, its Truth, and Mama: "Where did you first—When did you—Why did you—Were you—What do you remember about—Did you—Didn't you—Did she—Do you have—Tell me about—" Fourteen days staring at Dr. Archer's face of steel. Beneath it, curves and layers and blood, and white glistening bone. Fourteen days. Pills and needles and questions—fourteen days, con-sciousness blurred. Tired. Bound in white restraints, the straps cutting. At times afraid, fumbling with guilt, weakening. Suffocating on the doctor's pronouncements. DYING? Wanting! Wanting scissors, or a knife. Even a fork would do. Fourteen days, face to face with exhausting judgment; just to be free from Dr. Archer's moving teeth and tongue, rattling with their incessant inquisition . . .

He wanted night. Night with black stars shining. Endless shimmering night, standing on a balcony with Cassilda. Sweet, radiant Cassilda, smiling. Her pale yellow gown fluttering in the midnight breeze.

I'll never give up my Dream. Never betray Cassilda.

He looks at Dr. Archer. Sees the Truth standing behind him, takes strength from it. Hears another question coming . . .

I've been poisoned before. Let them come.

"Give me fourteen more days if you like. But I will never give up my Dream."

Cassilda, I have been faithful to you . . .

●

I am far saner than my captor—Doctor,
Thief! He took the book from me.
I spit on him!
I would bite and claw him.
Cut out His EYES.
Cut out His TONGUE. Pull out His TEETH.
Show him the Truth. See him blister in my gaze!
I would leave his flesh for the insects, his bones for the sun!
I would cast his empty philosophies in Truth's black flame,
    if only free . . .
        Free!—*Star-chasing, dream-chasing*
            in dream-time.
      There—on fire, I am a star—I devour the colors of space;
           my hand holds the infinite . . .

Cassilda, I know the Truth. I have seen the Place Where the Black Stars Hang in my dreams. Have no fear, Sweet Princess, I'll find you. I'll find a way through this maze of lies. I'll find the road to Carcosa.

●

First the careless orderly—on the white wall, powerful red words:

Dear Dr. Archer,
    I've been called to the Court of Truth by Cassilda.

Then the old-goat caretaker and his fat wife, curves and layers and blood, and white glistening bone. More powerful words on a white wall:

Dear Dr. Archer,

You wanted to see the Truth, to understand it. Never fear, one day, the Truth will come for you. It will stand before you and reveal itself. Watch for it.

Through the gate, looking back and smiling at Dr. Archer's office window. On the road. The long walk, frying in the leer of afternoon, under the blameless Big Blue Sky. Just another tourist with blinking eyes.

Rushing through clusters of struggling scrub trees and scraggly fields, slightly winded, but free. A road. Houses, not close together. Porches with disinterested shadows. A basking cat, not sight or sound of dogs. He needs momentary shelter and clothes. And a car. Picks a house with outdated apparel drying on the line. A kindly old woman, physically, not unlike his mother, gives him a cool drink of water. He shows her the Truth. Takes his time, peeling away the mask. Takes her husband's clothes, some food, yesterday's newspaper, and her car.

Two hours on the road. Driving carefully. Driving by motels and fast food joints, listening to All-News radio. Leaves the car near a busy truck stop. He gets a ride to Reno. Walks a bit, watching the cars flash past. He flashes his thumb in reply.

❈

Another shithole cheap room with a cheap chair and a hard bed—and the sounds of working hookers oozing in bursts through the thin walls.

Hand shaking as he reaches for the glass. Cheap whiskey. The solid shadow in the darkest fragment of the room swallows and lets the burn soothe him. The glass is too slow, he takes long draws from the pint bottle. He loves the burn, hates the fire of pressure behind his eyes.

Two fingers part the cheap curtain. Eyes that look straight into everything survey the parking lot—two pick-ups and a van—taking in the on/off neon, illuminating rust and dents. Next door a shout and the sound of a slap. Then a "Fuck you" and another strike. Muffled crying.

She probably deserved it, he thinks.

His fingers come away from the curtain and he turns to the bed. The flickering light of the TV flickers on the wrinkles and folds and long curves, pale and red. *She deserved it. She lied.* She smiled, then lied. Wanted money. *Just like the others.*

Two more pulls from the whiskey bottle and he turns down the radio's city songs and turns up the sound of the B-movie on the TV to silence the disagreement next door.

"Whores." *Sotto voce,* as hurtful and ugly as the breeze in Death's yard.

He puts on his boots and buckles his belt buckle. In the bathroom he rinses the blade of his knife and washes his hands, watches the diluted blood find its way down into darkness. Looks in the cracked mirror and traces the scorpionlike tattoo on his chest with his finger.

"Cassilda." A silent howl.

◆

His thumb flashed. A cloud of dust with the wind—no ride. His boot kicked up more dust. Twenty-two cars and trucks in the last hour and no ride. He was going to fry in this heat. Why didn't it ever rain here?

Didn't matter. He was on his way to the other coast. New Orleans. Jacksonville. Miami, it rained there. That's where she was. Someplace cooler. Six dead women from Barstow to San Antone and it had taken him this long to figure it out.

He'd seen Cassilda on the TV at the end of the bar; just once since he'd got out, just for a few seconds. She was as cool as autumn twilight. She hadn't used many words, but her eyes spoke to him. They said, "I'm waiting for you, Carl Lee." So he finished his beer and headed out. L.A. hadn't been a waste after all.

To no particular where, just went. Stepped right into August like it was a voyage or a baptism. Stopped in his cheap room, grabbed his stuff and left. Somewhere down the road he'd find her. The wind would take him to her.

The wind had taken him all across This Nation these past months. He'd been to Vegas and Illinois. Seen an Indian in Laredo, Texas, and niggers everywhere. Watched the dissatisfied compromise and the desperate cheat. He'd slept in alleys and along the highways; saw some crows pickin' at dead-cat-pie in a cemetery; hid from the rain one night in Ruby's Diner with Big Joe and Frank, watchin' the nighthawks drown cigarette butts in cold coffee while the all-night radio bedtime story barked sermons and scandals; fought off flies come to his sardines and bourbon picnic one afternoon while five gleaming kids ran barefoot through a sandlot yelling "Whee!" He'd seen the Grand Canyon, and screwballs whine about double-dealers. Heard crap enough to brainwash the boxcar hermits inta believin' their Mad Dog was Saint Teresa's piss. Been in and outta small towns and through railroad yards, walked by shy Spanish maidens, cowboy hats, and cotton galore . . . Worked or stole every once and again. He liked working better, but they would never leave him alone—always had to talk at him. Get this; pull that; over there. "So, what'dal-ya have? I ain't got all night" from twelve dozen skinny-ass waitresses who were as empty-lookin' as closed-down gas stations. HURRY-HURRY-HURRY. Like fast ever got anyone anywhere.

"Damn barstool sons-a-bitches, rattlin' so the drunk at their elbow won't know they're empty. Free Country, my ass . . . Squawkin' and bitchin' costs plenty."

But Cassilda didn't complain. Just one quick look that afternoon in the bar and he knew it. Nope, she wouldn't think of it. She was quite and re-spectful. Knew what to say and when to say it. Knew how to please a man. He knew she could cook and sew, and mind her Ps & Qs. Didn't scream no Holy Bible shit, wouldn't bitch and bitch and bitch about money, and sure wouldn't screw around with other men.

❀

The wind eased and a car stopped. Carl Lee smiled and threw his gear in the backseat. Willie Nelson was on the radio singin' about being to sick to pray. The young woman said, "Hi. My name's Laura Mae." And wouldn't shut up.

They headed East.

Carl Lee left her in a culvert in Arkansas. At the edge of a swampy pond he washed his hands and cleaned his knife. Forty minutes later he ditched her car.

His thumb flashed. Through Stamps and Crosett and Eudora. Stayed overnight in Onward, Mississippi. Another cheap motel with a cheap chair and hard bed, but it was quiet. He walked to the bar down the road. The bartender wore unsightly horn-rimmed glasses just like Dr. Archer's. Smiled dead-cold, just like Dr. Archer. He was quick to down his drink and go back to his room, away from temptation, away from questions.

Fully clothed. Knife beside him. TV off. Laid on that hard bed staring at the ceiling. Sweating; no fan, no air conditioning. Knowing she was wait-ing. Knowing she wanted him to come to her—Cassilda had everything ready for him.

He soaked a wash towel in cool water. Wrung it out and laid it on his forehead. He dozed.

Cassilda's fingers were cool. She had nice hands, nice soft hands. She didn't talk, just smiled, just like soft autumn sunshine. All this heat and she looked fresh as a daisy in her yellow print dress. The soft cotton moved with her. She handed him a glass of lemonade, beads like diamonds on it. She made him feel like a king.

He woke and rolled over. Looked around, rubbed his eyes, yawned. Thunder off in the distance. He went back to sleep.

His mother—thirty-four years of Arizona long nights—was wanderin' 'round the kitchen. Mutterin' to herself just like always. All that talk of Daddy, and lying men; rough hands and hard breath. She was skinning a rabbit. Blood on her hands. She wiped away a tear, left a blood scar. Mama called him. She didn't look up from the carcass, just called his name, "Carl Lee, you come and fetch some onions."

Mama was hummin' along with the slow country song on the West Texas radio station; at the bridge she muttered something about the curse of love. Both sounded like wind in the wire.

Out beyond the screen door by the gas pump, tires digging gravel, an old yellow dog in the back of a pick-up. The dog barked, flashed its teeth, and he remembered going hunting with Daddy. Twice. He was seven— "Old enough now." A doe each time. Daddy's Buck knife moved through the hide. Daddy peeled it back. The curve of muscle, white glistening bone. Blood. Carl Lee thought, this is what things really look like under the hair, and smiles—

He was wide awake. The late-morning sun lightening the pale curtains and the yellowing wallpaper. In the bathroom he splashed water on his face and drank a glass of water. He wanted a drink, settled for bacon and eggs and white-bread toast and black coffee.

On the road again. A ride with a quiet man in a loud truck. East. The panhandle of Florida. Soon he'd be in it. She was waiting. Only tomorrow or the next day away now.

Thumb out. Heels on hot tar. One town and another. Night. Still hot, not cooler. Red and white bar lights. Beer signs. He went inside.

Two drunk fools waltzin' across the floor, laughing. His drink in his hand. Reflected light in the wet rings on the bar. Laughing girls, curves and layers and blood, and white glistening bone. That's what they really looked like under the hair and the smiles. Movement in the mirror behind the bottles. He passed the whiskey over lips. Felt the burn. Washed it down with a beer, dreamed of lemonade. He left with a doe-eyed divorcée.

She unbuttoned her dress and let her hair down. Smiled. LIES—

All those sons-a-bitches jawin', Mama and her school-girl/movie-

*picture glamour magazine dreams, and her book learnin'—always talkin'
about romance stories she'd read and movies she'd seen, all of princes and
damsels and far-away places with strange names, and IF ONLY. That's
what drove his Daddy off—*

"It's OK, darlin'. Happens sometimes."

It happened. Curves and layers and blood, and white glistening bone.

*Mama, she'd lied about Cassilda and the book. And it happened.
Curves and layers and blood, and white glistening bone.*

Carl Lee sat in a cheap chair in her rented trailer. He drank her whiskey and looked at her laying there. She wasn't lying now. He put his hand
on her jaw and turned her head, looked at the truth in her eyes. He turned
on the radio by the bed, the slow country song sounded like wind in the
wires.

He tried to count how many he'd met. How many looked like Cassilda, but weren't. He shoulda known, the painted nails and painted lips
and bottle-blonde dye-jobs, and they drank beer—some right from the bottle—or whiskey, never lemonade.

Carl Lee heard the rain outside. Thought about spending the night.
There was still half a bottle left . . . But Cassilda was waiting. He went into
the bathroom and washed the blood from his knife. Washed his hands.
Watched the diluted blood find its way down into darkness. He looked in
the mirror and traced the scorpionlike tattoo on his chest with his finger.

"Cassilda," he howled silently.

Then he was out driftin' with the wind. Headlights approaching.

His thumb flashed.

❖

He deposits his small gesture in the mailbox. The fourteenth postcard
to the inquisitioner with cold dark eyes behind unsightly horn-rimmed eyeglasses. In powerful red words, each asks the same question:

Dear Dr. Archer,

    Are you watching?

(*for Alice Cooper and Robert Bloch*)

A Line of Questions

"Is journey's end beyond the endless crashing waves,
    or the turn?
    Is it in the house of ruin?"
One traveler on the road to yearning asked.

The girl with eyes only as deep as a mirror
    turned to him.
    "I see only rare colors in the shadows of
            Dim Carcosa."
Her pale smile was full of quiet departures.

She opened her umbrella—
    Beneath it, the Milky Way was a whirlpool of crystal tears.
He walked off
    to hunt in lake-mists rising—on the murmuring breeze—
    like the frayed edges of once elegant draperies.

"Which broken mystery comes next?"
    she asked, changing her tongue.
"What comes after the lost song?"
    the next in line asked.
"The fullness of dense fog and final sunset."
"I've lost Day in unfamiliar wind."
"Dissolution's endless melody is always breathtaking."
"Farewell, Remembering."
"Goodbye, Day," the oracle replied,
    as she turned to face the next
    unmasked, tattered
                stranger.

PITCH nothing . . .

Night, not dark—PITCH nothing . . . THIS room? / dimension? / *Enchantment?* was empty, or was it? He <u>couldn't</u> decide—he wanted to—he did! But in its cold hand, in the stillness, THIS stillness, he was confused. He wanted to retreat from THIS substance-invisible, he didn't want to be a victim in THIS unaccountable place. He didn't want to crumple under the predatory coolness. He'd had enough of THIS Experience. More than plenty—

He looked up, hoping [Need! clinging to it] to see the ghost of a chance or seraphim or stars— Shouldn't there be stars? There had been stars above in other places. He'd seen them, heard others mention them; he owned a book with their names in it. He'd looked through the lenspiece and seen them twinkle blue, and bright yellow, and red-orange, and white, pale far-away white.

It was this cold [CONFUSION] it was EXTREME and wearisome. And IT [the **BLACK**] gleamed? How could IT gleam? IT wasn't a color, wasn't a Thing . . . NOT a Form. IT didn't—<u>couldn't!</u>—have parts or guts or feelings [OR thoughts]. IT <u>couldn't</u> strike you. But it had. *How?*

"Damn!" It was like IT had a language. And some child—perhaps angry with the world—had translated it. And it made sense *somehow* . . . IT was self-sustainingandendless. THIS unfillable darkness was deliberate.

Deliberate as Fate. "Another cold bastard."

"I want out!" . . . "You hear me?" . . . "Now." Not even a swiftly thinning echo for reply. Only—THIS riot of bleak decanted, existing *before?* and *after?* and *outside?* everything.

He reached out, with no elegance and certainly not tentatively. If he could just touch a wall, or stumble into an object, he could feel his way out. He had to do it soon, before his numb hands <u>couldn't</u> feel anything at all. And that, he felt, was soon.

"Hello?" . . . "Hello?" "i seem to be lost." . . . "Can someone help me?"

"Please?"

He wished he smoked, had a lighter or a match. He'd get out—he'd burn his way out, if there were anything in here to burn other than his exposed hands and face.

He started walking again. Directionless. One step & another. Left-right-left. Just to move. Moving was good, it was like whistling—people whistled in the dark. He knew that. [*Don't they?*] You knew you were alive. He wanted to know he was alive—had to know. Wasn't there a stairway or a wall [some nook, or corner that could identified as having detail?] Or a door? Just one door, that's all he wanted—Just one door. If there was a door, there was a path to change. and change was a way out.

OK, he'd experienced it. Done. Fine. That was that—EXIT stage. NOW.

Still moving—*faster!*—walking, soon to be running. Then FASTER still—not up [that he could tell], and not down. *Around?* It didn't seem he even turned—not hot on the heels of his own heels; just moving . . . Or maybe he was running in place and couldn't see it? He stopped. Reached down to touch—nothing . . . He stood on [*nothing? It can't be. It just can't!*]. He stretched, shivered, twirled around, looked up[no gray, no flicker] looked down [only more identical **BLACK** nothing]. Rapidly blinked his eyes several times, as if to clear or refocus them. Yelled. No change occurred. He was still cold, still blind. Still surrounded by THIS scheming PITCH nothing . . . and Its intentions.

Didn't IT understand the effect it had on him?

Couldn't IT feel his surging swell of alarm?

"OK." "No more mysteries." "Silence your barren litany and fade now."

Why had he ventured into this secret? There was no money in it.

He closed his eyes to see if the **BLACK**ness would lighten/CHANGE. nothing—PITCH nothing . . .

THIS emptiness was more than dark. IT was transcendent blank, the directionless abyss All disappeared in. He couldn't argue with IT — couldn't frighten IT —couldn't shatter IT. Maybe IT was broken-hearted [closedinonitself]?

Broken-hearted, desirous Night—Isn't there some poem?

> '*Even Night,*
> *as radiant*
> *as a star and a kiss and a rose*

                    and the colors of a peacock,
        with her white moon
                and sad fountains
                and frayed rope ladder arias
        to absent, deceiving Oblivion—out sighing with the angels of Doom,
                has prayers.

        They flutter atop
                the sounds of bones and flutes and lost bells,
                        as she dreams
                                of gentle Morpheus
                                        and
                                            sleep.'

        Maybe IT <u>couldn't</u> understand?
        Make IT understand:
        How? "Don't You feel cold?" "Wouldn't You like to see/sense/
touch—?" "gray?" "Images?"
        No reply at all.
        How could THIS much space be so claustrophobic?
        How could THIS rampage of nothing be so absolute?
        Just keep talking: "Look." "i'm here." "Can You hear me?" "i'm sorry
i intruded." "Can't you forgive my transgression?" "i won't hurt You."

                                ✱

HE'D COME to the house at the invitation of
the old man. The old man in the bookshop
seemed anxious—he thought at the time—to show
him The Book. Once he saw it, he could tell
Tuey and that would be that. He wouldn't have
to hear about it again.
        This was Tuey's fault. The sly infection
left by his extended conjectures, the (occasionally absurd) debates on *Being* and *Nothingness*. And Tuey's damned book—

Tuey, A. H. 1955 *Religion, Witchcraft, and Science: Speculations on the Nature of the Night* (Hollister, Calif.: Mellaart House).

He rang the bell four times and waited. The old man said, "Come at 8—Sharp." Right out of an old silent screamer the door opened. And there was the old man—he too, right out of an old silent screamer. He was ushered in; down a series of long halls, paintings of wrong land-scapes cut like windows to gardens common men were gladly unaware of, hung only on the left walls. It seemed they wandered for miles, not talking, just walking; young coming after old, as if to catch up. He wanted to ask questions, but . . . Then they were in the muscular nightworld of a library, four enormous kero-sene lanterns suspended by thick ropes offer-ing limited plots of light. Four solid walls of books (row upon row, lacking recesses or even a single two or three inch hollow, but secrets/mirrors, exhaustive as wine—all wait-ing for the unfolding); no carpet, no desk, no chessboard, not even a bust, just four walls of books. Old books, big books, leather and cloth, red spined, yellow spined, black and indigo and sand (those bound in lighter skins were, or seemed, thin). The thin ones brought to mind Tuey's far-reaching collection of 17th and 18th century pamphlets on the higher mys-teries of This or the hidden leaves of That; each tractate seemingly written by Anonymous and bearing a seventy-three word—or longer—title in German or French.

There were two three-legged stools near the far corner. Not big leather chairs, perhaps constructed for Paul Bunyan or the nameless giants of some old legend from the young man's childhood, just two plain wooden stools. They sat, the guest and the old man. Face to face without a word between them; young seeking, old simply being.

A flat even voice, old pacing itself: "Would you care for something to drink?"

Higher pitched than the other, expectant youth quick to everything: "Thank you, no."

The old man shrugged. Then turned and spoke into the mouthpiece of a flexible silver tube suspended from the ceiling. "I'd like something hot to drink." "Nothing for my visitor." The old man smiled faintly but spoke no further.

Perhaps his voice was tired? Should he ask him? Should he wait a bit? (*OK. A little longer. Can't hurt?*) He watched the shadows on the old man's face and chest. He looked for an opening, an edge to pull on. But he just sat, waiting in the absence of sound. Even when he shifted on his stool like the edge of a shadow, NO sound. He felt like he sat with a refugee too tired from his forced march to speak.

He wished the old man had a clock with delicate chimes in this room or a snoring dog . . . (The room needed a roaring fireplace. Maple or apple-wood spitting and popping like hellfires ablaze would be nice.) or an old woman would slowly shuffle in with the old man's hot drink, coughing and clattering the tray. He wished there were a window—huge or thin or any—with crazy moonrays of white crashing through, wished for a sky with snow or rain, or the gusts of a mouser in kittenish pursuit of a dust dervish.

I know the old are quiet in their ways, slow . . . They have so little time, yet waste so much of it.

"So, young man" . . . "You want to see *The Book of Night*."

"Yes. Please."

The old man says: "The night of *this* world is merely a shadow of *Night*."

The younger man, familiar with autumn twilight, hiding places, and a Nevermore or two, nods as if he understands. But he doesn't understand.

The old man turns away and looks up, as if some Thing rests high in the shadows. "You do understand, I hope, Oblivion is not gentle." "It does not sleep." . . . "There are no sad fountains. No moons spinning light in the dark deeps. It contains no black angels hunting and gathering. Doom does not sigh. . . . Night is the Annihilator.—It stops the toils of the common."

"I would like to see The Book. To spend a few minutes browsing."

"Browsing?" The tone too similar to a laugh to be unintended, a laugh more instructive than any book. "There is little to see . . . But as you wish."

Suddenly there: an old woman, quiet as a silhouette, with the old man's drink—tea in a Russian tea glass on a small oval tray of tarnished silver.

She didn't speak, nod, or even turn to look at the younger man. Nor did the old man say a word to her. And like a thought aborted before it could reveal any splash of shape, any demonstration of intent, she was gone . . . The old man looked at the tea for a time. He took a sip, brightened momentarily, then faded to his old self.

A (long?) soundless gap (one empty minute or 6?). No words, no intrusive actions.

As if a slow fluid shadow, the old man

rose; his shape, wilted more than bent, seemed
hollow. Fitting, this relic embalmed in years
should be the shepherd of all this ink and paper. All the words of momentum, of action and
circumstance and success won and lost . . .
and he had The Book. The old man found The
Book, as if he'd been led to it, or solved a
puzzle. He didn't touch it right away, just
looked. As if making preparations.

"Yes, yes." Bobbing head, agreeing with his
words. "Behold nature," the old man muttered.

Dry fingers that knew error and pain, and
perhaps once beauty, before the angel of dusk
ravaged their immortality with thorns and hammers, eased it from the stack.

He carried it with two hands, carried it
the way a holy man would carry an icon. Halfway back to the stools he paused (looked confused—lost), looked up at the acute shadows
embracing the corner near the ceiling again.
Nodded, ever so slightly. His fingers shifted.
And he moved, now carrying The Book in a way
some carry a memory or a malady.

The old man handed the younger The Book.
(Torch passed, the younger laughed to himself,
careful not to smile.) Not a word or a mark on
the cover. The spine bore no legend. It didn't
look old. Not even worn . . . Just a plain
black book, not even heavy; seemingly too
slight to bear any Great Truth(s). Tuey was
mistaken—*All the Answers* in this? As a child,
he'd had cheap coloring books thicker than
this.

"While you survey the contents, I've a
small matter to oversee." Back to the younger
man, he stepped away. "I'll return shortly."

"Yes. . . . Thank you."

Alone with it. The essence of midnight in
his hands for the taking—his mouth was dry.

His brow damp. He suppressed a quiet "ALL-mine!" laugh. Allowed himself to smile (outright) at the thought.

He opened The Book. **BLACK,** not pages with words, just unintelligible **BLACK** inhabiting the arena between the covers, a torrent of luminous-gleaming gushing into the room. **BLACK** [all perfect] [blindness] PITCH nothing ... filling the world.

✱

Stamping feet—rapidly as if to scare off the cold as if to banish it with circulation. [HARDLY!] IT wouldn't even budge. It wouldn't even allow echoes. this BRUTE MOUTH WAS night? this STATION OF MISERY WAS THE truth? this BLIND GREED WAS all? He was tempted to call THIS aggressive wrongness demonic, but IT seemed/was?/had to be! outside physics and philosophy, free of function and mysticism, BEYOND understanding.

Out-out-out. "I want out!" ... "I'm life's flower, i thirst for light—" "Praise it." "Rooted to its unwavering tenderness, i need it."

"Please." "Return me to the tabernacle of lustrous light and sky." "You can skip the trumpets, but—" "Please?" "Unlock your birdcage." "and bid me good-bye."

"Please?" "Is there no waking from THIS solitude in otherness?" "i need time"—*Befores . . . and afters*—"Space with definition" . . . "i—"

"please?" "please"

Light. He knew everything lived in the light, perhaps there was even a place, a chaos [if you like] where everything began. But HERE? HERE was the End—everything ended HERE—cold, alone, empty ... Saints, demons, the failures and the revelations ... THIS thing? world? solitary without cell doors or escape was the sword.

Soul-deep in an exertion of questions and fear, he was slow. Cold had him, wore him to still. IT didn't mock him or see him as doomed. IT didn't take an interest in him. He was sore from IT, damned by IT. He tried to recall religion and the intent faces of the righteous ... He tried to fix on a god to pray to. But all was DARKNESS—cold PITCH nothing . . .

Silence, hitting brightly in a disquieting bondage. Losing even the creak of hoping. The "Where am i?" sluggish now. Bravado burned to death in THIS cold swollen DARKNESS ... Reaching for therapy in memories of light rushing, groping to recall free color laughing, a flash-dream of an angel, the lightning-echo stir of some safe domesticity stopped. Helpless. Tied in knots of failure. Forgetting to want to be capable again.

He wanted to sit. To lie down [ruin be damned!] and curl into a ball, hold his own warmth—or what was left of it—in his arms. If THIS sharply-focused indifference of stark [devouring] **BLACK** only had a name! Would IT hear him if he could name it? But The Book had held no names, no black marks set on paper ...

"i should have never—" Whispered, as he raised his numbed-dead hands to his lips to warm them. Little did it help. [at a loss for meaning] Burned by the chill, he imagines he hears a fluttering of wings, imagines he can smell the undreaming dead disintegrate in their crypts—wheels to run—laid out flat by his own feet. Crawling, feeling scattered ... His nerves graphic [as any aggression or humiliation] ... Feeling encased in everything (beyond reach. [Everything Here—*Wherever Here is?*—IMPOSSIBLE.] Wanting to surface in *Being* and *Time*—wanting full relief painted in charming codes—wanting THE BIG CHANGE and design; sky [blue or leaden, or filled with the lovely eyes of stars] or roof overhead, the hue and stain of measure underfoot, anything that charted balance and proclaimed industrious. Crazy with vows [NOT poems—no beauty, no beauty bright as a torch]. As much as he wanted to be done with THIS typhoon of dead calm, all he could utter was gibberish. Crazy with anxiety, ready to give it over to the idiot, waiting to croak and cry to O MOST GLORIOUS AND HIGH DEAR SWEET GOD for love.

Bastard, why hast thou forsaken me?

Trembling, shivering. He has eaten all the details of raw stillness. He has drunk all the bullets of the grave. He groans [sometimes empty puddles of silence], frantic desires from a jerking mouth [Oh—], moans [Oooooh—] in the needle-sharp dialect of panic. Groping, arms [blurred lines swinging] pushing hands in crazy circles—fingers [antennae] hunting [brushing over], almost moving past grazing an object. An It. Recognizing It as The Book—realizing he'd come in contact with The Book. He snatched it up. Held it as if it had rescued him. Just knowing another shape existed was warmth [mother's "All better now." kiss in his mind's eye]. This was his *Bible*—the first step to Homeward Bound. But this BOOK was the cause, the tumble from the furnished atmosphere of Earth to desolation, the Wicked Can't! POISON, endless hateful poison, that's what it was . . . He hated it. Wanted nothing more than to burn it, warm himself in its death. [*I'd love to see you writhe.*] [*If you had pages, I'd rip them out and rip them up.*] He closed it—snapped it shut [a blunt statement to hurl at the Awful Truth]. The **BLACK** was gone—vanished/*PTOOFF!*—just like that; the window opened—CLOSED.

HOW? WHY? He didn't care. He was back in the old man's library . . . Standing a few feet from the stools. All that running and he hadn't gone anywhere?

"Thank you." Whispered quickly to the midnight mask of shadows in the corner near the ceiling.

He was quick to set The Book on the old man's stool. Quick to step back from IT. Quick to turn away from IT.

He turned to leave The Book and the room, and the old man's house . . . The old man came back into the room and picked up The Book. He sat opposite the younger who stood. The Book in his lap like a napping cat. "Did you find it of some interest?"

His tongue couldn't raise words. (—if he could only say, "While you were gone—" "Supernatural?, hallucinatory—") He nodded and left.

On a street of rushing winds, headed toward city lights that changed the color of every picture show the eye said a huge "Yes!" to, he ran. He wanted to see people fall into the arms of their dreams. To (clearly, for days on end) hear voices—laughing or no!; to understand birds singing and modern, fragmented dialogues; needed to be outside with all the tell-tale signs of this big percussive life tooting and rumbling and abruptly buzzing, to smell coffee or gasoline or see a neon sign perform or the (lyrical summer) eyes of a young woman in love—he wanted to [BE! RESCUED!] see/hear/touch—as long as it wasn't cold! ANY movement or color or sound.

He heard a siren in the distance. Then a second joined in the alarm . . . A fire? Someone shot? A heart attack? Someone *Somewhere* was about to encounter Night—

Stock still. Wholly unnerved, throat rigid and dry.

Damaged. Sputtering thoughts clutching . . . Struggling with a hiss soon to be the voice of dust. Eyes burning with the weight of light, and fear—Slumped against a cold, dark wall, dread made him an indelible mural. He shut his eyes—gone lighthearted hands—gone paper rainbows—gone springs with sudden birds, open windows . . . Wrenched from the solid mosaic of configuration interlocked with method, his focus sickens and shifts in the cold, glutinous hands of ... **BLACK** filling 4 dimensions. **BLACK** overwhelming six senses. **BLACK** [all perfect] mountain, god, moment [all moments], silent, unmoving. and he [a small fleeting thing limited by mere perceptions] as blank and wordless/soundless as THIS so, so much, all too much, **BLACK** perfect image of obscene loneliness stretched out like a crazy mouth full of hunger words flowing.

Shaking terribly. Eyes tightly shut. Thirsting for Redemption, coveting Merciful God's good creations.

"I sought the Lord, and he heard me, and delivered me from . . . all . . . my . . . fears."

Eyes open—NO hint of yellowness . . . trace of red . . . splashes . . . or smudged/blurred images . . . or spots . . . or border areas of light . . . NO bands. NO uneven sectors. NO graininess. Just perfection [the Beginning, and the End] . . . NO horizon. NO rescue of rules in THIS cage of silence.

"O God—reprieve—just a meadow of sky—or—"

Oh God . . . God?

Feeling legless—stabbed—unable to wade through the dense arsenal of THIS godless universe. Not a cask of headstrong, not a pavilion of clever arrows, just a little thing blindfolded in the belly of the house of suffering. What he wants is the Old World [his fairyland nest of nimblesoft sensations], not the stranglehold of THIS crystal ball . . .

Out of lies, out of prayers (held close). The yelps absolutely still, the scream incubating. Drowning in THIS whole wide hazard. Everything left behind on the cardboard totem pole of Happened . . . If he had a map or a white cane. . . If there was just one stone or star in this desert . . . But all he possessed were the questions of the sick and dying and fears [the gold of Oblivion].

Dead still. Lights out. Cold. Dark silence.

"Mom?" [wishing for her exorcism, "See. There's no monster under your bed."] Trapped in a dark corner. On his knees. Whimpering: "all lost HERE." His mother's [soft summerBluesky] voice in his mind's ear: *"'The heathen are sunk down in the pit that they made.'"* How she loved the Psalms.

Repossessed by zero's fire he began to cry . . .

(*for Michael Cisco, who—gently—pushed me to*
The Experience of the Night)

I, Like the Coyote

and the sand-serpent
and all the other solitary wanderers
    —prey of the chilled emptiness
    of the Outlands,
know the voiceless arcades
of your abandoned cities
and the blood-blossom baptism
staining the dream rooms
of turbulent, treacherous
bandits
who wrecked the poem of day and sky
with their hunger and contempt.

We, narrow with misery and despair—
    moonshadows of the canyons,
    the keepers of torn secrets,
have tasted ashes,
shivered on the shore of unknowing, and
built totems along the dead roads of the hills.

In arid exile,
crumbling under the brittle gaze of the moon,
in the entrenched shadows
where the missing
is secreted away,
we—at this moment, still songs
    in the lonely fields of memory—
recall the garden
where we lived.

Blood Will Have Its Season

for Robert W. Chambers

On the stage of the Palace playhouse, four players mid-scene ACT ONE
of *The King in Yellow:*

THALE:	Camilla loves me.
UOHT:	Liar!
CASSILDA:	Camilla?
UOHT:	Ask her, if you dare.
THALE:	Who would dare, without the diadem? You're not so bold, Uoht. Have *you* found the Yellow Sign?
UOHT:	Stop your mouth!
CASSILDA:	And stop your bickering, you two frogs! . . . I will ask her.
CAMILLA:	I am not ready to be asked, mother.
CASSILDA:	No? Camilla, *you* could have the diadem. Then you could take your pick of your brothers, and we'd have an end to all our problems. See how I tempt you. The Dynasty would go on, and you'd be free of all this conniving. Perhaps, even, the siege would end. . . . Well, Camilla, speak!
CAMILLA:	No, no. Please. You cannot give the diadem to me. I will not have it.
CASSILDA:	And why not?
CAMILLA:	Then *I* would be sent the Yellow Sign.

✦

Outside the playhouse, light rain ending, and fog. Rat's eyes and other things prowl. Shadows imprison the struggling breath of the gaslights. Vivid autumn winds leave few in the grasp of peace. Oblivion's evil things ride through the streets, riding the lost into the ground. The lights of the cathedral are out. Cobwebs and murmurs find shoulders . . . Turbulent thoughts and ghosts walk.

This wasn't a night for cigar smoke and the polite conversation of The Club, no Lord Woodward woolen and endless, and Misters Clarenton and Grove bricks saddling him with slow dull fogs. Need made this a night for gin and tender pink cunt laid bare.

The card in his breast pocket was a siren's call. *Where the cloud-waves break,* he thought, his addiction hot on his breast.

This was a night for hunting and dreaming . . . And conquering.

A night for kings.

"You'll find the ladies delightfully inventive. They are quite happy to christen fresh inclinations," the stranger said, as he handed Henry Thale a card with a strange red marking on it. Intermission was over and the stranger was gone as suddenly as he'd appeared.

The card said I am a table set with a feast. "To hell with a late supper." His long spider legs set off for the banquet.

Quick through the midst of Respectability Henry Thale had come from the grandiose if bleak pomp of the play. *These just-in-from-Paris amusements are so overburdened with ennui, they're a bore,* he thought. *Roll back the fog and paint dim Carcosa red. Now that, I'd go for.*

He was out of the playhouse and quick to the cobbled curb where hailed a hansom, instructing the driver to take him to the address on the alabaster card he had been given by the stranger who called himself Mr. Fox.

The air was heavy and chilled and he was inpatient with the slow even pace of the horse's hooves. His hand would find no reluctance writing with the whip. The river, the sinners, and the sleepers behind fatigued curtains passed slowly.

Four blocks from his destination he exited the cab. Walking would be faster and it would stimulate the blood. His steps were firm. The barks and coos of the street whores did not turn him.

Halfway to the address he paused to press the flaring tip of a match to his cigarette. *All this filth. Perhaps that Fox is some devilish brigand who thinks to send me into some tight corner where misadventure or skullduggery might fall upon me?* But it didn't feel that way. Henry Thale was confident in his abilities to size up strangers, it had made many a business meeting turn his way. He ground the butt of his faggot under his boot heel and walked on.

Seven steps led him to the door where he pulled on the bell-chord and waited. A barrel-chested oriental let him in the house of lust. Rail straight a woman sat at a desk in the receiving hall. He walked across an expensive Persian carpet and handed the woman silent with summers past the card with the Yellow Sign emblazoned upon it. She pointed to a staircase. A tart who had been dallying too long in the flesh trade opened the door at the top of the stairs and escorted him to her mistress's receiving room.

Candles made pools of flickering light. In one to his left, framed against a wall of lavender velvet, two ladies of a certain quality reclined on a silk divan. Their hands gentle doves as they kissed and stroked each other's nipples. Bent over, a very tall blonde adjusted her stocking—he ignored the invitation of bare shoulders and full breasts. On his right there was an Oriental girl-child with a silver chain around her neck and an older woman who was dressed in Paris's newest and finest. Neither, to his liking.

Before him in the center of this court, on a chair of scarlet and lavender, inlaid with small ivory masks, sat the mistress of this harlot's house. She was reading *Titus Andronicus*—laughing low and sweetly, when he entered. Slowly closing the volume she handed it to a retainer. She did not rise.

"I am Mistress here. The Magus who sent you calls me Cynara."

"Cynara." It rolled from his tongue like the shadow of an image almost remembered. He wondered why she was masked. Some jagged mark of the past or perhaps a deformity? Hiding a face that might be recognized at some future function? He wondered why her mask was so plain given her ornate surroundings and luxuriant attire.

Thale looked into Cynara's eyes and she into his. She was surprised he didn't look at her breasts—they all did, marveling at their size and deep roundness, they found it impossible to keep their hands, and lips, off them, no matter what indulgence they had come to her to pursue. She turned into the light, like moons offered they shone, still he took no note of her abundant charms.

This one likes boys, or very young girls, she thought. *We'll see soon enough.* "Please sit." She pulled her chair closer to his. Leaned in.

Over neat gin, he talked, she listened. Then she stood and led him through a door and outside. The street was alive—with wooden carts ready for the hearth, and dogs, and rats, and garbage. And there were flies, in places clouds of them in whorls hungry for any maggot's feast. Even at this late hour fat old women washed clothes and bent older men carried lumpy bags. There were missing fingers, limbs, and blind eyes and disease that hungered after all that man is. The street was a factory of depravity, an open sewer. But he followed. For what he wanted, he'd followed her to hell and back . . .

"It's all for sale? Everything?"

"Yes, for the true seeker every pleasure can be plucked from these streets. The lovely and the ugly, first times and The Last, each is here. I could offer you—"

"Indeed you are lovely, but I like . . . my companions younger; tiny feet, shy, fearful smiles."

"Shy we have. Feet or quinny, that is for you to decide upon. All that is required is The Payment. And I can tell by your sartorial flare, you've plenty of *coin* to tender."

"Mountains." A dark powerful smile.

"Just a hill will be sufficient." The cold smile of a skilled player.

"Everything must be—"

"The particulars will be exactly as you wish. In this house dreams never slumber."

"Yes, Mr. Fox said I would be in the best of hands."

"You are." She regarded him with the most predatory of smiles. "Will your treasure be blonde and fair as a summer afternoon?"

"Pale and plain. What some might call mousy. Black hair—short, and slight limbs . . . Tiny rose nipples, and a new whisper of hair adorning her *untouched* flower."

"It will be as you desire." Her eyes laughed and said money.

"Some years ago there was a whore, Constance Castaigne. She had tresses colored in midnight's jet and the most delicate frame. Her skin was white as snow. She lived and plied her wares near the perfumery down the road from Doctor Archer's asylum. Often, before I went to her room for my grand tour of *jouissance* we took our pints, or gin, in The Baying Goat. Do you know the district I mention?"

She nodded yes once, her expression almost saying get on with it.

"Constance bore a child . . . I would have her daughter."

Cynara's eyes blazed. This would be more fun than de Sade's follies. The Magus would reward her well for this. "It may take me a few days to find the child you seek . . . Your private gala will take place Friday night."

"Friday. Splendid."

"Now, regarding the monetary aspect of this transaction. Shall we say, seven hundred pounds?"

"That's highway robbery. Seven hundred pounds for a street urchin? I'm not ransoming a king, Dear Lady."

"We're not talking about kings or ransoms. And a gentleman of your station must realize, a princess is not a cheap commodity."

"Indeed. And if by chance I alarm the toy, if the sun burns too hot while the sonata's wings flutter?"

"Frail things snap. Many are the cisterns which might be used to dispense with old plans struck hard."

"Just as I had hoped."

"Dreams are fulfilled here, as long as *payment* is made."

❀

Blasted, hungry eyes over bearded faces fallen down society's ladder into grimy blackness. Prostitutes and threadbare urchins who believe men are still—*only*—base, slack-jawed monkeys, stumbling in a Faust dance, reeking of mud and death. Eden, a cold whisper only dreamed of in the hard, cold pews of Sunday chapels. Each dancer weeping to survive the life eating life ouroboros. No what we will become, every day a black day peeling another layer of tears. Creatures great and small, yawning threads on winding streets of crime.

No angels, no art. The hue of gold is a dream frail fingers cannot grasp, the sun is a lie whispered about in the fog.

But there are skirts and pricks and teeth, a crowed mass of living rape, clawing at the first stair of the Marvelous.

Wet cunt and bleak eyes and depraved bellies are sick of this mad tea party gone ass-over-teakettle. The voices of violins drift no more. The flickering flames of candles have been tucked away for the night. Even the gaslight smears of thick, damp air are sick.

Cloaked in shadows to ward off the carnivorous ants and the groping lost, Henry Thale—cane-sword striding boldly, walks this theatre of Cain and Abel. Through the park with its phantoms to the bridge to his appointment he comes.

Under the bridge, black ink water slow and cold, leading to the sea by daylight; a bleak afterword to a long story, curling and dying to any witness this night. Cold black water, no words, no magic to be read on the back of its hands, but many holes full of old secrets. Ghost heads of flame hung on torches, underneath shadows, capes. Only the small echoes of sounds . . .

Down a long street with a bent spine, a street of dark hours. Past Soliliage and Dragon's Court . . . Thale remembered passing this street once before with Juliette—after the brandy . . . *blood will have its season* . . . She laughed and said, "Watch your step. That is the street that lost its dreamers. Off to shadows . . . Shorn of news, they, damned leaves, are the King's playthings now." Her remembered her lips—in full bloom, red for pleasure, and her eyes when they were cast down and beheld the desert . . . *every midnight tango sweet in his hands* . . . Past a tight shop that might have adjusted to its station more suitably had it been positioned in the Great Beyond . . . *fingers running* . . . The air seemed pressed down by a mighty judgment. Every sharp step was a bridge burned on this street . . . *she carried a large, yellow octavo book to him. For Yr Grace, she whispered* . . . Down a street where a bride, choking on last days, had signed her suicide note in her own blood. Down a street where plagues had drunk bereavement's whiskey, where awakened by the touch of blood ruffian and titan found nothing in The Secret of Leaving . . . *fingers running in the leaves together* . . . *every midnight tango sweet in his hands* . . . Juliette, spread wide under him. Juliette, after the scream, entrails cooling in the street. He cannot hold the dream as it slides from his hands into the blackness . . . *falling slowly* . . .

There stood the great door, more fitting for wagons and horses than men. Above, thirteen uneven widows; the four on the left only half the height of the others and oddly canted. . . . *petal to petal* . . . Before Mr. Fox's Tower he stands. Not a cross, or a gargoyle, or a script of flowing ivy carved into the weathered façade. Gray, as if painted by collapsing fog . . . *his handiwork, the joy of her complexities run their course, shone in the weak moonlight* . . . Above the door handle a scorpionlike etching. The Yellow Sign. So radiant in its fashion it almost laughed.

His lust stretched, but he did not touch the door of wrongs. This was a night to savor The Dreaming Clothed In Flesh, to blamelessly wash in joys and sorrows and stars descending. He stood there and smoked a cigarette. The emptiness of the street did not touch him.

If only it were late spring, the light birds in flight, young leaves reaching for maturity, the play of the glimmering sun on her hair—eyes shining, just so. Late spring when hearts are so active, every remark swift and served hot. A blind day . . . "'Black, black, black is the color of my true love's hair. Her face is something truly rare.'"

Soon enough, his balance tells him as he pulls the bell-chord.

The stern face of a retainer from the harlot's house greets him. He follows where the silent servant leads.

"Is all as—"

"You will tender the funds we agreed upon and then I'll take you to that which you seek," Cynara said, eyes hot in the cold pale mask.

Thale places a folio of bills in her silk-gloved hand.

Pale yellow fingers count the money slowly. "Good. Every detail we discussed awaits you in the room at the top of the stairs."

His eyes follow the stretching candlelight ascending the stairs.

From a small table at her hip she pours brandy and hands him the glass. "A very rare vintage to celebrate Your Wedding."

"*The Book?* Was a copy found?"

"It rests on the altar in the room above."

He takes the glass from her hand. Sips.

Before another word can pass from his lips Cynara is gone.

Time and shadows are heavy curtains. Midnight drinks deep.

Up. Damp, cool stone walls. Grime, sizzling with pocks and blisters of mold, paints intermittent sections of the walls. Green-gray shadows striped with black, thick and luxurious, gleam. Up four stories of slow-curved stairs to an attic . . . He stops at the foot of the landing. Breathes evenly to slow his racing heart.

There are dead moths on the floor. The planks are painted in dreamlight. The brass key in his hand breathes.

A grandfather clock with no hands stands as sentry beside a heavy door with rusted hinges. With a single step he will be outside this world of full-blooded lies. He takes it, entering the once elegant tower room—a land, a secret life, abroad—of empty masks that trouble no sky with their hollow gaze.

In the center of the room, She, transformed from refugee of streets little better than carcasses for infirmities to bride. He, dressed in his finest, the loving, jubilant husband come from the gloom to farm the pure, raw sugar of the field, a moment from *after this*.

She had been bathed and delicately perfumed. Her hair shorn, short, boyish. No paint had been applied to her fingertips, no rouge brightened her cheeks or full, ripe lips. With ribbons of yellow silk she was bound to the devil's chair. At present she was gagged.

Red and yellow flower petals carpeted the chessboard floor. Scented black candles dripped hot wax. He danced around her. Swayed. Watched. Whispered, "This is a night of quicksilver dreams. This night is music."

Paused, sat at her tiny, white feet. Whispered to her again, "How I ache to beguile you, Dearest Camilla?"

"Oh, you and I . . . We shall taste all the delights shut fast behind the gates of Carcosa."

A moment in dreamspeed passes. He rises, standing silent.

A thin black veil is tied over the girl's eyes. His hands, smooth, warm, ready to whisper phrases in the garden of kisses, rush to the knot.

"From illusion and shadow I release you. There, My Sweet, I cast out dim and give you light."

Her eyes were large, wide with fear. Her lips trembled.

"No smile for me, my love? You'll soon open and give me all I desire and when my hand presses its years to your supple flesh my smile will light upon you."

He fell to his knees, his hands clasped her pale foot. His lips pressed to her arch. "Tiny little doves. Tender white doves." He pressed his cheek to her foot. "Are you ready to fly for Daddy?" he whispered. His cheeks were flushed, hers ashen.

He thought she should have worn yellow ballet slippers. Thought how much he would have loved slipping them slowly off her feet. Imagined them lying on the floor, poems an arm's length from the fairy tale curve of her soft heel.

"Would you care to hear of the marvelous where wideness dances? I could spin tales of bereavement and betrayed lovers . . . Of The Departure and The Whiteness. Of masked galas, leaves and dust crying in the corner, or plots hovering in the bed chambers of mothers, dream homes burning at both ends . . . Better still, I shall read to you before we glow in the fragrance of each other's desires?"

He walked to the wall, a vast mural of a lake where a black swan rode the current of autumnal fog painted upon it—"Do you see how the light shines like a kiss upon the lake?"—and stopped before a glass case. From it he took a large, yellow octavo book.

"My wedding present to you shall be a poem or two from Our King before we sigh upon our bed. Yes, I can see how your eyes shine with delight at the thought of The Flowers of His Sacred Breath gracing the opals of our poets' hearts. The delight quickens within me as well, Dearest . . . Ssssh now. There is no emptiness at this edge."

The cover of the yellow book opened gently. "'I journeyed far down away into another country where it was all one dim and vague lake, with a boundary line of clouds' . . . You see, Dearest, here is another rare bird—

sadly gone, who opened the lid of The Book and slid past web and labyrinth and all the goodbye days inlaid with dust and passed the padlock of
seeking stars, soft and quiet, and sat in the whispering towers of Carcosa.
And here he writes, 'There arose in our pathway a shrouded human figure,
very far larger in its proportion than any dweller among men. And the hue
of the skin of the figure was of the perfect whiteness of the snow.' Imagine
the fruit he finds fallen upon the floors of the Old Towers at the End of the
World. Perhaps we shall be met with his greetings in Dim Carcosa?"

Tears scream from her eyes.

His dark was erased, cured. "Ssssh. As you waited in your room, I
spent my afternoon in the trance of prayer."

She tried to force her voice through the red ball-gag. She shook her
head no.

He threw the book to the floor. Its leaves were open. The Yellow Sign
burned on the page.

"Are you listening?" With a slap, cruelness rose. "I give you the flame
in my eyes. Expect miracles." Hungry voice, volcanoes growling.

The wind and the river outside the tower went silent. Time had no
hold on this gallows. He stood and removed his pants, unbuttoned his
shirt, and cast it aside. "Did you know I served in the Great Army?" He
wheeled, his stiff prick in his hand. "I have killed many and soon you shall
feel my sword. What do you think, Camilla? Are you ready to serve The
Dynasty? In her time, your mother's generous bottom served under my
sword for weeks of nights, but I grew tired of the obedient ... *She loved
me so—she would beg, with tongue and breasts, and variety. All those
nights I took my exercise in the tickles and laughs of her loud "Yes!"* ...
Did she never tell you that blood will have its season?"

He rushed to her side. With a stern hand turned her face.

He reached down and grabbed a handful of petals. From above her
head they gently tumbled down upon her. "A thousand petals of yellow and
scarlet I give you as a bridal bouquet. Shall we love?"

With searing fingers her clothes came off—childhood's end. In the
candlelight, his moon-bright eyes declared his love for her soft curves. His
smile declared his ardor for the unsoiled cunt that lay behind soft wisps of
black hair.

... *fingers running* ... patrolling. He etched diagrams on her soft
belly with his quill-tongue. He spread the honeycomb of her blooming
womanhood. "I would taste the rarest honey. I would empty the mill. Oh,
dearest, how my fingers yearn for the undertow."

... *fingers running* ... His lips found velvet. "Warm." Twitch ... *fingers running* ... Brandy on his breath. Sparks blooming. "This fire you have set within me. I give it back and more."

He untied her and pushed her down on a divan of curling red ivy. Tied her wrists—her arms spread, angels wings opened. Placed his hand upon her inner thigh. Rubbed his prick on the outer coastline of her pale ass. From behind he entered her. Throbbing eel slamming split quim, riding, the reins of her hair directing her course.

He untied her and turned her over. She was too shattered by the storm force to resist.

From the side of his boot a knife flashed. "Another sword for you, My Love. Will you serve this one as sweetly?" . . . . *petal to petal* ... With a flick of his wrist the knife removed her left nipple. He sighed and placed the bloody rose upon his tongue. "Ahh ... *Flesh of my flesh.*" Swallowed whole his communion wafer. "Flesh."

... *every midnight tango sweet in his hands* ... There were hard kisses of teeth and fluids on his canvas. Etchings were carved into pale, tender flesh ... "I am the wolf who turns wounds to psalms, who, in the cold thirsty hour, dines on childhood's limbs and leaves sobs turned to dust for the ghosts drunk in their canals of disgrace." And he laughed his wolf laugh.

She trembled under the hot waves of his raw fancy, burning and stormy. The whole of her budding breast was in the dragon's maw. Her nails cut into her palms.

Frenzy loosened, blood occurs ... *every complexity sweet in his hands* ... The tiny dancer—prisoner, victim, followed, page after page, where wrongness led ...

Calves and thighs burned by sweat. Shame capsized by wickedness ...

Gestures of scorpion hands washed in subterranean intrigues. The coldest touch. He plunged the blade into her wet trough of Venus-honey. The knife began its translation. Depravity, a slow right twist. Whimpering. The worst written in blood. Then he eased it out of her torn sea.

"And now there is blood on this sword. How sweet you are to give your very all to my dearest treasure."

He removed the faded, frayed yellow gag from her mouth. Her mouth opened, her eyes remained shut fast. She couldn't catch her breath, couldn't find the voice to scream.

"Such a quiet, dutiful child."

There is blood on the floor.

The salt of her tears at the corners of her open mouth. He holds a mirror to her face. A mirror with no glass. The last chapter almost written.

"Goodbye, dearest. You will not deal with angels in the Place Where the Mysteries Are Rubbed with Ashes, but phantoms awakened by your perfume, their waiting hunger will come to you. They will take your dreams and leave despair lying in the corners with dust."

The poet, lost in his dance of dreamspeed, spins. One last kiss of his knife. No echoes. The poet's pen lies silent on the floor.

There is blood on the floor.

Wandering aimlessly around the still life, a jigsaw harlequin, red and yellow flower petals stuck to the checkered spots of her blood that cover him. Her legs and cunt bloody. Blood on her breast where her rose-nipple should bloom. Wet tears drying on her cheeks above the blood smile he'd opened on the soft field of her pale throat. Her eyes cold. His hand strokes her hair.

"'Black, black, black is the color of my true love's hair,'" he murmurs, almost singing. Then he laughs, his arm draped over her shoulder as if some broken angel's wing. Laughs, hellfire wild and low. His hot breath dreaming on her cold shoulder.

The door to the field where plagues burn opened. Cynara looked over the carnage that lay on the killing field. Thale turned, looked at her. Eyes, the wolf still in hunger, still chewing its passion, flashed with recognition.

"I have been faithful to thee, Cynara."

"Yes, Thale, in coin and currency, but now blood is required."

"More blood?"

"Blood." She laughed. "*Flame begotten of flame*—desolate, requires its payment."

His eyes cluttered with the terror of The Truth. His thoughts whisper words that have no voice.

There was a blade in Cynara's hand; the twin of the blade he had used on his daughter—he recognized the Yellow Sign etched on its hilt. The blood rushed from his face. Carcosa burned like a kiln before him. It bound him in stone paws filled with time. He saw the white moons, the metropolitan sprawl, kettle-black and lying like a cluttered yard of potbellied baseburners with sky-wounding towers like chimney stacks capped with crooked-peaked witches hats. The wind, soft and flecked with the strangled clamors of distant objects, moved and still he stood—hard as an inscription set in a grave marker—yet he was on fire with fear.

. . . *petal to petal* . . . The knife was a hammer in her hands. . . . *every midnight tango sweet in her hands* . . . As she cut, again and again, deeper and deeper, her fingers scooped his seed from the dead girl's corpse and were quick to place it inside her womb.

The Dynasty must be preserved.

There is blood on the floor.

Moments earlier a vision in the finest cut of red silk, a demure vision no crowd of city or country folk would believe spends her nights on beds of diseased shadows fucking demons, she has gouged out his eyes with the knife blade. One stride and she steps on his left eyeball, popping it. With her other heel, his right is truly blind as well. "Deprived of triumph, I send you to your life in Nothing as blind as you were here."

She cuts off each of his fingers. They lie with the petals at her feet. "No door in the Blackest Labyrinth will you open."

There is blood on the floor.

After the scream he was still, entrails on the floor, cooling. Hot as the passion of any prophet or demon, she shivered. Cynara removed her mask. Eyes closed in near rapture, she licked what remained of his spent lust from her blood-stained fingers. O'er the roiling cloud-waves of Hali, Camilla's laugh rolled.

❧

Wearing the diadem of Succession, Camilla—unmasked—beams. Laughs, low and sweetly. The tread of a murmuring breeze is in the barren branches. Pressed to a slim white bole stands a brooding man in fox fur. She walks to him and clasps her brother's hand. His brother's seed in her womb and her Mother's plot warming her thoughts, she flashes smiling eyes at him.

"Lord Uoht, cast aside all thoughts of power struggles. Your brother and his spawn have taken the Winterboat to another shore. Would you care to walk a bit in yonder dim glade?"

Taking note of the cool, radiant diadem he smiles.

"And will we now, finally, talk of The Wedding and joy?"

Hand in hand . . . *petal to petal* . . . *"Yes, dearest."* . . . *every midnight tango sweet in her hands* . . . *"There will be joy on the night we wed."*

(after reading James Blish's *More Light* and Robert Bloch's *A Toy For Juliette* back to back)

mr wind sits

Brillig spins its gleam. Seven silver frames—webbed together & dusty—
hold seven smiles. The beheaded nymphets in the grainy photographs
brighten. The worn edges of yellowed curtains waltz quietly above the head
of a black kitten lost to mouse dreams as mr wind gradually breezes around
the room; the carpet is a map of his travels. He stops at the window and
looks out over the garden and the dark, thorny hedges and the brook to the
wilderness beyond.

"Somewhere games are being played."

mr wind returns to his desk and reads a footnote for the sixth time.

"Somewhere games are being played."

He looks over at the row of silver framed photographs. Grainy black
and whites taken in dim light, but he sees the blonde curls, the sunny afternoon blue eyes. He hears the pleasant April laughter of each.

Twilight—like a shrunken old man settling into his bed—recedes.
Midnight and The Need are closer. mr wind lights seven waxlights and
continues to read of things aloft, things postponed, and things obedient.
He thinks of *we* and unfolds into deeper. The clock moves forward and he
arrives in deepest . . .

*a little street. Not deserted, simply
thin. Lilies and blue bells and butterfly petals bursting, sailing in the
sleeves of gentle porches. On other days conversations rustle like sparrows.
Many are the windows arched with holidays grown up. Dreams live in each
doorway . . .*

*The ball is red. It rests
unmoving on a radiant green lawn. She—*"Alice," *he whispers—is sitting
on the steps. No all fall down, no dollies, no wreath of friends. Moments of
gladly have found other pockets. Still as the lamppost, his hands are folded.
He peers, waiting for Now. Whistling, he floats down the street toward the
park. She looks up, trying to catch the fabulous sparks of his song. Open to
new she follows . . .*

The grandfather clock, old in his father's time, chimes. mr wind looks
at the slender silver hands that have danced with years, but they are not

wings. There is no joy in the land of waiting. He looks at the face in the 7th frame; the fawn eyes, the softly pointed chin, the button nose; those gently smiling lips of rose. Returns to deeper . . .

She—"Alice,"   he whispers—, *a dazzling angel of nine, whistles the chorus of his song. He whistles back, smiles, waves. He drinks the beam of the slender little bird.* "Dear, dear, Alice," whispered from a narrow smile. *A shiny silver piece appears in his left hand. Palms flash, fingers dance; here—like eyes suddenly open, exit, there & back again. Another trick and a third. mr wind & His Alice, crowned with clouds, whisper and laugh quietly. They sit in swings of rope and board in the thick, calm shadows of wild pines. He begins a story*—"On a leisurely, golden afternoon a quiet man captured a gentle little bird in the lenspiece of his camera . . ."

He sits without. The after of serene dreamtime is weak, gold passes into winter. The air is very still, cold. A delirium of seven voices thrash in his soul. A cyclone of fire sways in his blood . . . Night is pierced by the arrow of dawn.

"Somewhere games are being played."

mr wind sits. He stares at the silver hands of the grandfather cloak and waits for Now.

(For Joann Izzo)

The Prisoner

Ears and toes, and all the naked rest of him, burning with cold. Raw, but not empty cold. Cold. Filled with hate. It seeped through the stone walls. Thousands of eyes burning with hot, hard hate and by the time it finds its way in, it's turned cold.

It wasn't always this way. In The Before he was famous, loved. He had women and money and parties thrown for him, by the women, by those in power. He was loved. His every word. Loved. Repeated, sang, read. And reread. He was a national hero. In the Before . . .

But the woman died. And the police told him to put his shirt on before they took him to the jail—dungeon. Then came the lights. Bright. In his eyes. Burning, never off, burning with hate. Because she died.

But he was sleeping. After his drunk and their fucking—at least his drunken memory of it was them fucking, and then sleeping it off. Sleeping right next to her . . . Covered in her blood. His kitchen knife on the floor by his bed.

But he was sleeping, he didn't kill her. Why? He'd wanted her. Wanted her beautiful, naked ass shaking under him and she gave him her all. Gave and gave until he couldn't take any more. Why? She said he could have her again. Anytime! That's what she'd said before he fell asleep in her arms.

Where did it all start? With that book? The old black man's book. Full of damning things. Full of stars and secrets and power to be had if one had the nerve to . . .

"All the things That Were will be again. When touched by prayer, They will swell and reach out from the Endless Dreaming . . ."

Him and his damning love of books. And words. All those magic words, flowing . . . Flowing like wine. It made him drunk. It made the women he wanted drunk. Drunk enough to fuck him. All those words. The poetic, the damning, the vile and beautiful stretched out as lush vines painting addicting dreams across the pages. Words that made you cry. Words you wore like skin. Words that were answers.

He loved to swim in them, to hold conversations with and about them, and to watch them dance until they drown. Words full of zero, and rain, and stones. Words that built, inhabited. Words as food. Caravans and roads of words. Air. Could one ever get enough air? That's what they were, air. He needed them to live. Needed them to get money to buy wine and scotch and nice cars and houses on the beach, to attract the women who came to him to fuck. He needed to breathe.

But outside they were building a gallows, a wolf that would steal his words. And when his words were gone, they planned to burn his books— every copy of every book. Disembowel his words with flames. They told him so. Laughed. And spat upon him.

They told the gathering crowds to bring matches, to spit upon him when he burns.

All over words. And the dead woman.

They loved her too.

She was a star. Of screen, of stage. She sang, she made them cry, made them all want to fuck her.

Yes, she was a great fuck. The best. He'd admit to that. But not good enough to die over. Not that good. No one was *that* good. Just because her skin was a palace and a market place, just because she was a sculpture of pleasure bordering on rapture, that was no reason to die. He could have twenty a day who were 8½s to her 10. If he wanted, he could have one every hour on the hour. He could have them in pairs, in trios . . .

✦

They still burn men for their crimes here. They don't buck tradition. That would be spitting on the Law and they loved the Law, every word of it. Every word their father's father's father's fathers had spent ten years quilting together, each phrase exact, but no less poetic than the song in their hearts.

This was the land of words. Magazines, newspapers, books. Every city had at least ten libraries, every small town, two or three. Here they didn't teach their children math until third grade. But reading, understanding words, that they taught from the first day of school.

He was the grandmaster of words and they were going to silence his work. But they weren't *his* words. He didn't write the book. All he did was translate.

He couldn't believe The Muse would do this to him. Not to him! He was her hands, her voice. She needed him to feed the dry, dying hearts of the masses. He was her loved and perfect son. She wouldn't do this, not to him.

It was Them. Their small minds. Timid, afraid. Afraid to reach out and touch something new. Or in the case of his translation, something old. To rediscover that which was lost. The stupid fuckers, all for a few words. A few words they said were dangerous. Dangerous visions. The words infuriated them, made them howl.

And they made someone plot against him. Maybe someone high in government circles? Someone came in during the night when he was sleeping, drunk, and she was drunk too, he knew it. And they killed her and made it look like he did it.

Well, he didn't do it. He wanted to tell them that. He never hurt a single of the 1,000 women he took to bed, so why would he destroy the best fuck he'd ever had? Why would he destroy the whole of his rich, beautiful life over those words?

❋

The old man from the desert had a shop on the corner. A small shop like the others in the old quarter. But not like the others around it, the others sold colorful robes and simple carvings, trinkets for babes and sisters and wives. In the old man's shop, the shop under the sign of the crow and the moon, sat reliquaries and soul bottles and wonders brought back from the wanderings of the sons of Adam. And there were other things, but mostly, the old man sold books. Old books from old places.

And the lover of words, the grandmaster of words, always wanting more words, wandered in. Walked the tight corridors, quickened as the roots of lost cities flourished in his glowing eyes. Within the span of a few minutes he'd placed a bulky volume on the counter.

"Good afternoon. Would you please tell me the price of this?"

"The price of mystery? As high as any life."

"It would be nice if it was a little less dear."

The old man's eyes darken, but he smiled. "Call me Ishmael. For I have seen The Urgent Leviathans as they roil—hot and wild, as they rock and reach and clasp through the unending, ageless ages. I have seen them in The Great Black Nothing as they sleep in the fathomless Still. They have painted my eyes and the heart in my breast with time . . . And space."

Seen the bottoms of too many bottles is more like it, he thought.

"I have breathed in the dust of their dreams . . . The Demons of Fury will come and even the thunder will run from their voices."

The old man should be the master of bones. Bent and wrinkled, he walked like a keeper of graves whom the sharp sun had removed too much of.

It was all bookseller bullshit, but he was snared by the crocodile's drifting voice.

"I know you. They sometimes call you the Grandmaster of Words. They say you've a passion for wine and the ladies."

"They say many things about me."

"True. True . . . one so famous . . . *your life must be hard.*" Spoken firm, but at half the volume. "Today it suits me to let you name the price. If it is fair, the book is yours."

He felt like he was making a deal with the devil. Too low, he'd lose. Too high, he might lose something else. But he wanted the tome. He couldn't read it, but it spoke to him nonetheless. The hell with the money. He made a half-educated offer. The old man smiled. He wrote a check and felt glad and satisfied.

His nights with the text began. By the light of a soulless moon he slowly came upon the keys to open the leaves. And there followed ten other moldering tomes rooted in Greek where he rediscovered pieces of the lost language and in the moments of rebirth began stitching together that which was forgotten. Repeated phases he discarded as he boiled down the translation . . .

When the sun came up he took no note of it. He stopped taking his daily swims on the beach. Stopped drinking. Stopped dealing with the pleasures of flesh. His eyes in its heart he searched to give the text a mouth. And the words came. Dark words of warning. Words pulled from the rusted depths of secrets. Words to wake the ignorant from their sleep of unaware. Words of Torments That Were Hidden in caverns shut fast by that which was not remembered and now ready to wake and walk the world. To undo it. To leave man and his triumphs and marvels undone.

What was locked beneath the journey of the roots and the worms he opened. Freed.

This was a book of the immortality of the stars made flesh.

And like a plague it spread. His new book was an instant bestseller. The whiteness of his pages in every hand and the black marks that flowed across the pages on every tongue. On porches and in coffee bars they spoke of it, reviewed it, handed their copies over to other hands, to other eyes.

In another time the book would have been forbidden, but this was the new time, the time of pure freedom. Let nothing be obscured by timid hands.

He was #1 on the bestseller list. Flowing from party to party to gala he heard her name everywhere. Every woman he fucked held her cigarette like her, did her hair like her, talked like and about her, wanted to have lunch or a drink with her. He went to the premiere of her new film. They went to dinner. Laughed, held hands, whispered in the rarified air of adoration. Then, star to star, equally hot, they went to his beach house to fuck . . .

❋

They cut off his hands. Cauterized the stumps with the white-hot flat of a sword. The sword they used to chop off his hands.

They pulled the ball-gag out of his mouth and sheared off his tongue. So he would utter no foul curse or spell.

Only blood filled his mouth.

They thrust a nail in the center of his forehead. To be certain his inner eye is blind.

"He'll not deal with demons any more." The hooded guards laughed.

His tongue and hands were cast in a pot of boiling water. Thirty minutes later they were pulled out and throw on the fire.

Secured he was led into the court room. The judge had said the evidence was too damning, too overwhelming. There would be no jury. And he would be allowed no defense. No words would be spoken on behalf of this monster.

"Witch, I find you guilty! You have robbed us of our most beloved treasure and born a nightmare upon us. I sentence you to burn. And all your books to be burned with you as well. Never more will your cancerous burdens of shadow eat away at our hearts and foul our minds. I would burn you this very minute, but the people need time to come and witness the passing of your unholy existence. At noon in three days you will burn."

And they came. Vultures, buying up T-shirts, bringing copies of his books to add to the pyre. Vultures, soaring on wine and beer, shoulder to shoulder, waiting for the carnival's main event. Reporters from far and wide came, ready to fill the daily journals with words of his demise.

And high noon arrived.

The crowds roared and cheered. Babes sat on the shoulders of their fathers. Women who would have wasted their marriage vows on the rack of his lust just weeks before came to hiss words of revulsion. Cold beer warming their libidos, gladdened men smiled at the prospect of all the women who would soon be searching for new beds and new lovers.

A gray door opens. Ringed by soldiers he emerges. A wind of hate fills the square. Two thousand hands are thrust into the air. Each holds a page from one of his books. The pages are torn in half. And torn in half again. They snow upon the ground and are trampled under foot.

With a rope woven of leather strips he is led to the pyre of his books. Tears stain his cheeks. His despairing eyes are filled with his books. All his joy, all the days and nights giving birth, clothing them, never giving up the ghost . . . all the struggles. The awakenings and the wakes, the straw in the garden of the worm . . . letters, islands, the treadmills and the fallen angels . . . all the beauty, the larks tongues in his ears, laughing, crying . . . all the flights, wings open in the blinding rays of the sun . . .

From the crowd, a match, and another match . . . 6 become 9 . . .

He strains in a frame of flames.

A boy nudges his way through thighs and knees and emerges from the crowd. He unzips and pisses on his books . . . An old woman renounces him by throwing a copy of his first book at him. It hits him in the chest . . .

The colors of his covers blacken. The tender insides open and curl in the flicking serpent's tongues of flames. The smell of the flesh of his books burning fills his nostrils. Whiteness, his words on wings of smoke, blown to nothing by the wind. The screams of his tortured words fill his ears.

Then the fire touches his skin . . .

He would scream if he had a voice.

An American Tango Ending in Madness

A century in seclusion with the green birds . . . The humors of the lantern as sedatives . . . And she misses having shoes . . .

The darkening sky shouts.

"The tiles here are so cold." She wiggles her toes. Almost smiles at the movement. "I've grown pale here."

Still she walks the garden. Bare feet gently pushing aside the black, curling leaves of the Winter Tree . . .

Black hair and a crown of dead black moths. Her cloak and parasol wandering from vault to headstone to dry fountain. She stops at a gray-blue marker. "I was once like you." She opens her parasol. Her face and shoulders now shadowed from the gaze of the moon.

The ring on her finger is so heavy . . .

She returns to her rooms.

Curtains flapping in the breeze, flapping, as the hazy yellow sun rises over the swirling dust.

She put down The Book and put on the mask. She never read with it on. She wanted to face the Truth face to face.

There are six bodies, the bodies of children, lying near the closed gates of the courtyard. This journey in the leaves had been profitable . . .

She was sick of being under house arrest. She wanted her freedom and the sooner the yard was full, the sooner they'd unlock the gates . . .

✸

Susan, blonde, slender—fit, black hair and ample in her dreams, believed Fredric was a werewolf, tearing at the throats and breasts of harlots who wanted his money and to sit beside him in the queen's chair. Their fine dresses of red and black would hang in her closet. Whether in darkness or by candlelight, their flourishes would waltz in his bed. When they entered the museum gala it would be their arm in his arm . . . Each pursuer would gladly push her into the abyss to be the nightingale that sat on the rainbow.

The glow of Fredric's power and vast financial holdings called to them.

But she was first in this court. And first she would stay. By act or word, she would not be swept aside to some final chapter of pain. She could see what lie behind their masks. And her poison was the most deadly. Let them find another pocketbook to steal from or let them die. She was master in this game and enjoyed licking their blood from her hand.

She loved watching his firm muscles move against her flesh in the mirror. Loved watching his lips kiss her secret curves. Just a little grass, and sometimes a glass of brandy or a bottle of wine . . . and a whisper . . . and she spread her wings . . . flying . . . guiding him with her hand . . .

The candles have gone out. They sleep . . . The brittle light of the city drifts through their window. In the bewildering labyrinth they dream . . .

Fredric chases a rabbit. He's lightning running on windblown feet, chasing his dinner, the sweet skin of the hind legs flooding his nostrils . . .

She is a stone mouth biting Death . . . The inquisitor's hands are full of bees. They fly from his rope fingers and fill her empty shoes . . . Susan reaches down. Her shoes are now black roses. At her touch, they swoon.

✦

The line of questions comes. One by one they hand her their note—
One line, one short question. She smiles and points.

"You may pass," she whispers.

Most turn slowly. They all follow the garden path to the suicide chamber. Hands folded quietly in their laps they sit. Wait. Reflect. When a bell rings or a bird awakens autumn's gleam with song they rise from the simple wooden bench and enter the chamber.

Each traveler, man or woman or child, leaves their mask behind on the bench. After they have passed into the chamber a pale man walks to the bench and removes his mask, casting it into a slow stream where it glides toward the lake. His bone-white hands reach down and pick up the mask left by the last question. Without a word he places the mask over his featureless face.

It is ever midnight in the park.

The questions slowly stroll into the park unseen by The World outside . . . and never leave. Beyond the gates, The World continues to laugh and drink, or sunken in solemn doorways, cry, and grind out its toils . . .

The next question appears. She changes her tongue and points to the slim doors, which open like unfolding wings, under the golden dome of the chamber . . .

✦

Susan was a librarian once, a writer, when the words weren't too unsettling to put on paper, and long ago, when she attended art school, a sculptor, until the chilled morning the hearse that carried the body of her idol and mentor, and lover, passed her in the street.

After that, she took her father's money and went in search of a new life.

What she found was Fredric's bed . . . and in it she stayed these last six years. There were no children, there never would be, but she always had dogs. A pair. Always a pair. One large and having a dark coat. The other, half the size of the larger and white or light tan in coat.

And they always had romantic names, nothing common. Zemo or Zeus for the large canine and Camilla, her mother's name, or Cosette for the one with the pale coat. Never a Mike or a Bob. Never a Missy or Cupcake or Bubbles.

Unless she and Fredric were playing in the mirror, or on those afternoons when she read from The Book, they were always at her side. Sentinels. Teeth ready to save her from any attack.

✸

The curious tails of the kites in the park have stopped their circus dance.

A street of deeper blue. Shadows and ripples consider further away. Twilight walks slow, leaving gentle footprints.

A gallery window under a yellow sign. The lights are still on. Fingers from her past touch her shoulder. A voice of a long time ago whispers to her.

The exhibition is titled In the Year of the Dragon. Two of *His* sculptures are being shown . . . Her fingertip caresses the cheek of his life mask . . . *So long ago the soft moments happened . . . She sees the "come follow" eyes of the hearse driver . . . She is as frozen to that corner as the streetlamp . . . A crow lands on the empty spot, a moment ago (a lifetime ago?), occupied by the hearse . . .* She hears a piano and a sad voice singing, "'Leave dreams to the dreamer.'"

There is an empty space on the wall of her study. So quiet this image of her mentor, her former lover, now gone to dimmer glades. She buys it. Rushes to a cab. Rushes home. Hangs it on the wall of her study. Her fingertip caresses his cheek . . . She reads to him. Reads from The Book he once, a long time ago in his small room in Dragon's Court, read to her.

She can feel his fingers stray . . . then, angel to her demon, play in her darkness . . .

✸

After the battery of rampant caws she must endure at the luncheons, for decorum and Fredric's sake, Susan loves to sit in the park. The quiet breeze treading the leaves, the light bird song, the sun fluttering on the hair of children free of error and worry and toil, soothe her nerves. For a few minutes or an hour, she's free of the trials of perverted ugliness that oppress her. Free of thoughts of Fredric and his line of endless whores.

But the alarm of her wristwatch comes and she must return home. To not have Fredric's dinner ready and waiting might send him over the edge.

On the table in the foyer, under the vase of day-old roses, a note:

> Susan,
> Called away to the court. One can't avoid Truth, or the judge, can one? I'll be staying at Don's place in the Hills if you need me. His number's in my rolodex. Back on Thursday. Don't forget the party on Saturday. Can you pick up my tux?
> Love, F.

Another trip to SoCal. The third this month. Another star requiring spin and counsel. Another starlet requiring his less cerebral services.

She should cast out the werewolf, take half, or take a lover . . .

Instead she takes to her bed . . . With The Book.

Zemo sits at the doorway. Colette lies on the floor behind him. They never enter the room when she reads of the sweet cool shadows descending on the Dragon's Wood.

The wind rises. Its voice whispers, "Come back."

She sets The Book on her nightstand. Unties her hair. Unbuttons her shirt buttons. Slips her panties off . . . Her fingers call to demons . . .

❀

The longest day . . . A piano, harvesting an autumn eulogy. The sad notes, postcards from a long-stemmed trance, drifting as if from some other world, find her waiting under a tree soon to bend under winter. The bones of a nightingale litter the ground before the headstone. She moves the skull forward a inch with a toe . . . Under her pallid mask, tears have dried on her cheeks. The ring on her finger is so heavy . . .

She unbuttons her blouse and offers her breast to the wind . . .

❀

She is locking the clasp of her diamond necklace ... *She comes in from the weather. She stands in the doorway, drops the small bag of groceries ... sees Him hanging, shirtless, barefoot, from the pipe ... the brown rope tight about his throat ... The Book of the King of Wisdom lies at his feet ... She takes the book and flees ... His cold life mask lies on the table ...*

Fredric smiles at her in the mirror. Kisses her bare shoulder.

"You are truly beautiful."

She smiles and thanks him with her eyes.

On the dining room table rest their masks. Hers, a timid bird of green feathers, flecked with blue. His, a rabbit face.

He hands her hers and laughs. "Shall we?"

❀

Drinks in manicured hands. Champagne. Gowns and tuxedoes. Masks; angels, demons, comedians, animals, ghosts, owls; blue and red and white and black face; jeweled and beaded, painted; some with wings, one with insect eyes, one of the laughing sun; smiles and leering grins, rejoicing ... A band, blue and low, swings slowly ... Warm-toned greetings, as if this was a pleasant country and these were nice people ...

Behind black curtains at the rear of the great hall they disrobe ... Down a circular stairway, he, a tiger of sure step, she, somewhere far off inside ... They step into the Garden of Sugar ...

The room is sparsely lit by antique lanterns that cradle short black candles. Each lantern is hung from a rope. The uncarpeted floor is a black and white checkerboard. Each white tile has the image of a "compass" in it. She focuses on one, thinks it whispers only to her. "Come home," it says. Black ceramic bowls of strawberries and white grapes and white ceramic bowls of cocaine sit on the mirrored tops of low tables ...

Every body, young and not so young these days, fit and firm, tanned or pale, hirsute or expensively waxed, or aging and sagging, naked, except one; a man in a Lone Ranger mask and white hat sports a leather cowboy holster with two silver six guns and a bullwhip ... 100 firewalkers with remodeled bodies, redesigned by 100 knives in London and Phoenix and Miami ... The smell of $200 cigars and marijuana is in the air ... The music of the band upstairs piped in. They're playing "Ships in the Night." The clarinetist quotes phrases from "The Nearness of You" and "Makin' Whoopee," the piano and the double-bass seem to say, "Me too." "Me too." ...

Fredric leads her to a large black sofa collared with red roses. He gives her hand to a tall man in a pale yellow mask. The stranger opens his fingers to take her hand . . . She thinks his fingers look like rope. On a red sofa, collared with black roses, across from Susan and the stranger, Fredric sits with three young women . . . The pale redhead in the dove half-mask is on her knees, her mouth and tongue at play. Green Man mask facing the ceiling, the dark-skinned brunet lies cooing as Fredric's fingers stroke her Venus-clef. The other redhead, in a Janus mask, slides his mask up and pushes her nipple into his mouth . . .

Susan watches Fredric's episode while the man in the pallid mask unceremoniously fucks her without a word or sounds . . . His breath reeks of gin. She wants to cry, to scream . . . Wants to be across town . . .

She is staring at the ceiling . . .

Wants to be far away in a pleasant country . . .

This is all a mistake . . . I must get out of here.

✦

The Truth and the Hunger, images dreaming in the mirror . . . The moon, here, freed from its exile behind the clouds . . . A quiet cello dreams between blue promises. The slow dance blooms . . . A flower nursed by a different river, she, born in a different country, was born to bloom . . . in someone's eyes . . .

She is naked, lying on the bed, one leg raised. He stands dressed only in an unbuttoned shirt. He passes her a joint, exhales . . . He sips brandy. Stirs it with his finger. Circles her nipple with the finger, then licks it.

Fredric has never asked about the small, red scorpionlike tattoo on her ankle. Something from her younger, wilder days in art school when she ran with that sculptor that hung himself, or maybe something from one of those artsy plays she adored and was always reading or running off to see.

Postmodern, multilinear bullshit! Surrealistic bullshit! Fuckin' avant-garde, what about dialogue and plot? All that slow moving gibberish— He hadn't let her drag him to a play since *Titus Andronicus. More artsy bullshit. Madness, rape, dismemberment, revenge.* He'd rather see a movie with plenty of jokes and lots of tits.

He took another hit off the joint. Looked at her feet and her ankle. At the tattoo. He really didn't care when she got the tattoo, or how, or where, he loved the thing. Loved kissing it. And she knew what he wanted when he pressed his lips to her tender ankle.

He lifted her foot and kissed the tattoo. Her fingers eased down her belly . . . He watched—in the mirror—as the long, slender demons danced in darkness . . . When she had finished the dance she sat up. Fredric, gorged on her scent-in-full-bloom filling the room, eyes still observing the hungry game of skin in the mirror, rubbed the head of his cock against her nipples, slowly rubbed the shaft against the undersides of her breasts. She held her breasts together for him and he pushed and pumped between them until he was spent . . .

✻

She circles the suicide chamber . . . The sky is gray. The Phantom of Truth rises from the bench and walks to her. He reaches out for her hand and leads her to the bench. She sits. Unbuttons the buttons of her blouse. Reaches under her skirt and slides her panties off. The Phantom of Truth kneels before her and takes off his mask—his face is a skull. She closes her eyes. His fingers part her Venus-mound. He puts his head between her legs . . . His fingers, angels to her demon, stray . . .

✻

"Fucking spies. Why are you always watching me? Does he make you? Do you report my comings and goings to him?"

Zemo cocked his head.

"Oh, you understand me. Don't you? I know you do."

Cosette, sitting behind Zemo outside the kitchen doorway, backed up at the harsh crack of her voice.

"Do you whisper in his ear when I'm sleeping?"

Susan had been walking the cold rooms of the house all morning. She'd had half a bottle of wine and a few pills . . . She'd had Fredric's pistol sitting on the kitchen table for the last three hours . . . She'd had enough. Of Fredric. Of The Guilt. Of The Lies. Of having to fuck other men while Fredric watched her. Had enough of having to watch him fuck other women . . . Had enough disappointments . . .

"Fuck him!"

The half empty bottle of wine shattered against the kitchen wall. Rivulets of red run down the wall . . .

Red. Dead babies . . . Her father's blood . . .

Her father throws The Book into the fireplace. The flames take it. He raises the glass of brandy to his lips. One last sip of this life . . . Places the barrel of his pistol to his temple . . . and travels to another, far, country . . .

She comes home from her date. The light is on in father's study. She goes to say goodnight . . . He is in her arms. She is crying . . . Screaming . . .

She reads his note: "Good-bye, Day." Is all it says.

Red. The whole of the world red. Bleeding. The whole of the world, cold and dark, ready to strike . . .

Goddamn fucking red; her muddy skirt, the babies— Her daughter had had doll's eyes . . . All the eyes and prying fingers following her . . .

The dogs are standing, barking. Zemo two steps closer than before.

"What the fuck are you staring at? Shut up! *Please* . . ."

Susan picks up the handgun, walks to Zemo. Blood and brains and bones and a bullet exit the back of his head. Rivulets of red run down the wall . . .

She turns to Cosette . . .

"You little bitch, you're just like . . . *Them*—Do you watch him fuck his whores when he brings *Them* here?"

She shoots Cosette . . . Blood and brains and bones and a bullet exit the back of her head. Rivulets of red run down the wall . . .

The gun barrel is in her mouth, but she can't pull the trigger. Thoughts of her father stop her. She drops the gun . . .

Blood and brains . . .

Red . . .

Her Shame . . .

Red . . .

"Shut up!"

She gropes for another way. One that does not require her own hand . . . She can't go *that* way . . .

Nor by rope . . .

First her father, one shot to his right temple. Then her mentor— teacher, lover, hanging from that rope . . . shirtless, barefoot . . .

The car is running . . . She fans the gas pedal . . . Exhaust fumes fill the garage . . . Her eyes grow heavy . . . *She sees her father and her former lover on the street under the Sign of the Dragon . . . They wave.*

She stares vacantly. She sees black roses . . . *Sees a pleasant country . . .* She's coughing . . . Something heavy, hot, sits on her chest . . . She slips her shoes off . . . Unbuttons the buttons of her blouse . . . *She sees her father and her former lover, angels . . . Sees dead babies, angels . . . Hears words that have no sound . . .*

Cold tears are drying on her cheeks . . .

✦

Bitter October. Migrant birds—swept by the sun, far from the river . . . a long time ago dead as the sad stars, but with names in its mouth . . . ashes . . .

Footsteps . . .

White halls with white tiles. White shoes, white pants, white coats. White nurses in white uniforms. Pale nurses with plain features and lifeless expressions . . . Bright white lights shining over head . . .

Susan in a white dressing gown, sedated and restrained in a wheel-chair, sitting by the window. Susan, so pale and still, framed by a sun that bleeds to death in the arms of scrub-covered desert hills.

Fredric hands the doctor The Book.

"Two years ago she asked me to provide the funding for this. I showed it to a producer I know. He told me it would bleed money. I told her no. I should have said yes." *Should have said and done a lot of things. God, she looks, so . . . Hollow.*

"In these past few months, she's often read this thing for hours on end."

"I've looked in it a bit since she . . . Her teacher gave it to her. There's an inscription inside . . ."

"You'll take *extra* good care of her then, Doctor. I need not remind you of who I am and what my wife means to me," Fredric said.

"She is in the best of hands," Dr. Archer said, adjusting his unsightly horn-rimmed eyeglasses.

Archer knew who he was dealing with, knew how powerful and wealthy this man was. And Dr. Archer knew his discovery of the Carcosa Syndrome could bring him fame. Nothing would happen to this one . . . Now that he had a copy of The Book, the secrets to Carcosa and The King in Yellow play would be revealed to him . . . Awards and dinners and grants must be sure to follow . . .

Archer thinks of his *other* patient, escaped a year ago.

Perhaps there's a way to create a dialogue with him through the press and get him back here? Having both subjects here to study would guarantee my success.

"One thing further, Doctor. The ring Susan wears is *very* expensive and very old. I know I should take it for safe keeping, as it was my mother's and my mother's mother's, and Susan knows how very dear to me my mother was. Please understand, I see the ring as a sign. In my heart, I know Susan understands through the ring, how much I *need* her. Guard it, and my wife, well."

"Rest assured, I shall watch over them as if they were my dearest treasures," Dr. Archer said. He recognized the Yellow Sign on the face of the ring and knew it was another piece of his puzzle . . .

Fredric looks at Susan's bare feet, remembers their last night together. "One thing puzzles me, Doctor. Why don't the patients here wear slippers or shoes? I'll not have her taking a chill."

"Over the years we've had several of the facility's guests try to leave, without permission, of course. Our policy of not providing certain of our patients with footwear discourages any thoughts of long walks. You might think it somewhat odd, but it works." *For the most part.*

"In regards to her recovery, where do you plan to start?"

"When the time comes, I'll begin by exploring the issue of her father's suicide and the unfortunate circumstances she's undergone in her failed attempts at bearing children. And I've no doubt, her mentor's suicide is tied in as well."

Fredric thought of the three cheap abortions she had in college, the damage they caused to her womb. He wanted a drink. Two. He remembered the last three occasions Susan was hospitalized; the two miscarriages, and their stillborn daughter. He wondered if he, at some future date, would have to tell Dr. Archer about their sex life, about how he used other women and The Parties to control her . . .

❖

Her eyes survey the faces of the travelers as they gladly pass through the slim doors into the softly swirling cloud-waves.

The moon shines whitely and falls, gently, upon the lake . . .

In a room of soft heirlooms she sits in a large, stuffed blue chair. Her bare feet are tucked under her.

On the floor by her chair, black and white drawing of swans, slow as night, sail back to the place of touching.

She whispers from lips—tattered, dry garments, midnight tender, midnight cold. Her words, each a playful thief laughing, each a window, each a vessel of not coming back . . . Her words dance from the closed leaves of The Book to dim Carcosa's phantom gardenvale.

Spring skies come . . . no more . . .

(for Susan McAdam)

Orchard Fruit

Seen it too many times. The Kennedys, Elvis, Lennon, Princess Diana. Pick a celeb—even a minor one—and make them gone. And *bing-bang abra-alaka-sha-pocus!* Instant fame, and the feeding frenzy.

These days it seems everyone—and I do mean *everyone*—wants to know about my dear friend, Tom Brown. So they call and send letters, fax and e-mail, and even, with their thrusting microphones and Cyclops-eyed cameras, ring my doorbell. So hear it is. *Hopefully you'll leave an me alone now!*

Fifty-two million+ *Chabs* books sold—second only to *Goosebumps'* sales records for a children's series. The stunning art for the national campaign against child abuse some years back. Half a dozen best-selling posters—you should hear some of the offers I get for the original of *Lunatic Receives the Gift of Steam,* and his Giger-suggesting rendering of my Cthulhuvian snake-goddess, Kassogtha—like I'd think of parting with it while I draw breath! (I'm donating them to the National Art Gallery when I check out.) All the CD covers—what was it? Eleven, twelve million copies of The Road to Madness' *Backsliding into Pandemonium.*

5'8", one-sixty, brown hair. Middle name—Sewall. Drank his coffee black; said Loreena McKennitt sang like an angel (He was right of course.), and poets get the colors right, but the image is too often unclear; chain-smoked; thought PC was the worst kind of hogwash; liked the night sky without the moon, but full of stars; came up through the fanzines (didn't we all back then?); had a passion for artichokes I dare say was larger than Bob Price's legendary passion for pepperoni pizza, and was forever tending a bug sanctuary he called a vegetable garden.

When he was young—rough—and desperately searching he drank some and lied a lot. Wasn't much on film, but would bury his nose in a novel, loved to swim, went to church every Sunday, and was curious about more things than I care to remember. Most of all he was a painter. That's right, a painter; he *needed* to create arresting nightmariums on canvas, wood, and paper. Nightmares that scared you so bad, your dead grandmother on the other side could drown in your cold sweat.

He was also one of those expectant souls who need love as much as they need food or air. There's more, a confused, quiet-for-a-heartbeat-then-right-straight-back-to-hungry whole life more, but—

Tom lived in an old converted barn up in Maine; beyond a fairytale village with a white clocktower and nature's open green gardens and more than a few cows, out in the woods with the owls and the beasties, big and small alike, and the Mangler, a big black side of teeth and fur that slobbered all over the floor and did nothing but bark like he had a nail in his paw every time I visited. He was married about a hundred years ago—a beautiful woman, Margie, with a masters in mathematics, who treated you like her favorite uncle even when you spilled coffee (or tea in my case) on her brand new carpet, and who could bake a cherry pie to make you cry—but like many of us he blew it. So he lived out there with Margie and that damned dog and painted.

I still remember our 1st meeting. At a con in Providence back in '97. We were both hungry young bucks with some talent (he had about 200 ten-gallon paint buckets of the stuff) who dreamed big and laughed quick and right out loud. Well, you couldn't smoke in the hotel so we were standin' outside in the near-broiling sun puffing away. We introduced ourselves and things clicked. So we wrote to each other and called on the phone. I made him a character in the novel I was laboring over, and he painted—brilliantly—a few of the monsters I animated with squirming fugues of phrase.

Two years later, I had my first bestseller and Tom was doing covers and the like for everybody who was anybody. (Who could forget how he outmuscled Frazetta on the cover of Price's tour-de-force *Conan Against the Gods,* or the Miró-on-black acid of Ligotti's long-prayed-for return to the Noctuary?) The next decade and a half was a celebration, bright size and full. Recognition, a bit of fame, and money—not mountains, but enough to live without any economic fears.

But somebody turned the page. Actually, he forgot himself and everything he held dear. Screwed up one night in London with a buxom young admirer.

After Margie split, he started into painting moonlit cemeteries and open graves, and those caskets with—

For all of five minutes I was happy he didn't take to the bottle. (That was my way of handling things back then.) I though he'd find his way out of the hollow lands the way I finally did when Sue died.

He didn't.

He got rocked hard and fell ass over tea kettle into true madness.

His paintings had always been a furious clarity of unbridled links between death and sex and mythic imagery, but now something new and determined, something that blurred all sane thresholds, echoed a hypersensitive devotion to a darker ecstasy. The imaginary worlds and denizens of his past abhorrent shockers had never left the viewer with such a deep and wholly unclean bother. But these new loathsome accuracies— diseases, to be truthful—after looking at one, which I *will not* describe, I felt like a rape victim I'd seen portrayed in a popular film; I wished nothing more than to scrub myself until the violation was worn from my skin.

Upon being confronted by Tom's disturbing, and, I strongly felt, disturbed new work, I called to check on him under cover of praise. What I encountered was distance. It was like looking one of Lovecraft's cosmic monsters in the eye, all the excited conversations and quicksilver triumphs we'd exchanged seemed now as lost as the waters of Mars. How it was then would be never again I feared.

Faced with the hunger of his poisoned dreaming my concerns hardened to worries.

Then the trips began. Night after night he'd sit in the manicured orchard of bereavement and repose near the edge of town. He didn't drink there, nor did the tears come. He just sat by the back fence, a wire border limiting the bustling wild, staring at the uneven, bubbling weave of West Brook.

The summer passed and rumors popped and flittered about him wandering the cemetery howling the brittle utterances of a certifiable lunatic. By the following summer, his less than melodious lamentations of inconsolable grief escalated. The Heathers, local socialites without luster or any shard of compassion for anyone without blueblood or visible fixtures of money, having their second dinner party of the season interrupted, called the local constabulary. Three days later one of his banshee-echoing, post-witching hour rants at the distant moon woke Mayor McNaughton's cadaverous wife from a deathlike sleep.

Tom spent his first night in jail. I wired bail money.

Judge de Philips levied light fines and dispensed mild warnings, but by Lammas Tom was roaming the covered furrows again. Now wide-eyed and worry-lean, he looked like one of William Beckford's roaming nightgaunts.

Hell, I know everybody's lookin' for love—lost love, new love—but on August 4th they found him in a grave he'd dug up holding the cadaver of the recently interred Plarr girl. He wasn't engaged in acts unthinkable—sexual—just holding the damned thing; the cop who telephoned me said it looked like a mother holding a dialogue with her dreaming child. "Yes, that's right. Just sitting there whispering to her as if she could hear him." Thankfully, no one wanted to press *serious* charges.

That's when they called me the second time, and despite being an emotional mess in the middle of a bloodbath some people called a divorce, I decided to move up there for a few weeks, or months if need be, and straighten his ass out. Or at least see to it he found proper psychiatric care.

So there I was—stuck in the verdant wilds of One Horse Dorp, Maine—living half a mile away, spending every waking minute trying to bring him back from the danger zone. Thought I was getting through, but—

One afternoon—deadlines and editorial mishaps ready to take me out—while fast faxes were flying back and forth between my rage and my editor in New York, he slipped away. When I first noticed his car was gone I thought he'd gone to the store—I knew he'd run out of coffee and I'd bitched about being low on smokes. Two hours later, as twilight shadows gained form in the house, I realized there was a leak in the boat. These days, Tom hated going out, excepting his obsequial ventures on the lawns of Stroudwater Cemetery. He wouldn't have gone to town and stayed for over two hours. I lit a smoke and decided to give him an hour to return before I unslipped the dogs.

Now I've never been the outdoorsy type—I'll take the labyrinthine innards of an abundant bookshop or the hearty whorls of a neighborhood barroom—I like cement just fine. And just because I write dark tales where bloodletting and the supernatural laugh away the foaming festivities of their marriage in foulsome cellars on decomposing sheets of purloined human skin, doesn't mean I like to visit graveyards, especially at night—I'll wait till my date with oblivion, thank you very much. But that night I did. What choice did I have? I knew where he'd gone.

Fearing for him, at times foolishly I assured myself, I sped to Stroudwater knowing somewhere in the back near the bristling wilds lay the brook and his roost.

Muttering damnation (you must understand I hadn't been near a graveyard since the morning I dusted Sue's coffin with a handful of dirt), I came to the site of his continuing nocturne in the full bloom of dark. I parked my car outside the heavy gates and looked upon the promenades were we exile love to dust. A slaughter house, or any other butcher's theater, would have stirred less agonies in me, but I passed through the gates and walked into the silent shadows.

My abrupt darts of thought and fear became wild images of ghostly apparitions ejected from sepultures, premature burial, and my dead wife's rotting face accosting me as I walked the stone-lined lanes. Add my distorted moving shadow to the firm abyssal shades cast by marker and monument and you can guess I was scared on a level only children know.

Puffing my way through two cigarettes and cursing myself for having started whistling of all things, I came to the cemetery's back lawn. And there, beside the oldest of the vale's bittersweet cathedrals, as still as the surrounding decorative statuary, Tom stood. I called to him and he turned. The fat pearl of the low moon tinted harlequin hues upon the ravines of dark meditations and despair carved into his face. I called again, hoping the voice of a friend would be an empowered spell vital enough to break the misery of this bound in torment nightwalker. But as if I was too distant to be heard, he turned away and reaffirmed his grip upon a shovel, and I noticed the dirt on his hands and clothing, and the mounds of unearthed soil.

"Digging again. For what?" I whispered, though my jaw and fists were clenched in anger and shock.

It was then that my fears turned to legal complications. As I wondered if he would be better served by being arrested again, and hopefully placed in a facility able to free him from the bonds of oblivion's drapery, he moaned in tones gone foul.

I stepped back, for if the bones of the dead rose up before me and danced with the Devil himself I could not have been more flabbergasted, for indeed the dead did rise. Having clawed their way from, or having been ejected from below, ripe ghouls ambled from the subterranean depths beneath Stroudwater to clamor through the airs of blackest night.

The timid boy in me froze, for there before the cold matter of fact man I'd become, stood the Morlocks of my childhood's most intense fears. Slightly hunched, yet upright, the troupe of single-minded beasts of claws and fangs and savagery, had come with burning bellies to feast-day.

As they erupted from the ground before him, like subway commuters quick to leave the lower depths, I retreated a few steps. Tom did not.

Like a fool long parted from his wits I did not flee at the sight of several female forms, each naked as the night sky, hideously revealing moldering muffs of matted hair and withered, dangling breasts, and most horrid of all, desiccated leprous flesh and milky red eyes, ringing my transfigured friend.

They swooped down upon him like a murder of crows intent on the splattered remains of some roadside rodent who'd lost his poor judgment, and a mad dance by moonlight, a waltz of grotesque swirling began.

Unbelievably, though I ordered him twice to run, he stood unmoving in the center of the Devil's coachmen. His head was titled back, mouth opened in an O, hands outstretched—palms up, as if in rapture—

I swear his breath was still. Blissfully drowning in the swell of his epiphany, he reached out, living flesh to rotting casings, to embrace the trespass of his executioners as carelessly as I might to turn on a light. And the surgery of their touch commenced.

Slow were the cuts. Paths of blood grew and spread like groping vines of ivy as it flowed like black wine in the moonlight. The slimy tongues of the living dead suckled on his clawed-opened flesh, but he did not retreat in pain and fright, nor did he cry out for the she-demons to grant quarter and be gone. No, to my utter revulsion, he extended his arms further to offer the gluttonous blasphemies the fabulous artistry that ran through his veins.

He didn't scream. In fact his moving lips appeared to mirror the guttural laughs and pleasured moans of the ghouls.

I stood there watching, as if the image was a cartoon, or behind the glass of an aquarium, distorted, untouchable, and unreal. I was as motionless as a nightshade or a mountain of the distant glowing moon taking in their appearance.

There was no breath or whisper of a breeze, yet their hair, faded, bleached, or bled of color by age, rustled like nests of mussed cobwebs in a strong wind. And I could see their teeth—serrated rows of crowded black and yellow shards of pointed bone. (He would have stood a better chance among sharks, I thought.) These were not sweetly scented angels; their hideous forms were a song to the eye compared to the stomach-turning stench they exuded.

The tallest of the affronts to all feminine grace and beauty stepped toward the circle surrounding him and barked something rougher than any fast foreign tongue. The others stepped back from their sucking and licking and kneeled with bowed heads like fearful supplicants. Padding damp grass the troupe's doyenne of blistered, warted, and pocked skin circled him twice before pausing. Face to face—red eyes to glazed eyes—her eyes tightened. She seemed to be surveying him.

Certain of the coming death blow, I looked at the ground around me for some weapon, but found none, and my fear and confused disbelief reasserted their petrifying grip on me.

As she examined his wiry contours, for what hellish purpose I was certain I understood all too well, I, horridly mesmerized, took in the details of her form. God, her nose, or the half of it that hadn't been eaten or rotted away, was a curved beak—seeming quite capable of rending flesh. Her bony shoulders and near-skeletal arms were scarred by the marks of sisterly nipping, perhaps over unearthed spoils. The ravages of something akin to leprosy, and misshapen warts were as abundant on her taut buttocks and long thighs as lichen on a cave wall.

Seemingly with speeds almost faster than sight, her black-nailed fingers—sticky with desiccated carrion—were upon him; pinching and probing and poking in their unorthodox explorations. Finally, she reached out and firmly grasp his phallus. Then after considering it with the judgmental scrutiny of a horse buyer at auction, she looked into his eyes. A smile—can monsters smile?—came to her torn and maggot-eaten lips.

The she-ghoul nodded and he nodded back.

She stepped forward and placed her hands on his side as if to dance with him, then bent as if to impart a kiss and instead took a bite from his chest and chewed it.

The dry tightness of my throat forbade my scream. In revulsion, I stepped back yet again and found myself pinned to the hardness of a stone cross. I prayed to its master for protection or invisibility.

She continued to feast upon him, taking a series of bites from his chest and shoulders. All the while her talons pressed into the flesh of his buttocks, holding him fast to her mock rutting. After consuming the fourth or fifth walnut-sized chunk of his flesh, she reached down and brought her sagging breast to her lips and bit off her own nipple, which she chewed on for a time. Then, as if she were a mother softening food for her offspring's tender digestive tract, the ghoul vomited the pasty hash into his open mouth. And by all the gods in every heaven and every hell, he swallowed the food she offered.

Spasms racked his body and he shook as if electrified. Finally, his voice, or the pain it contained all these months, returned in the form of a scream, and it fell upon me as black rain in the pit of souls. And he slumped—his head upon her shoulder, certainly lifeless. But he was not dead. Clasp tight in her arms, embracing the thirsty kiss of his ghoul-queen's maggot-tongue, vitality returned to his ravaged shell. A life-creating vitality I could and would not fathom.

He'd found the love he so desired—*needed.* Yes, needed; for the one thing that Thomas Sewall Brown had been unable to live without for all the years I'd known him was the love of another.

In the stark illumination of night's pearl he turned to briefly consider me. I looked in his reddening eyes, and he in mine. His mouth—gone was the humored smile of my fond recollections, replaced by unevenly-fanged jaws—opened as if to speak, but perhaps his words, if he had any, would be of no value.

The she-ghoul nudged him and snarled. With her talons around his wrist she tugged and stepped into the disemboweled grave and he followed.

The others, dismissing me with unhinging looks and barked snarls, were quick to follow their queen and new king.

After a time I walked to the maw of the tunnel to—*where?*

Looking down its throat I saw only black. I desperately wanted to call out, and for the slightest moment I thought to follow—to bring him back. But what was there to bring back to the sane world of clocks and common toils?

Confounded in the heavy weather of fearful and bewildering emotions, and sudden murderous anger, I left the ribbons and shredded swatches of his bloody clothing, the shovel, and the imprint of the dance in the damp ground. Before the sun found time to rise I gathered my few belongings and left for the cement security of my home in New York.

A few days later there were questions regarding his disappearance and the possibility of foul play, but I dismissed them easily stating my inability to reach him and the demands of my editor had sent me home in angered frustration.

You might name me mad—or worse, holding my recollection nothing more than a way to cash in on our friendship and his fame. Think what you like. His departure under lunar light lives thick and crisp in my frail thoughts. It shook my comprehension, as all startling and undreamed-of encounters must, but I was awake, and sober.

I have never returned to Maine, nor have I entered another orchard of the dead. For I have buried to much of my heart and found no fruits for my toils.

I have also stipulated in my will that I wish to be cremated.

(*for the CoffeeGhost*)

The Songs Cassilda Shall Sing,
Where Flap the Tatters of the King

For SusanM, worthyWorthy,
C'cyss-kohe/COFFEE*ghost/beelze*BOB/*Saletti,*
AnKh-S, Carlos OM, *Th*-ill,
ST.eve——s . . .
& all those HOWL(ers)
& Our Lyricist and his r-p-o-p-h-e-s-s-a-g-r

"All the Stars Are Dead Now", © 1994 David Tibet/Current 93,
Ourobouros Music
Used by kind permisson of David Tibet

S usan left her small-minded town for that Anotherwhere. In Anotherwhere there was motion and . . . escaped, kindred spirits. Beyond the Mom, apple pie, and Superman affectation of the rusty actors in their endless cycles, there were things she wanted to see, and things she wanted to hear, and say, and—more than anything—DO. She wanted to find The Underground. The one *Alternative Press* and *Pluto's Orchard* and *Catharsis Magazine* raved about, the one college radio, ever exploring new vibrations, sent out like Plutonian ragas. Many was the night she dreamed of being part of that flourishing culture where everynight was an October midnight, and a component of the post-industrial nation, who, painted like exquisite corpses, danced like pale-skinned iron birds running from rust.

Born, certainly not asked—sometimes *goddamn*positive, not even wanted—she needed to be away from Stale St. Endless Domination with its whitewash of clean and safety. She wanted her passions to soar on the forbidden wings of soft midnight. Wanted to own the firmament. Susan ached to break free and find one revelation—even a tiny one. She was suffocating and wanted her due.

F riday afternoon on the chessboard, every elaboration splashing. Distortions, fabulous disappointment, demented tactics or predatory intentions angling, all-too-public executions blasting like car horns, anything you could name elbowed its way along the avenues. And she, in midnight-black and full of imaginings, moved through the patterns of the city.

Susan—NOW/in this new city with a new life/**LILY**—hit the concrete citywalks on a cold day. She carried a few fears, $723—her fortune, her Ouija board, and her fragility wrapped in a black on black aesthetic. Inside her knapsack lay her blood-red pens and journals of poetry—black shadowy weaves of heartbreak and gloom. Past the hustling pimps and social throw-aways swarming the bus station, and past the bad karma of the human condition tossed like damaged goods into moldering doorways. Past subway maps and flyers for Jesus and extremes rattlin' to take it apart and barstool saints in conversations of one and acres of redundant and magazine stories come to life and the numb of shrill SALE assertions in windows. And on every corner, either available or ducking the wind, greed and hope considering career alternatives. Lily moved through the ruins. She knew the street address of Café Morphine.

On the bustling auto-da-fé with 100 taxis barreling to the next traffic-crush and the squads of lemmings being herded to *whoknowswhere?,* big, dark innocent eyes fed her mind with the huge of it. It loomed; gray, brutal vibes, overpowering. Its buildings were as intense as the sculptures of a hurtful hallucination. An ill-junkyard perhaps, openly mocking one's self-assurance, but this was IT. Here you could let your emotions escape your skin, you could create a dance with your pain.

Lily smiled to herself—she was gonna roll the bones. Re-made/remodeled, she was ready for tomorrow's ports of call and all the surprises just waiting to be opened . . . and the Answers! She was going to find a Goth band that needed a singer-poet and on a darkened stage, sur-rounded by the sinister freeform, in the drama of flesh and soul, that deliri-ous impromptu of ghosts and ecstasies rattling, she would find the glow of heaven.

As Lily walked/hurried/side-stepped the pandemonium, she dreamed of Cassilda. Cassilda harnessed her pain, and made something of the chaos—you could hear it in the songs of SYS. Lily heard it. Every time she pushed the play button and the bootleg cassette began to flow across the heads of the small black Sony Walkman® she heard Cassilda escape the damnation of this decaying society. That's what she needed, to be far from the oppressive gray lands.

In the devil's club she'd find bandmates—soulmates—and they'd pin buoyant, swirling sounds of brooding brightness under her haunted sara-bandes, and she'd sing & she'd mend & find happiness & peace, & even love—not just fucking, but love, real love. She'd find an oasis of sanity in this sinister cartoon of madness, and a cure for her torments. And the Man in the Moon and *ALLtheREST* could go to Hell!

All she needed was to find Café Morphine, and guitars flowing over drums, and there in the synth-wash and the lights, the brothers and sisters who were sick of The Housebreaking and being branded "LAZY CUNT" & "WORTHLESS MOTHERFUCKER".

"That's all I need."

A nd she found it. After the 1800 mile bus trek from her parents' prison, beside a dull-white cafeteria with red plastic seats that called itself a restaurant and a grimy-faced shop with a chain-link veil that sold used books and CDs. As yellow as the sun it stood—

Café Morphine

Café Morphine ... The hand-painted sign with its weathered Eyes of Haroeris ... And inside, wide & long & 2 short flights down ... Catacombs. Bricks. Plank flooring. Exposed pipes now painted black like the veins of some unseen beast—

Once owned by an ex-wrestler named "Sharkey" until the fire in '61. 57 burned alive one night when Cass and the Muckrakers raised the roof. Formerly the outpost of pimps & hepcats & Finger-Popping Daddies & pill-poppin' grifters & the Commie sex-maniacs with long-stemmed reflections of Soul Francisco's mari-juana-hipsters & those rejoicing sparrows illuminating long-lined mysteries from truth-teared eyes of naked jazz & the cutting points of view of mellow shaman with fanciful fables of Tangier and the art-grottos of Berlin and the grub served in Barstow's hoosegow and when Ferlinghetti had said Allen said Jack once—

Café Morphine ... once Villa Delirium—HOWL all night, cut it up—until the fire ... But even after being boarded up for over 2decades, its name, and the pursuits of this new unconstrained generation—HOWL all night, let it bleed— hadn't altered.

Lily read the pasted-on announcements.

7th
Daddy's little Whores

Today—tonight

8th
The
embarrassed **Personalities**
of
GOD

&

In Some Small Darkness

and next Thursday—She couldn't believe it!, but there it was, right there in plain letters.

14th
SYS

"The Society of the Yellow Sign." Whispered from her lips like a prayer come true.

Cassilda's band *was* playing here. The Internet had it right.

Now she just needed a place to stay. And a job until she could form her band.

Lily drifted. Just walking, sometimes at faster speeds. Looking. Trying to take it in and sort it out—measuring it on her bullshit meter. She ate a sandwich, washed it down with a bubbling Coke, and waited for night, when the club would open.

She hung down the block watching the door to the club. Some few— "Employees?"—entered and the beerlights in the window came on.

Before the shrine five came together. Then six became nine. Two more over there. And five off to the left near the maw of the alley. Now 20 or more waiting. The covens had gathered. 10:06 by her watch. "It's time." She moved toward the rustling. Nods & looks & mouths pink under black lipstick. Hellishly thin under black & black & bitchy was the dress code. She turned to look at, to quietly revel in, each self-portrait of freedom—

Denizens in corpsepaint & gender-benders in black lace. Leather/rubberware S&M demons—*ever*hungry. Vampyros lesbos, lips as dark as wine. Siouxies & androgyny. Hedonism & nihilism—pick a toxin. Borg-weds-Barker black on black stitched to black. Chiffon & crepe. Demonic tattoos etched in scar & ink. Mascara & piercings & crosses & pentagrams & onyx & unvoiced questions & oblique expectations; all tinted by the streetlamp's ivory gauze, they, like tethered ravens, waited to step across the threshold.

Mina & The Hanged Man & TheZipperZombie & Locrian & Esmeralda & Ghoul Von Malice & Countess Bathory & Mistress Absynthe & Edvard & Claire Voyeur & Eva Obsession—Lily backed away from one who'd christened himself Necro. She wanted to be far from the creature in the strategically ripped *Reverend Marilyn Manson is the Antichrist Superstar* tee. Far from his fully displayed malice & rot-yellow teeth & rankbreath close enough to induce puking.

A lovely, shadowy waif, was beside her. Big bright eyes. Black lips smiled and formed a word. "Hi." Head cocked, curious.

"Hi." Tentatively replied.

"I'm, Tess." Another gentle smile.

"Lily." Hopeful, forgetting to be guarded.

Tess looked at the knapsack and the suitcase.

"I haven't found a place yet." A small, helpless shrug with the explanation.

"So I see." Smiling, remembering her own coming out. Tess felt the fear of the 1st day. "C'mon, I live around the corner. You can crash on my couch."

Lily followed the slow breeze waltz of her savior.

"Eaten?"

"Yes. A little something."

"Good. Put your things there."

And they went back to the club.

Past the bouncer, down the stairs, through the huge black doors with their stars & sigils, into the warm cavern with its stage & tables & candle-light & gaunt rustling shadows milling in black-on-black art-crypt. Swirling, gigantic music—Medusa Cyclone's "The Smith Can"—danceable, alive & edgy as lightning.

Backlit with flickering candles, the pair of girls poised in a shaded corner with drinks—iced vodka. Near the safety of a wall, viewing the ropes.

"See, *THEM.* That's Byron—a royal, dangerous ASS—and his ghoul-pack of sick, cold things. Stay away! They're *blood*-drinkers . . . And thieves when it suits them. Byron says fuck AIDS. Only Lestat lives forever. The rest die when they die . . . Hey, there's Boo!" Tess smiled and waved at the Edward Gorey rendering of Count Poe in the tattered cape. "*C'mon!*—You'll like him. He knows everybody worth knowing."

And she was off, faster than a leaf in the wind. Like a good shadow Lily followed closely.

Boo swayed softly—head back, eyes closed, arms up like a tree—to beat the of Collection D'Arnell Andrea's *"L'Aulne et la Morte."* The amiable nightshade turned. "Tess!" A gentle hug and a kiss. Smiling soft brown eyes.

Lily liked him right off. He felt *right.* And looked good.

"This is, Lily."

Boo's eyes considered her. "Hi." Bright. Friendly. Like Tess'.

"Hi," Lily said through a nervous smile.

And so, on smiles and flowing music, the night, and the imaginative expressions of Halloween and tragedy—nearly half of them anyway—and Lily danced.

Coffee and day-old bagels in a clean kitchen. Oh there were cobwebs high in the corners of the small living room and the sofa was borderline-ratty, but the kitchen held no collection of old fast-food wrappers and waiting for the trashbag clutter. Who cared if the kitchen table was a wobbly-legged card-table, the chair (needing a coat of paint and missing two back spokes) was solid. And Tess looked cozy & normal in her sky-blue nightgown of flannel. Lily sat with her hands cradling the warm mug of coffee, vaporizing her ghosts, and Tess' calico kitten, Pyewacket, stroking her bare ankles.

Five days out of prison and in HEAVEN. The dream life. Not some shimmering reflection of some otherwhere, not some visionary impression glimpsed on the ceiling above her bed back in Endless Domination, but here—Hands-on real and rightNOW. Beauty could come from pain. They WEREN'T "socially inept"! They WEREN'T "oblivion seekers"! They WEREN'T lost in some abysmal evening enduring only the reckless soliloquies of the fallen! *They weren't!* Brightness found ways through the cracks. Dreams could come true.

Two days later Lily had a sales job in a Goth boutique run by Tess' friend and had moved into Tess' spare bedroom. She'd purchased a boom-box with a CD player and two used CDs (the first two volumes of *Heavenly Voices,* which she'd left behind when she fled her parent's prison), red pushpins for the rip-repaired-with-tape poster of Black Tape For A Blue Girl she'd come upon, an inexpensive mattress, make-up, and few appropriate clothes, and a ring with an imitation yellow topaz—her birthstone. She felt the ring was fitting, for she had been reborn. Her share of the rent paid and some food in the fridge, $73 & 83 cents left till payday, and in three days SYS would be at Café Morphine. Bright, revitalized, Lily was going to see Cassilda & SYS perform.

"Everything's so purrrrrfect," she whispered to Pyewacket. Lily was certain she'd be in a band by next week and in love by the end of the month—perhaps with soft-eyed, Boo. When she closed her brown eyes she could see it all flickering on her lids like a silent movie.

Tomorrow & tomorrow came and past and the day drew near. Then it arrived and inched along slowly.

Twilight—FINALLY! The excited bustle of preparations— "Everything must be right for Cassilda." Lily's expectant thoughts reached out like the tendrils of an overgrown garden. She played her SYS tape; twice, then thrice. And again—Overjoyed, she reveled in it. The primitive simple pulse of the kettledrum, the repeated single note phraseology of the reverb-saturated distortions voiced by the guitars, the harsh, cyclical wavers of electronic fog summoned by the keys, and Cassilda's apocryphal articulation of sweeping poetry, rich in timbre—painfully bittersweet, nearly silent at times, then soul shattering, the death wail of 1000 vampires wasting in solar fire, SYS' rigorous declaration was intensely alive, inexhaustible. Disorienting, it was a complex amalgam of pagan delirium and death. Lily sang along in a light, aching voice. Tonight she would whisper along as Cassilda enabled the holy texts. Tonight there would be a royal ball in the court. Lily had her ticket, her black-lacquered nail traced the bold red stamp of the Yellow Sign below the letters SYS. She looked at it while she sang harmony with Cassilda's, for the moment fragile, soprano.

"Songs that the faithful shall sing,
Where flap the tatters of the King . . .
The coiled thread unravels—"

Tess, announced by her biting clove tobacco, was in the doorway.

Lily ran and hugged her. *"LIVE!* I'm going to see them *live!"*

Tess faked a frown and corrected. "We."

Lily squeezed harder and kissed Tess' cheek with full round lips like ripe fruit. "We," she gladly agreed.

The dark club, painted in shades of gray and flatblack to resemble the exposed stone bowels of some sorcerer's castle, was nearly as black as it had ever been. No candles on the tables, no neon lights. No flash or flicker or strobe. On the stage dozens of thick black candles burned in two enormous iron candelabras. There sat the uneven wall of black amps and a blood-colored gong with the Yellow Sign emblazoned upon it and a monstrous kettledrum. Two electric guitars. A five-string bass. Two electronic keyboards supported by thin black metal legs. A small, straight-outta "The Phantom of the Opera" pipe organ. But no microphones.

Lily panicked. Muscles tight, goosebumps beneath her apparel. How would she hear Cassilda? Then it struck her—like being told your dog had died—Was Cassilda sick? All this great luck soiled by some bug, or accident—it wasn't fair! Some other setback she'd handle—willingly accept if she had to, but, *Please!*—not this.

No. She'll have a wireless mic. That's it! THANK GOD.

The DJ played a brooding organ piece by Paul Schütze. The introductory organ invocation faded and a semi-demonic "Call from the Grave" from Aghast rose to fill the void. Lily absorbed Nebel's witchly utterance. She wasn't Cassilda but she was good.

Lily, hand clasped tightly to Tess', fidgeted. Her sharp, uneven bangs played across her eyes like wind-whipped black branches cutting the shining face of the moon. The wait was agonizing. She could barely breathe.

Molochai, the DJ, sensed it—he saw it in every thirsty eye. Let them wait. Make them want, NO, *need*, the salvation of SYS' funeral mass. And for nine minutes and seven seconds he nudged the throng's desire with Current 93's impassioned requiem "All the Stars Are Dead Now." David Tibet's ecclesiastical delivery rang through the club—"*Dead! Dead! Dead! Dead! Dead! Dead!* **Dead!!!**"

With a vulture's eyes Molochai scanned the assembled faces. "Corpse-paint. How fitting." They were consecrated. Cassilda would be pleased.

Lily didn't want to hear David Tibet sing about the Last Days, she wanted to hear something gentle & bittersweet. Something like This Ascension or Bleeding Like Mine or Love Is Colder Than Death or The Moon Seven Times—How she adored Lynn Canfield's kindly voice. That was it. She was going to ask the DJ to play "Her House" or better still, "This and That." She wanted cascading whispers not screams—Something they could dance to.

Lily wore a long dress of the palest yellow; it was almost a robe. She wanted Cassilda to see her, to think she was beautiful, and *worthy*.

Tess, in layers of softly fluttering black lace, brought Lily ice-cold vodka in a glass with a fluted stem. Boo was off to score some grass for the bittersweet after. The girls smiled at each other and giggled quietly. Moonlight Cinderellas dreaming, they were at the ball. This was their night.

No music played. Molochai wasn't in the booth. In the radiance of darkness, between impurity & the divine, the crowd with their medicines & powders waited. SYS would be on soon—They knew it! In another minute. Perhaps two, or even five, but soon.

A tall man in an ivory-yellow cassock with the Yellow Sign stitched upon his breast stepped on to the stage. Many marveled at the line of buttons running gaunt-neck to booted-ankle, they appeared to be fragments of *real* bone. His head & face *completely* shaved his ghost-colored skin mirrored a bleached skull. If any countenance could be said to be deathly his would most certainly banish the consideration of any other. He did not look at the wanting creatures.

Rushes of whispered speculation arose. Was this Baron Uoht? Could he be the one called only, Thale? Maybe he was The Stranger, or Yhtill, or the one said to be unnamable? Like the members of the thoroughly secretive avant-parodist band, the Residents, the identities of SYS were mystery-shrouded unknowns.

There were six in the band; five men (by their habiliment and seemingly cenobitic demeanor they might have been clones or identically-outfitted quintuplets) & Cassilda. They had names, but offstage NEVER spoke—NO interviews, NO chats with fans after shows. NO photographs. NO proper recordings, only hand-labeled bootleg cassettes which bore no signs of their origin. The band NEVER dallied with groupies or carried an entourage or drank or ate or were seen before or after shows. They simply came and went like an illusionist's enigmatic apparitions. The lives & times of the Legendary Pink Dots were as precisely documented as the Beatles in comparison.

Without so much as a nod or a cough or the bat of an eye Cassilda's bandmate opened a Bibleblack tome. He closed his eyes as if to concentrate or pray before speaking. "She, our radiant sister, full with the wisdom of Our Father—*the true and* **only** *God*—has written the 'Inevir Decrees' in the *Vèniavd.*"

Another band member, a doppelganger of the first, appeared and struck the gong with a long bone.

Again the first spoke,
   "'On that perfect and holy day,
   when falls the Night of All Nights,
   when men must whisper,
         Goodbye, Day—
  He, Our Father,
  shall stand in the lush garden with his desires
         and *overwhelm.*
  His judgment shall be delivered!
  This is the law.'"

On, his slow, chilling monotone reverberated. Passage after passage underpinned by pressurized silence.

Was there any member of the conclave unaffected by the truth of his dramatic recitation? Each, blood-drinker and beautiful nightshade alike, stood statuary still, as if weathered monuments in a garden of bereavement. It seemed Tibet's doomsaying voice —"*Dead! Dead! Dead! Dead! Dead! Dead! Dead! . . .*"— had, like the skeletal finger of the Reaper, marked each as it moved through the shadows.

THEN, without the aid of stage-tricks, concealing fogs, or dimmed lights, the remaining members of the band were suddenly on the stage, instruments in hand.

THE ILL DRONE OF WHITENOISE UNDER NAPALM-RIFFERY/joined by/**THE TOLLING THUNDER OF THE KET-TLEDRUM—A HEARTBEAT. HUGE. AS EVEN AS MACHIN-ERY.**/then—instantly/**THE EXPLODING-MAGNUM-IN-YOUR-**

FACE OF A JACKBOOT BASSLINE/and/THE RAZOR-BLIGHT OF A BLEAT-OF-PAIN-GUITAR LEAD SLASHING—

Cassilda stood there in a billowing yellow robe, tattered at the hem and sleeves like rags weathered for 100 years. Cold as any mummy or vampire, the fierce queen, her silver-shod staff of power held in her right hand, surveyed—encompassed—the flamboyant assemblage. Above the dissecting table of aural hate, hard as a raging cock, the demon queen roared.

Counterpoint to Cassilda's ravaging press, banshee-guitars rose up, screeching like the damned singin' out in The Pit.

Often the sounds of the city burrow into your brain like grave worms. But sometimes they suddenly confront sensitivities as sharply as the gleaming edge of an arcing razor. The hell-storms-into-your-town malice roaring from SYS gashed ears like the latter. SYS' bass-heavy message was on the march. And it didn't plod, it swaggered in its jagged pummeling—Just as if it had a mission. And it did! The shit had hit the fan—**BIGTIME!** The *NewThing* was out of the box. Yep, bet yer dead-ass. It jammed & rammed & (surerthanhell)slammed. And if they didn't step aside—FLEE—S*uper*quick—more than two screamin' guitars, a bass & drums, would be in their faces.

BUT they COULDN'T MOVE—Cassilda held them in the black.

The spot offed and Cassilda's prayer decayed.

A motionless moment. Breath held. Expectation.

The storm-chord hit like the first salvo of a blitzkrieg. Aerial missiles of aural napalm and hot metal poured over and penetrated the crowd, vaporizing all but this moment of power & dark burning rapture.

Waves and spears of STEAMROLLERHEAVY rock rolled over the hellraisers. Then came the whirling/fLaShInG/searing MEGAwattage of strange lights lashing and fanning in synchronicity with the volcanic soundfire.

POP-POP-POP it ripped into 'em. Their fear gushed out like blood fleeing the pressure suit we term skin.

The black was banished. Exploded. Eradicated. A sharp, tight spot hit the skull-moon face of Cassilda. Perhaps in the bowels of Hell the slight movement of her facial muscles and jaw might be a smile, but here on Earth, even in this den, it was the cold salivating promise of the harshest rending death. Shark-black eyes open full and wide, projecting psychotic madness and hateful blasphemies, body, arms, and hands as tight as piano wire encircling a dying man's neck, Cassilda's razor-etched maw opened to deliver the word.

"Slaves of pain & DAMNATION!
Rise and adore your New & Only MASTER!"

Eeee-yowaaaaaaaa! They were outta their seats—as if their asses were on fire. UP! Fast & Hard & Ready as cocks! All were willingly branded by her command. Forever to wear the sign of the King. They loved it!—BUT!—But . . . still they were full of fear.

"In hate, and with malice, the King has bought your soul.
YOU, Death's OWN,
are but crumbs . . ."

Boots stomped. Burnt throats howled. A frenzied gallop of kickass, combat-ready, eat-'em-alive surging running wild, the beat rode the torture road.

Street-hawked chemicals, adrenaline, and pure unfettered angst melted to fear slammed through the concert-goers' veins & souls & brains as Cassilda sang.

The sun shook and the earth cracked, murderous indignation rose to challenge and consume Heaven's light as Cassilda sang on, delivering one ferociously-gritty plague-spell after another.

As suddenly as a 90mph/head-on/car*crash* the band stopped grinding their hell-hammer riff.

Cassilda, the King's beautiful and perfect daughter, spun to face—

An image of great feathered wings of dusky light spread wide. There hovered pure malignity—The King, arms fully extended, welcoming. What little could be seen of the exposed gray flesh of his hands & forearms & face appeared as desiccated as a long-interred corpse in hot dry ground. A carcass denied the preservation techniques of mummification.

Wide, blasted-eyes. Fear-dry throats. None in the hall showed their fangs. Tight jaws and tighter urges tense in their waiting. The stillness of near silence—a few seconds in duration, a few lifetimes in impact—suspended like a waiting noose.

Then the breach, the slight fracture. The low-register bellow of a single chord issued from the pipe organ. It rose and fell like the subharmonic breathing of an unseen leviathan in great rattling breaths. As the vast five-cycle exhaling was expelled, thin gray/white wraiths, hideously twisted and skeletal, streamed forth from the black pipes etched with the King's cipher. Bolts of jagged fire hounded their fleeting arcs. In pain the fire-lashed specters writhed in the devil's rodeo until they were ripped apart by the teeth of invisible rending winds.

The demonic members of SYS knelt head to chest before the image of their King. Hands clasped together as a fist, burning tears from clamped eyes, each adored HIM.

Cassilda arose and faced the crowd, her voice the ambush of the poisoner.
"Suffering children of mortal fire—
Flesh is the mask.
Behold the divine hour,
When flap the tatters of the King."
Her whisper ascended. A song and prayer across urban abysses, Cassilda's
adjuration flew—finding force, power in its need.
"Come to us, Lord of the Grave!
Come to us, Grim One!
Come to us, Truth.
Ruler of all, behold the anguished flesh awaiting—
Come NOW!"
Enjoined echoes. The crowd embraced Cassilda's cry to Hell. Short-
ened. Hungrier. *"Come, Truth! Come, O King! Come, O King!"* The free
chant of the anvil chorus. The stomp. Doom walking. Wanting. Rapid
heartbeats lashed to the wheel of heavy need. Hearts painfully aflame. Now
LOUDER. A demand. *"Come-KING! Come-KING!"* Thunderous.
Desperation raw.

ON & ON & ON the black petition pressed. Out of the hot arena.
Winding & turning. Left/Right/Right/Left & straightahead—thoughtfast.
Wheeling around rats sifting mounded garbage and jagged brick angles.
Over—under—through—Past speeding taxis and parked cops—Deeper
into hard-walled streets weathered by man's neglect and mutability—Past
pissed in alleys that mirrored 12-dollars a night compartments—Past broken windows and the shattered dreams of the city's ejected scatterlings
bludgeoned with disgust's rough laughter—Past lives sagging with all the
forward&backward&aroundAGAIN—Forward & forward & straight to
the far/too/fuckin'REAL to be a mere nightmare overTHERE the call
hurled. Fast to the target. From senders to receiver—
Into the sky—
Past the moon—
Past stars of every color & configuration—
Ash light . . . clouds . . . formless shining *superclusters* . . . ex-
panding margins . . . unimaginable cataclysms . . . diffuse rings . . . dwarf
& spiral . . . tightly bound broods—
Past arrogance, notion, and hardship—
Though measureless black
lagoons of emptiness to the Place Where the Black Stars Hang—
Delivered.

The plea, how it aroused the gluttony of the King. He heard the summons, hoped for a fat table. He turned. Head back, bathing in the feverish want. Motionless. Raw want as hard as hate's pure heat. His unknowing conscripts awaited. His heavy boots marched forward. Change a letter and the deep toll of his footfalls would have sounded like doom, change the pitch of his breathing and its rasp would have sounded like a slashing razor.

From far, cold Carcosa he came.

The King came to his table.
There was spread

l
i
f
e

Without
master
or cause
or purpose
it exists.
It rapes the heart.
It's as heavy as facing guilt in the mirror.

they felt they were lost in it—blind in a labyrinth of traps set only for them
they were right
they stood on the heights
each alone

hands empty of everything
except. . .

FEAR

And each, on their feet or on their knees, having heard the word of the King's priestess, having felt the cool stroke of the King anoint their brow, gave up their breath and their souls. And having acknowledged the unavoidable Yellow Sign, death's sigil, each troubled young mortal shed the last of their desires and expired.

Lily beheld it all. Tess & Boo, and even Byron & his ghoul-pack—desiccated, sucked dry. Picked clean they all lay like scraps. Lily, baptized in the pure wild truth, was the last standing.

TruL(il)y

a

l

o

n

e

This wasn't the Cassilda Lily came to see, *to worship*. These weren't the SYS songs she loved—knew—not the ones on her bootlegged tape. She desperately wanted Cassilda to sigh the victorious rituals on the cassette, those so hauntingly akin to the ceremonial minstrelsy of Ordo Equilibro. This wasn't supposed to happen on the way to heaven! Where did this sudden turn come from?—And WHY*?????* She'd come so far. Why couldn't this just subside and be swept away? WHY?

To brave the windmills for a mere glimpse of redemption, and—
And she emphatically didn't want death. NOTNOW! She'd lived through
                                        —the rape by her
brother's beerguzzling college buddy,

                              —and Ann's stupidOD,
                              —and the ridicule by the
cheerleaders & the sluts,

                              —and her own bungled
suicide attempt.
                         She came here to find life, to bloom and be glad to be in the arms of a beautiful young lover who gave his treasures as freely as his perfect kisses. Lily didn't want death, she wanted celebration.
                         But the King—call him Doom or Destiny or the Grim Reaper or the Collector of Souls or Cessation or simply, Death—wanted her for his celebration.

Open, everything inside OPEN, but there were no miracles in this touching. Stealing all the warps & processes flourishing within her, the invader took every self-portrait, every meditation, all the montages collected for rainy days. GONE—devoured—the Lord's Prayer and the name of her favorite TV show. SO TO—the taste of pepperoni pizza with EX-TRAcheese

... worries over *frizzy* hair

... rain

... shame/BLOOD, but no outer tears her 1st time—
Toofast/Toopainful. "Is that all there is?" Later, much later, laughing at it
... neighbors

... the near-hysteria of spiders crawling on her
... the name of the white flowers she brought to the cemetery
and placed on (Dear)Ann's grave

... knowing what month followed June
... cinnamon ... quarters for ice cream

... Alice's adventures   ... gloomy wet
weather afternoons in the house wishing for The Cat in the Hat
or the sun to pop up

... beads ... language/round poems like innocent lullabies

... indifference
... anger
... Aunt Joyce's flattery   ... why she left home

... chanting peepers ... barefoot summer, running

... each visitation of golden blustery autumn
with it's
kaleidoscope dance of boisterous leaves,
and
bounding, bustling "My, aren't you just darling."
ghosts & princesses & OLDER-FRANKENKIDS scaring the little ones
right outta their SWEETdreams,
and
the BIG**FAT**HUGE glowing jack-o'-lantern on the

front porch with rows of candy corn teeth

> . . . Tess' smile
> . . . gorgeous Boo

> . . . being alone

> . . . color

> . . . want, emphasis   . . . lies—

NO MASKS/NO LIES!

Lily/trembling mumbled as her hot tears ran. Something was shaking her—IT had hooks or talons buried in her lungs. She couldn't breathe. IT/Agony's cyclone—all thorns and poison—tore at her belly, scraped cheek & breast & nipple. SHE WAS A STICK IN A DOG'S MOUTH. This was it? *THIS?* sharpness was the dance?—THE END of voyaging?

Pain & pain on top of pain on top of pain. THUMPthump—THUMPthump—THUMPthump THUNDEROUSLY*fast,* her heart was choking on its own fear. She was cold. SO VERY(unmercifully)COLD & weak. Frail, quickly unraveling—No hope/No dreams. Overcome by the cacophony/clamor/noiseGRINDING & the shock & the crushing feelings of disappointment & the claws(SOVERYTIGHT) of the raven. *Nausea.* PARALYSIS—*The claws?* A whimper(not strong enough to implore) be-fore—

Her head hung, dangled gallows-style/neck snapped. She couldn't feel her body. Insidedeep there should be texture, petals, ALL the this&thatmar-vels of living flesh&blood, NOT the UGLYtortures of this vast infinite crush.

> falling,
> she was falling.

Lily lay there extinguished. Nothing in her eyes. Cold meat among the dead flowers.

And Cassilda, Death's demondaughter, glowing as exquisitely as any angel ever rendered in poetic strokes, now in the bittersweet voice Lily had so dearly(*so verydearly*)loved, sang—
And the King laughed.

Café Morphine. Just another stop on The Tour. And tomorrow? Who knows? That newly opened Black Metal dungeon in Moscow?—or that deserted warehouse the Vampire Underground used as a concert hall in Paree?—or that steamy club in São Paulo?—or—

Who can say? There are so very many ripe gardens of pleasure these days.

On the street the marching gaunt clad in black & black & angst-unbridled spanned a single step on the uneven, cracked concrete. Then half of another. His finger pushed the play button of the boombox he carried, and Cassilda sang—

And in far,
cold Carcosa
the King laughed his laugh . . .

The Night Music of Oakdeene

For Brian Lumley—
Whose rich songs carry us to all the strange lands of night.

(*Prelude.*)

They say day and his penetrating herald, dawn, have restorative powers, but night, mute, unknowable night, has her *chansons*. Perfumed with dread and deception, agony and disbelief, their refrains are sung in every language, by every soul who passes into the dungeons within her autumnal skirts. The verses sung in Oakdeene are many. Whether cursed, sonorously mumbled, hurried or spittle-barbed, or sweetly promised hushes, they all, finally, fall into the inescapable dominion of night's languorous opera house of forgotten threnodies and bones.

As heavy as the unavoidable truth night fell on Oakdeene. In the graphically lit depths of the asylum which both inmates and employees called Hell, the sequestered inhabitants felt night's caress and heard her whispered promise.

Fear, night's first-born, walked—its hunger bathed in the sanitarium's sharp bouquet. As fear's footfalls echoed along rigid hallways and found ways through walls, Oakdeene's rodeo of discordant lamentations rose to fill night's unquenchable desire.

(*Langsam.*)

A flash of silence. Spirited clatterings. Wired counterfeit-calm and muffled ephemeral rumblings—resonant bolts followed by their pressurized absence. The stale, over-warm air hung motionless except for Nick Garrett's coiling blue exhalations. Shaded apprehensions clung to paint-armored walls.

The sweat under Quick Nick's collar brought back the memory-immortalized sensations of another cell block and its stifling August heat.

"No wonder they call this place Hell. All that moaning, and the heat—Christ! It's like being slow-roasted." *Just my luck—stuck in Hell in August.* "Shut up, Asshole!" *Bastard's nearly ninety and he whines like a kid* with a scraped knee. Ought to put 'em all down. Save everybody a bundle. Ain't none of 'em worth shit. "I said shut up!" Same loony babbling every night. No wonder those two quit last month. Hell, if I wasn't in this jam—

Hell quieted for a moment and Nick Garrett went back to his "only D-cups or BIGGER" publication. Lighting another cigarette, Quick Nick, as he liked to be called by his elbow-bendin' buddies at Coe's, flipped through the pages of the September issue of *Big Bold Busts,* quickly passing the bleached blonde posing as a Nordic snow bunny and the freckled, punked-out redhead with the Stones lips and tongue tattoo nestled in her deep cleavage. Nick was looking for some action, but it better have dark skin.

Passed the small black-and-white ads guaranteeing to straighten out just about any kink, passed the "How to Find 'Em" text. Another page and another. Centerfold—

"Now that's a set!" Brickhouse Betty—just what ol' Doctor Love ordered. A couple of big soft ones to rub away my blues. "48DD. Heaven. Pure heaven," he said, pruriently admiring the young black woman's breasts through a passing breeze of hotly exhaled smoke. "Just a little squeeze and a big sloppy kiss, and Betty be ready to play love rollercoaster."

10 P.M. The clock tore Garrett away from Miss September's abundant charms.

"Time to see if the spooks are nice and comfy."

With his softly jingling keys swaying at his side Nick started his "top of the hour" check of the cells. About his neck and shoulders, like a garland of skeletally thin specters performing a pantomime of doom, the smoke from Nick's cigarette slowly whorled.

"Another fine mess you've gotten yourself into." Stuck in this God-forsaken dungeon with Ed Gein's whole fuckin' family. "Well, the British side anyway."

Nick glanced at the form on the clipboard.

Giles, Ian. NMI

Born: 13 March 1951. Stoke-on-Trent.

Incarcerated: 27 September, 1975.

Level B. Cell 1R.

Serial sodomy/Child molestation/Kidnapping/Murder/Suspected cannibalism.

"Ain't that some fuckin' rap sheet." I can think of a couple of ways to fix the little prick's ass. Could hold a lynching party for his pecker with pi-

ano wire—stand 'em on a orange crate and slip the noose around his prick.
Kick the crate, and oops. Then I'd pound a railroad spike up his ass while
he's lying there bleedin'. Wonder how he'd like a little turn-about-fair-
play?

Angrily disgusted that Giles had been declared criminally insane and
allowed to live after the fever-pitched trial, Nick turned away from the cell
of the monster camouflaged by smooth cheeks and tender eyes. "Convicted
of *eigthy-eight* counts of brutality against kids and they let this fuck live?"

He crossed the corridor and peered into 1L. Ronald T. Shannon appeared asleep.

Look at him. "Sleeping easy as a babe. You'd think one of 'em would
have trouble sleeping," Garrett said, thinking about the four murderous
women who were reported to be rooming together in Shannon's head.

Nick moved on to 2R—John Lawrence's little piece of Hell—and
took note of John the Gardener's distant stare. Lawrence had taken up
residence when the bodies of three middle-aged spinsters, a child, and four
dogs, were found fertilizing his roses. Garrett turned away. There stood the
door of 2L.

2L. Martin Spellman. Garrett hated the ancient old man and his incessant moaning. And, worse, when he wasn't moaning or a board of catatonia, Spellman reeled off speaking-in-tongues gibberish as if he was trying
to ward off the apocalypse.

"Freaks. Wacko-*freaks*. Obsessive-compulsive, paranoid schizo-
phrenic, and the flat-out unzipped, we got 'em all. Murderers and scumbag pedophiles." Quick Nick Garrett shuddered and instantly chastised
himself. "That's *their* word for it! They don't love kids—they rape, torture,
and enslave. It's abuse. Pure fuckin' evil."

Nick stood as hard as a fist. His hooded eyes darkened. Unmerciful
thoughts placed him back in his hometown behind the dilapidated garage
on Mumford Street with Tammy Hughes tears on his shirt and his hands
around her incestuous father's throat. The face of the monster changed.
Back in stir providing cover for the shank that found baby-raper Stanley
Teller's mid-section.

It's like Johnny Psychoseed's been plantin' by moonlight. And it ain't
just in America. "Hell, they had Jack the Ripper over here long before we
started growin' 'em," he said, forcefully butting his cigarette with his heel.

Nick continued on, taking note of each inmate's status, marking the
forms appropriately, although not neatly. He read the riot act ("Shut up or
you'll get muzzled. And a couple *real-gooood* whacks.") to Lloyd and

Merrill who were again exchanging nightly invectives. Andrew Stewart, the Falkirk Ripper, spat at the door and gave Nick the finger as he passed 6L. Garrett instantly replied, upping the ante with both fingers and a sharp comment, "Hey, you dumb-asshole. I'm out here. I can still rip a piece, so go fuck yourself!"

Half of Nick's charges were asleep, and the others about as quiet as they ever got. All in all it was a typical night in Hell. Back at his desk, boredom was elbowed out by a sudden current of agitation. Pissed, as he hadn't encountered an acceptable willing body in over a month, Nick put the soft-core magazine away, planning to take Miss September up to his room after shift change and mentally fondle her right into the pleasure zone.

As Nick dug through the drawers for another Hourly Status Report form he found a tightly crumpled-up ball in the papered depths of the bottom right drawer. Jammed in the rear and somewhat flattened by old notebooks, assorted reams of odd forms, and over a dozen magazines—most of which were close cousins to his pictorial selection—the balled-up paper piqued Garrett's curiosity. Using his thumb and forefinger as pliers he liberated the paper ball from its prison and carefully uncrumpled it; straightening it somewhat by rubbing it against the rounded edge of the desk. Almost flat, he turned the page over and looked at the unintelligible handwriting.

Sixth Sath-lat-ta? He wondered, looking at the bold pen strokes. "'*G-he 'ph-n-glu-i*.' Huh? '*Yibb-Ts . . . tll*'. "Fuckin' Grade-A wacko gibberish." Must be something one of these psychos wrote. No wonder they're over the edge.

Nick stared at the four lines; all of which ended with the word, Yibb-Tstll. He tried to pronounce the visually brutal words, but they wouldn't come.

"Waste of time," he decreed, sentencing the page to the trash.

Garrett poured himself a mug of hot, but hours old, black coffee and lit a mentholated cigarette. Twenty minutes later the abrasive words were still fingering his thoughts. He took the page from the wastebasket.

Yib-b?-Ts-t—ll? Yib. Tst? Stit? Uhl? He played with the syllables until he felt he had it. "Yib-STIT-uhl?"

Howls erupted from the cells as Garrett's utterance echoed down the corridor. Pain raked its way out of the throats of the confined—the terror-blinded pain of the all-too-knowing.

"Shut up—or I'll give ya something to piss and moan about!" Friggin' murderin' psychos. "If you were human to start with none of ya would even be in here." Better. "Now keep it this way!" Shit, they're quiet—every damn one. Yib-Stit-uhl. What the hell does it mean? Screw it—who cares? Yib-Stit-uhl. That I'll remember.

Garrett dumped his cooling cup in the sink and made a fresh pot. He was in a better mood. His new verbal cudgel gave him a potent weapon to beat the pained moans he detested. As Nick began mentally ticking off the laundry list of every hostility cultivated, an idea arose. The residents of Hell had repeatedly scalded the unsuspecting with their violent offenses—

Then fuck 'em. They like to hear screams that hit ya like thunderbolts—fine. They love to see the trembling on their knees brutalized—OK. This Yibb-Tstll gibberish slammed fear into 'em like nobody's business. If I repeated it over and over I could drive 'em nuts. But then I'd have to hear their screamin'. But if I taped it, and had headphones, or earplugs . . . These monsters deserve a taste of the suffering they dished out . . . Yeah, I could tape it and just keep playing it back. Yeah, like that weirdo classical guy Anita used to listen to. What was his name? Steve—Rich? Reich? Whatever. *Come Out.* That was it. Over and over and over and over and over like a friggin' chant. Looped she used to call it.

Two nights later, after a shift filled with bent demonic laughter, twisted prayers, and absurd threatening demands for freedom, Garrett decided to purchase earplugs and implement his "fitting little torture."

In the store buying the components of his torture device Garrett smiled. His "fitting punishment" was gonna hit 'em like an anvil—"Yeah. The anvil chorus." Nick laughed.

Wednesday's shift began and Nick, earplugs firmly inserted, pushed the play button of the portable cassette player. The volume control knob set at a reasonably firm eleven o'clock, new batteries ready to deliver the punishing mantra, the night music of Oakdeene commenced.

(*Andante energico.*)
"'Ghe'phnglui, mglw'ngh ghee-yh, Yibb-Tstll,
　　Fhtagn mglw y'tlette ngh'wgah, Yibb-Tstll,
Ghe'phnglui mglw-ngh ahkobhg'shg, Yibb-Tstll;
　　THABAITHE!—YIBB-TSTLL, YIBB-TSTLL, YIBB-TSTLL—'"

Over and over and over and over like a drunk that won't shut up, the words of the Sixth Sathlatta looped as if they were the inexorable laughter of Satan reverberating through every level of the Inferno.

Immune to the howls of the demented and damned, Nick made his rounds. At every cell's 6″-by-6″ inch surveillance window he paused to smile or wink and shout "Yibb-Tstll!" at the blasted-eyed, cringing inhabitant.

This tour isn't gonna be so boring after all, he thought, soon adding his laughter to the chorus of agonized despair.

The repetitious chant, no longer imprisoned within the tape, sprayed its aural cyclical throbbing through Hell. Blooming as if it were an actual performance from Philip Glass or Steve Reich slurred by fulsome chemicals imparting imperfect symmetry, the persistent pulse reflected off the hard surfaces of the corridor walls—echoes bounced and multiplied imitating a minimal composition of gradual phase shifting. Slowly the outré chorus built. The modulation of Nick's taped voice altered as the slap-echo fed off itself in Hell's concert hall.

Quick Nick's voice became three. Then four. And the choir of Nicks continued to swell into a complex mire of payback sculpted tongues. The repetitive layers of vocal-*concrète* extended, intertwining and obscuring. The candle power of the overhead lighting quivered. The air temperature dropped. Nick's pulse beat in time to the tempo of the clattering litany that seeped into his ears. The unnatural rhythm of the magnetically embedded invocation intensified. The trance music bent notes, as if they were tuned wrong, as if they were "The Black Angel's Death Song." And the rhythmic influence was as waves crashing from the forever of distortion on to consciousnesses dented and unwitting. The bottom grew fat and rubbery. It became a drone that squeezed through air with the subtle pressure of a python flowing over uneven branches. The harsh, hurried scatter of words became the strange language of an intolerably strange dream tunneling through and condemning modern sensitivities and traditional disciplines. The middle register was a nearly pure wind of white noise, and the onrushing spikes and barbs of the higher frequencies played like fits of awkward madness drunkenly quarreling. All the opposing activities, high, low, and middle registers, as hurried as cheap carnivals or fleeing mice, spoke at once. Each banging its blurred dramatic pitches of feedback louder than the last.

Burned to gutturally coarse wails the constantly locked-down inmates of the asylum's lowest level played nightmarish counterpoint to Garrett's unrelenting recording.

Twenty minutes passed as Garrett's voice became eight strong, then ten.

(*Allegro vivace.*)

In his cell Martin Spellman, who decades before had held Nick's position, stepped out of his fear-induced catatonia. He fought to quell the discordant vocalizations that fell upon his ears like acid. The future, no longer something quiet under glass, inched along carrying the past. Step by step the necromancer's cutting narrative of exaggerated absurdity advanced, bringing confusion enhanced. All too well Spellman recalled the nightmare the Sixth Sathlatta had summoned from an unknown beyond. All too well he recalled the face and form that had driven him beyond the door of the normal and ordinary. Spellman tried to count the voices: eleven. Thirteen were needed to call forth Yibb-Tstll. Beyond his door Nick's voice became twelve.

Nick stood center stage, both star and victim, in an opera he was completely unaware of. Removing the earplugs, Garrett heard Martin Spellman's voice join the chorus. The adept called. Thirteen—the push into the thin air of stupefaction, the descent into breathtaking secrets revealed.

(*Scherzo. Schattenhaft.*)

Nick Garrett looked and all was nonsensical, uneven, and eerie, as if he'd somehow been imprinted by those he tended—caught in the thickness of their demented sentience. What if the aether that colored rainbows now took form and began to dance like a three-legged curse on a mushroom with taps that sounded like clattering knives, and then taking notice of Nick, stopped to talk? What if all the psychedelics from all the drugs were spliced together? Decades of hard life in cheap downtown hotels and wrong alleys that led to state-furnished housing hadn't allowed for this. Surely, he felt, he was gone from the earth. His rusted-tight earth of mercurial cons, hard stances, and carnally willing playgrounds of adventure (after proper lubrication with alcohol and a few pearly lies). This place was impossible, except in someone else's imagination or macabre dreams. Here the sand was washed away, and all was front to back—Swift and Carroll off their hinges in this loft of shadows rising.

"Dream?" He toyed with the word, but fully understood he was awake. Confused, uncertain, and bent by all that flickered before him, but awake in this place the sky was green and the shapes twisted and ripped. Here where the "sci-fi-jungle-planet tainted by bad-acid" panorama was a hostile factory of discordant buzzing all he'd been taught, all he was certain of, capsized and was wrecked. There were clipped howls and siren barkings beyond the foliage; the music of some devil's black demons—they too aptly fit the distortion.

He shivered. This was the stage where phantoms rashly danced as gods of thunder. This was the pinewoods singing the deliriums of infamy ablaze. He stood there, alone in the unnatural contrasts, as small and frightened as a child.

He stepped back, as if the solitary movement could distance him from this dimension beyond the edge. Nothing changed. What castle of horror had he conjured with his thirst? And it was for *them*—the iron maidens and rack and ropes he'd imagined, they were to bend *their* minds, not his. He'd paid his debt. He'd only killed to protect the innocent, not to consume them. This—this scathing cold shot was without justification. They were supposed to be cast low. They were supposed to be the mish-mash of flesh and bone and energy that fed the armies of the notorious—not him! He was supposed to be safe and sane. He was supposed to be warm and fascinated in the arms of Brickhouse Betty—not exiled to this metropolis of destruction.

Quick Nick turned 180°. The verdant, slimy-wet congestion of clashing foliage was gone. This new vista was desolate. Burnt or blasted—either way harrowing, this was a contaminated wasteland somehow pulverized into powdery dust and pebbles.

There was motion in the vast clearing's center. His eye caught the rapid rotation of blurred greens. Cloudy emerald, forest, lime, pea, and a dozen other shades, all running together. Some screaming their brilliance, others almost bleached out.

What the hell is that—*Thing?* A tree of some sort? An animal? Some building arranged with mistakes and scissors, or some hallucinatory sculpture?

Unwillingly he stepped forward. One invisible push or tug compelled him. Another step and another. His feet dragged across the scoured barrenness. He demanded his feet go no further. Who's controlling the strings, he wondered, finding himself closer to the spinning form of green which towered perhaps three or four times the height of a tall man? What conference of the dislocated gave stature to this deformity? And why?

"Why?" Why—

Closer and closer still, until he could discern—

(*Finale. Prestissimo.*)

Eyes pinched closed, Nick's head shook.

"I won't look. I won't look. It's not there—I won't accept it." It can't be.

Eyes flung open, expecting the sunshine of reason, it was still there.

The spinning *thing* slowed. 300 rpms, 230, 110, 90, 60, 40 . . .

Pounding heartbeats were consumed as winging seconds. His hardness, inspired and pressure-built by prison and the Street, weakened. The inhuman madness stopped its slow pirouetting and faced Garrett. Eye to eye with nightmare, he began to crumble. He wanted to cry out, but to who? Even the concept of "Mommy" was now an unknown before this nether-thing that carried hysteria.

Hellfire-red demon eyes—seemingly unattached—slithered like rapid spiders across the wet sheen that covered its decaying head. There was a corrupt orifice in its forehead—And a smile.

This was no plant. Plants didn't—couldn't!—smile. Nick heard terrified laments and pressurized cracking howls dimly echo the endless call he initiated . . . "Yibb-Tstll! Yibb-Tstll! Yibb-Tstll!" Quick Nick was caught in the loop, another fragment in the vast air of echoes. This was what they called to—this *creature*. Him.

Yibb-Tstll's sickly grim grin, formed of vile appetites, settled on Nick as if it were the sticky vapors of abhorrence. As if it were thick fleshy draperies nudged by blustery breezes the cloak billowed and flapped. Skewed edges flicked and fluttered. The neck-to-ground cloak of green parted. Green gave way to black. Beneath the cloak's dominion, loathsome winged creatures of phantasmagorical reptilian design clung to distended black sacks.

Somewhere deep he begged to forget the unforgettable. Yet there it stood. Had he asked for an impossible feat?

Nick's rollicking carnal fantasies of fleshy, sweat-covered black boobs fled before the bloated mammilla of this shuddersome harm. Lumpy, purple-black pus oozed from the gnarled dark nipples of a hundred pendulous teats. He gagged, choking back bile, knowing the viscid fluid to be far worse than the bitter black brew he'd come to detest in Coe's.

At that moment he desperately wished he'd fallen into another life. Perhaps some firm component of the commonplace, where the 5 o'clock world's big black whistle would send him to home to meatloaf and boiled-to-death peas, kids complaining of being overburdened with homework, bills, and later, a light comedy on television. Nick wanted to be out of here—behind bolted doors, or playing pool, or laughing at a stupid joke—anything. Anything at all. Stuck in the rain with a flat, or playing a losing hand of 21, or—just away from this occult of new sights. Garrett's fleeting wish was kicked aside as the faceless battish forms flew from their writhing breast perches below the opened cloak, assailing him, mind and body. Nick's rangy arms, oddly waving about like the slight limbs of a marionette controlled by a drunken puppeteer, ineffectually flailed at Yibb-Tstll's horde of buffeting children. Beneath their biting weight he collapsed before being forcefully cast into the awaiting cloak. Quick Nick, enclosed in the cloak's nearly light less interior, found the irrationally fingered hand?—of an appendage, more branch or tentacle than arm, thrust its probing tips into every orifice of his head. Garrett's death wail met extinction still a prisoner of his obstructed mouth. Bones snapped like dry twigs under the feet of trophy-blinded hunters and flesh was rent.

Thirty-seven minutes and thirteen seconds after it began, the horrid utterance on the tape was suddenly silenced as the inexpensive cassette was eaten by the inexpensive tape player.

(Coda.)

The summoned destroyer withdrew and the echoes decayed. The corridor lay mute as Oakdeene's fiends clamped their eyes shut and exhaled.

Nick's meandering claret made nary a sound as it flowed toward Spellman's metal-skinned door. Enervated, Martin Spellman turned away from the half-eaten shell of Nick Garrett and fell on his bed to silently begin praying for a peaceful death.

Another verse of the inexorable song falls silent, and night, even in the severely illuminated bowels of Oakdeene, her shielding cloak of darkness drawn tight about her, hibernates the day away. Lost to her cold dreams, she awaits the alarmed cries and panicked laments that arise at twilight.

Dogs Begin to Bark
All Over My Neighborhood

When I'm not hunting monsters, carrion-eating ghouls, Dracula's children, and assorted were-creatures and desperate things that crawled out of magic mirrors [key the creepy, cheese-o horror-film music]—last week it was a pair of lesbian succubuses—hey, it's the 21st century, everyone's got a new kink [and no, the name's not Van Helsing], I read Spillane.

Go on, Asshole, chuckle away. But if one day you meet Jack the Ripper's mutant cousin come down from Neptune or back from the dead in a back alley on Dead Street—yeah, that place where the sun don't shine—I'm thinkin' if you get lucky and find the exit yer gonna call me and not the Ghostbusters.

Starts with a scream . . . someone adds bass and drums and a rushing piano. Jazz. Night horns pressing. A shift in the wind. Dogs barkin' in the neighborhood. Sirens. Red lights flashin'. Shit's flyin' fast—someone might end up in a hospital bed with loose molars and 87 stitches holdin' their midsection together and some fool will end up at the bottom of a staircase with the garbage. Blood and guts. And cops in cheap suits . . . Fragments. Duets. Freefall. Portraying one of last's night victims, a lost clarinet squirms under the autopsy knife . . . Some guy who crossed the wrong street in the Twilight Zone is not going to wake up. Some street lonesome, working for a rock of razorlight, just picked up the wrong trick—bet his name's written in worm-eaten sigils in the Book of the Dead—she's not going to wake up . . . Maybe there's a stripper just come outta a gin joint for a smoke. Inside a crowd out for a good time, until the walking fucking dead stop in for a late lunch of raw ribs and fresh blood . . . Thunderstorms. Cigarette smoke. Life running through someone's fingers as they try to hold their guts from slidin' into the gutter. It's fucked up. Like some blasphemous carnival of the grotesque where the sideshow attractions come from Hell and only having a three-day pass they ain't wastin' time . . . Violence. Shadows—all up in it—gonna gitcha. Things to be dealt with. Whistling in the dark ain't worth a fuck here, pal, so zip it. Evil laughter. Squonkin' horns tearin' through a dark blues line. Something spilled. Something red and wet . . . A guitar full of rain notes . . . and there's the drums again. And windows are breaking—the glass looks like diamonds on the wet pavement. A Phantom of the Opera organ and a siren sigh fill the alley . . . Some strange shit here. Sergio Leone smoked some bad weed laced with midnight dust some mad wizard bought—paid with his soul—out on the Devil's Highway. Ain't no preacher gonna show up and invoke God and save yer ass here. Ain't no white voodoo knight with a mojo sword comin' to send your John Q. ass back home to yer soft cotton jammies with laughing Snoopys and yer fuzzy little kittens. Yer just about fucked—if you believe in a Higher Power start prayin', not that I've ever seen it do a damned thing . . . Piano at the pace of a Frankenstein scream-shot. Then I'm there in the weak streetlight glow. Black suit, black hat. Cross, silver bullets, a spell or six I stole. Garlic—comes in handy with some of these things that look like calamari that need a few more minutes in the oven. Knives blessed by shaman and bishops. Whatever works on this object d'occult. The drums kick up and the bass walks a little faster. Shots are fired—a bang so loud yer dead grandmother on the other side thinks about callin' the cops—DUCK! Some fuck-faced monster is currently in serious need of a dentist after trying to hold a conversation with the five tight-grouped shots I just used to adjust his smile, but most dentists these days don't have after hours calls . . . So I whack the thing that looks like a reject from some '50s sci-fi creepy by amputating its head or with a silver bullet dusted in van-van powder [I'm not chargin' ya extra for the extras so shut up] from my quick gun and you get ta go home. Maybe sweet little Joann or faithful and rock-solid, church-going Nancy meets you at the door with a hug and a peck . . . I get to hit a bar and hit on a vixen with an ass that can start a revolution and eyes that stop traffic and clocks as sure as Michael Rennie in *The Day The Earth Stood Still* and get told, not politely, to hit the skids. At least one of us got lucky tonight . . . A haunted sax cryin' in black and white. Rain on the bridge, in my shoes. That's my luck, rain on my hat and tears on my shoulder. I'm walkin' in the rain. Smoking a filterless nail that's certain to kill me if I make it that long. Headed over to Earl's—"*The Tums are extra.*"—Greasy Spoon on Yancy Street for bacon and eggs with extra grease . . . There's a bottle of single malt on my desk back in the office and I have a bed there too. Life's just fuckin' grand . . .

My number's on the card. Keep it handy. With all the shit in this nasty world, packed with bitter once upon a times come back fer another bite at the apple and throbbing nightmares, these days ya just never know when ya might have need of a shamus with a map of every blind alley and sinister sidewalk in the Dark City That Only Sleeps When Yer Dead . . .

Why do I read Spillane? 'Cause in my line of work all I see is blood. Yeah, plenty of guts and bones too. Usually starts with some poor, naked dead girl who looks like she made out with a meat grinder on her way to a date with the Boogieman down in The Zero. So I read to escape. Why Spillane? Because the guy who is me in Mickey's books gets the knockout babe and every once in a blue moon walks away with enough cash to take a vacation on a sunny beach where the beer is cold and the hotel rooms are cozy.

In my line of work you take what you can get.

[*after John Zorn's SPILLANE*]

Chasing Shadows

Arms flapping, no even-measured runner's stroke. The electricity of fatigue sheathed in tight wet cold. His balance, never trustworthy or surefooted in night's dungeon, spinning like beads jounced in a rattle. He slips and stumbles. Around a corner into darker. The wind and its companion rain pushed away, or perhaps simply fooled by the sharp turn. He is full of tiny scurryings and fears that maneuver within him like dirty things brought closer. Chilled, he leans on the wall for support, trying to seal the shutters that allow judgment and vitality to flee his body. He fears to look at the street; the cobbled pavement beyond, now full raging sluices, rushing to the rusted grate of the underworld.

Had it been an hour—a draining crossing of the city with chiller-cinema nerves in flight—since he departed the warmth of the tavern's quick laughter and glowing revelry? Had it been that long since his meeting with his filthy assailant?

The complexities of chance confounded him. All he'd done was sought company after missing her; a mere smile. Perhaps a voice that could turn him, if only for a moment? But not *that* voice. Certainly not that dark and hateful tone ringing like terrible secrets rich in needs not suited to civilized men.

There was a scrape and a scratching. Deeper in the alley's nest of darkness there was a muted clanging. A can's lid spilled by a seeking cat perhaps?—Hopefully!

He inched toward the alley's entrance, cautiously staying close to the wall in shadow. The rain and the wind raced, as forceful as the wicked madrigals of ravens they bullied other sounds to silence. With ears alive, attuned, he could not discern footsteps.

Hailed because he, passionately in his cups—quickly harvested by loneliness—had dared breathe the lyrics of a song. What had he done to agitate that thing? Merely sing? How could his voice have traveled any distance in this implacable riveting?

"Damn drink! And damn circumstance."

Again the words—her words, came back to him.

'*Strange is the night where black stars rise,*
And strange moons circle through the skies,
But stranger still is
                Lost Carcosa.'

Damn the fled vixen—her eyes like soft, dancing smoke under night-dark tresses. Damn her and her false promise; she taught him the words. Damn the memory of her charms, cajoling his desires with her robust lips and knowing warm fingers on his wrist soft in their need. Need of more than her memory had forced him into this night.

On that lost night of sharp-cold spread wide he should have gone with the round-eyed red-head; she asked only money for her ample favors. But no. He'd looked away, only for a moment, and there the other had sat. Familiar and waiting, wrapped in a dated, once elegant fabric of pale blue, alone in the corner behind the saddest expression, she was a portrait he couldn't take his eyes from. He could see her as an artist would, back against a soft curtain, heels to buttocks, long pale arms hugging knees, fragile chin resting on chest, lips—lost without kisses—held together near sobbing; a frail, yet beautiful child frightened and alone. Her need was a breath and an elixir; one he needed. Perhaps due to the tavern's dim light or his smudged desires, years longer than her age sat on her. They did not steal her beauty, but hued it. All his options were dispelled. The bold freedom of drink, pressing and needful, had pushed him to attain the rarer, softer flower.

Damn his tormented loneliness, pushing him from his soiled asylum of thick dust and soulless dead souvenirs. Damn the maddening frustrations that ran as dizzy things on this night saturated in gothic thunders.

Why had he agreed to listen? Why had he walked into the soft garden of her voice so like the mystery and revelation of a first kiss. Were her dreaming eyes so haunted, so very beautiful, he thought to save her and—what? Find a lasting magic—that desperate longing of old maidens and wounded poets, and finding it discover salvation—for both of them?

He imagined her light perfume was still on him. It aroused the pressing memory of her full kisses. But the image was broken by his tormentor's shout. Above the wind-borne din it roared. With all the force and gestures of an episode in madness it plunged through the storm beset streets.

How could that man—Man? Not man! Never a man; he wouldn't accept it. More thing of the sewers, or the grave, with that rank tattered costume as thick and matted as vermin fur. How could it pursue him? He'd certainly outrun it. And more certainly, left no tracks in his wake. And why did it come, and keep coming? He was not the son his lunatic shadow declared him to be. Accosted by the vile madness suddenly spewing its craziness upon him he had tumbled into the rush of the storm. The raw waterfall freely took him, and he sailed, bumped and fast, down the raging corridor.

He needed to be home. Behind his door and windows and walls fortified with his dead things. They were firm and unmoving. Oh they ached, at times loudly like images of sacrificed ancestors, but they did not threaten or disrupt; long ago they had learned to behave after a fashion.

Against the sullied wall, searching the downpour as if lost to a trance of deep mystery, his disorderly uneasiness mounted. It filled his heaving chest and darting eyes. Home. He must be home—now. But which way? Where lurked the filth-caked indigent who shambled through this drenched wilderness of coarse backstreets, and incredibly appeared dry—untouched?

Could it be, even the whipping sheets of rain, sweeping the defenseless streets clean with penetrating assaults, found some way to avoid the menacing affront? Were the massed, stinging droplets frightened by that rangy, erect danger—most likely criminally insane—which must have slithered from the sewers?

His decision made he moved quickly. Ratlike, bouncing and close to the walls, he made his way.

And he was in his room. The substantial door bolted. He examined the walls and the souvenirs that appointed his desolate cloister. Still the same. Nothing had moved. No hand had imposed its intention upon his dusty pavilion.

He was quick out of this wet clothes, fearing they brought the lunatic's taint to his sanctuary of old furniture and still photographs. Dry, he fought to quiet the painful drama of disquiet with the amber contents of a bottle. And with the liquor warming him, his thoughts turned to a night past, a night now a visionary memory of her beauty emanating and wholly exalted.

A single chance meeting, as perfect and delicate as a figure in a globe, until she ran. How many days ago? He looked at that night of rain and moon and embrace again, as all desperate men under a spell must, and asked what had happened before her departure into midnight awakened?

✦

In the tavern they talked for a while. Their words caressing like gentle fingers. After the wine and the words, he'd brought her to his loft. Something sweeter than speech and iridescent was between them; its text more than stirring, almost hypnotic.

She longed to hear him play.

He opened the dust-covered case. He paused, his back to her. Could he? Could he touch the smooth dark wood and let the music like whispers flow? Could he give it voice to let the tales spin like exultant ceremonies? He knew she waited. There was his heart and his past. He offered it to her.

No longer stranger to stranger displaying poses to hide ache, they looked upon each other. The dull shabby room held that which passed between them. She stood in it; a blessed, tranquil saint, teaching renewal and holding all the hushed prayers that filled the cathedral she adorned.

She placed her long fingers on the viola, almost touching the strings. She held it like the Blessed Virgin held Christ in the Pietà. *Her eyes opened, her lips parted, he took her smile as she looked at him.*

"Please. For me?"

He could not resist.

Five years since he'd played, but he played for her. Looking in her eyes he drew inspiration. Her smile was soft. His largo a bittersweet reply.

She had seen him play years ago, she said. Another song, a haunting piece that brought tears. She could not recall its name, but remembered its soft melody. For a time it had saved her from her grief and her sin, she confessed. She hummed it for him. Then began to sing. She'd added words; strange haunting words. The words fit the sonata as a man and a woman fit; both sides of the one melted together—trust and passion alight—permanent, for once joined neither could stand alone.

It was the Sonata for Viola Solo, Op. 11 *by Mad Sclavis, who had been committed to Doctor Pifarély's asylum of undisguised wraiths after his wife, Arienne Cecile, had taken her own life; her contorted body laying beneath the balcony as cold and disfigured as the stillborn child she'd clutched in desperation for four hours. Tormented Sclavis, who they said, closed his eyes and cried himself to death. They said his last and only words were, "Goodbye, Day."*

He played for her as she stood by the window an angel in pearl moonlight. His angel? What welcome lie did he embrace, hung before this woman like a bleak cross, wanting and needful. Could her wings fan away the resident gloom? Could it be he was now awakened, and somehow worthy again? After the first refrain, she sang along—a clear, vibratoless so-

prano; not trained, but rare and glove soft. And elusively familiar. Exile and bereavement married in harmony. He was bewitched.

The subtle complexities of the nuance-rich sonata rose and fell. There were moments stilled to motionless calm as the melody moved like waves from anguish to serenity. The composition was a kiss of blustery desires and errors taken, it was infectious and profoundly sublime. At its heart lay tragic ordeals and numbing loneliness. Her words did not burden or alter it, they were a mirror.

> *"'Song of my soul, denied—*
> *my voice, from cold, fragile solitudes,*
> *shall dry, echoing the heartbeat that breaks*
> *with each rushing wave, upon the shore of*
>   *Lost Carcosa'"*

Eye engaging eye, she sang, he played.

The sonata ended softly. He set the viola back in its lavender-lined case and she came to him. They stood in moonlight etched by the peeling casement, then they were in each others arms. Her breasts were virgin moons—pallid wonders that stilled his breath and stroked his heart. He thought he'd cry.

She did.

They made love, his breath giving her life, and hers to him. And for a time, embraced by something he could feel but could not define, he lay consumed in the rapture the poets sing of. But there was the clap of thunder and the rain came like rapid hounds stretching out fleet steps in pursuit of hot red blood and she fled.

He thought to cry out, but his throat was dry and would not obey. Confused, he just stood there as the door closed upon her image. Like timeless black waiting he did not shudder or move and time moved as a man moves by vulgar compositions in a gallery of mad deeds. Focus returned, like thirst or a needle or the bite of a rat panicked, it was sharp. She couldn't be gone—not yet, not now. Then in the rain, he rushed after her, moving quickly like an affliction quick to own all in its path. Across the stones and curbs and through doorways asking. Asking after the memory of pale blue and ink-black hair.

✦

The days passed, but her memory, warm and demanding within him, would not. The sun bled to death and he stood, head down in his troubles at his window, watching the long vapors of darkness settle. Seven days had gone by since his collision in the rain. Heavy with them, he had counted every acute hour. Bound in complicated fears he stood at the door, twice in the punishing hours almost strong enough to travel through it. His back to the barrier he twitched like a startled rodent. Then frustrated by limitations—"If only there were another exit from this warren"—he, like a thin sentinel searching fog, found himself at the window frosted with his breath. His need was simple, and he wished he was dangerous and could force an oath of submission from his fear. If only he were immortal—

He could see the procession by moonlight, marching unevenly like strange stiff-legged marionettes to war, the gathering in the underworld. He saw the spider-jointed demons at the ceremony; the feast—grotesque heads splattered with their own blood plopped on filthy platters; the nakedness of warrior and shaman—black angels with ancient voices; the hideous tremors of their coupling in the darkness flecked with littered bones—

He knew where this contaminated beast which hounded him was born. If he were immortal he would simply pass by.

Pass by? Unchecked and untouched?

Surely the monster which had manifest itself in the wild hair and great winter-coat of a madman had passed into some other pursuit. The violent creature, belonging to a dimension more harrowing tale of the fantastic than simple grim fairytale, one of wolfish revelries and the shadows of disorder, must have been struck by some other echo or possibility illuminated. Yes, of course! There was the truth; after seven days the flutter of some other innocent passerby's gait must have drawn its attention like a flamboyant ensemble.

He slammed the door and rushed to find her. His heart's need his only map. His mind was a thing of teeth, opening and closing its mouth to shout of starvation. He needed her as the man lost to the desert's vacant sands makes water his new god. Only she could deliver him. All speed, he was in the chilled rain. One disagreeable street, not dry for days, was exchanged for the next. A bitter shout, not aimed at him, but as jarring as the Devil's laughter, awakened his dread of the tattered, filthy man. Even as the agitated cry burned out, unwanted memory—the resonance of the crazed-demon's bellow—clipped his heels.

The straightness of the streets pulled him along, but corners—

crossroads waiting to unloose every annihilating sin, trouble, and murder—became the worst unknowns. He paused before each black, filled inside not with the slight butterflies of unease, but the drowning. Would death descend unheard on vulture's wings, or like the raging heart of a crematorium, surge as the roar of a radiant fever? Yet, too filled with all the symptoms of his enterprise to turn back or away, he braved each conflict. And finally he was around the last.

There was round laughter in the tavern where they had met, but not hers. He moved along. Light had vanished from many windows. The fullness of darkness drifted like unmoored islands in the hollow lands between shrinking tenements and dismal lot. Padlocked shops with chain-web veils became empty warehouses, and the wind picked up.

Lost in this world. He felt disjointed by the weight of it. He paced and was soon sick of the circles.

Then the enemy was beside him.

"You have been lost for a long time, Thale."

It wasn't his name. He knew it. What was it? Thill, perhaps? But not—Thale? Yet, it rang like an old melody he played well, but had misplaced. It wasn't his name. No this phantom awakened was mistaken, he was certain of it. But it was familiar, correctly fitting the hole left by that fallen from his memory.

Why?

He almost asked, but instead chose to run. He had to; this singleness heavy with the currents of madness smelled of the whirlwind and wailing bonfires—they were on his breath like strong drink. Around the first corner and the next he fled. Through soot-choked alleys lined with throwaways and broken things. Glass splintered under his heel. As he rushed passed, papers flew like frightened things. He was fast, then faster. He must find home again.

A fog rose up and blanketed the pavement. And the thinning buildings lost solidity and receded. His pace hurried.

Home. He must be home. He must. But which direction? Which way? That one, the frozen lawn of teeth black as strange weather brewing? The other, a narrow carving through a squat gathering of bungalows and two-stories sleeping in the dim stain of a few streetlamps? He stood in fear of the wrong step, then chose left—the other, shunning the sagging rows of bruised façades with steps and porches like broken jaws and windows like flawed mirrors. He flew like a free laugh, headlong at the speeds of rushing wind marching, splashing through silent puddles, leaping, wheeling to avoid all that had been cast off and out. Turning and turning, sliding along a street curved like a laughing mouth.

Stop—look. Move, then stop again. Right then left. Full of ferocious miscalculations he turned and turned and turned. Another right, into a dead end. He folded back and moved on. All about him changed and changed again. And again, like moving mounds of fog in winds, thick then thin with oddly shaped holes—hungry quicksand deeps. Tendrils sprouted like horrid black-branched trees made only to snap necks. On he moved like stories and songs rushing pass sleeping ears.

More than fear drove him now. Curiosity, and some faint feeling akin to rage arose and jostled his homesickness. Another step, then two blurring to four—a bewildered rat in a maze. Running over bridges and soft earth. Fogbound and tortured, and still running. Terraces and patches of weeds were ignored as he pushed passed. Unrecognizable whispers and wooden croaks like strange haiku from things with no names were all about him. Another bolt of rapid steps. Atmospheres of possible sprang up like civilizations only to fall into ruin.

He pulled up and stood firm. He made fists at his sides. He clamped his eyes and mouth shut and shook himself. Schizophrenia? Juju? Or perhaps some fever that stung reason like spirituous drink? What clutching distortion sent its roots spreading like beams from a lighthouse? How long would he remain a slave to this torment?

He moved on. Things that should have happened long ago and stayed still as the surface of a morning lake were beside him. There were faint impressions of melting snow cascading and an empire of glazed-eyed gypsies celebrating with seven loud songs about hot red blood and predatory violence overwhelming screeched arias.

He remembered a madness rich in racking tears. How many riots of crashing waves had it lashed him with? He ran desperately, his hair and the edges of his coat autumn leaves in November winds. Then he saw the moons; heavy twins of lusterless pearl low in the sky. They stood before him and shone. He felt they shone their sad greeting only for him. They reflected the reminders like intrigues that filled the empty monastery he'd become. His forgetfulness fell away.

For a time he just stood there.

Soon the stars came out; black stars. The sound of muted waves crashing came to him and he ran again. Home. He must be home. But in which shadow did it lie. Home, the need of it was everything. It was a hungry worm in his belly.

He ran and the white moons stayed with him. He stopped. His running seemed endless and pointless. Tired, he sat, his back to a metropolitan sprawl, kettle-black and lying like a cluttered yard of potbellied base-burners with sky-wounding towers like chimney stacks capped with crooked-peaked witches hats. The wind, soft and flecked with the strangled clamors of distant objects, moved and still he sat—hard as an inscription set in a grave marker—yet he was on fire and felt light. He let his breathing fill him.

"Home is where the heart is. And yours was broken only by distance."

Again the assiduous enemy and his eyes like sharp medieval arsenals. He stared at him.

"You wonder if I'm Truth."

He knew the voice, and those eyes, though now—like his own—set behind a mask. His stalker's garb had changed, filthy greatcoat for tattered yellow robes, but it was the same pursuer nonetheless.

"I know you are turmoil," he said without rising from his rocky seat on the shore.

"Ah." The tone was as sticks beating the grass.

Their gaze was long. One expecting, the other as difficult to known as a new language.

"For a moment you yearned for brightness and motion. You were pulled away by a song. We turned and you were gone," the figure in yellow said.

"Gone where?" In a moment of confusion he couldn't recollect the otherwhere.

"Chasing shadows in the other world."

And as it was said he remembered the day and the invitation of the dim music as it lingered, and how his feet had stretched, following the waning echo. But he no longer cared.

"Camilla, who was also lost for a time, has returned. Shall we—"

"No," he replied, gazing up at the black stars suspended like ripe plums. He listened to the waves break upon the ageless shore. "The dynasty can wait. I'll just sit here awhile."

The robed figure in the pallid mask nodded and walked off.

Thale did not turn. He closed his eyes and listened to the sound of the waves which came in crashing repetitions like heartbeats.

But the Day Is a Tomb of Claws

Clayton Stanley looks out his window and sees the City of Night—one minute, cursing the hard belts of Afterwards, the next, holding its head in its hands, trying to hold the shipwreck afloat . . . Sees, and hears, Jive and Hustle, wired, drunk, ready for the carnivores woven of almost, as they work their way from dance to dance. They leave the scent and taste of tears and blood in the asylum . . .

New York, L.A., New Orleans, Boston, and Chicago—they transform by night, but San Francisco is Night. Pure as lies. Titan, demon, wizard—all in one, and none for all! Sure last yesterday The City had soul-flower hippies and sunshine by day, parks filled with free music celebrating the bright blue above, and last week it was honest if you didn't count those the ringmaster marked for downward. But when the sun goes down, it's grind all night; hearts panning for gold in the swift, roiling current; sex with the next one; and companeros; and it's never too late; and snowblind suicides; and D-cup vampires with cloven hooves and a hot jones for stolen emotions; 1 A.M. asses and whirling red police lights working the traffic; and yer new-in-town wrong word and there's Dr. Weird opening the Hereafter can and yer standin' on ouija ground; jazz and party noise and clouded hearts in sunglasses to ward off fingers that ate too many dishsoap movies; tits and bullets and stained teeth, and crowed bars filled with cigarette smoke fog and hot eyes come out to play, to breath deep . . .

San Francisco. Every poison and every pleasure—gorgeous or slow, or constructed of illusion, shoehorned into the churning storm.

Unsparing. That's The City of Night.

Fuck those who get in the way.

Clayton Stanley lived right in the poisoned heart of it; crackwhores with extra bounces of dead, bloodshot eyes too brittle to make it downstream, holes damned with Not and a hundred miles deeper than Alice's. Hell, if yer up for the excitement there's even a morning sunrise, but you'll have to stay alive all night to see it. Every night the howlers were out begging and clawing, pressing and trying to chew just enough to make it until to-morrow. He stayed in. *Every night.*

Terrified of *any darkness* from an early age, he lit six 95-watt light bulbs in his large studio apartment every night to ward of the spreading shade of grave and headstone, and the claws that hid behind the wet stones in the cellar of his memory . . .

His sixth-floor window open to the baying street. Sirens ran to clean up the spilled lust and wham-boom of dangerous visions of this affair or that shuffling. The wind came coughing in from The Bay and its hot grasp kicked over every once-iron-now-rust body-frame and dumpster-diving Buddha. Made them little more than shitass-poor dirt farmers after the blind teeth of a twister cleaned its plate. Cleaned the shine right off of it.

Terror walks the street by night. Looking in eyes and coats for pieces to eat. Unrelenting, a cold, hysterical wind, working over every tattered and squirming contour. Torture sways. It watches madness, waiting for the fall. Drop your guard, your armor, your shield, and you're meat.

Night is supreme, but the day is a tomb of claws . . .

No longer a young man, filled with the immortal abilities of the wanderer, he spends his nights with the TV or thoroughly researching and writing his tragic comedies that could hit you in the crotch or make you have to stop to catch your breath when you weren't laughing. And there's his music. In Rio with Roxy and Virginia Plain, or on the boulevard of broken dreams incarcerated in the Gloomy Sunday Bar & Grill, drinkin' shots of strange weather with Marianne and reviewing ghosts dances in bored bedrooms—*in every dream home a heartache indeed,* and perhaps, if he's in the right mood, exploring the thrill of it all on some lost continent; hours and hours and hours of blacktop ballads and wild gifts snake-bit by the big black sun. And he has books growing on every surface. Varley and Lupoff and Clark Ashton Smith. Lovecraft and Frank Herbert, and the contexts and consequences of Najovits and a hundred other histories of ancient Egypt.

But all that doesn't mean a thing. It's all orbits of quick pleasure to soothe that which he misses. And swears he no longer needs, or wants; the sunlit desert sand. It still burns within him. It still turns his gaze to The Distance. His fingers can still feel every soft white grain . . .

Sitting among silver and brass candleholders, the dreaming voices sifting what is shadowed by the moon. Clayton as a younger man—thirty years ago, eyes and heart wide open, ready, reaching, for skies of glory, and joy.

Irem. The three days walking the ruins and broken pillars . . . A small cavern—tomb?—the moon cannot touch . . . The amber statuette, no more than the size of his pack of cigarettes, he smuggled home to the

States . . . The ancient statuette with the scorpionlike hieroglyphic imprisoned inside . . .

That's what his words sing about, the sunlit desert sand and those nights, drawn by the bite of the ruins outside the tent flaps, of wanderings. And the torment he brought home.

Clayton came home, braided hand, heart, and purpose to a beautiful young man. They were in love—deep and dear, despite the storms and the crumbs that came, sometimes on hands and knees, sometimes for weeks at a time.

The studio apartment left them no room for moments or space alone. Together every waking or slumbering hour they were face to face, thought to thought, in what started to distress them as Forever.

They made love. Sat and talked and dreamed and laughed away Saturday mornings and Wednesday nights. And they engaged in mostly soft forms of war. This night to that, adoring or murderously threadbare, with no door between them, they loved. Drunk or sober, elated or filled with Fuck That and Fuck You, they filled every space, every minute, between them.

The sun of a July evening sank . . .

Clayton Stanley was drunk and tired, the publisher's rejection blistered his fingers. His lover laughed it off. "Fuck him, Clay! He's an ass. Get a part-time job for now and we'll get over this financial hiccup. Then you can try to find another publisher."

"You're such an inconsiderate ass when it comes to my writing. This was the third publisher—do you see a line of editors fighting to ring the doorbell?"

They meet by an oversized window open to the street below. A siren wails by. Someone shouts. Clayton's lover's hand comes up, flashes. "Snap outta this bullshit!" His fingers leave red marks on Clayton's cheek.

Clayton pushes away the angry eyes, the angry words. His lover turns an ankle and . . . glass shatters. He's out the window. Six stories. Falling, slowly. Groping hands. Glass cutting. Cutting face and chest. Arms swimming at odd angles. Shards of glass peeling blood and energy. Cut by a hundred pieces of glass he curses Clayton on the way down. No scream . . .

A crowd around the body. Careful not to touch the blood. The crowd stares. Murmurs. A buzzing of massed voices . . .

Cops and repeated same versions of the fight and The Fall, over and over. His room is an interrogation room. Reports. Hot needles in his eyes. Cigarettes and tears. Shaking hands. Guilt's venomous hard grip squeezing his heart. And another cold, hard cop in a cheap suit with questions . . . A sip of cold coffee . . . Walking to the sink, he does not know why. Walking to turn off the TV. Walking in a circle around the sofa as if he could get somewhere. Walking to the bookcase. Clasping the statuette to his chest with shaking hands. Tears fall upon it.

Then alone in the night.

✳

Night after night he sits alone in his room. Raw, his throat, his eyes, the unhealed scar in his heart . . . He stares at the statuette. The statuette stares back.

Never once has he touched the statuette since That Night. Never moved it from the deep shadows of the bookcase which house many an Egyptian tome.

A July afternoon of raw sun, burning . . .

Drunk again. Tired. Fingers sore from racing toward his editor's deadline for his latest novel, Clayton stares at the white screen of his laptop—CHAPTER 16 and not another word on the page. He needs coffee and a cigarette. Maybe an aspirin or a banana for his empty stomach—when did he last eat? He taps the mouse, clicks save . . .

Pulled by the TV, he rises from the hardback chair in his smudged kitchen. Ten steps to the edge of the carpet. Standing, compelled, by the flickering image, so alive, on the screen. CNN is playing footage of a young jihadist, fist and voice raised in pride and anger . . . And the young man is a dead ringer for Clayton's dead lover. His open mouth cursing the Infidels is the open mouth of his falling lover cursing him . . .

He sees the statuette. The statuette sees him.

Quick to it. It is hot in his angered hand.

"Fuck you! A thousand times, fuck you."

Stanley is at the window.

You didn't fall, you jumped. You left me . . . Fuck you. You left me.

And he flings the statuette from his open window.

Watches it tumble to a stop.

He stares at it. It stares back . . . His heart is breaking again. He cannot be without it, without him. Clayton Stanley can't let him be gone. He was supposed to be here forever. They were supposed to be together forever . . .

The statuette is calling to him. He leans out the window . . .

Without a glance and he's in the street. In the sun. Standing in an empty parking space, staring at the last vestige of lost love lying on the curb. In the middle of the afternoon, sweating in the animal heat, Clayton bends to recover the only physical trace of his love.

Voice of late seasons, singing as if to itself, of dead souls, stretching the name of his dead lover . . . over and over . . . and over.

Beams of pure, hard sunlight pierce the statuette. Some *Thing* within it flares, sparks . . . Some seal, center, opened by the raw blaze of sun-fire. The pain imprisoned within reaches out . . . A wavering aspect of bent light blows around Stanley. Some unseen *Thing* hangs in the dry, hot air . . .

A buzzing of massed voices . . .

Cut . . . A wide arc across his shirtless chest . . . He feels dizzy and hot.

And cut again . . .

Three vicious slashes on his cheek . . .

And again. Forehead opened, nearly to the bone . . . A terrible buzzing—hot needles in his ears. One voice, his lover's—barking curses, curses of vengeance from a night three years gone—loudest in the guttural buzzing . . .

There's a hole in his chest, his knees buckle . . .

And cut again . . . Perfect raw cuts . . . Nancy and George and Veronica, stupefied, stare in disbelief. Wu Man screams . . . Liu hides her face of cluttered years in her hands. James, squealing, and Henry and Fernando, sharp and broken, run like hell. A cluttered hum in a mumble. Short, sharp murmurs. Ned and Ralph, teeth-chattering, and fifteen others are rooted in every distortion of fear to the ground their silhouettes shake on.

The moments are a blur. An unseen hand paints in blood; Pollock on a blood bender—red, a dagger of primitivism, splashed this way, dripping, spattering, destroying biology's canvas . . . a chaos dance, faster and faster . . . splintered bone juts from pale and bloody skin at odd, inhuman angles . . .

Pinned to the ground, one supporting arm desperate to raise its body from the razor-stoning . . . Clayton Stanley struggles in the web . . . no voice or hand intervenes . . . he spits blood . . . and an eye falls to the dry pavement . . . a finger, in three bloody pieces, lies beside his eye . . . he can't lift a finger. . .

His one functioning lung is on fire . . .

Shaken. A marionette arm sways, rubs against a deep furrow in his thigh. His leg jerks, his severed, booted foot remains two feet away from the stump . . .

An invisible force pulls his jaws apart. Bone snaps . . . breathless . . . a femur nearly clean of tendon and meat . . .

Some invisible force—*Thing,* with teeth, tearing, ravaging. Agony—a searing desert-born agony . . . a wave upon the rocks. Life run to ground . . . chunks of flesh cast aside, so much unwanted matter under an angry sword. Life unwound and undone—absolute. An image of Hades, not of a man . . .

Blood and pieces fly . . . a death by a thousand cuts. What resembles a carcass torn and dismembered by jackals litters the ground . . . An empty beer bottle shares the thin slice of shadow made by the curb with Clayton's cleaved hand . . .

A new voice howling in the chaos-choir of massed buzzing.

The flies, and police, will soon come . . . Only the flies will be satisfied by this smear of hostility left in the wet meat on the killing ground . . .

Frightened, curious eyes at the edge of the unbelieving crowd. Eyes, many times in a maelstrom of anger, that have imagined her lover and his witch-tramp given to the cold empty hours of the endless drifting in a fashion of blood like the one she has just witnessed. But she is not completely repulsed. Rather, her eyes are locked on a small object several feet from the blood pool of the dismembered shell. It winks at her. Calls her.

A jerk of the hand, she is quick to take it up and put it in her pocket, thinking, hoping, this curious statuette—gift, will please her lover and turn him from the bed of his witch and return him to her arms. Her face is flushed, she feels dizzy and hot.

A lover of ancient Egypt at heart—her two-timing lover owned museum quality replicas of a canopic jar depicting Beloved Royal Wife Kiya and a large bust of Akhenaten—he had been to see the exhibition of 55 objects from the tomb of Tutankhamn several times when it was in L.A. and would be captivated with this relic, which she feels, speaks of mummies and howlings in the desert. Yes, he will be pleased indeed. She knows just how and when to present her gift of devotion . . .

He will love the gift—love her . . . or the ancient necromancy she believes inhabits the ancient statuette will turn its burning gaze upon him . . .

(for my friend, Stanley C. Sargent)

In This Desert Even the Air Burns

(*for Karl Edward Wagner*)

Early one vicious morning. The air a thirsting panther.

"Me and . . . "

All the old man had was a black and white picture of her, the broken yellow lines in the road headed to who knows where, and the need to put the heavy stars to sleep.

"her."

A ghostly incarnation of Dylan was on the radio singing about love driving him insane. Not his first time. Might not be his last. It wasn't the old man's last. Not by a cold million miles. The desert motels, desolate nests burning in the solarfire, and the dry brush blew by, looked they were headed somewhere. Everything out here looked like it was once headed to some place else. It just never got there. Most often it paused in the long empty, ducked in a sliver of shade to escape the absolute sun, got snagged on memories and never got up.

The old man stopped and got gas. $15.23. Bought a Coke and a pack of smokes. $3.74. Almost out of silver. Completely out of gold. Opened the glove box and checked his gun before pulling out. He was old, yeah OK, but he wasn't stupid. Not this go 'round.

There'd be a doorway before it got too dark. A bed. A TV with old news he wouldn't really listen to. He'd get eggs with cheese and onions or a burrito for dinner. Coffee. Black. Hopefully fresh, but if not . . . And he'd lay there in the motel room [or pace around in circles] and wonder.

Third of a bottle of whiskey and he still wouldn't be able to forget her. Not on this road with the phone poles stung out like prison wire and the haunted complaints of tomorrow on the wind. Not while his eyes could see the shadows and the things that were locked in them.

It was a room for not going fast. A room of narrow failures.

The wind was outside walking the road. By a broken gate that had never seen an island it turned, howled for an old lost love. He pulled the covers tighter. A song from yesterday's jukebox moved slow in his thoughts. He burned in the cold. The ghost of midnight cried questions of right and wrong. Church bells were ringing.

The old man turned on the light. Looked at his boots. He wished they knew different habits. Wished they played dumb and just went along with the dance.

He turned off the light. Wrapped his head around her face. A million miles back and still he had to face the lie. He took. She took. Neither could wait. Neither did. He didn't dream. Tossed and turned. But didn't dream.

When he woke he was still sick. Love. Sometimes it was six foot long and just as deep. It came. You said it would put your mind at ease. Then close got closer and things got blown into a million pieces. Rock yer baby. And she rocked you. And there was paper. And scissors. No one won. And a million miles had passed.

Before became nowhere. Then was outta doorways. So you left. Didn't take anything but a broken heart and a maybe a picture of the fire.

Then came the trains and the river and Baltimore. You sleep when you can. Tried not to gamble.

Tried . . . to drive straight. Begged night and the painful kisses of the whiskey to bury the bewilderment.

But on some dirt road where they closed the door, you found you were headed back to the last time. And yer boots started leanin' back and that black and white picture turned into a bird flown away.

Yer standin' there just taking up space . . . hands lost in your pockets. Thought there was something there, but no one was talkin'. And there's no one to trade places with. And there's a sunrise starin' at you, offering no future and no sermon, and the appetite of the hole just gets deeper . . .

And the ramblin' starts again . . .

Fargo . . . Ensenada, mariachi and wanna-be matador too hung-over to play . . . Austin . . . Eden—someone thought it looked like it . . . Eudura, a lightpole by the jail . . . San Antone . . . Towns little more than small hives outta words and for old times sake . . . oceans of sand without limits . . . alone and gaunt, a little ranch squeezed hard . . . a little one-room shack, might be a coffeepot and a cup and a saucer come from the East years back on the small hand-hewn table—the nails that held it together might have started rusting . . .

Ramblin', hardship to next tomorrow morning, and all the mistakes down the line. You see sin . . . and ashes. See old ghosts—too hot to run from close range conversations with old lies, sitting on weathered old porches . . . waiting . . .

Indigo darkness stretched out thick, swollen with dry. Half a mile stretched into half a state. Impulses sick of hide and seek surging to move on . . .

Sun a lion that won't let you run away. Sand and desert sky with no history . . .

The road . . . flat today for a while. Rocky later on . . . all day too hot dragging on . . . the sun's a scar and the sky's got nowhere it needs to be . . . there's no water out here. No world to get to here . . . the cactus laugh when your burden goes by . . .

Time comes. Whispers. A hundred years. A hundred years traveling with an old injury. Barrels of whiskey gone jar by jar . . . A hundred squirms, aches, crawls forward weakly and the inexhaustible details of the puzzle last longer than a long time . . .

The old man looks at the black and white photograph of her. Even figuring on the clock her once saint-like face didn't look a day over a million.

The wind offers no warm embrace . . .

It's late. His pistol is sick of waiting. He smokes his last cigarette . . .

Looks at her picture one last time. The wind whispers, "Once in their castle beyond night . . ."

Dusk. The scent of alone thickening . . . twenty miles from Calexico. Far away not far away . . .

You won't be wrong this time.

Not this time . . .

✦

Once in their castle beyond night . . .

You were out . . . burning affairs filled with darkness. She took off with your brother. Headed West into that small, rotting sunset . . .

Never saw it coming.

You looked at your hand. Didn't have a needle's eye of light between your knotted fingers. Picked up your gun . . .

Put on your boots of Carcosian leather.

A million miles ago the door closed. You remember what went. But you still don't know why . . .

"*Cassilda . . .* Why?"

Sunday waist-deep and thick on the ground. The tired old sun setting into the dry ground. Nightwinds with blood on their lips soon. Outta whiskey and full of

"Why?"

(*Bob Dylan "Dreamin' of You"*)

And She Walks into the Room . . .

Freight train or bullet they'll kill ya. A woman too. That body might look like paradise, legs right up to the penthouse and chest that could shut E. F. Hutton up, but in there somewhere is a dagger. And she'll use it on you. Mask on or mask off, when the need hits that pretty little heart with the spring action brain you're smoke—ptooff! Don't be fooled 'cause she's not wearing any clothes.

Perhaps she breezed outta a mentholated cloud in a gin-joint, walked to the bar and leaned right into your heart. She was decked out in red—right down to her toes, the same shade as her hair, or you first saw her under a corner streetlamp glowing with voodoo-moonlight in Hell's Kitchen, raven tresses and black coat, either way your dignity took a powder and you jumped into the flame without blinking. Wrong move, Foolish. That play-mate softness coming across the room right now is a cat woman, part villain, part black lizard, all angel face and full-on red death. And that smile under her sparkling Cabo-blue eyes is about to vanish. And you with it.

Maybe we should step back a bit? Take a long, second look at the room. Let's slip back . . . Nice hotel. Long-stemmed Aprils in the peacock vase and fragrant candles and a bed you're hoping to spend hours in. High balcony with a great view of the park. Remember walking arm in arm with her there last weekend? Her feet didn't touch the ground and you were dizzy. Her eyes addictive and full of anytime, her lips were parted. And you? What about you? You were incapacitated. And two minutes from now if you don't get yer ass out that door yer about to be permanently incapaci-tated. Shut in a brute black box and dropped in the zero for a night without end. My buddy, Otto, calls it The Big Dirt Nap. And he should know, he works a shovel over at Rest Haven. And he's got a souvenir, some call it a scar, from his first hard glance at the pagan scenery in Aphrodisia.

Starting to get the picture? I hope so, 'cause the clock is ticking. Relax. That's a good sign. When it stops, that's bad. Very bad. Got that? Good. Now to the really important stuff.

How you get out is the easy part—RUN!

How you got here is something you might want to examine before you commit suicide. I'm not pushing here, but Mr. Tick-Tock on the desk there lifespan is drawing to a close. So get to it. And get out.

❦

"Word is your financials are stretched thinner than a forgotten wish."

"So thin there's nothing but dirty business between the two nickels I got."

Erle, the sometimes pawnbroker, sometimes thief and pickpocket, sometimes loan shark, smiled. "I kinda bumped into a case of beauty and brains just out of the rain and she was in need of a match. Seems she knows someone who knows me and it winds up she has this job and wants to know if I know someone who might slide in an open door and grab a little something she left at a sick friend's."

"I'm guessin' about half a beer went down and my name came up."

"Second beer."

"And you mentioned I drive a Ford and like Caddies?"

"Might have come up."

"And the Looker with the brains said she knew a place where a man with the right hands could pick up a Caddie on the cheap."

"B. I. N. G. O. I gave her your card."

"And for this I owe you how much?"

"Not a dime. You've kept me in lamp-oil for a long time now and I'd hate to see you out of touch."

"And the twist is?"

"Straight as Abbott's delivery. The job will put you right, and you'll keep my flame burnin'."

"Sounds like a plan. Provided she purrs right."

"I think you'll be the one purrin'."

And he was right. Right from the first look.

Some women got the looks and legs and rear carriage and that luminous twinkling in their eyes yer willing to steal to be able to afford, but they're missing something. Maybe the walk. Maybe it's the smile.

Most of the time it's The IT!

Rene had IT in spades! And then some.

Twenty paces away and your knees are in an opium trance and you wouldn't find room for This Week's Harlow if she walked in with cash and roses.

No, one look—the first one, and you've been kissed by an angel. That stone wall you call a heart takes a flying leap, surrenders to yes and yer vacationing in a very pleasant county. Yer eyes are engaged to that long-stemmed kiss packed with curves and charm that just flashed in your mind.

Peacocks bow, orchids bloom on the pyramids, Then begins . . .

♠

Sidney Rollins came in from the cement, picked a booth in the back, ordered a beer, and kept his eyes on the door. He knew what he was watching for. But when Rene Girtler walked in Karoli's Poseidon's Lounge even the moon got dizzy. Every splash of laughing smoke stepped aside. She came straight to the booth. Smiled. Sidney stood. When he started breathing again, he smiled back.

She sat down.

He melted into his seat.

They talked. The deal was struck.

Rene left. Sidney sat ensnared in fast thoughts of sinful pleasure for another five minutes, then he went looking for the doorbell she wanted pushed.

7A. The penthouse.

He pushed the button.

Back to back dizzy. Skip the sweet smell of success, this one . . . Well, he hadn't won the Irish Sweepstakes, but he didn't care. Not with this view. Laurel Hasler was a perfumed angel that left men breathless. Those with big ideas, the spineless, handsome, outlaws, the quick-witted, her hypnotic magic got inside their head and stayed there. A dozen Hollywood directors and twice that number of Broadway producers had called her curves as thrilling and dangerous as Mulholland's and her eyes sexy, exquisite, and spellbinding. She'd passed on the offers to be fetishized and pierced by the eyes of moviegoers sitting in darkness soaking up dreams of light.

Sidney Rollins was a sponge. Soaking up every inch of this dream. His face said, dumbly, "Ah," his thoughts: *Absolutely entrancing. She's . . . otherworldly. If her brain's half as sharp as her body is lush, I'm putting down a deposit on a twenty-bedroom villa and staying home for the next thirty years.*

He was here to lie and push hard if need be. To find and return a makeup case, an heirloom. But standing at the door of Valentine's Day Sidney wavered.

"Mr. Rollins?"

"Yes. Sidney, please." The last word a plea for bread from a starving man.

"Sidney." Her voice, pure bedroom laughter. Alto set deep, low, and hotter than a flaring match head hitting an open gas line.

And he was on fire, blazing away with expectation. For him it was say goodbye to the boulevard of broken dreams. Sign him up for a long incarceration of love in the afternoon and a marathon of kisses with this perfect stranger.

"Please come in, Sidney."

The gun for hire enters the lair of the femme fatale . . . Trying to remember what it was about Rene that knocked him out, Sidney followed her to the sofa.

They talked. Had a drink. He decided to play it straight with her. She laughed in all the right places. Was packed right in all the right places—from the front, sideways, he thought if she stood on her head in an Emmett Kelly get-up she'd still send fifty men to the morgue with massive coronaries.

Sidney told her everything. If there was such a thing as love at first sight, he'd come down with a monster case and didn't want to blow it by spinning a web he'd later fumble over.

"I understand," she said, thanking him with a smile. "But I fear you have been duped by this woman. Do you think I need to steal? Just look around, I can have anything I take a shine to. I have met Miss Girtler. She is a very envious woman and a gold digger to boot.

"At a luncheon two months ago she saw my compact and asked about it. I told her it had been in my family for five hundred years. She asked if I'd be willing to sell it to her. I said no.

"Displeased does not even cover her reaction.

"Would you please tell her you were unable to acquire it for her? I'd be happy to pay whatever fee she offered you."

Their fingers grazed over the ashtray. Sparks. Smiles. Her perfume hit him like Brahms and whispered, "Baby."

"Do you hear many confessions in your line of work? I'm sure you do. I have one . . . I would like to spend some time with you. Get to know you. If you're interested?"

The reds in the room were flowers, the blues interludes with angels, the yellows and greens peacocks, tails sparkling with the kiss of evening stars. He was weightless, and open, in a tango of romantic notions involving touching and dynamite. Sidney's blues bugged out for long ago and far away.

"I'll return her retainer tomorrow."

"Splendid. Perhaps we can have dinner after." Her voice a whisper of secrets shared.

"Just name the place."

"Here, if you wouldn't mind? My cook is excellent and I do not go out very much these days.'

"Would sevenish suit you?"

"I'll be here." He wanted to say with bells on, but just grinned like a kid who'd just caught a Babe Ruth home run ball.

◆

"What? Are you out of your mind? You just fell ass over tea kettle for a woman who's 500 years old. And you're passing up the biggest payday you've had in five years. For her?" Her red lips offered something other than money. Something volcanic.

500 years old? Laurel isn't a day over twenty-nine. This cupcake is a total loony.

"How's that? 500 what?" Out like a condescending spit of laughter.

Scorned. At this point she was ready to play any angle to get the compact. Rene changed bridges and tried to flood him with truth.

"The mirror inside the compact steals souls. That right? Some lady demon lives in the mirror and drinks souls. The owner feeds this swollen hag-thing sins and souls, the owner stays young. Got ta tell ya, lady, I'm not as fuckin' stupid as I look. When I go to the movies I like a good war picture where the good guys win and the hero gets all the kisses of the stacked babe he just rescued. I don't go in for the creepies. I've seen enough women with black eyes and bloody lips and more than my share of dead bodies to sit and watch some made-up shit about things that are dead walkin' around eatin' the living. If I get hungry, I grab a cheeseburger." *What a nasty little atom bomb.*

"She's bewitched you and you don't even know it. If you don't get away from her you'll wind up dead. Look, I'll double my offer."

Smiled, full of heat and promises. "Maybe throw in a little extra." She shifted, no Morse code, straight on. Offered another opportunity, another chance to make her his bed and blanket, to be his slave or a Parisian whore.

He didn't bat an eye. He had other horizons on his mind.

"Double. Triple, makes no difference, I'm not buyin'. So pick up yer check and hit the bricks."

"This isn't over." *Pearls before swine.*

"It was good for me too."

✦

Foggy. Not a night to snap postcard pictures. Strong black coffee in Big Joe's all night diner. The rainbirds on shore leave. Bastards—with gold teeth or no teeth, nighthawks, and spare parts whose first kiss was a wild ride on the long way home from the local hoosegow. A waitress—bottle black over gray and three kids and thirty years passed Betty Boop cute—with bunions, just trying to live off small change. A new Cadillac and an older Rolls at the curb. Two women, dessert for the eggs and sausage crowd's ashtray-backstreet heartbeat.

The window booth in the corner. Two women better suited to The Plaza or The Met. One in diamonds and gold. Laurel Hasler, voice as smooth as forty-year-old single malt, blonde. A frown from her and you'd drink yourself to death. A no. You'd eat a bullet. Young. Ageless—timeless. Not a hair out of place. You couldn't build one this flawless with three wishes and God on your side. One in black fur and silver. Rene Girtler, dark hair, divine eyes, curves to put goodnight to sleep with a smile on its face. Lips as lyrical as her voice of honey. Not a wink over twenty-eight.

Two angelic faces at close range. Grit and spurs under freezer burn hard expressions. Storms under blouse sleeves. Coils and mountains ready to tear each other apart. Two minutes. Not a word to disturb the aimless cigarette smoke in death's yard.

The coffee arrived. Black as their hearts.

"I've tried to be nice about this. I offered a fair price."

"And what is the going rate for immortality?"

"The effects of the mirror will last you another 500 years and you could live like a queen on what I've offered," Rene said.

"Money? I already live like an empress and I can buy and sell countries. *And I don't like competition.*"

"I would never bother you."

"Your existence bothers me."

Rene's expression said bitch. "You think you've turned him?"

"He's wearing my lipstick on his collar." Laurel's smiled hummed.

A smile from a loaded thirty-ought six. "Then why was he fucking me last night?"

Laurel's face was black as the heart of a backstreet brawler on a mean lowdown.

"He told you he was busy on some case or errand, didn't he?" A body shot to a bad liver. Rene's smile widened. *Just one more push and this bitch will be in the cold ground.* Rene took off a white glove. The bullet is chambered. "He asked me to marry him." The diamond, flowers on the grave.

On the third finger of her left hand, under the black glove, was the diamond's near twin. She'd been betrayed before, every two-timing liar who couldn't keep it out of another woman's mouth was a skeleton. If she had a tank she'd run over her with it. And backup two dozen times for good measure. He'd put his hands on This after what she gave him. He was dead. Then this cat-thing was going to die. Very slowly. She'd sell her to a slaver she knew intimately. His establishment in Istanbul would weather her in hard yesterdays. If she ever looked in a mirror again, she'd scream. And if there was enough time in between tricks, she'd slit her own throat.

But her fiancé, Sidney Rollins, was first . . .

❋

Rene lit a cigarette. Exhaled. Smiled—no hint of summer or sun, etched from torture and greed. Sidney was about to be a loser's train song tripping over memories. He'd be back. Begging. Laurel had swallowed the lie about him asking for her hand. Probably thought they'd fucked too. They'd fight, nasty as two drunks, their heat turned to hate. He'd lose it, push her or slap her. She'd throw something at him and throw him out. And he'd come running. Rene knew how to show a man she was made for his pleasure. Knew how use the fugue and the tango to dominate him with forever. She wasn't losing out to some 500 year old slut. A few nights with her red shoes under his bed, and his pulse pounding in his ears as her tongue of fire captured his flowing ecstasy and then she'd send him back for the compact. This time he'd get it for her.

The street was filled with night-jazz. She saw the glow of a bar. Wanted the make believe of plutonium hands pouring sugar on her weakness . . .

❋

Yeah. That's how you got here—One lied and one sucked it right up. Forgot to think. Just let yer heart do the talking. Stupid move, dontcha think.

Mr. Tick-tock's 'bout run his race . . . thirty seconds ain't a long time, but you can get out of that door . . .

If yer still thinkin' a tigress can change her stripes, forget it. This cat-woman's smile has been lost behind her fangs . . .

Fifteen seconds . . .

Ill-fated ticking, destined for the rustle of blackness opening its eyes. My buddy, Otto, reads poetry, likes to quote the stuff from time to time. If he was parked in that chair I'm willing to bet he'd say something like, 'we are blind clockhands climbing toward midnight.' Just take the 'we' part out, 'cause you're the only passenger on this hellbound train.

Lights down: The William S. Burroughs Bedtime Story Hour on Dead City Radio broadcasting black tar excerpts of the Apocalypse—*"Bullets quoting infamy and the destroyer on the way in. And on the way out. Cold splashing from buckets of fire and you're here to go—Gone, baby. Gone" . . .*

And she walks into the room . . . Heaven, passionate and dangerous. Lips wet with venom. A phantom in black sheer silk. Velvet claws no longer in long black gloves.

"Darling, come into my arms."

Never seen that face before, have ya? Lemme tell ya, the mirror has.

Yes, I can see you like what she's done to her hair . . .

There's a corridor on the other side of the door . . . But you're on this side and her open arms, leafless autumn branches of ghosts and thorns stretching, are waiting . . .

In a few seconds . . .

(after a batch of Tom Waits and sunnO)))&Boris ALTAR)

a certain Mr. Hopfrog, Esq., Nightwalker

"Yes," said a certain Mr. Hopfrog, Esq. His whispering hand—nails painted in stripes of red and black—resting near his hat as if he had to leave.

"I wish Stanley was here."

"I'd call him back if I had that power." A space lay between us. It grew. He looked away, out the window. His home was in the West and it was calling him.

"It's very cold here—lovely in a northern way, but cold. Stanley wouldn't like it. Not at all."

I knew he was right. He always is. Even about Stanley . . .

Later we left the books and crossed the threshold. Away from the city lights to Robert's grave to talk about the next time.

❧

He had *That Edge*. They all said it, in words, with looks, to his face and behind his back. Whether in his changeless room of starlit on and on or out in the trance of the streets he wore his edge in praise and damnation. Praise resting on his shoulders like fine sunlit doves. Damnation falling from him as if unwanted rain. It was an edge born in a thousand mysteries and ten-thousand trials, an edge he earned at black doors and in endless circles. Day or night he wore it well—proudly.

But he'd never worn it with me. He'd never waved it at Stanley or Robert. With us he was always, Dear, Sweet Hopfrog, glowing in the rich soil of our shining eyes. And for that we loved him well. Even on the nights of wormwood hunger when he failed to beat The Assassin.

❧

All those nights he climbed the winding stairs and sat in the aerie and talked to The Devil of pasts submitted and futures to be rode . . . And more. They sat right on the floor on a rug of furious colors. All the signed papers yet to be collected, the tears of autumn trees, littered around them. Black steel eye to loving eye, surveying names marching on the chess board. Power to power, black to light, in a game flavored by loaded chance.

As the din of the Hourglass of No-Time turned the weathervane from shadows to My Soul to Keep to judge of the dead, they—masks off— traded bleak and ruthless for soft bluffs and valor and fire. Sometimes there would be a smile, sometimes one would tip the scales with a blaze of rain.

The two warriors had glided through the shadows for a long, long time. They knew every stain in the meadow and every wound buried in the mirror. Like the chill of the soft moon their footsteps had passed through many an empty window. Many were the things set in tar and whispers they'd faced. Their hands knew Saturn-red blood and smoke and the name of each and every thirsty crow waiting in the branches for the fruit to collapse. They both brought magic to the solemn game of souls.

"I'm watching you," The Devil would say with a hot red tongue.

a certain Mr. Hopfrog, Esq. didn't move a slipper or a paw. "So watch. If the river flows long enough perhaps you'll see a candle bloom."

The Devil scowled as he scratched his head. a certain Mr. Hopfrog, Esq. laughed. He so enjoyed baffling the Devil with nonsense, which The Devil believed to be cryptic tells, if he could only decipher them—But he never could.

On this night, my friend smoothed out the hem of his skirt. "That's much better," he said. "I so dislike untidy and its folds."

"You will burn under my foot one day," The Devil replied, rustling a contract painted with an unsteady hand.

"Time twists. One can never tell under which stone the birds have hidden the key."

Another heated scowl from The Devil. Another butterfly-soft laugh from my friend.

There they sat. The Devil's tail, red and curled and quiet in the moment, resting in his lap and a certain Mr. Hopfrog, Esq. big hands on knees ready for any flick of tricks. They played a game drunk with names . . . And places, labyrinths of black leaves and dark corners painted in the end-wings of vanished voices.

Seven contracts done with and it seemed the night had just begun . . . Several more read by the bruising snake tongue. Several more blacked out and burned.

"I love this night. You haven't saved a one, *little* Hop-frog. Did the dance of bright sun and blue sky tire you today? You knew we had a date, you should have rested."

a certain Mr. Hopfrog, Esq. threw his star-milk embroidered slipper, which caught on The Devil's left horn and spun. "I'm awake enough. Play your next card."

No diamonds or clubs did this devil hold. But spades . . . Spades to bury the dead, he had plenty.

With a great indigo smile bending the winter between them, The Devil gently removed the slipper and placed it back on Hopfrog's foot and then The Devil laughed—swift and fierce. From the bottom of a moth-dream bag he produced a contract Our Dear Sweet Hopfrog had never seen.

"One if by rabies . . . This soul—by something a bit more fun," The Devil said, slowly shaking the old parchment from side to side.

a certain Mr. Hopfrog, Esq.'s eyes could find no escape from the to-be-cast-down-into-blackness name the parchment had devoured at the signing. He'd taken Stanley, and Robert, and now—his shark-eyes steel sharp with laughter—The Devil said payment for My Sin was due.

A sky of thundering hopelessness festered around him, a poison filled of ghosts and knives and tasks of blackmail brushed in hot strokes. Filled with dust and hatred it snarled. Cold black lies opened wide faced the ma-gus, winding and rewinding all he knew. He was in a hole—a torture room, a panting tomb in a grinning boneyard and his hands could find no door to push me through.

"What will you trade for your friend, The Rat? I *might* accept all the little flames and their shiny a long time agos littered here at my feet. All those childhood sonatas to burn on the wheel of fate . . . That I might take."

With the tip of a talon The Devil burned a hole in my contract. His smile roared. Then the dissector's finger burned another and another. "The worm awaits companionship and I await your *best* offer, little Hopfrog." The edges of my obligation blackened as The Devil's finger danced on the record of my poisonous misadventures of sword and teardrops.

He knew what The Devil sought; alone and without complaint he heard the song of the blackbird. Ever the loving, devoted soul and friend, a certain Mr. Hopfrog, Esq. pulled ripples and mouths and mazes from his sleeve and traded his wreathes and complexities for my flight.

✻

The breath of Night swells. Its wings—tasseled with streaked screams and tears—open to spread the ink chill. Through the Door of Skin, where only the ceaseless sky is witness to the molting of all that twinkles, steps the Nightwalker. On the Road To Forgetting, vultures, floating in high circles, gather above the courtyard where time is buried ... And we find a certain Mr. Hopfrog, Esq. gone off to waltz on Night's darkest page ...

(for my friend, Wilum Hopfrog Pugmire, Esq.)

The Black Litany of Nug and Yeb

Äma bl-Nug ol Äma bl-Yeb!
Ttak cls iro Züür.
Ttak cls iro Züür.

O Masters of the Black Fires Concealed
Rise o'er the flights of dim mortals sleeping.
> *Nug and Yeb, Great Dragons black and red, come prepare thy Father's table!*

O Bringers of the End of Man's Allotted Time
Extend thy ill-frost that here and beyond might be cleansed.
> *Nug and Yeb, Great Dragons black and red, come prepare thy Father's table!*

O First Issue of She Who Is to Come Bearing a Thousand Young
Now lost to thy stillness of discomfort, spark thy Doom-Engines Black and Red.
> *Nug and Yeb, Great Dragons black and red, come prepare thy Father's table!*

O Great Hammers of the Scouring, arrive with thy Black Fires wild,
Clearing all spaces for the Terrible Masters Outside deprived.
> *Nug and Yeb, Great Dragons black and red, come prepare thy Father's table!*

O Angers Fuller Than Thunder whose concordant verdict crashes as a wave,
The frail earth lies ripe for thine age of starry-fire.
> *Nug and Yeb, Great Dragons black and red, come prepare thy Father's table!*

O shadowy Nug, uncover thy cauldron-black torch at the boreal pole
That the Divine Punishment may be born in all glory.
> *Nug, Great Dragons black and red, come prepare thy Father's table!*

O Servant of Abhoth, Yeb of the Whispering Mists,
Bring forth burning, thy round furnace red inhumed in the pole austral.
> *Yeb, Great Dragons black and red, come prepare thy Father's table!*

O Twin-Spawn of Yog-Sothoth, in thy nightmariums bound,
Strike with thy noisome Black Essence overbrimming.
> *Nug and Yeb, Great Dragons black and red, come prepare thy Father's table!*

O Sum of Destruction Complete, indulge thy Lords' will
With pact eternal cast.
> *Nug and Yeb, Great Dragons black and red, come prepare thy Father's table!*

O Both Sides of the One, the charts divined accede,
The heavenly facets shining, are set in the strict aspect foreordained.
> *Nug and Yeb, Great Dragons black and red, come prepare thy Father's table!*

O Issue of those Harms Tremendous fettered to strange-time most abhorrent,
The Sign made and brought through all the days is as a fever risen.
> *Nug and Yeb, Great Dragons black and red, come prepare thy Father's table!*

O Dreadful Gods, in thy cold sepulchers deep amongst the black maze of stars,
Heed this appeal, made with arms spread wide in thy acolytes' wanting, and arise.
> *Nug and Yeb, Great Dragons black and red, come prepare thy Father's table!*

Äma bl-E'rhibib ol Äma bl-Kähi.
Äma bl-Nug ol Äma bl-Yeb!
N'dr Ir'cculgra Tchcr Ürcti L'mü.
Ttak cls iro Züür.
Äma bl-Nug ol Äma bl-Yeb!

Erendira

for the Grandmaster, Andrew Vachss

I've sent more monstrosities than I can count into the black maw of doomsday—enjoyed doing it. They maim, kill, injure, off to the gallows they go. I'm not God, never bought into that, but I'm firm on An Eye For An Eye—fuck firm, it's carved in stone. I don't believe in peace, but balls-out wild out doin' what thou wilt, go fuck yourself with something jagged and when it's bleedin' good and proper jam a white-hot poker up there. I'm all for order and you don't have to set law to paper for me to enforce it. There's Right and there's Evil. If you don't play fair I fuck you. Fuck yer gray areas. And I don't give a rat's ass about why some assbag sides with the Darkies. If yer one of them, yer meat—same way they see us, meat.

Jam yer money. That's not why I do this. And you can stick buying my way into heaven. Like I said, I don't believe in that shit.

I left my interment in The Catacombs about a hundred years ago. Headed South and East. Heard the livin' was easier there. Ain't. But what did a frightened seventeen-year-old kid know. I left Erendira in The Catacombs. Wanted to take her with me, but she said no. Said it with tears in her eyes, but it still came out no. She was too afraid to leave her Mom alone in the Darkness. Broke my heart. What little bit of one I had. The Darkies had taken most of it, piece by blood-soaked piece, years ago. So I left.

Down four flight of stairs. Out the door . . . on a street the color of a cigarette ash . . .

Over the bridge to further away. Walked and walked. Like many of the journeyers you see on the road to the South, I stole to eat from time to time. Never took food from anyone's mouth or hands. They've got to live too. But I took what I needed to keep walking.

When I got to The City by the Bay I channeled my pain, became ruthless; it was pretty much that or die. I learned to kill—quick hit and I'd be gone. Became a master. There and gone—with a knife—with a gun—poison or drugs or a car—an ice pick, or anything handy. My hands have done the work too. It's all part of the craft. Learnin' to be cold is the hardest part. But my heart was buried in cement to start, so it kinda came easy. If you could call fuckin' someone's life easy.

Workin' for Braga made a lot of things easy. No one in The City wanted to fuck with him. Sure, some said he sat behind that big desk play actin' with his Mr. Big cigar and his silk tie and his silk shirt and his King of Everything monologues, but he'd sent more people to Hell than the Darkies. Still does. I'm the boatman that punches your ticket. You lie, cheat, steal, fuck with him, offend, or anything else that pisses him off, he sends me to end the trouble. All kinds of trouble—human, or . . . And no one is more effective in cancelling darkness than me. It's almost the only thing I do that gives me joy.

I worked for Braga because I wanted a piece of quiet. You can't get much anywhere, but I wound up with a little spot. There's a small dock and pelicans and Rona can run on the beach, sometimes I throw the Frisbee to her—she likes the red one best. No one comes around; too rocky to swim, if you were stupid enough in dip yer toes in the water, there's monsters in there too, monsters that make sharks look like guppies. And the few locals here know I'm Braga's Reaper. They stay away. Far away. They look out for me too. Better to have the monster on your side than after yer ass.

✦

I told Braga I needed some time.

He put down his Mr. Big cigar. Looked at me like I was nuts.

"For what?"

"Something personal."

He laughed, just a touch unhinged in it. He's a pretty good actor when he tries. Braga uses his hands a lot. They always say the same thing, "Another burden?"—comes off like why me?—and "It's not easy being the King."

He had his why me hands out. "I ask you a question and all I get is two words."

"You asked. I answered."

"That's all I'm getting?"

"You pay me for taking out the trash. You've got a line of suits to say yes sir and whip up bullshit answers."

"And you think I can rely on Pitt while you're off chasing fucking rainbows or whatever?"

I didn't say a word. Braga and I do not see things eye to eye when it comes to Pitt.

"Pitt's a dog. Does what Pitt wants. This is about me. Well, ain't it?"

I just stood there. He knew I wasn't going to say a word about Pitt. Braga knew the last guy who said something bad about Pitt to me was dead before he finished his sentence.

"Shit. I'll never understand why you look out for him. You're the coldest motherfucker I've ever seen—colder than me even. *If that's possible.* But you look after him like he was your goddamn baby brother. You walk in The Shit for me because I pay you, but for him you'd do it for free."

I lit a cigarette.

Braga knew I wasn't going to get involved in a conversation about Pitt. He'd been there the night the guy said Pitt was a worthless, slow-headed douchebag. Seen me slit the guy's throat for the offense.

"Jesus F. Christ! What kind of time?"

"Much as I need to fix a problem."

"I've got friends and connections up North. One call to Metheny, or Steg, I could see to it anything—*anything* you need gets *fixed.*"

"I said personal."

"Fuck I heard ya. So go." His hands fanned out in another why me gesture. "Fix what you need to fix. You get jammed up you call."

I didn't say thanks. He don't pay me to be polite.

❋

My car was headed North on the I. Home. A place I ain't seen in a lifetime. A place I try not to think about. I try hard. When I was a kid it was all darkness and teeth. Doubt anything's changed. If it has I'll deal with it.

Braga says I'm the coldest bastard walkin'. I walk in, down IT goes. Guess that's about right. All that shit that burned away my humanity—My Life, well, send black to the blackness. They were meant for each other, not to be here among mortal folk. Blast the shit out of it and try not to get the greenish goo that passes for blood all over your shoes. If that's cold, that's me. But Braga ain't talking about me offin' the Darkies. When he says cold, he means people.

I don't kill women or kids. Braga's a villain; pimp, junk peddler, into numbers, imports or exports, guns, or pretty much anything, that's his bag and the humans he deals with are the same. They're the ones I take down.

They're predators. Darkie or human, a predator is a waste of breathing space and I'm the fresh air inspector.

I rather be cleaning this house of Darkies, but work is work. The Darksiders—succubi, shaper-shifters, gobins, transhumans, banshees, trolls, vampires, and 100 other kinds of foul shit—are here to stay. Everybody says so. The papers say it's a war. Dark against light. All the conservative editors, preachin' bible black Believers shit, say Hallowed Be Thy Name's Angels will come and we'll be free of this Satanic infiltration. Bull-*fuckin*'shit. Every year there's more assaults and more sightings—they only come out at night, my ass! When I was a kid in the North there were maybe a few attacks each week. Now-days, there's a few attacks every hour. North, South, East and West, these monsters are everywhere. It's spread. Spreading.

And it's sunk its fangs into Braga's business. Last week a guy into Braga for five-large got ripped up and ate. Braga went ape-shit. He's lost nearly a quarter of a mill this last year alone in uncollected debts because there was no one around to collect from. 90% of what I do is hunt down these monsters that snatch the cash out of Braga's pockets.

Overbosses, they don't like to be called crime lords or kingpins these days, everywhere are sufferin' from it. Even where I'm headed.

Might have been wise to let Metheny, the overboss here, know I'm in town, some might see my return as a threat. But I wouldn't walk across the street to piss on him. We've met. He backhanded a waitress at one of Braga's pow-wows two years ago and I might have stepped in and replied on her behalf. Story goes she wasn't the only one went home that day with a swollen eye—c'est la-fuckin'-vie. Bad blood there. Fuck it.

Never one for bastards down to small change, postcards of the blues, or pasties and G-strings, I skipped all the heigh ho and the shore leave braids in Midtown. Checked into The Labyrinth on Montgomery. 3B. Near the elevator and the stairs. I'm not good with tight corners. Plans, even good ones, bug out and I like options. Fluid keeps you breathing.

Made a call. Pitt's cousin-in-law, Lovano set up the meet.

I went to dinner. Nothing fancy, salad, steak, and fries with black pepper gravy. No dessert. No alcohol. Paid my tab. Went to the lounge and had tea. They didn't have Darjeeling, but I'm not on vacation.

The Sha Quartet meditated over some "the stones in the pentagonal garden should never be placed carelessly" zen-jazz composition. The alto player's cherry blossom phrasing impressed me. And the bass player's flock of twilight steps damn near gave me visions of star-isles in dreamtime. The drummer knew of the tiger chase, mountain rhymes, and how to fold a fan. The piano player was a mage, drifting from the tolling of the wind at dusk to bits of August, the tempo and rhythm of the stars were in his fingertips, and in his heart. Four or five times a year I entertain brief fantasies of another life. Enjoying music is a part of those waltzes in "If time" I don't let out often. The "ending in blood" business doesn't leave much room for them. And it's dangerous.

The place was mostly commerce types and hookers. I'm half-ghost, half-smoke. If they even notice me, I look like I've got nothing to trade. They left me alone.

Eight P.M. Two hours to wait. I let Sha's rite ease me through the first hour.

In another life . . .

I walked into Blackwood's precisely at ten. Saw what I needed to see and walked to the table where she was sitting.

Erendira was nearing forty, as am I, and not at all what I expected. Twenty years had changed a lot of things, but not in the ways I figured. Gone the girl, the hints of womanhood, the innocence. In front of me was a woman who had struggled, achieved. Everything I loved was there, changed perhaps, but right there. Everything. And much more. Glad I hadn't chosen architecture as a career, as I hadn't envisioned this future.

I wanted to say the years have hardly touched you. Said, "Hi." I sat. Searched for another word. Felt stupid. Waited for her to talk.

"You've become the man I pictured."

Talk about wanting to be somewhere else. I've spent most of my adult life as stone and right that minute I was lost, sinking. Felt like there was nothing to hide behind.

"I'm sorry to have used our . . . *friendship* to bring you here."

"Never feel sorry for anything." *Especially this.*

She sipped her drink—coffee. Took out a pack of cigarettes. I could tell she was struggling with whatever she wanted to tell me. I hated that she felt uncomfortable.

"El Diablo." She exhaled wandering smoke the color of the grave. "And his wolves."

I could feel the knot in her heart.

"Killed Mom."

The thing that had held her here and kept us apart, her mother, gone. Erendira had given up everything to stay and help her Mom and the Darkies had taken her. I was stone again.

"Once you loved me. You are the only other soul I've ever been close to. I gave up . . ."

She looked at me. I knew the end of that sentence.

"I want you to find them for me. And kill them."

I nodded.

"I have saved a little money."

"I have no need of money. I came here because you asked for me. I came here to see you. If Hell had barred the way I would have come."

Her eyes smiled, said thank you, said—I thought—I love you.

"You'll do this *thing* for me?"

"Yes."

"When this is done I want to talk to you. There are things I want you to know."

"When this is done."

She took my hand. Squeezed it gently.

"Thank you."

I got up and left while I still could. Didn't look back. Wanted to. Couldn't find the courage.

It took me three day to find El Diablo and his wolves. You track these things long enough it gets easy. They think people are too scared of them to come a-callin' so they're careless. I'm detail oriented, I can't even spell careless. But I can spell dead.

I found them in a wounded skin of a tenement that had not survived the riots of its enemy time. Playtime for the fuckheads involved torturing two small kids. Their whole lives added up to maybe six or seven years each. A boy and a girl. Fun and games before din-din. I fucked them up. Bad. Put 'em down without putting them out. Wanted the kids out of here before I went to work. I had a message to send.

I put the kids in a cab and went back to the blackboard. Ice pick, knife, and a hammer. Spent four hours writing out my message. Left it for The Street to broadcast. In this town bad news gets around. By this time tomorrow every alley and diner and burned-out shell storefront would be talkin'.

Guess the whisper-stream will say the body count was three and after 100 no one wanted to count the rest of the pieces . . .

I went back to The Labyrinth. Showered. Changed. Tossed my soiled clothes. Went and had breakfast and tea. The waitress found me some Earl Grey. And when I had ratcheted my courage up enough, put in the call for Erendira.

I waited.

Room service brought the coffee and my tea. I sat and waited.

There was a soft but firm knock on the door. I got up and let her in.

She sat and I poured her coffee.

We smoked. Not a word between us.

When she finished her cigarette her eyes asked.

Yes was all I said.

"I told you I had something to tell you." She unbuttoned the top two buttons of her blouse. There was the cheap silver necklace I had given her when I was boy. "I have never taken this off. I have never forgotten you. I have never married. Never taken a lover."

I know as much about death as the Grim Reaper. Hell, he and I are brothers. I don't know shit about love. It's the only thing I fear.

"The day you left I vowed, one day when Mom had passed I'd find you and ask . . . if you."

"I have always. Never stopped."

She smiled. The relief pulled years from her face.

"My promise—vow, was if you wanted me, if I could find you, you and I would go away." Her look said if you want to.

I did.

"You remember that picture of the cactus you gave me? That's what I want. A little house and sandy hills . . . And cactus outside the windows. I saved some money."

I never grew anything in my life, but I was going to find out if you could grow or transplant cactus.

"I don't know how to—"

"We'll find our way," she said.

"Go home and pack. I have arrangements to make. Do you have much to pack? Sell?"

"I have been packed for three days."

"Two hours tops."

She left. I almost kissed her on her way out. But I chickened out. I had never kissed a woman. That seventeen-year-old boy I was in a past life had kissed the girl she had been and that was the last time I kissed anyone.

As she walked down the hall I opened a room I had shut fast. Inside I locked on the image. I was going to need that image the next time she was close to me.

I dialed the number I have for Pitt.

"Pitt. I need a favor."

"Done." Before I could tell him what it was.

I told him where the money was. Told him where and how to send Rona. He told me when to pick them up.

Braga never understood the glue between me and Pitt. He wasn't there when Pitt's daughter hugged me and smiled that first time. Vicki was downskid. An angel. That little girl never had a bad thought or word for anyone. And she loved me, instantly and totally. Loved me as much as she loved Pitt. Don't know why, but I never cared. She did and that's all that mattered.

The Darkies broke into Pitt's house one night when he was out of town on a job for Braga. They killed the babysitter, made a meal out of Vicky. Broke Pitt's heart. Worse it destroyed his soul. I found them. Had 'em tied down and I had cut off their hands. Bashed out their fangs. Then bad as I wanted to send the monsters back to Hell—bad as I needed to kill the fucks, I walked out and called Pitt. Sat on the place 'til he got there. He looked at me. Nodded. As close to thanks as it ever came. I left them to Pitt. He knew it took everything I had not to take them out myself. He understood how dear Vicky was to me.

He'd never whisper, scream, or utter a word about where I was going. Braga could set him on fire or fill his veins with chemicals, he could spend a week breaking every bone in his body. Pitt would never break. Some debts can't be repaid and some things are worth dying for.

♦

I was once shipwrecked in a storm of evil hours with demons. That was then . . .

Rona loves the desert. So do I. It's so clean. Every morning it's like a painting. Every evening the setting sun serenades the cactus. Erendira cut her hair short. I love it. I love her.

The day after I kissed the bride I began to grow a beard. Three summers and Erendira says it still tickles. Her eyes laugh when she says it.

Having spent twenty years between the pages of a book, the creased picture of the cactus I gave Erendira when I was seventeen is now unfolded and framed. It rests on a driftwood mantle over our bed.

Hell (and its denizens) may have come to Earth. But it has not come here.

(after Nik Bartsch's Ronin—STOA, and HOLON)

An Engagement of Hearts

Matters of the heart, how they play on the mind.

Cordelia stared at the perfumed correspondence she had unintentionally happened upon, and its flowing penmanship and fragrance too curious to set aside, just finished reading.

> *My dearest Denis,*
>> *I wither without you. Come to me as soon as you may . . .*

She read every unbelievable word again.

> *. . . My darling, you must know my nights are the blackest depths of unease while you are away from me. Be done with her as we planned, and hurry to my arms! I remain forever and always*
>> *Yours faithfully,*
>> *E———*

Yet another dream broken. Her thoughts turned to previous lovers, each in their time dearly beloved, now interred beneath stone and rich loam stitched by the passing of the conqueror worm. Soon to be alone again. Deceived, and then forgotten; perhaps one day, laughed at by the scheming pair. Cast aside—by Her Denis? Grotesque, and unthinkable! But the truth of it was in her hand.

Cordelia Pierpont Buchanan's face was flushed, her eyes moist with salt tears. Outside, beyond the patterned lace from the Continent which accented the windows of her comfortable home, rain from thick gray clouds hid the vista of bright-flowered Washington Square. She turned from the gloom and surveyed the sitting room. Fine sculpture, paintings, expensively-bound leather editions of poetry, furnishings worthy of the finest houses in Europe, servants, she was surrounded by fine amenities worthy of her class, but the hues of the room suggested only the dusky twilight of some bleak October.

She had money and property, her father's swift dealings and her mother's inheritance had seen to that. And she, befitting her station, attended luncheons and the theater, and the balls—

That's where she met Denis. At a spring gala on the roof of Madison Square Garden. She well recalled the sprightly music, the dancers whirling; the champagne—an excellent year; the spiritualist, Eva C., and her mysterious mediumistic energy (fakery, hocus pocus, many harshly stated after her demonstration, but Cordelia delighted in the romantic imagination at play); the expensive, flamboyant costumes—Denis with his cigar and sword, in a Venetian mask of canary silk and matching cape, a Musketeer from the pages of some romantic fable; the risqué conversation with Evelyn Nesbit about Yvrain's robust nudes, "And there is, Yvrain's friend, Denis—quite handsome and charming. He's said to be quiet popular among the Bohemian young women of Paris."

She should have stayed home and read the essays on Ibsen in Emma Goldman's *The Social Significance of the Modern Drama*. But Cordelia attended, and drawn to him—instantly infatuated, she laughed and danced in his arms and fell under his spell. Some termed the liaison scandalous, but she cared not. Cordelia heard the whispers regarding his past—a libertine with a host of unscrupulous dealings on the Continent, one of *Them*. She knew what lay behind the polite smiles and sudden silences, but she listened only to her captured-heart. "Prudence and propriety be damned!" it cried.

Eight months later they were engaged to be married. And with the full force of her womanhood she loved him. Naked in his embraces, freely giving herself over to carnal sensation, she found no shame in the union. Naked before his eyes—blushing not, posing for his poetic strokes upon bold canvas she entertained only adoration for his genius. Their conversations were easy exchanges of promised bliss. And when he was gone from her she reveled in the hours spent in her boudoir delighting in thoughts of "Our happiness."

And so it had gone for eleven ecstatic months. She, transformed, with her idyllic plans, and he, all artistic urges and impulses, creating beauty in his studio on the Lower East Side. Of course she visited, but never unannounced; to disturb him would be unthinkable. And when he found time he returned to her, those nights and afternoons, waltzes of uncontrollable desires, filled her heart with thrilling souvenirs. Color returned to her complexion and the nervous flutter over lost love passed. She felt young again.

When he was absent she whispered his name, and waited for tomorrow. Obsessed with the silken heat of his touch, she walked from room to room, wearing his promises like the rarest jewels.

But this? This?—*Now?*

Thirty-four—feeling centuries older—and still unmarried. And with this notice in her hand she feared she never would be.

Well, if *She* wanted him, she could have him. Let them be together. They planned to do away with her, to turn her mind with a yellow bound book he had given to her; a book said to drive all who read it into the maelstrom of madness, and many, to their death. Cordelia, who simply hadn't the heart to spoil his birthday surprise for her by telling him she already owned the volume, saw Denis as he handed her the slim volume—"I am told it is fabulously delicious! It was banned in Paris—every copy is said to have been confiscated, and promptly burned. They say this drama drives its readers into every manner of derangement. Imagine ... *something* banned in Paris? How delightfully curious." The conspiring lovers hoped, besieged by the poetic lines of death and suffering, she would take her own life.

'*Be done with her as we planned . . .*'

And a mere three months ago, she, without a living relative to survive her, had had a new will put in place, leaving him in possession of the totality of her very comfortable holdings.

Cordelia had suffered in the past—Denis was well aware of her agonies; the wicked tribulations, the infamy of betrayal and the unconscionable lies heaped upon her by other lovers. Denis knew, for she had told him, holding nothing of herself back, she had lingered in the delirium of denial and those moments like a coma of melancholia, until her lurking suspicions of treachery were confirmed. There had been a writer, then a poet, each drawn to her beauty, and she was later to discover, the money left her by her father. Each in their time, drifted from her, and finding themselves suffering delusions unchecked, although she hired prominent alienists to attend them, took their own lives.

Her head down, her distress turned to anger—

'*Be done with her as we planned . . .*'

Cordelia saw the words. They were a threatening knife. A change of fortunes would have to be fashioned.

With the letter in hand, she climbed the flights of stairs to the attic. At the far end she knelt before a heavy chest which had once belonged to her father. Setting the letter on the floor in a sliver of sunlight, Cordelia removed a key from its hiding place beneath the carpet and opened the chest.

Had it come to this?

There was a shadow in the corner beside her. Thin and long and bent, a wicked mockery of a man. The true silhouette of her lover, or the manifestation of some miserable curse? she wondered. The ghastly impulses which had possessed her parents—bringing them to a bloody murder/suicide—had been unrestrained evil, and this continuing affliction of unfaithful lovers she suffered, was this family cursed?

She took the object of onyx and gold from its velvet-lined case. Rising from her knees she stepped to a small bookcase which held a dozen copies of *Le Roi en Jaune*. Her finger caressed the spine of one copy. Denis and his trollop would have her where reason ebbs—and *dead* . . . "Never!" she shouted to the mocking shadow as she rushed from the attic.

❖

They had spent an hour in each other's arms. He rose kissed her brow, and without looking at her, promptly left the room. Denis was more than quite content with Cordelia's distance as they lay together. He believed the lack of unbridled vigor in her lovemaking was caused by the play beginning its work upon her.

Denis stood to the side of the doorway. With his heart pounding and a conspirator's hot blood rushing through him, he listened to her read from the outlawed drama. First, her voice soft and weary, then sharp, almost shrill, as if terrified. He smiled to himself and thought of his beloved, E——. Soon they would be here together. Soon all this, and more, would be theirs.

Cordelia knew he lurked, as darkly as Poe's demented murderer in "The Tell-Tale Heart," just beyond the casement. So she performed for him, just as she had in bed, thought it took little in the way of acting to dim the flames of her carnal appetites. It was all to easy to feint some degree of derangement. She was confident she had adequately concealed her design and he now believed her to be succumbing to the poison text he had given her on her recent birthday.

But as he listened, the strange, monstrous words began to vex him and he dashed from his post. Although he had only heard a scant few lines, he understood why the French authorities had declared the drama unwholesome and vile. Two glasses of scotch to quiet his nerves and he still could not drive the chilling words from his mind. Denis was more certain than ever their plan would work; no one could possibly confront the whole of *Le Roi en Jaune* and retain their mental balance. And if she did not—would not—do way with herself, he could always push her from an upstairs window and claim she jumped. With the book as evidence who would doubt her derangement. Cordelia's housekeeper and serving maid would testify to her having read it, and he knew she had told at least two friends she owned a copy.

It was obvious to him she was on the path; all he need do was wait.

❧

The afternoon was suitably cold and windy under gray skies. She quietly laughed to herself, thinking only fog and drizzle could appoint her stage more fittingly. Cordelia stepped from the cab and looked at the flourish of tattered urchins darting along Delancey Street. She was seeking just the right messenger. A few curious young girls spattered in dirt passed and stared, but she quickly waved them away. Cordelia surveyed the faces of those without means. There he was, a boy, deathly-thin and skin paled by lack of nutrition. Cordelia hailed him and he approached.

"I have a task for you."

The boy nodded his interest.

"You will take these to the following address and give them to Mister Denis ———. You will say to him, This is a gift from your beloved, Cassilda, who waits for you in dim Carcosa. You will then reveal this object and say, Behold the Yellow Sign. You will leave it and then depart. Can you do this?"

He nodded rapidly and smiled at the bill in her hand. Cordelia handed him five dollars and the address. His eyes flashed and he bowed deeply to her.

The boy knocked and waited. After a time he knocked again.

A fleshy young woman, resembling one of the parading whores who lustily cooed and offered their charms when the streets were darkened, opened the door. "Yes," she hissed.

"I have a delivery for Mr. Denis ———."

"I'll take it," she snapped.

"Sorry, Miss, but I was told I have to give to himself."

E——— admitted the boy into the studio. Denis was standing over an unmade cot and buttoning his shirt. His feet were bare.

"Who is this!"

"A delivery for you, Sir. A fine lady paid me to bring it."

Denis looked at E———. She looked at him and shrugged.

"What lady? Her name, boy."

"She didn't say, sir. She was thin, she was—like my mother, and dressed very fine. Had light hair like sunlight, and soft brown eyes."

Denis knew it was Cordelia.

"She said to tell you, 'This is a gift from your beloved, Cassilda, who waits for you in dim Carcosa.'"

"Waste no more of my time, boy. Give me what she sent and be gone!" His hand was out.

The boy uncovered the onyx and yellow gold ring Cordelia had given him to deliver and thrust it into Denis's hand. "'Behold the Yellow Sign.'" Handing a parcel wrapped in brown paper, which appeared to be a book, to E——— the boy dashed from the studio.

Denis looked at the ring. "The Yellow Sign?" He turned the ring in his fingers and looked at the scorpion-like engraving in the onyx face. "She's sent me the Yellow Sign." He laughed and showed E——— the ring.

She looked at him and smiled. "It's working. She sent you this! The play begins to exact its toll."

Denis had to agree, the proof of Cordelia's blooming derangement rested in his hand. "Cassilda," he murmured before breaking into quiet laughter. He knew the name was one from the play. Listening outside of Cordelia's bedroom he'd heard her speak some of the character's lines.

After unwrapping the copy of *Le Roi en Jaune* and showing it to E———, the pair discussed their future. Their manipulation had taken hold, Cordelia thought she was Cassilda. Denis put the ring and the play on a shelf and sweeping E——— up in his arms carried her to the cot to finish what the boy had interrupted.

✤

Timing the appearance of her episodes, Cordelia performed for Denis over the next two weeks. She quoted passages from the play, and called him Thale once when they lay together. At odd moments she seemed gripped by inexplicable compulsions. Twice at the breakfast table she asked if he knew how many of the great talents who had committed suicide had used knives. "I should think poison is less of a bother," she stated flatly before he could reply. In the library one afternoon she stood by the window for nearly an hour, waiting, she claimed, to watch a wondrous parade of furies led by Hecate and Thanatos pass by. She played at being bemused and forgetful, mumbled abominable vagaries—naming dead Carcosa and the ebon light of the Hyades, and during supper one evening threw a quizzical tantrum before falling into a deep melancholia which lasted for three days.

Denis was delighted, but began to express what he felt was the appropriate amount of concern for her to the servants. He worked hard to distance himself from culpability.

Seeing his plan working so well and so quickly he returned to his studio and E——, only to find her sobbing. The book he had placed on the shelf lay open on the cot, and E——, naked, smeared in painted distortions of the foul symbol on the ring, lay in shallow ponds of spilled paint on the floor of the razed studio. At the sound of his entrance she wheeled, wide-eyed and raving.

"You've been with *Her!* Admit it! You've been fucking her!"

She flew to him, fists battering his chest and shoulders.

"Admit it! Admit it."

Her fists were at her sides. She seemed to be struggling with herself. Her eyes darted from him to the cot and she mumbled, "You were mine. Only mine." Then her gaze caught the unhinging curves of the Yellow Sign on the ring she wore and her offensive resumed.

Denis was quick to attempt to arrest her aggression with a bear hug and a calming denial, but E—— was utterly possessed. With a knee to his groin, she freed herself from his hold. She stood before him and screamed, "You've been fucking her! How could you betray *me?*"

Without warning E—— picked up a chisel and slashed his chest. Astounded by the attack Denis stood there in shock as she plunged the instrument into his abdomen. Only when he lay bleeding on the floor did he recover enough to attempt to crawl away. But now a feral beast was upon him, repeatedly plunging the instrument into his back.

Denis lay there, bleeding and battered he felt himself slipping away.

Then she stood above him with a knife he sometimes used for whittling. Tears were in his lover's eyes as she slit his throat, and severed his genitals. "This was mine! You gave it to *Her!* How could you? It was mine!"

As his body cooled afternoon passed into evening. E—— sat on the floor beside him and rocked like an exaggeration of a frightened, angry child—arms tightly crossed, hands upon her shoulders, chin to chest. She shook and shivered, and sometimes lay in a tight ball, her nails digging into her upper arms. Many were the low-toned moans that sounded like the distant whining of a wounded dog. Minutes would pass in silence then she would suddenly whisper long commentaries spiked with protests of disbelief and cruelty. At times E—— rose and paced circles around him, cursing his infidelity. She hurled paintbrushes and palette knives at him and poked him with broken pieces of canvas frames. She spat upon him, and kicked his lifeless shell, and then would lie beside him, holding him tightly, and cry.

Some hours passed before her demented outbursts subsided. E——— looked upon that which her rage had wrought and screamed. Shocked and confused she examined her bloody hands and the ring she wore. In a moment overcome with horror and grief she rushed to the window and jumped.

✦

The wind in the cemetery sounded like a choir of solemn mourners passing the earthen temples of those dissolved. Cordelia walked along the manicured promenades, from fiancé's grave to fiancé's grave to fiancé's grave, placing a single, wilted yellow rose upon each marker. They, gone from her, were now and forever death's true companions. With word and line and stroke they had sought to uncover beauty and expose truth. She wondered what pageants their talents had discovered in doom's yard.

In the failing light of late afternoon, smiling, gratified by her ability to uncover and deal with fabrications, she sat on a bench which overlooked the valley the perfidious trio, once, each in his time, her beloved, resided in. As if they were favored children just put to bed, Cordelia began to read to them from a well-worn copy of her favorite drama, *Le Roi en Jaune*.

"*We have not any secrets anymore,*
  For schemes and plots and plans and all device
  Have now worn old and thin, till time hath stopped."

The current of her quiet laughter echoed softly in death's garden. Three disloyal beaus and their adulterous harlots justly dispatched, and tomorrow was another gala . . .

Perhaps—

An Event Without Knives or Rope

A slow night, exhaling . . . darkness, shadows in the shadows . . . and living things . . . and hunger . . . A distant siren. Need calls out to demons . . . The rules of the game laid to waste. Life on the bottom shifts.

An alley straight outta the '30s, it's face is out of laughs, out of questions, dead . . . garbage cans, soiled windows—cracked and sleeping . . . wind stretched pages of a newspaper with another week of crimes and no answers . . . cigarette butts left by bad luck and trouble . . . the air is dry, hot in the mouth of summer . . . His clothes are torn, dirty, his hat a waste of time, it can not hide his guilt . . . A bottle, its voice run away with understanding . . .

Blood . . . there was strange weather and trouble . . .

Every night of the week he's out. Lost in the plans of drink, looking back in vain . . .

Beer and cigarettes . . . maybe a piece of ass. A sad tone to the thought. *One more drink . . .*

Two hours ago a barstool . . . a lonely conversation . . . they leave, she and he, off to find a bottle and a quiet place, maybe to fuck . . . she's more in the mood than he . . . a liquor store filled to the brim. she hands him money for a bottle . . . around a corner away from the lights . . . He brushes the cigarette butts to the side, he lays his rumpled suit coat down for her, they share it, share the indifference in the bottle. Never spilling a drop . . .

Parked . . . whiskey as if it had purpose . . .

He has his hand in her pants, she has him in her mouth, a little flame on her lips, some part of it reaches the place under his lapel . . . He opens his eyes and sees feet. No sound, just there . . . Thick legs covered in fur . . . and hooved . . . Hears a growl . . . Her head comes up . . .

"*Again.* Always fucking anyone . . ."

"You never want me. You fuck your witch-things, but never touch me." Snake eyes hiss.

"If you were not always drunk we might . . ."

"Make it a ten-some? I'm not some covetous bitch on your totem pole. And I'm not a ghost."

"I've warned you about this."

"YOU SON OF A BITCH! Waiting for you to tumble in from the streets every night is living? I can feed myself and have a little fun doing it … I've had enough knifes buried in my heart." Flashing eyes, claws—suicide. The air, suddenly brutal. Something under her dress rattles.

He pushes his back to the wall and clutches his chest … squeezes his eyelids shut, puts his hands over his face …

"You want to be alone. Then be alone." A hoof stamps. The business end of claws eat holes in her neck. In the dialect of insult and injury, a frenzy of red stripes … a ragged half scream …

Blood, on his lapel, on his shirt, white two days ago … blood on the garbage can, on the brown paper bag …

Muscles bunched, tight. Hooves and scarlet-matted fur and horns and claws severe. Flaring blood-red eyes—galleries of unwanted abominations and sulfur, look at him … He waits for the grasp, the deadlift … knows his head will, in a second, lie—torn, bleeding and sideways—beside hers between his knees …

"Humanity," the contempt spit on him.

A hideous, great black beast straight outta some hell … Demon-spurred tail, swiping side to side, walking away to some forgotten corner of dust … and skeletons mumbling … some corner grown stiff under the cast off time of terrible crows …

An alley from the '30s … hot with cold blood … and something dead …

He looks down the neck of the bottle … nothing in there … He drops it and runs screaming … Stumbles, scrapes his knees, turns his wrist, jams a few fingers … of course, promises—"Dear God, Everything and Good"—to *never again* …

(for S. T. Joshi, *fingerpost*)

One Side's Ice, One's Fire

Vex had blue hair when she came to the obscure town . . .

Vicar Street, more Nightmare Alley if you ask me, was wide open with old stores that had been asleep for a long time and telephone poles covered in last chance handbills. Exploited by tough tomorrows and inconvenient yesterdays that didn't survive the hustle, skinny-ass night-gaunts in terminal shoes walkin' The Row . . . Women picked up by lies—the melody blurs, takes a fist to their youth, their antennas break, they wear and get dropped in tears. Sour is the breast milk on the birth certificates here. Everything, in and out, top to bottom, clouded by ugly chaos on a madass bender.

Spillane's the coroner here, he fills out the reports—never writes cardiac arrest as cause of death. Met him once, he was on a call—triple homicide/suicide with a carving knife (common as rot-gut confessions and the flu 'round here), said, "Everything here is loaded. Except the church bells . . . and we could use more rain. Helps clean the splashes of murder and hate from the streets . . . Every night furious says fuck the consequences. The joint is a primer for hopeless." I agree with his review of what the plow leaves in the Petri dish.

It's all a parade of shit and fury, considerations not even attempted; soaked in scowls, summer's crawling, trounced with both hands while its down; bare mornings sacrificed on the full moon; notorious hearts and minds hanging on short cuts that end in low life; history disrobed, every fixture conquered; dawn's lips, a foundry of detritus; in their grottoes over cut-rate bottles of subterranea the neighbors rattling about weakened-to-the-point-of-nil, discharged tokens still panning for Godot; Forever groans. Doubled up, it pulls the rag-covers over its head, afraid of the thug-stones of Did; rank with ache desolate right at home.

The chaos moon leaned forward, looking in windows. Nothing here is airtight. Dark, slow fog hugging the corners of threadbare everydayness and loud scabs. Drop a match here, or scream, and the whole stir-crazy place might blow, clean up to the graying outlaw vultures having coffee on the lip of the flat-roofs. The whole broken shitcan an opera in rust and ashes. Twenty-year-old hopehead or old lady, tinker, tailor, sentimentalist, rusting derelict, dock worker or ex-freewheeler reduced to begging, here, where the lonely have a field day in the open arms of broken glass and rituals emptier than The Void, you pay for your ticket in blood.

. . . Vex went to the address on the letter . . . The letter had mentioned loyalties . . .

And a dirty trick . . .

Where she went . . .

I came in a bit later . . . (the package that arrived after Vex went said PAY NOW) . . .

The Blackwood Hotel, last seen as elegant a century ago. Some say leave your brain functions at the door. By the look of it, most do. The staff's eyes are cold as lizard skin, their tongues excite no heat. Every name badge reads L. Kafka. The corners of the carpet reek of piss. The paintings in the dungeon-lobby are a wild slosh of when rampage blew. All the doors are green. This place is a mistake sliding into sickness. A goddamn weird place if you ask me.

I'm in, probing. Getting responses that add up to shit. My eyes roar. Theirs say, why hurry? Finally, after they see the lightning of my weapons—hard marshals who never say sorry—in their garden, I get the room number . . . I take the stairs. Doors with threatening faces of fire thundering in the hall. A pair of red children's rain boots in front of the door. One, having stumbled, lies on its side. Vex had very small feet. My pulse tries to catch up to my sinking thoughts. The air smelled like rotting paper, and food, someone in this dim, graying fortress had amnesia and had left something out, perhaps on their way out to an outing in the woods, or the zoo.

7D. The door wasn't locked. I went in, sidestepped the trinkets. Closed the curtains. I'd already seen the street. Circled the dried pool of blood and locked the door. I didn't send out invitations and didn't want to draw company just yet . . .

I pulled a hardback wooden chair over to the wide stain of dried blood. Sat. Stared at it. I listened for trickles, or echoes. It pulled on me, but stayed speechless. It was Vex's blood. I could smell her. Without teasing her blue hair (for an effect I could never understand) Vex was 5' 10" and a smidge, barefoot. 119 lbs. girl loses that much blood she doesn't live. Cold angry shadows behind my eyes started going wild. Some hardcore shithead thought I'd play the ransom game. OK. But I'm paying up with pain . . .

The apartment had suffered. Someone had come in here and given the maid a permanent vacation. Fueled by adrenaline their amok rate went up and the poison came out. Their violent ad-lib of acid rain had licked everything, scraped it unclean. The volcanoes had unpacked. And not quietly. I was pretty sure they didn't have a permit. Flotsam come to a miserable end. I sifted the shore like a trainee studying for a test. I have a good imagination and don't get confused, I knew they wanted to be PAID NOW, knew they were serious, I just wanted to know who to send the payment to.

I found a map and several markers, all torn in the shipwreck. Pieced them together. Had a blueprint. Walked out on the American street that had divorced Norman Rockwell—based on the weeds and the peeling paint (and the reek of puke and piss), I figure it and its shark lawyer took 90%. I went looking for the nearest bar. Oil greases wheels, booze greases tongues. My Berettas had questions and they're intimate with many dialects, greasy or not. I didn't figure any of the conversations they were about to engage in would be extended.

Tight streets. Hot as an oven. A jazzy pop song about being *Dead! Dead! Dead?* oozing out a half-open window. Not a scream in earshot. Tight streets. An itch that can't sleep in this sentence of dust, tangled and fraying and fading behind decades of disrespect. Really looked like someone should send in the clowns, or a least a cleaning crew.

You live around here, with the hunger-chiseled street-poets and the cunning junkies and the dime-store gangsters and the madmen smothered in apparitions, you get sick of the running black fire and the cold. Lots of the inhabitants here scurry off looking for plain old room temperature. Can't say I blame them. You think it's easy around here, step right up! Let's see how long you can hold your breath.

The shift winding down the night on Amnesia Street was swallowing sour dreams; at this hour you take what you can get. Two bars had a chokehold on the corner. Perched like Castle Frankenstein on the North face of the corner, The Limbo was a gloomy place, part Hammer Film set, part dump. On the southern shore, The Cocoon looked closed for vespers, or some other ethereal plot. One clan was vampires, the other, angels who had punched out and gone feral, most had sheared off their wings (maybe it was some tribal thing?). Murderous dispatches came out of each cauldron, hit the streets and folks tried to pawn top, bottom, and middle, just to keep breathing. This was Ground Zero in a turf war for blood and souls.

I wasn't planning on giving up either. I lit a cigarette and pondered which joint to ply my supernatural powers in first.

BLINGed up and bouncing, a crew decked in sartorial advantage pulled up in a white Caddy and went in The Limbo. Half my cigarette later, a tight pack of unforgiving fang-boys parked their red van in front of The Cocoon.

Eenie . . . meenie . . . minee. Go . . . I've seen a lot of red. It doesn't bother me. Tucked in my wings and tail—I never wear hats, so I couldn't do anything about the horns, and walked into The Cocoon.

Everyone in the place was dressed in red, head to boot, or sandals or stilettos for the ladies. They drank from red glasses and smoked red ciga-rettes. How fuckin' quaint and uptown. Me, I'm a basic black kind of guy, denim blue or Earth-tones on my days off. I skipped stopping at the bar and walked to two men seated at a chess table of red and white pieces. The white queen had just fallen. Dropped the small package dead center of the match. Lit a smoke. Exhaled.

"I'm investigating payment plans," I said to the tombmeister. He could tell I was not the waiter.

"It's always good to consider the details."

"Mr. Muth, isn't it?"

"Who is asking?"

"The guy with the fat briefcase full of money." Even a blind bluesman could have smelled my well-oiled Berettas. Heimdall heard what they were whispering to each other.

"I very much enjoy currency." He ground out his cigarette butt. Took his time. Like I was supposed to read the gesture for the fine print. Smiled coldly. "And I could always use another handyman if you're looking for something to keep you busy while you're in town?"

"The illegal atmosphere in the windowsills around here might be good for my health."

He looked at me like he was drawing blood. The first time that hap-pened to me was a blonde, the second was five inches wide when I was sur-viving some hardcore in prison, the last time it was LOUD. Mr. M, as he liked to be called, was neither A, B, or C, and none.

M, the alpha blood-junkie, was tapping a claw on the rim of his glass of blood. (I got claws too. Got 'em from Dad. Mom's side of the family wasn't deadly, just dead.) He drained his glass. Made a little show out of it. Behind him, a twisted little toady, just into his fangs, drummed on the back of a chair. Like I need rim shots or drum-rolls to get the point.

"Might I offer you a drink?"

"Doesn't appear you have any Earl Grey and I don't go in for red. Clashes with the color of my skin." *And I do not care for messy eaters and drinkers.*

"I've an errand to tend to. I'll be back. We'll discuss your offer."

M pointed to the door and waved.

I walked outta M's little patch of Hell and crossed the street. Wanted to see what the ex-Heaveners had to offer. I also wanted to double check my information. I like my tally sheets tidy.

The Limbo they called it. My mother would have said close the door and clean it. Just like ex-smokers, one minute yer a filthy little sonabitch, or in this case as they were all women, daughters of a real bastard, the next, spittin' a different agenda, you preach like a righteous mutha on a jag.

The floor was asphalt, cracked and pitted; a broken white line ran down the middle. Realistically painted, the too-close belly of a blue-tinted full moon covered the entire ceiling. It was dim and yellow and pressed down and tendered its opinion with the closeness of an open grave in serious need of a through scrubbing. The white table tops were star charts. Guess they still had a thing for open sky.

There was a lot of passion in the place. Every HOT!-HOT!-HOT!-Perfect Ten ex-do-gooder eyed their sword after looking at me. I guess being the only tomcat in a room of bikini-clad femmes stirred something that wouldn't be nice if it hit the fan. Or maybe the horns and tail kinda got their backs up, old wounds, scars that won't heal. This side of the coin or that, I really wasn't concerned either way. Green, red, blue, thick or thin, blood's blood. It flows, you wash yer hands. And if it stains your shirt there's lots of haberdasheries around.

Every pretty face in the joint was painted up for Doctor Tarr & Professor Feather's Asylum Parade. They were drinking cold gin and absinthe in The Limbo. Every model-thin beauty in the place was loaded. So were my Berettas. They may have been seraphim up to goody-goody with thirty-seven Hail Marys on top at one time, but they were soul-suckin' zombies now. I don't give a flyin' rat's ass what stripes a predator's wearing, you piss in my yard I'm sending you the cleaning bill.

I sat on a train a while back and the woman beside me was reading *The Grass on the Other Side of the Fence Is Greener Because There's a Cesspool Under It.* You pick whatever side turns you on, just be careful you don't burn your fingers when the shit comes out of the oven. Me, I walk my own line. Sure, it gets windy up on this tightrope once in a while, but I'm OK with edges.

Two women were playing chess. White and red pieces. The red king was one move away from checkmate. I walked over to the table.

A leggy blonde with the face of an angel in a white fur bikini (every ex-angel in the joint was decked out in a white bikini—guess they were rebellin' too) gave me the eye—the Clockwork Alex one that had eaten a lot of chaos and liked it. Her look had a river of blood in it. Said I was on the menu. Guess she figured my red skin made me kin to the bloodsuckers across the street.

I kept my hands at my sides. No need to stir things up just yet.

"Evenin', ladies. I'm new in town and was hoping you might ease my discomfort with some information on a very unpleasant affair."

"Are you *fucking* drunk?"

"Oh, to walk in here you mean. Nah, just a sightseer looking for a simple kindness."

Serious. "We don't do *Kindness*. Try the Catholics down by the bridge. I hear they're still handing out Do The Right Thing icons." Sharp as steelwool.

Cold bitch and her witch cult.

"Sorry to have bothered you, Ma'am."

Her eyes, both poetic crime and a storm, dismissed me. The fatherless circus orbiting around her seemed ready to growl or worse, the swords at their fingertips were dragons readying mountains of ugly speech. I noticed a spot of drool on a mouth that promised death.

In the Hot Zone love stories between angels and demons are forbidden. It looked like Little Miss Missfortune and I weren't were never going to make bedsprings sing.

I saw what I needed to see. They didn't do a thing to aid Vex, so . . .

I may be red, but I see things as black and white. You're a help, or you're The Cancer. When I arrived here I found I like hummingbirds a lot, so I went to medical school.

Before mad and ready to kill turned to bleed I hit the exit.

The hardened pain I was wearing stood on the curb with me. I smoked a cigarette.

A shitty little corner without hope. One side was ice. One was fire. I didn't concern myself with excuses. Walked to my car and got the hammers and protests I had received from a G. I. I know who had written a few dozen Army manuals on bomb disposal and KA-POW! If I'd learned anything about life it was editing—slip in too many spices and dinner comes out of the oven tasting like a big turd, so I fired things up . . .

I put M back in his box—burned the fucking thing. Burned his bar and his crew with him. Walked across the street and turned the lights out for Little Miss Missfortune and her blonde, blue-eyed angels too. Vampires and angels, none of 'em breathe bullets too well and they sure don't hold up well in extreme heat. Dad always said our family's nightmares are written in blood, and though I rebelled—the showdown involved heavy gunfire and blood (Dad's, not mine), guess most would say I'm a chip off the old block.

I lit a smoke and looked around. The whole shebang asleep in a blast of silence.

I kicked the top off a fire hydrant and washed the ash and blood off my hands. Lit a smoke and walked back to my car . . . The wind came up. Offered various gestures. I let it develop, didn't bother to wave. Never hurts to dust things off . . .

Misery . . .

And woe.

Decay floats. The maggots wallow. Thousands of nobodies and tons of trouble. The outcome is dark and lonesome. Even the comic books are full of it . . . A sprawl of midnight cowboys and black widows on the mean streak express, all haunted night long every layer tortures . . . A whole pack of dark pictures, containing no answers, no glory you can win . . . Anonymous ends for easy targets . . . Ghost orgies in syringes of white-hot sludge. Down here in the crazy dusty moments, to the parasites with the razorblade eyes and suckerfish mouths a day makes no difference. The rats know how to swim and they know how to swallow, manacles can't hold them. Let it ride or step away, it's all touched by crimson. No one gets to fix things and no one gets to leave the theatre . . .

Another pock mark in the foxhole. Even though everyone here is stark-raving mad, Wonderland this ain't. Never will be—I can't clean it up that fast.

It's windy.

The moon comes out. It's holding rehearsals for Oblivion . . .

❦

Vex wasn't my lover. She tenderly kissed my forehead once, but that's as far as it went. She made me tea, held my head and my hand. Looked after me after the shotgun kicked me out of my neighborhood with a loud splat. I told her if a tornado ever came down the street call me. She didn't . . .

Vex and I are on the last train home, but only one of us will see the roses bloom in the backyard next spring . . .

The rain turned to snow. Cold and wet. The trees in this garden are bare this season. The view is undisturbed. A lot of people would call it pretty . . . Now Vex's just another dead girl. Laid neatly, isolated, in a cell of blackness, she will never come in from the cold. She died on her knees. I'm on my knees at her grave.

If I could shed tears . . .

A Spider in the Distance

They sat there quietly. Their feet in the warm, still water of the pool. The wandering wind did not enter the courtyard.

"What do you wish for?" she asked.

He was slow to turn, slow to move his gaze from the peace of her unmoving feet. "At this moment, nothing. Being here with you is enough."

There had been another love and terror and the long despair, then he arrived and calmed her. She took his hand in hers. "I do love you."

His eyes smiled in the soft playful light.

You, and being with you in this garden is treasure, he thought.

She did not want to send him, but it was not a question of wishes. There was only need.

She put her arms around him and laid her head on his shoulder. There would be the rest of this day and tonight. The distance would come with the sunrise . . .

✦

Distant now are the points of friendship. Next to the stones a spider had come down. Far from home and the warm blue hands, in search of prey he came to the midnight pages. The waves bid goodbye to his boot prints.

The wind came to whisper details.

It was only a few miles to the corpse of the poet and The Mask. A few miles of stillness, dark and cold and waiting.

Spider stood in unwelcome midnight-nothing come down from the sky. He did not stand there in the loneliness long. No help would come. Ever hungry for words, wolves and hawks and teeth would come seeking slow ships. Spider hoped she was right about him being ready.

The path was sharp, but he had been to banquets on webs before.

Under the darkening stars Spider took out his compass and his map. He looked over the open field of stones and saw the undertow of the night winds, saw the sails of other seekers turned to rust. Twisted, dry wrecks of trees, bent snakes curled by the smiles and bane of winter's giant rage littered the stark expanse. The wreckage was filled with the bleak echoes of crows and autumn.

"There is a gate by the mound. Try to get through quickly," she said.

"I know how to be quiet, and deadly, if need be," he said.

He moved her ring to the anointed finger and unslipped Razor. The day he met her, came into her peaceful courtyard, he placed the sword on the mantle. For ten months it laid quiet, the dust came and slept on it. It was clean and oiled now. His hand and arm no longer felt the strangeness of parting, the balance was restored. All the meadows Razor had painted thick with red sat on his straight shoulders.

The moon was a hungry goblin, its light ready to rend. Spider moved among the stones and broken trunks, Razor attuned to any inclination of hidden snake or poison. Shadows chilled in endless hours reached for flesh and bone.

The first mile passed and the black mouth of the second now lay behind him like a frozen lawn. He could see the mound in the distance. The stones thinned, short scrub grass and barren patches of sand eased his march to the threshold.

Spider circled the mound very slowly. Stopping only once in the jet shade of a felled trunk to survey the archway.

The silence and stillness was a great weight. Nothing here twitched, nothing of the sun left its letters here. No raven or demon or echo of the games of the abyss, no grim sentinel patrolling, nonetheless the shade of evil hued this—trap. All the accounts written of this place spoke of it in frightened whispers.

In the land of his birth, magic was poison and Spider hated it and hated the violence it had brought to the now devastated city of his birth. Demons and devils and flesh-eating carrion that walked by night, he'd faced each under fading stars and blinding mid-day sunfire and now standing before this gate wondered if his practiced steel could carry him through deviltry and home again.

The hole in the soil was ribbed, as if dug in steps, a foot or two in the hard earth pocked with stones then the next excavation. The hands that had dug here were not swift and the tunnel they burrowed was not straight. But it was large enough for a man to walk upright, most of the time.

Spider was sleepy and he could eat, breakfast was almost half a day back, but the hours that led to the road home were still before him. He would consume them and eat when he reached his ship. His burning torch fed his steps.

He stopped from time to time to listen and look for footprints or other signs. Only dim echoes of his own footsteps came to his ears. He moved on. The sour flavor of the air made it hard to breathe. He came to a place where the walls gave way to wider dark. He let his torch hunt the floor and the breadth of silence. No sun hurts this ground . . . nothing, nothing . . . empty.

Spider followed the wall, the blood in his arm powering his sword as it fathomed the bare air until he came upon another opening.

He entered and tapped his sword upon the wall, listening to the echo. The cavern was enormous. Spider stretched out his arm, extending the feeble light, and walked forward. This chamber of the underworld was empty and malignant. He felt the different hours that formed its emptiness.

This is all too quiet, he thought.

His torch replied with bones. Whole and in pieces, armor and leather beside them. A sword an arm's length from a ripped leather bag much like his own.

One set of remains became two and there were brothers for the scraps fallen from the basket of life.

And after another dozen paces, fresh bodies, but they were not men. These hyenas were once women and children, but some ill desert magic had turned them. Eaters of the dead, dead themselves, this was the obscene party that had cleaned every contented delight and unrolled quarrel from the dead men who came to this tomb. Arrows, by the tens and tens, feathered the freshly grown carcasses of the ghouls.

Spider bent to examine the corpse of a thing that had once been a woman. Afraid to be corrupted, he did not touch the blood around the wound, but knew it to be fresh . . . The first arrow stung him, biting the middle of his back. The second hateful pronouncement, lower. Seven more, systematically, followed.

He was down. Noise, the sound of warriors came to him from three sides as the arrows fed slowly.

Faces in the light. Soldiers. Drawn swords, hard faces. A few murmurs. A brisk laugh.

"Were you looking for this?" A leather-gloved hand held the unadorned ivory mask. The Mask he was sent to find. It flared with secrets.

With his eyes he spit at the man who cost him his life.

Deep in the swelling cold, the hard cavern floor a black bed . . . *She passes through the room, leaving a hint of summer sun with her scent. Her "come follow me" eyes laughing, the heat of her bare footprints an open treasure map* . . . A last fragile thought, caught before it can slip across the distance. Then he died.

Two soldiers tested his death with their boots.

The Captain put The Mask in his leather bag and they left the chamber swollen with death.

✦

Four months and he had not returned to her side.

There had been no word and the ship sent to find him had returned, the captain saying his boat was found burned and wrecked on the coast. They had searched, only briefly, the darkening, ragged weather made their departure from the cold barren shore a swift need.

"You looked for him for less than half a day," she said, another good-bye breaking over her shoulders. *Spider, will these winter rains never cease?* She thought of the summers he had painted in her heart. *Tonight, in my bed, I will dream of you . . . of your good-bye kiss.*

"There was no trace of him. There was no proof, but he is lost. And with the condition of his vessel I knew he did not survive what, or whoever, attacked him. Fearing a troubled passage, I thought it best to save my men and my ship."

Camilla frowned and tied her hands in a great fist. She should have sent an armed group with him. She should have told him everything . . .

In ten days the King of Alar would arrive to talk peace, or to wage war. If she did not wear The Mask on the day the King of Alar came to the peace talks, the war would continue for another millennium. To look upon his face unmasked was the highest form of disrespect. And it was said he cured every insult, every dispute, with the bark of his hungry sword.

Even if she sent a hundred swift men this very moment, they could not return The Mask to her in time to forestall the spurs which would walk in Carcosa in ten days.

Ages ago, in an act of defiance, her mother had taken off The Mask and sent it into the West in the hands of a poet. Sent it to be hidden away by a madman.

Midsummer behind her, Camilla faced unknowns. She climbed the stairs and stood on the terrace, looked at the cliffs and the waves below, the sky, the garden. Spider should be here beside her. Mornings filled with good should smile on them. But she was a prisoner in a dark cell and she was frightened. She looked into the lake and feared what looked back. Not for the first time she wanted to be invisible. Since that stiff twilight hour when Camilla placed the ring on her finger and assumed all authority in the realm, she has sent a hundred men to recover The Mask, thinking one day she might don it and propose an end to this war with Alar. Not one had returned.

Countless times she had visited her mother in her rooms and the conversation had turned to steam as she struggled with the misadventure that would prove their undoing. She would never understand her mother's inexplicable act. Camilla knew the prophecy and believed it, but if The Mask were in her hands, her enemy the King of Alar, could not discover it and place it over his face.

Had the king's minions found The Mask? Was he ready to wear it and thrust Carcosa and her people into bitter servitude until the twelfth of Never arrived? Would he set foot in these halls, not to talk peace, but to place what remained of the royal family under the sword?

No dawn overlooking the sea. The sails of Alar were in the harbor. The soldiery of Alar and their hooded king came—returned—to the court.

He wore The Mask.

She burned with fatal emotions, trying to find words to accept the defeat.

Black eyes glazed with violence. Swords flashed. Thunder, unchanged, returns to her halls . . . Her brothers cut down. Beheaded, in the space of a few moments of fire.

The King's captains laughed over what they had laid down. They spit on the half-naked body of her mother, dragged into the hall, stumbling and bloody for all to see. Wood is brought into the hall. Chairs are broken, a fire started. The heads of her mother and her two brothers are thrown to the flames.

"You have served me well and long. This thing of Carcosa, I give you." Alar pushes Camilla to his captain.

The King's captain spits on her, says, "No man of Alar will soil himself with this Carcosian whore." His sword speaks broadly in her belly.

On a floor that had broken ten thousand calendars she lays like a common abomination. Camilla's eyes reach across the short distance to Alar's masked face. A harsh laugh splashes from his smile, closing the argument between them for all time.

Hands that were cold yesterday remove The Mask and cast it to the ground before her. "You thought to buy the soul of a king with *this*." An abrasive boot triumphantly shatters it. "Your desire forever lives in the mud."

Her lips snap open, dribbling with ashes. Her words are too wet with the impossible to hear. Further broken, beaten down. Time and the sane closing . . . *She holds out her hand to Spider. "I'll be back soon, Camilla. I will bring flowers to your room."* . . . The last thing she sees before the winterboatman takes her across the distance to to-morrow is the scorpionlike, scarlet tattoo on Alar's cheek above his cold smile.

Blacker now, the sky turns dark with rain . . .

PAIN

for one of the true masters, Ken Bruen

Lot of moon up there.
Lot of pain down here.
In my knees, my hips.
My thigh's on fire.
Lower spine a white-hot lava pit.
And the chill comin' up the valley don't help.
I'd light a fire, but that would bring them here.
Sooner.
I think.
They're coming. Been comin'.
For days now?
Can't tell.
Between the bouts of pain and the dizzy spells I'm having trouble with time.
I haven't heard 'em yet.
But I feel it.
Feel it like the blinding tightness behind my left eye.
Hard to move when all this pain flares up.
Turns into a weight.
A machine that chews. Like it has a single purpose.
Guess it does.
Hard to move.
Lost a lot of blood.
I'd lay down, but that's a thing I never learned. Chin up, bite the bullet.
Move . . .
Maybe that's why I always had a thing for The Blues.
Lot of life in that pain.
Hanging on and holding out.
Hoping for . . .
Hope.

I'm a little too far down the line for that now.

Cancer.

Insult

or penance?

I'll be fucked if I know.

In my bones.

Spreading.

Too far along to cut it out.

That's what the first one told me.

The second too.

I said: "Jesus FUCK."

Lit a smoke right there in his examining room.

The dumbfounded asshole started to say those things will kill—

I laughed and shook my head on the way out.

Went to a young female experimentalist—cutting-edge, tops in the field—

Hat trick.

That's why I took the job.

One clean fast job and . . .

Go die on some quiet warm beach. Jacked up on the best drugs Big Money can get its hands on. Maybe my feet up in the afternoon. Maybe Champion Jack Dupree singin' "Take it Slow And Easy" on the box. Maybe a pretty young nurse who will give me a moment's pleasure in between the roaring slabs of Lightning.

Don't want to spend my last days screaming for Mommy.

She was a bitch.

Slapped me around. Blamed me for Dad leaving.

He was a fucked-up drunk.

Liked to slap us around.

I never missed him.

She did.

Miss him.

Bad some nights.

When she was drunk.

Then—

She'd fuck me up and . . .

Fuck me over.

Cancer took her.

She gave me a lot I guess.

So I took the job. Sat and listened to Magnus's long winded explanations about The Thing I was to snatch.

Bullshit.

Academic hogwash mumbo-jumbo.

End of the fucking world paranoid conspiracy theory

and

total lunacy.

But it was a pile of money.

Opened his safe and showed me The Green.

Let me count it.

Said: "You put IT right here on my desk and that's yours. Go do what you like."

I drank his bourbon—"A special, *private stock*," he said. "Packs quite the punch."

I lit a cigarette and said: "Done."

His fuckin' eyes lit up.

He gave me the keys to an old Land Rover and the address.

In

and

    out.

Quick.

I already had the gun and the set of picks.

In

and

    out.

Quick.

Sidedoor.

Second floor.

Gallery to the left.

Smash and back down the stairs.

Out.

Forty-minute drive to the pile of cash.

But I didn't figure on the pain.

I got in easy enough.

And IT was right where he said IT would be.

I smashed the glass.

No alarm.

Grabbed IT.

Turned . . .

PAIN.

In the teeth of the Lightning.
—Light headed
—Dizzy
—Lying on the floor
—Eyes tearing up
—Blurry
—Doubled up
—Racked
—The FIRE
—Every ounce, every cell being preached to by the SLEDGE-HAMMER fire
—Shaking.
I heard footsteps.
Managed to get my gun out.
Leveled.
Ready.
Security guard came in.
Old guy.
White hair.
Could barely walk.
Went down with the third shot.
Didn't move.
But—
"FUCK!"
IT was broken . . .
Shattered crystal. Old and expensive shit, now broken worthless cheap shit.
The rods inside spilled across the tile floor.
Some were broken.
Lying at odd angles. Glowing.
Wisps of smoke . . .
A low howling from somewhere not near . . . nightmare dogs baying . . .
"FUCK!"
I'm outta there.
Sirens.
Guess there was a silent alarm.
I didn't take the road.
They'd be coming from the road.
One way or the other they'd stop anything coming their way.
Went into the woods.

Backroads over the mountain.
I'll put the barrel of the gun in his mouth.
He'll open that safe.
Or—
That's what I thought.
Fucking Land Rover died.
So I got out and ran.
Pine branches slapping my face.
In
and
     out
of uneven patches of moonlight-treated ground.
Tripped over a rock I didn't see in the sharp-edged shadows.
Slid.
Head first.
Fucking damp clay.
Down the hill.
Rollin' and tumblin'.
Ass up in the air.
Banged.
Turned around. Head first.
Over roots and wet grass.
Scraped.
Bend my wrist nearly backwards.
PAIN.
A splintered piece of fallen branch jams into my thigh.
Deep.
PAIN.
Pretty fucking deep.
And I'm not moving.
Tried to pull it out
and
the Lightning hits.
Lying in the cold damp clay. Eyes tearing up. Doubled up.
Racked.
Shaking.
Arm.
Hips.
Head.

Thigh.
SCREAMING.
I scream. Half a scream anyway.
I'm bleeding.
Pretty bad.
Figure I can bleed out
or put one in my head.
They're hollow points.
Do the trick well enough . . .
No soft sun on a Mexican beach.
No everything is gonna be alright . . .
Not now.
Cold sad moon.
He's got The Blues.
Covering me with them.
Cold cold ground blues.
I nod to him. Half a dim smile.
We're the blues brothers . . .
I'm cold.
I thought I knew the rules.
Wet.
I thought I knew the rules.
And
I hear them coming . . .
I see Magnus's eyes light up. See his miser smile as he talks about IT.
His hunger for IT is cold.
I didn't see that before.
Just saw all that money.
But I see it now.
I see the look on his face as I downed his special private stock.
His cold smile.
Long ago and far away . . .
The hot tone of his voice . . . The rush of his oratory as he talked about
Einstein and John Dee and the Fourth Dimension:

"I was enlightened by a translation from The Book of The Black Name . . ."
"Hounds athirst."
". . . 'wings of alchemy' . . ."
"Demon dogs."

"Tindalos . . ."

"Angular time . . ."

". . . the functions of a prosaic existence . . ."

". . . a parallel life . . ."

"The events in Partridgeville . . ."

and weird fucking names or words—phlegmy, broken, I couldn't spell or pronounce with a gun to my head.

Thought it was all bullshit.

Fucked-up voodoo timewarp shit.

Eloquent and complicated.

But fucked-up plain old bullshit.

But not his money.

I'm no fool.

I thought I knew the rules.

Shame on me.

The pain eases.

Finally accept what I need to accept.

Always have.

In blues songs hard times often lead to the killing floor.

And the cold cold ground.

I've sang along with Muddy and the Wolf and The Hook a thousand times . . .

Men are sailors on the sea of fate—

You get washed up where you get washed up. You can waste your time dreaming about changing your station,

but—

I light a cigarette.

As close to Last Call as I figure I'll ever get.

They're coming.

Let 'em come.

I ain't got no place to go.

Couldn't go if I wanted to.

No money

to go.

Can't walk.

Can't even stand.

I'm having trouble with time . . .

Lot of moon up there.

He looks sad.

Like he's got hard case of the blues.

Lot of pain down here.

They're coming.

I can hear them now.

Coming like lightning.

Coming to take away the pain. Just like the pretty young nurse with the needle . . .

Old Man Mnieckowski lived next to door us when I was a kid. He had a dog, a friendly little cocker, Rusty. Sometimes he'd come over to my front porch steps and put his head in my lap. I'd pet him . . .

Dream

   . . . the soft warm sun . . .

   of

   green fields

   or kites with magic fluttering tails

   of superheroes

   and baseball games and hot dogs and peanuts and Coke

   of owning a shiny red wagon

   or a fast bike . . .

Dream

of

   a street with white picket fences and a green lawn

   and no rats

I loved that dog like he was mine.

I hear them clearly now.

They must be close.

I wonder if they have names.

A Night of Moon and Blood, Then Holstenwall

Du musst Caligari warden ... Du musst Caligari warden ... *Du musst Caligari warden* ... Du musst Caligari warden ... *Du musst Caligari warden* ... *Du musst Caligari warden* ...

✱

"The wheels ... Can you hear them, Herr Doktor? *Listen.*"

✱

With purpose, the wheels turn slowly—on and on to the next Where. By day, and when needed, by night, over slight round-tops and by wall-thick hedgerows the lumbering bulk of wagons traveled, weather and time faded reds and blues and yellows dimly proclaiming, *M. Night's Traveling Theatre of Marvels.*

Mere feet from the little traveled road a wolf had left the small bones of a rabbit, and hours before the loner's repast, a murder of crows had swiftly passed over the brittle grasses tanned by a long hot summer ... Into a silent field of eager weeds and stunted saplings never to become mighty boles, came, at the edge of nightfall, a carnival. The only song from the train-in-single-file bearing the flamboyant phantasmagoria was an ever-grinding moan and sigh of wheels. The caravan came to rest as if it had sailed over the mountains of the Great Beyond to the shores of Tomorrow and was awaiting admittance.

Fires were lit and the weathered wagons positioned. In the twilight, the rain-bled reds and gray-hide grays and deathbed-pale yellows looked like weary elephants come home to die after their forced march. In a havoc of rushing sounds, hairy, muscular men with scars and sweeping mustaches and slinky ladies, once full of promises for the strutting young dandies with bulging pockets, began to construct the fantastic from threadbare canvases and twisted poles.

The fun asylum bloomed in the moonlight: uneven lines and torn folds revealed grotesquely distorted faces hidden in the deteriorating stripes, while colors of every color beckoned, "Pick me!", and behind flaps, in the unlit arenas, treasures and wonders for simple minds and small eyes.

Some of the exhibits waiting (to say hello) were real—two majestic white stallions, one lion, one bear, one elephant. And snakes, pythons and asps and cobras. And among the bright tents and fluttering flags, each seeker—*compelled, overwhelmed*—would find a Wolf Boy, and a sea-green mermaid with icy-blue eyes. A tall, tall man and a short fat woman, Madame Zala with her Old World accent and crystal ball, a professional pickpocket, and a hypnotist. Games of chance and feats of strength, tricks and treats—rides that whirled, clownish jokes and pamphlets and snake oils, all were soon to be offered. There were whimsical costumes and hungry dogs running . . . and glimpses at strange relics and exaggerated dramas, illusions come to life as the pump organ played . . .

And in a wagon behind the torchlight and all the other wagons, a jaded practitioner of an ancient carnal art. All would be bright, or ominous, for the silver coins of the curious. By noon tomorrow the siege would begin.

The ringmaster walked in the strong moonlight. No clouds. No threat of rain. Low, in harmony with the warm southerly breeze, he whispered, "Step right up my friends. Step right up—for THRILLS! Or . . . *Shocks.*" He could hear youth's *ahhhhhhh*s and burning coins jingling. He smiled.

"Tomorrow. And tomorrow night. And the night after . . ."

In the sleeping town beyond the hill, children, besotted moths— Konrad and Karl, Florian and Anna and a hundred others, fitful in their beds, dreamed of the gaudy performances the new morning would bring. The World Outside their dusty village was but a dream away.

Stars chilled by the black canvas of the heavens did not move above the Earth—but fireflies, like the warm decorations of spring poems were nimble as they moved like hungry fingers in the valley.

On the boards of his crudely painted stage he was poised. As still as a statue in an old museum. Staring, gazing on the faces of a thousand ghosts who had stood before him and stared back in amazement. The clawing features of a few hopeful, but melancholy acrobats sucked in the siren promise. The doktor's smile was a hiss, death-stern. With a theatrical gesture he struck his crystal-crowned, crooked staff seven times upon the stage and listened to the muted thundercrack echo. There was no fire burning in the braziers set to the left and right of the small stage, no exotic fragrance from

foreign towns filling the air with Eastern mystery, that would happen tomorrow while the anxious eyes collected before the unopened curtain
waited and whispered. Though he uttered not a word, Dr. Caligari heard
his voice boom in the silent tent. With a grand sweep of his gloved hand he
whisked his mad-hatter top hat from his head and bowed slightly.

"Ladies . . ." He smiled.

"And Gentlemen . . ." His features were weighted by a detached and
bitter expression.

"Children . . ." Another smile.

"Step right up! Beyond, in the ink of night, lurk spirits . . . But here."
He pointed to the lightning pinwheel painted at his feet center stage. "In
the minds of men, waiting to be transformed by the POWER of my *voice*,
lie delights . . . and *nightmares*."

A thousand times in a hundred towns he had sent men scurrying in
fear, had charmed ladies with Prince Charming visions. And tomorrow he
would do the same. But tonight . . . tonight, the leering moon whispered.

Not far away, just over the round top of the hill, lay the quiet cottages
of the quiet town and the reveries of its sleepers.

Caligari removed his eyeglasses and rubbed his eyes. He tugged on his
earlobe. His thoughts turned inward, tightening about misshapen emotions
that knew no balm. Deep in the brittle resonance of images remembered—
his hands twisted, the opportunities missed, his accomplishments crushed.
The last puppet and the one before, both failures, but this one—*Cesare . . .*
Cesare, the flesh of his spirit, would be his masterwork. Caligari would etch
another entry in his diary after Casare's nightwalk.

❀

After the children had been put to bed, and salt had been spilled and
nemesis bellowed, and wives and maidens had whispered their prayers, and
(some) lusts were stated, and (many) cups emptied, the town slept. On this
poisonnight of low-hung moon there was no fog to press against their
unlocked windows.

The figure, lean as a viper, seemed to float along the contorted bends
of the narrow street. From shadow to deeper shadow it surged in curved
flight. Climbing, navigating a canted roof, disappearing in the leaden shadows of a stunted tower damp with mourning.

Softly rushing.

Then hovering. Leaving no reflection.

Deeper it pressed into the horrormovie tunnel of uneven streets. Nightblack locks as coarse as a witch's midnightnest moved like slim branches in a yawning breeze spilled from the dirty world of some other-night. Eyes as empty as a broken clocks seemed open mouths of silence. Noiselessly, the figure eased around small pools of dirty water, casting weightless shadows in the weightless pitch. Even when framed in smudged pools of wind-fluttering light cast from waxy streetlamps, the lean night-walker, clad black on black, seemed a cancer, a little night colored only by its own angles.

Intense and clawed, it came to drink.

From window to doorknob to window the sleeper made his way through the hours. His dagger big with death, ready to grasp the light it caught in pain. Upon a jagged stairway, framed in a diamond of moonlight, then after a stiff waltz of puppetlike steps, engulfed in crooked shadows, fast violence followed the tilted line; testing, seeking. This handle and that sash . . .

And beyond a pane there in a drunken-brushstroke of moonlight coming ashore—white pillowcases, a layer of raised clouds over white bed sheets, a curtain of softness framing the angelic womanchild.

White reflected in Cesare's eyes. Cold—hard, bent, full of soon—enters the room.

Inside, ready to take tomorrow, Treacherous smelled Fragile in her stillness. His red-hot mouth stiff with empty space. Balletic steps of small movement. Four feet from the bed. Not a sound on the stage. The width of the invader's claw a dark beam on the woman's slender neck. Blank eyes stared at closed eyes.

Would they open?

Would her dormant lips find voice?

At the bed. Rigid. A fingertip away. Steel shifts. There is no protection in sleep.

Edges court edges.

The likeness of darkness rustling thrust its inches into the breast of a sleeping daughter, never to be a woman, never to be a wife, never to become sleek and leave her baby-face to the yesterdays of childhood memories. Dreams are revised, facts and theories lost. Interacting, white space made explicit by the attention of black, mining the open ground. Bone and cartilage were harmed.

Bright red. Fiery red. Blood blossoms stain the tomb quiet room.

Her heart is taken beyond the edge of the world.

Outside ruptures inside as relations untie meanings. Wet hands, desire expressed. To act. Fear raped by RAGE. To know. Life annulled.

Silence covered all but the fragrance of black breathing. She sucked in air with each sharp thrust, but the currents of agony gagged her voice as they filled her wounds. No white scream! Not even a whimper for mercy or to God as she lay locked in the feast of the glutinous shadow. The monster with frozen eyes poised above her. It searched her frozen eyes.

No fire, the bowl was now empty.

Its rapture past, the redthunder words of hate written, its arms dangled at its sides.

Like a vapor it withdrew.

Caligari's instrument lay in eternity's cabinet. Dead until the next performance. Caligari's corpulent jowls were pushed back by his smile. He focused on the contents of the cabinet then turned to record the bites and jolts of tonight's drama in jagged lines in his thumb-worn diary of sins.

Night fades . . .

✸

The rickety wagon rocked; it had rocked—side to side, front to back, wind and rain and torturous sun for the last eight days. Dust from the other wagons of the caravan sent dry fogs into the fields. The sun rose high in the sky, illuminating the hills of Holstenwall. Tomorrow began the annual fair, Caligari wondered which Veronika or Viktoria or Hermione would attend his next production? His eyes grew madblack and he smiled like the light of Pierrotmoon.

✸

"Ha! He smiled just as you do, Herr Doktor—*What?* Yes. I've taken my medicine today. Never fear, I am completely cured. I was merely trying to entertain you.

"After all, this was only a story . . . ."

Under the Mask Another Mask

The wind comes off the Hudson. No vengeance in it. It doesn't care about spectators or pathology. An unbroken lethargy of grim heat under the backhand of an August skyline. Keyless journeys of circumstance in this knotted crucible trampled by turbulent decay . . .

Shifting half-truths reconfigure The City's civic armature. The inconsequential exaggerated within the voyeuristic no-growth . . . All the blind spots of The City filled with chaos metamorphosed into simple struggle for the fragments trying to outrun the tomb, and every minute—day after day after day—losing speed . . .

Across streets, playgrounds for savage experiments of agitation and necessity, unfiltered depravity out shopping the landslide, sifting what's goin' on, for hard currency, for alcohol or razorlight chemicals, for mindless expressions of fun, or just to kick boredom off the street . . .

No reprieves. If it's on the serving plate they're gonna take it . . .

Arianne's returning from the Blue Cove Bookstore, from a heated experiment of phantom soliloquies delivered by an up-and-coming poet of The Void. Trying to remember the kiss of each phrase, fearing it to be another theater of comfort that rounds an abrupt curve and becomes a lonely coast disintegrating in ashen shadows and dust. Her ears are still full of his gin and embers voice spilling like a last call.

> *From each death The King's misery narrows.*
> *He breathes*
> *And phrases of Oblivion*
> *Fall from his spreading wings.*
>
> *Before his eye days collapse*
> *And the blue stories of evening,*
> *Once loved as spring flowers by the light,*
> *Weep no more.*

Her hands clutch the autographed book. She's late.

. . . A broken heel. The shadows tilt with new edges. The firm lesson of hurried making its point then vanishing without sympathy . . . Walking again, not hurt, inconvenienced. A landscape changed to bumpy ups and downs . . .

Around a corner that lost its daily light, a corner of dismal concrete edges. She is surrounded by shadows of the exhausted dipped in lawless. Lamps pasted in handbills give their weaken light to the restless hours. Newspapers and cardboard cups buoyed by bouts of the wind's hard hands roam while the hunger of slow private shadows gagged by black's motionless monologue mutates. It's a network of hard lines and bitter deeps, a clenched masquerade drifting until it comes upon a heartbeat.

Something grotesque awakened in a doorway Arianne hadn't noticed. Something now erect. Now three—harsh reputations churning in riot-colored garments—walking. Three brick-solid predators with hostile masks below baseball caps with stylized recipes she can't read. Biting voices. Hands surface to play the game of dominance—She is thrown into the pot. Pushed. She, another thing cast to the ground. Kicked, without explanation . . .

Rough hands, taking turns and two knives for clipping wings. Cannibals hungry for opportunities, stunning weakness in the slaughterhouse.

Skirt off. Dizzy, panicked. Panties off. Dizzy. Panicked. Blouse torn open. She sags under the weight of a choking hysteria. Two beasts hold her legs apart, then come the fast stiff points thrust upon her, as thorns, as weapons, as venom striking deep. Contaminated in the crossfire of an act of violence . . .

Half a dozen slow thunderstrikes of cold, hard applause from the tallest attacker now merely observing. And the ringing:

FUCK THAT BITCH GOOD!

Fuck her *up!*

Be cool, *bitch*—it's only a little in-and-out. Bet'chor hot-fat-pussy stored it up for THIS.

GET THAT ASS UP IN IT HOE!

Her eyes slapped by portraits of the raw nighthawks feeding. Dreams gone in the undertow . . . Blow after blow, her face and all the hopes and fears and tender joys behind it, altered, sting by sting, from its former poise . . . faces of yelling teeth working. Sharp white teeth under wild eyes of resonant laughter. First comes the brutality of the ice-age, then the mountain, and harshest of all, the machine, each destroying. Broad backs climbing, taking . . . a thousand hands carrying out the sentence.

She tries to kick as if her legs could shout STOP, but they're yanked back into place before they can even mumble. For her effort she's punched in the eye, winces.

Weakened.

Nausea. The foul taste of genitals in her mouth.

Contaminated. All her summers now windblown, sliced away, changed in a gash of red, in a rite of knife. A mouse frozen in the jaws of searing predators. Staring, with her one unswollen eye, but not seeing. Blindfolded by fear. No daylight. Tears, but no spring to pawn them to.

Congratulatory laughter.

A pack of cigarettes comes out . . . and from an oversize pocket, lighter fluid. Her face is wet. Her hair reeks of accelerant . . . A black hand casts off a match. Fire, the true god of man and Hell. Her face shattered, bent into a million pieces—transformed by the burning hammer. Her voice can't concentrate beyond the scream.

Arianne claws at her face, scrapes it against the ground until the coarse gray leaves furrows on the field of scorched flesh.

Her sobbing digs no hole she can crawl into.

The cloud of laughter above dismisses the clock. The stench of compulsion and burnt prayers smothering the breath trickling from her . . . A moment of frozen quiet . . . incapable . . . the ground drinking her blood . . . The map of her life ruined. Staring at freedom on the cold shore of a broken bottle, but her fingers are broken. Arianne can't reach the sharp glass and The End it offers . . .

Wounded by little drops of night the stone face of the moon departs.

She loses consciousness . . .

✦

Hideousness is what she sees. Ordinary gone in the mirror inlaid with crime. Contaminated. A death face of burned and scars and acid friction, a mask of proportions she has no ability to comprehend. Each scar slings a white-hot flashback of the gruesome battlefield. Arianne can only view This piece, or That bewildering sector. The old whole, calm and graceful, beautiful many said, gone. Gone, the bright, unblemished pearl that used to smile at her from the mirror. Gone—all the days found in soft and tender. All her sweet days gone in this chaos of confusion—in this obliterating black hole—that answers reason with Nothing. Gone. This face before her is a phantom, a false unrelenting lie she can't step across. She wants to blink and send it away.

She tries, eyes CLOSED/eyes OPEN—no ruby slippers. Tries again. And again. No trip out. He hands are fists . . .

About to gag on the GODDAMN turning into a scream . . .

Eyes drowning in the depths of the mirror, reaching for a theory or a technique to piece this grotesque puzzle back together. Clawing for a new brain and a new biology to fly above or around this final expression of the unwanted circumstance. Getting nowhere in the projected entanglement forced upon her by the now unbandaged face.

Strong drink, by the pint, by the shot, by the bottle. Hiding—hiding in the living room—hiding in the bedroom—hiding from widows and the dilated night and the overwhelming silence she can't wipe away. Hiding— in the hands of slippery books—in instant questions—hiding . . . In the bottom of bottles, witnesses to her thirst . . . She sees visions of Hell, a plague of black and fatal in the mirror. Always running to the naked mirror and finding dizzying, frustrating shadows in the corruption it manifests . . . In an empty room dragging each hot liquid finger of whiskey teeming with unexhausted enemies into the ghost drift of lost . . . Hiding in the bottom of bottles and the voice in The Book of the void poet.

Her sleep is troubled by the gray voice of the wind carrying darkness. Then comes the touch of words held out by yellow hands. Like bells from somewhere she has never traveled, a Tomorrow she longs for, ringing with, "Let it go," quiet—without conflict comes to her. It settles on the canvas. Soft wings glow, murmur. Soothe. "Do not lose You in the harbor of lone-liness. Take up the Truth."

Awake. *The Truth.* Rushing to the mirror. "Truth." *The Truth? Un-covered . . . Cover this in Truth.*

The retreat into a different light . . . untrained in this visibility . . . ab-sent of self . . . of self . . . Self?

In a different light . . .

✸

Another night of claws tearing deep, another season at a desolate cross-roads where no deal with God or the Devil can be brokered—Though she tries . . . Searching the bottle for amnesia that does not come, for former— or sunlight—or a pulse. Searching the mirror—Yes LOST, seeing Sum-mer again LOST. All the heart-shaped little things, spilled—soiled and eaten by the hunters—scarlet and terminal. Patternless scars crossed this way and that on this mask of shame. Searching the mask of guilt for what has departed. Searching for the undetectable in confusion's tar. Searching that which can not be explained or washed away in the mask of anger. Leaning over the toilet her guilt and shame blows up . . .

She wants to be cleansed.

She wants to set back time.

She wants to stop screaming at the dirty expressions performing in the mirror.

She wants to have never left the apartment That Night.

She wants REVENGE! Arianne wants to mold the skin of horny cocks with the thickness of a blade, to seer sour eyes with darkness. She wants to melt her anger in their furious deaths.

But what she has is the mirror, its cross-examination—stone after stone, repeating deformity, pressing its interlaced outburst of disgusting, laughing as the firestorm of violence replays before her eyes—laughing as the nuclear act, again and again, breaks her spell of beauty . . . What she has is the mirror and its critical tongue. The looking glass points, shouts and Arianne glues her eyes to the humiliation it blinds her with. In its web, traumatized pieces that can't come back from the chunk of night that slammed into her, pieces that now scream loneliness and hate, a slope of coarse rags hobbled by the raw bolts that raped her beauty . . . Everything broken, burned. Pieced together—never to blush, never to brush away a stray hair. The end of self-discovery. Her old face now a lost limb. And she runs to the yellow words of The Book, hoping they can grow it back . . . But they slip from her fingers and Then comes again and goes on and on.

The scream of a monster brushes her shoulders . . . A fountain of doomed teeth in the mirror screaming.

Scars. Scissors—she picks them up a hundred times. Sleeping pills to close the cracks. The bottom of the unhelpful whiskey bottle smashed into the face in the mirror, now shattered like her face. Minutes in the swarm of the jigsaw. This piece. That. Eddies, black and red, raw and quick, formed in Hell and shit and pox. Unrelated parts look out at her from the mirror. Something different there . . . The mask of some other.

Arianne runs from the room. Trips on the diamondback ripples and haunted labyrinth of the hall carpet. Back to her bed . . . Clutches The Book to her breasts.

Do not lose You in the harbor of loneliness.

Her eyes are hiding behind a fortress of tears.

✦

An after-hours appointment in a white room in a white building.

The odor of good-bye in her voice, "I am a victim," tumbling from the wide slash of once-exquisite canvas now torn apart. "Breathing, but blind to the exit.

"I'm searching for The Truth."

"About you, there are many. Or more rightly put, if one stops the masquerade, peels away the fairytale, only the Truth is left," the repairer said.

"The Truth. The *one* Truth. I've been reading of a place where troubles are over . . . The friend of a friend's sister, said—"

"To see me. And The Book you mentioned told you to, what?"

"It echoed a dream. Both said to, take up the Truth. They said one must peel away this mask and don the King's."

"Yes, I see."

"And—"

"I can show you the way."

The back of his white coat to her. Arianne watches the whiteness dance, watches his pale hand open a white door.

On a sliver tray rests a pale, silent mask. Her eyes find comfort in its unblemished smoothness. She want to caress it, to believe in its wholeness, but hesitates. She knows she must cast off one before taking up the other. Arianne removes the dark veil she has worn day and night since the performance of the wicked removed all musings of calm and bright from the future. She sets the veil on the silver tray. Black and bone white, different routes, side by side.

The oval whiteness in Doctor Peltonen's hands. Smooth and ready to wear . . . slowly placed on her face . . . a shade falls upon her face . . . warmth. Settling, bonding . . . comfort . . .

Eyes closed. No thoughts of supermarket aisles or the beach or the rescue of library stacks. No thoughts, webs, of dishes, or fault . . . Black and black . . . opened. *And I . . .* Another light. *And I . . .* Different light. *And I . . .* The landscape transformed. *And I . . .* New senses flashing. *See . . . dim images full of time and water and things that were . . .*

His white coat. Threadbare at the sleeves. The square white mask tied over his face. Her hands take off his white coat, his white shirt. Pale white skin at close range, canvas for the fluid ivy of tattooed script etched in ink upon his skin. Arianne's eyes scanning his arm—

Star of my exile,
echo the heartbeat that breaks,
with each rushing wave,
upon the shore
                    Of Carcosa
. . . flowing along the curve of his shoulder—
        Gestures of mercy?
        Under this exiled moon?
        Scars and embraces—Myths and mysteries!
        Forget sin and rain,
        Lighten your burden—
        One push will reveal the places of forever . . .
She removes his white slacks, reads—
        The raven rests in the winter tree,
        yet the bole finds a season to grow . . .

His pale hands remove her clothes, read curve and layer, downhill and between. Closer underway. Pacing, assembling . . . Absorbing.

Rendezvous in sleight-of-hand. She in her mask, he in his. Her soft eyes trembled. Her soft breath breaks upon the waves of script. His lips tremble at her touch. A kiss . . . a low laugh . . . Each wanting more, each taking more . . . Each seeing, absorbing the silver Truth . . .
        when the whiteness falls
                    in cold Carcosa . . .

She is chewing the strange, bringing it closer, learning new directions. Excited, arched, brushing, in a sigh of eyes they read each other, gnaw at the irresistible as if it were a cautious prayer dripping with slow spacious dawn in the cold air of the white room. The slow rush of a snake's hiss wind breathing, he moans . . . She, reading the curves of something as it bursts from a beyond she reaches to discover . . .
        It swallows so many suns . . .
She can't understand it or speak it yet, but it's coming . . .
        Carcosa,
                wide is the white light, the whiteness . . .
She spurs his sleek nearness with thrusts of words translated from his flesh
. . .
        Good-bye, day.
Her winged fingers brush over the soft arcs of ink-etched words . . .
        Night walkers

frolic in the dreams of the changeless spectral flame
of midnight . . .

Absorbing every word . . .
  and spread open
  over their drained breast shut fast,
  marvels of the ancient night never over
  entrenched
        in the elixir eternal . . .

Each veil peeled . . . stars . . .
  Your eyes twinkle with the wormwood emblem in the sky
  that speaks my name . . .

lips, hair . . .
  the lake awash in cloud voices . . .
  out of the storm
  and into the harmony of yesterday . . .

roses, chalices . . .
  cloud voices in the water
  they sing of glamour & finished . . .

lips, so warm, awash in cloud voices . . .
  Beneath Demhe,
  where frail dreams erode . . .

kisses writing in soft dreamspeed . . .
  Star of my exile,
  echo the heartbeat that breaks,
  with each rushing wave,
  upon the shore
        Of Carcosa . . .

fashioned from a radiant whiteness, Truth, intense and intertwined, so sweet . . . Arianne is hollow no more.

Orgasm.

She has paid in flesh . . .

They dress. He in white on white. She back to suitable street clothes.

He brings her a mirror. Places it in her supple hands.

Eyes open . . . The mask of Revelation, softly covering the injury—another face. The *True* face.

"I see . . . Another world."

"Carcosa."

"Beyond the dunes . . . Unique . . ."

"There, Cassilda, you may cast away the loneliness." There is a knife in his hand.

"This is the King's hand. It listens to Day. Its borders shape the dull beasts for The Termination. Its radiant light stops Day . . . The children of the sun glow with stains of hopeless damnation. This is the time collector that gathers their sin and sends The King's jewels to their cool rest."

Doctor Peltonen puts on a yellow glove. He picks up the black veil and drops it into a container for waste.

The relief the blade grants warms Arianne's hand. Its correctness feels like a sky.

"It has rubbed the light of discontent with The Law."

Her breasts swell. Her eyes shine. Arianne's fingers tighten about the future, absorb its focus.

❋

Somewhere in the night.

Beyond the dunes, beyond the cloud-waves and the crooked-peaked, bitterblack towers of Carcosa. She is part of the landscape. She walks in a garden of Winter trees, dead moths at her feet.

This is The Night of On and On, the end of errors. It eats light and weaves it into stories of rain.

"So you shall, Child."

She turns. Sees—

The Yellow King on his throne

Arianne swoons.

"My Servant has given you the spider's thread I forged in a furnace of moonlight. You will return to the Other World and stitch the light of the children of the sun to my tapestry. With friction you will take their brighter and cure this abominable disease that tatters my form.

"You are the Maiden of Ink. In skin, you write the melody to soothe the poison that swells within me."

She kneels. As if an obedient bee on a flower, her soft lips kiss the frayed hem of The King's yellow robes.

❋

Arianne comes from shadows, from smoke and clouds . . .

Another gray street paralyzed by means to an end. A smack of predators, loitering. Their poised cravings thick and hard. She crosses their sweaty off limits . . . The results of their surprised situation she leaves for the simple appetites of urgent waste collectors coming up from the sewers in their cloaks of scabs and matted fur . . .

Another night, another waltz of scarlet hunting. Another hateful Thing that used evil as a form of amusement damaged and now forever part of the hard, unmoving landscape.

Marching through the places where time grinds. Writing GO! with her knife. Sending bitter to the mound. Each time she laughs . . .

And another dead thing and another, each time leaving her mark of inches in the howls that went in and never came out.

Again

. . . and again, Arianne, dressed in the somber fragrance of the moon, sends each repulsive page of evil to bed with Blackness . . . An endless night of the blade—her blade drains the river, the handle nourishes . . . She comes as a phantom, rushing to slash tendons and hands and dead crotches . . . The radiation of every cankerous smile she smothers. The "Gon fuck you up" of each rough nightbeast of grim and disrepair is their handwritten suicide note which she signs with windmill arcs and jagged furrows loud with blood . . .

She leaves dust and nothing for the spider and windows to measure . . .

Each once malevolent carcass she burns (whispers "Lights out" with the tongue of an angel as the fingers of fire play), tattoos in flames, as treatment, as proof of life undone, but the revenge for the perversions engraved on the face behind the mask is temporary.

And after . . .

To far cold Carcosa . . . to sit at the healing hem of The King's robe . . . exciting in His Masterwork . . . licking the wisdom of His Elixir . . . *Leave nothing but bones of ivory,* he whispers in her heart.

❀

A street, old age rotting in its belly, of spilled darkness and disappointment too straight to be a labyrinth. Triggers and slamming knuckles and minutes squeezed until they were all out of clemency. No sorrys. No exits from the Last Exit. Deals and blame (hissed between FUCK YOUs) and quicksilver tricks and vultures and the unfading footfalls of the unspeakable pressing at every window.

A death dealer with big arms and devil-mean boredom in his hands stands in the shadows. Arianne sighs, smiles. He tastes the coming game and stretches out . . . She has It trapped, fastened to her gaping blade . . . Cracked and bleeding margin to margin, staggering, her prey falls to the shadows. Judged . . .

She laughed and laughed . . . Laughed—her she-wolf howl of fire laugh. Her joy dripping with The Truth . . . Arianne stares at the unwilling, pleading *Don't* . . .

A question from the thing with the one way ticket exhaled before dying, "Fucked-up-Bitch—You tryin' ta-be some masked superhero?"

"I wear *No Mask*."

She stands unwavering over the dead death dealer, exalting in the fire, listening to the soft curves of the flames. They quiet her tears. The cold wind at her shoulder slithers away from the fire's unnatural nimbus.

. . . A body spilled on the hard ground, a body with a face of fire. And Arianne and her knife above it. The hollow-pointed assessment of a fresh-on-the-streets, young cop brought to bear. He'd seen ski masks and do-rags as Wild West bandit masks and stocking masks, but this flat, bone-white mask without a mouth was like staring at a wraith. He scanned the empty face—couldn't make out the eyes, locked on the hand and the bloody knife. Notes the curve of breast and hips.

A woman? "Drop the knife and step away from the body.'

No response to the hard instruction. She does not turn away from the song the flame whispers. She can smell yellow flowers chilled in The Final.

"Do it NOW."

She turns to face him.

Re-accessing, head-to-toe. His emotions play on his face. "I'm not playing here. *Drop the knife.*"

Under her mask she was smiling. The beacon of The King shone in her heart. He would not let her be taken down by a man. Arianne takes a step toward him. And another . . . Raises her knife.

She's got to be crazy. Or stoned—FUCK. Wired—damned near scared shitless. The fact of the blood-steel threat not hesitating. Advancing. "Stop!"

Too close now.

Fuck.

Two shots explode—strike, expand—shred within. She goes down.

Kneeling over Arianne's dead body. No pulse . . . His breathing slows.

More than curious he slowly removes her mask.

No make-up or eyebrows.

No mouth.

No nose.

Not a scar or a blemish. Utterly smooth this surface, pale yellow and devoid of any human information, expressionless and lifeless as are her eyes—sclera, iris, and pupil, completely yellow. No white, no black, nothing in the solid field of yellow to measure the laws of nature by.

He puts a finger on her cheek. It feels soft, but not like skin—

He runs his fingers slowly across her forehead, across both cheeks. Not human skin . . . Remembers the lustrous whisperings his fiancé's silk blouse unlocked in his fingertips the first night her caressed her.

"What the *Holy* fuck?" He will not surrender to the inhumanness of the blank face and crosses himself.

✸

In far
     Cold Carcosa

    The King sheds no tear.
    The face of another jewel,
Needing repair, ventures near . . .

(*for S. T. Joshi*)

W a t e r   l i   l i es

for Robert Bloch—who gave me Jack and Juliette and Norman

W a t e r   l i li es
 floating.
Stamen up—reaching.
Gems of dew, shining on their velvet skin.

W a t e r   l i li es
 They say Monet
was a genius—
They should see mine, floating face down.
Gems of blood, shining on their velvet skin.

 They say Monet
 was generous; the light, the daring—
They should see mine, pale fingers reaching.
Floating like
              W   a   te r   l i   li e   s.

Yvrain's Black Dancers

They, *the Fellowship of the Yellow Sign,* attuned to their darker temperaments and the tenor of the elegantly inscribed invitations sent by Doctor Archer—oddly not present for the festivities, had painted red rings of rouge around their eyes—bizarrely tinted their cheeks in vivid yellow and mournful blue; and in the candle and gaslight glow, as the blue-gray tendrils of cigar and cigarette smoke reached out like marsh fogs, the court of refined revelers seemed more things cloaked in pallid convictions, than merely several of New York Society's affluent brought together to view Boris Yvrain's new work.

Gathered around it—some less than arm's length from direct physical contact, a heathenish circle of worshippers, lacking only the outward activity of deliriums whirling, they stared, each more a thing of statuary than the marble piece Yvrain had recently brought to life.

Earlier, before the black shroud of velvet was lifted, they had amused themselves most carefully; politely disciplined laughter flowed between sips of wine and cognac as they appeared to dally lightheartedly in the gaudy Madison Avenue apartment. Voices now quieted, though their strong features, unmasked at its unveiling, spoke of concealed passions roused, disdain, and fearful hostility.

Dare I touch it, each silently asked. But no hand or step moved toward it. And none dared back away; their own agitated longings forbade it. Black as any darkly stained mahogany carving from Africa, Yvrain's *The Black Dance of Xandres and Sianith* held the nine collected more tightly than any desperate mother's hand.

Had the often volatile and always vehement, inventive genius abandoned discipline and reason to release this bold structure which more than suggested secrets better left unspoken? Had he, riveted by confounding visions whilst enjoined in rites base and unspeakable, formed relationships with spirits of the dead to unearth this grievous fusion of male and female copulating? The viewers had not answers; they were merely witnesses to the strange exhibition, caught in its world of feral festivals.

The male form, Xandres, a gaunt death-demon in a devil's mask celebrating its mastery of fertile soil channeled, rode the robust clinging thighs of Sianith—wanton as any poetic drama illuminated in a vision. His head was thrown back, his savage eyes, laughing a volcanic outburst. And Sianith responded in kind—her head was thrown back, her full lips an abyss opened to discharge a moan pitched as sharply as any desperate scream.

It, He—*Xandres*—that cruel king of darkness, had great wings and six curved horns and three grotesque tails (each whipping like lashes at her raised buttocks), and skin, folded and frayed like a tattered robe. His pocked and hideously studded member was as a three-headed viper, the thick middle head—an oppressive terror unendurable, penetrating the lamprey-flower of Sianith's charnel-ripened womanhood, the other two heads, hungry mouths stretched wide, harshly clamped to the barbed-tips of her scaly breasts, which she offered—taloned fingers thrusting the blistered globes forward—as if for nursing.

And she—*Sianith*—the tiger of starless night hunting, the poisonous womb of death, absorbing his unfurled eel-meat, was as brilliant and harrowing as any pandemonium of unspeakable torture.

All the things of night flowed from it; every requiem poured out like tears, every twilight now dead in time, every frailty, every subtle mediation explored, yet forgotten, every rape and crime and depravation committed, as the echoes and ripples of decay hatched from the rat holes of nothingness—and sharpening, washed over each elder. Yet it drew the ring of observers—jovial grins cast aside. It spurred wild charges of desire within, as each empty soul—polluted, willingly impregnated—fixed upon it, watching its ruthless dance.

Yvrain's vengeance was thrust full upon their greedy thievery—with lies and mere pennies they swindled his works from him, preyed upon his desperate circumstance. But no more! He would no longer be a slave, a mere footstool, for he had found the Yellow Sign and struck a bargain with the emissary of the Tattered King. Now it was his turn to be lord. From the *Black Dancers,* scorn and loathing, the blood of Yvrain's payment, poured.

. . . vibrating with raucous screech and distant twitter the flutter of madness' black wings roared in the silent room; bare feet padded worn, dry earth, and the heartbeat of the drum, full of fever, raced. And as vulgar beasts they turned upon one another. Hands, now blunt, clawed paws, the males tore at the delicate fabrics covering the females, cuffing the other males aside to be at the pale flesh exposed. Tattered silks and woolens lay

like dead things on the carpet. Blood flowed as the five males battled over the four women—the bald, spectacled banker, a corpulent obscenity of flesh—tangibly delighted, writhed upon the tiniest woman, her rose nipple, meat in his great slashing mouth; the beak-nosed composer gleaming, his voice a bell of intoxication as he sodomized the shipping magnate's fleshy wife. The women—vampires, demons, jackals, witches, moaned as they were assaulted, the men—vampires, demons, jackals, monsters, barked. And growled.

The orgy of raw wantonness became murder. Bejeweled fingers clawed eyes from their sockets, bellies and faces became works of art torn from the walls of Hell. The shipping magnate's hard ardor, slipping from the intimate folds of the composer's mistress, found its way into the mouth of the petite blond. Her polite white teeth rejected the savagery with vicious scarlet. Cigars burned cheeks and carpet and tender once hidden places. A pocket knife came out, flashed, and began painting in wide strokes splashed in screams . . . fingers curled . . . faces, breath lost from them, turned cold and ugly . . . neckties became nooses, gags, bonds . . . bear-jaw hands were clamped to throats as teeth and muscle sacrificed all to obscene invitations . . . In the blind hour of the wind that burns, hair was ripped out in chunks . . . Every carnal décor of Hell was sampled as the very air turned sour . . .

On the drunken-voiced revelers howled. And one by one, each— tethered by compulsion, exhausted by their exertions in blood and madness, was taken into night, while perched upon the summit of the Greek column of bone-white marble the luminous, laughing *Black Dancers* twisted in their dynamic ritual.

❖

The heavy folds of black velvet curtains parted. Unmasked, the darkness that is Doctor Archer and Boris Yvrain enter the room . . . The skeletal hand of Doctor Archer comes to rest upon the artist's shoulder.

"Well, Boris, it is just as I foretold." The doctor lit a cigarette and watched tongues of aromatic smoke leap from light's gaze to shade deep. "Is it not?"

"Indeed. The Truth has been revealed."

"Now, about your next work—"

No Exit Sign

No rain. No prayers. No whisper soft prayers fastened to the tongue.

Midnight is a sea. A tortured song of the past. The silence is armed with death . . .

Moonlight. A slimy street. Disease. In every door. In every nook. Thick as scrawled swaths of dry soap on darkened windows.

Moonlight. Crashing in the room. Filling it like a drunk who doesn't give a shit who's watching or what they think.

Moonlight. Staining everything.

Blood stained everything. Every thing. Blood—loud and fresh—everywhere.

A head with no face—the skinned face thrown in a corner-tomb with no memory of yesterday. Dropped with the other garbage. Cash lying around, two thousand in small bills maybe. Cold blue steel. And dope. A skinny underage girl with a dirty spikeneedle still in her arm—slain. Naked.

The light is dry. The blood is black in the dry, cold moonlight. A voice from the street comes through the broken window. "Fuck you!" as if it will heal him, cure his blues. Cure his pain. "fuckyou." Lift him up . . .

No. no. no.

no.

The Bottom. Black . . . pitch . . . Not on any map.

down so low

so low

The Zero. Red spilled in black. The hole of All-Night, pain rushing in, rumbling with evil and errors and every worn out, burned out spasm ending in misery.

Red. Red again. Same old trouble lit up with the alchemy of claws and teeth and claws and the great open leech mouth spreading its sky of predatory blackness.

The dung pit of Nothing. Cold as the face of the moon—another inmate in this earthquake.

No way to heal this stir-crazy claustrophobia. This . . .

Fate? Crime? Wrong turn? All or none. Fuck if it matters now.

Same old demons. Same old blues. Again.

Again.again

Damaged. Screaming. Trapped in forever, stuck in this furrow of Last, every hand clawing, every bloodshot eye drowning in venom.

Red.

pitch black . . . Red.trapped

Tired of all the monsters and enemies and shit that gets in the backdoor. Tired of dreaming about sunshine.

The pounding.

The questions—laughing, staring back in dirty windows. Sick of this life in prison. The confessions.

How many mocking faces flicker in the mind's eye? How much vindictive red laughter rings in the ears?

Convict—toss and turn. Convict—turn and toss. Can't sleep at night. Every night. Convict—toss and turn. CONVICT! Moonlight or no light.

The welfare line for free government cheese and powdered milk. Eight years old. They spit at you. You can still feel their eyes burning on you . . . The big fat kid hit you, took your milk money. Every day for a fucking year . . . The kids in the nice clothes from the nice homes laughed at you. Whispered, "Fucking Welfare Trash." . . . The bleak teachers who thought you were stupid and senseless, a dreamer. Headed for jail, or seamy circumstances, or warrants, and finally out of adjustments, a dead end . . . The girl you met who walked out of the Revolution Lounge with you on her arm. Laughing. Smiling. On your way to a 2 A.M. breakfast, then a quiet place to talk until the sun came up. She took one look at your car, saw the crescents of flaking rust on the dented fenders, laughed, before she went back inside the club. You went home and drank a warm beer and a half bottle of Seagrams . . . Faces. Words. Looks. Poison. Years and years of defeats. Eye, heart, veins, mind, full of them . . .

Suffering. ANTI-love/ANTI-accomplishment. Living memories of pain . . .

It won't do. It won't do. It won't do . . . I want. Wanted . . .

PAIN. Incurable. Bitter.

It won't do. It won't do. *It won't do.*

Convict (Too tough to cry.) Convict (Too full of the lethal street to let it out or let it show. Toss and turn . . . Can't sleep.)

It all added up to the blues. A hardcase. Then the blues went black. And mean.

Cold hard mean.

Alone. Alone.

Alone.

Nine lives, hell. You used up dozens. Tried booze, pills, a gun—twice. Stepped in front of an oncoming train. Jumped in the bay at high tide once, didn't fight the undertow.

Alone with the pain. Old pain. Turn and toss . . .

Face to slanted, hungry face with the moon. One of you had a knife.

A twisted night of mad ghosts coming out of the woodwork. You move. "Now.now.now. your time.now." Something got lost.

"Fucking NOW God-damnit!*now.*"

Red flowing from both wrists. Cold and black in the moonlight.

. . . And a hand. And a soft laugh. "You think you can escape me that easily?"

Focusing. The Change—The Coming Back . . .

The hips.

The belly . . .

The breasts . . . HER. *Again* . . .

The ANTI-incantation: "You."

"The anger and the fear drive you to this absurd scene. A poet of the storm lost in cold moonlight." Teeth, white as the skull mask. The kiss. Her energy in you. Signed. Sealed. Delivered. Fixed. She brought you back. Again.

"I am the current and the forge. You flow where I send you. I say when the wind blows. How many times will you try to escape? Stabbing yourself. The razor blades. Poison and the guns when the fever takes you."

The protest: "I'm sick of killing. Tired of—"

"Kill? Eradicating predators is a gift."

Loudly: "Killing is killing and I've had a bellyfull."

She points to the body on the floor. The body that has no face. "That pimp took a coat hanger to her, filled her with poison for three years. Sold her every night since the day she turned fourteen. He fucked her while she bleed and beat her when she cried. Punched her when she begged him to stop. Told her he'd feed her to the rats if she didn't swallow. I made you so you would feel *their* pain. You are Justice."

"I'm a murderer." *Bought and paid for.*

"No. They are vermin—Cancer. You are my knife."

The convict finally looks up. There's her face. That shiny white skull, it seems to laugh, to find satisfaction in the bent and torn shell of the coarse street hunter, gutted, stripped of life. That face, theatre, and that smile. Staged and serious. Noble and evil, a fantasy, and haughty. That smile, a widespread trick, both trial and critic. That smile that feels like a gun pressed to his temple.

But it's not a bridge to quiet hours. . .

"You open your wrists or jump from some roof and I come and sent you back to this morgue to evict the cannibals."

"Fucking oblivion. I can't get there—you won't let me, and you can't fill it with the guilty I put down. I don't see why you won't let me sleep. You had others in the past—hundreds, yes? Let me go, you can draft some new warrior. I'm tired of all this shit."

"Soon."

"Soon for me, or soon the way you count it?"

Steel, no grin. "Soon."

"Let me put a bullet in tomorrow."

Steel. Insensitive to the yesterdays lying on the table.

No breeze in the room. It might as well be a vacant lot or a deserted shack on the outskirts of a ghost town. Just piles of crap and garbage and the two dead bodies, the stray girl bleached by junk and her master, both discarded. More garbage.

He hopes the dope-pale child covered with fresh bruises and old scars found Quiet. But he wouldn't bet on it.

The convict looks down at his boots . . . his hands . . . the blood . . . the knife that has drank a hundred souls. "*JesusFuckingChrist*—I didn't sign a fucking thing."

"You wished. That was enough."

"One fucking thought when I was eight or nine and that set the wheels in motion?"

Cold truth. "One *Prayer.*"

"I took it back. Sat in church and said I'm sorry."

"You didn't mean it. And you didn't Believe."

"I . . . thought I did. Doesn't that count for something?"

No bail, no escape. Her face says no.

He drowns in her expression.

No sleep this night. Not this time. Two dead and hours of moonlight to fill.

Hand on the doorknob. It turns, opens in the cold grip of his surrender.

The hallway, another frontline of dangerous, is nearly lightless. Black-on-black-pitch overhead. Black-on-black-pitch down in corners of parasite dust that never heard of remedies.

She blows him a kiss for luck.

Her smile, the color of a struggling streetlamp, a blur of seeping smoke, touches him. He almost turns. His last question gone, ashes. Forgotten.

The convict steps off the decrepit stoop. A street, a piss-marked territory of hard-scrabble, leading to another wasteland street without a tomorrow. A street that hadn't seen the police in a week, or maybe it was a month. A lawless street where the sky, bewildered and tired of carrying water, has gone away. A street flat as the offending facts that repeats vicious like it was a mantra—Today is yesterday/Tomorrow is today . . . Same old blues. Again. Same old wind blowing. Again.

Midnight (not on any map). Midnight. No hint of sour clouds. Midnight. Crippled and blind. It doesn't hear the sirens. Doesn't hear the screams. Doesn't care how anyone feels. Midnight, a demon mask that never had a voice, never had a Sunday feeling . . . Death row. Cheated by the crypt-purr of the apocalypse, ghosts(with no names) rattling and trembling and sore-pocked crackwhores(with no names) and deal-breakers(with no names) about to be flushed and pawns(without even a number to mark them) panting, worn thin and gray shadow torn, each and every one out of their caskets, hunting and gathering for a flicker, or the murmur of a chance in the flotsam and ridiculous cheap illusions("One of these days." "One of these days.") sharp as a sword . . .

Standing there in the fumes of This Was (there will never be a glimmer of morning here), listening to the hollow sorcery of the semi-human spiders, the convict hears gunfire. Turns to its precision and walks.

The knife in his hand cackles . . .

Lovecraft's Sentence

The following material was found on the hard drive of my estranged brother's computer after his mutilated body was discovered by the police three months ago. Strangely enough, this tale and all his worldly possessions were left to me. Believing his fans would more than likely want his final work, although it reads more like a hastily written draft than a completed story, I have placed it in the hands of his agent to do with as he wishes.

—Rev. Jeffrey H. Anderson III
Birchvale, New York

Editor's Note: For all his many barbed faults and short comings Ian was my friend. His tragic death will leave many deeply saddened; myself included. There are those who perhaps will think this unfinished piece should never see print, that being said, the friend in me overrode the editor and I have decided to print the draft exactly as it was found.

Martin J. Jameson, Editor
HAUNTINGS and HORRORS

'At dusk, the wild, lonely country guarding the approaches to the village of Springfield in north central New York seems more desolate and forbidding than it ever does by day.' That's a line from a Lovecraft tale, or a slightly doctored version of one. (Okay, so it's Derleth. Sue me. I didn't know back then.) For the better part of twenty years you've read openings like that from me; *The Blood of Angels,* which I'm sure you remember (it sold almost two hundred thousand copies and the film received an academy award nomination), started—'It is true that I have sent six bullets through the head of my best friend.' And my third novel, *An Arc of Doves,* in which every chapter began with a line from Lovecraft (the title borrowed from a Harold Budd/Brian Eno composition), began, 'It was on my seventh day out of London that I reached the place in America to which my ancestors had come from England over two centuries before.' Only a hundred fifty thousand copies of that one sold. No film yet—there's no sex, not even a bared breast, and they've repeatedly told me the sporadic emotional violence "won't carry the plot without giving her a good slap, or better yet, a kick or two." Wanna bet they make it after I'm dead? So I ask you, have I ever written anything, other than a poem or two, that didn't start with a sentence of Lovecraft's?

Of course not. So, why start what's to be my final tale with that line? Well, it seems fitting, as I sit here taking what may be my last look out the bay window that faces the open fields beyond my property to the southwest, watching the sun lose altitude and waiting for him to come.

God (now there's a laugh), it's unhinging, to sit here and know, to wait. Yet, that's what I'm doing. What else is there? My end seems certain. Perhaps you think I should run. But where could I go? London? Maui? Perhaps you'd advise the dense forests of South America? I don't think they'd be far enough. Is there a mountain peak hidden by clouds, or a cavern buried so deep? No bars, physical or spiritual, protect the inmates of this asylum Earth from the ocular scrutinizing of . . . Perhaps it would be better to end it myself, but I cling to the hope that maybe, just maybe, I'll find a way out of this with my skin and, if I'm lucky, my sanity.

Maybe I should backtrack a little . . . for the sake of clarity. That's funny; how much clearer could things become? Frighteningly clear, I'm afraid.

OK. My name is Ian Anderson; no, not the cat from Jethro Tull, although I've always loved a couple of cuts on *Benefit,* and played the hell out of a good portion of *Stand Up* in my time. Fresh out of high school, some twenty years ago, I suffered a bad fall and injured my spine, makes walking a bit painful and lifting impossible, so it seemed the family furniture business, was out of the question. My mother, as I was unsure of what career to pursue, suggested I write. Since I was eleven, penning entertaining, but irrelevant stories has always been a love of mine, so after a year of convalescing from my injuries, mostly confined to my bed with little more than my thoughts and books for company, I bought a typewriter and began.

The year was 1975. My inspiration was *The Year's Best Horror Stories: Series III.* Actually, the book (which I still own) contained two stories which inspired me; Brian Lumley's "The House of Cthulhu" and T. E. D. Klein's "S. F." Klein's writing knocked my socks off, but Lumley, his story and the otherworldly gods in it, well, I was hooked. I had already worked my way through the accepted mythologies (Norse, Greek, etc.) and Marvel Comics (as you might expect Thor and Dr. Strange were my favorites), and was currently a big science fiction fan, my apologies to the speculative Mr. Ellison. Searching for adventure beyond the incarcerating pale blue walls of my bedroom I had previously raced through every Conan, John Carter of Mars, and sword and sorcery tale I could find, until I came across Bob Heinlein. He generously gave me my first telescope, and it was *Time for the Stars*. Like a satellite freed of gravitation I flew.

I was young, and like the young pursued my own gods; gods my parents raged against. And what gods they were! Heinlein, Burroughs— Edgar Rice (not William S., there'd be time for him later), Howard, Carter, Herbert, and Tolkien. August gods creating life and worlds of wonder on the printed pages held in my always-hungry hands.

Still, something was missing from my armored dreams of youthful immortality. I had yet to discover fear, but fear is a cunning adversary; somehow it always finds a way, through persistence or careful planning, to cross a man's path. In Lumley's tale a chord was struck, and it wasn't a feel good Broadway melody. Hell, it wasn't even the Beatles. It was as if Frank Zappa, Sun Ra, and Iannis Xenakis had attended a tea party in Dachau and the ash tainted brew had been hard to swallow—dissonance ("smash, and clash, and bash, and bust, and burn") reigned as fear found a new home. The boy was spooked, and he was curious.

Lumley led me to Lovecraft, and Lovecraft led me to Derleth and the others. They in turn pointed me toward Arkham House and deep into the dark woodlands, swamps, and oceanic realms of Cthulhu country.

Lovecraft's Mythos, it seemed to me then, had everything: it detailed the past and doomed the future. It became my first real philosophy course. It, the Mythos, does after all answer the two basic questions of philosophy: who am I? And, why am I here? The answers: I am food, and, I'm here to be harvested.

Somehow, knowing this, I managed to grow up a bit. Some said "not much," others adamantly voiced the opinion "not at all."

[*Editor's Note:* Due to what I believe is a computer anomaly a small section here is unreadable.—MJ]

Later I studied Plato, Descartes, Kant, Nietzsche, de Sade, and Crowley (as well as the philosopher musicians, Dylan, Ochs, Cohen, and Davis—don't laugh, there's a lot to learn from Miles—and the black-clad, gentle decadent, Reed), all while absorbing a spot of this and a dash of that. With the doomed outlook of the Mythos and a more than passing interest in the nihilists, and their country cousins, the existentialists, I chose my totem; the raven. Pass the Amontillado and quiet the needle-stuck-in-agroove Nevermores please. Using the sharp needle of adolescence and the frail blinders of ill perceived immortality I gathered my threads and, with an unsteady hand, wove my quilted credo of darkness.

Below the thin crude fabric, there was nothing. A flash of heady color, the caress of intoxicating material, and when they're gone, they're gone—ashes merged with dust, caught in cyclonic winds. Alone in an unmade bed, physically sated yet yearning, I found myself drunk in this play some term living, stumbling for meaning. Out there, on the edge of something, searching with microscope and maps, desperately calling, at times so loudly I feared my voice would shatter. Arms outstretched, thrust upward—deep into the night, but there was no hero; no cavalry arrived. No answer was delivered.

Emotionally I'm a coward (two short-lived attempts at America's preferred social game—marriage—and a failure at both) and as for the rest, it's hedonism, fueled by fairly vast sums of the all-American greenback all the way. I don't believe we've been here before, or there's some great after, or any after for that matter. I feel forced, by the short sight of time and evolutionary mechanics, to seek the arms of angels, here, while I breathe, and to join the chorus of rapture, now, while I can find voices to harmonize with.

And so to bask in impulsive whim and obliging lagoons I write. Monday nights, and then from Tuesday to Thursday, saving the weekends for taboo and paradise.

Sometimes work and the need for research calls me away. Last year, responding to the throaty moans of the muse, and editorial concerns, I journeyed to Ireland, the lush garden homeland of Yeats, for a few months. And I did work, I produced; still, they have radiant young women and libation. Somehow I managed to salvage the trip (two short works—I never did finish the novel about the Phealans of Kilkenny and their family demon who fell from the stars) as I traipsed though village and vale singing my lonely nightwalker song.

Then came London. Soho is a banquet, a feast for the physical senses. And Stockholm—chilled evening streets warmed by blue eyes and dark smiles. Someone should have seen my eight-week Dylan Thomas impression. Actually wrote a damn good tale regarding one delightful little, shall we term it a dark interlude, entitled "Make Me Feel Alive Again," but couldn't find a publisher in this era of politically correct disguises (whatever happened to saying what you think, and telling the truth? Guess they're on an extended sabbatical, or maybe they're dead). They (my publishers) told me graphic eroticism (so it gets a bit brutal—look at what's selling these days) and the Mythos don't mix and they sure won't sell. C'est la vie.

On raged the wanderer, over the next rounded hill, around the next fleshy curve.

Bored, or perhaps frightened, to journey's end I fled. Home, with a weary heart and tired eyes. Home to find a moment, a respite, away from restless fingers and the yearning cathedrals of flesh. Home, where I bolt doors and draw curtains, where my cats (got three of 'em: Sly—of Family Stone fame, not Stallone, Fripp, and Miss Grace Jones. Gracie, for short.) soothe my wounds. It was there, in the steady-as-a-rock comforts and quietude of my sanctuary that the uninvited visitor called.

It was close to eleven P.M. when the odd happenings began to occur. I had just finished—after missing two deadlines—a thirty-three-thousand word jaunt through the arduous legal battles undertaken by a cult in the Finger Lakes region of western New York who wanted to worship Hastur the Unspeakable openly (partially inspired by the Waco barbecue and a couple of local incidents that involved Satanists, adolescent girls, and drinking urine from canning jars. Wonder if they had Sticks McGhee playin' in the background?) when my reality changed.

Announcing my visitor's arrival, although at the time this fact was unknown to me, a series of blackouts occurred. Electrical winkings really, but after a few minutes things settled back to normal. It almost seemed laughable to me how five or six sudden on-off bursts of lighting which plunged me into momentary darkness could unsettle someone who writes macabre tales, but it did.

Slightly spooked, I returned from the fringe with ice—I like my scotch cold. Back in the living room I use as an office, I took note of a dramatic change in the air temperature. A deep chill gripped me, as if my air conditioning system spewed arctic winds, even though it wasn't on and it was mid-July. Cold moist vapors swirled about my feet and ankles, slowly rising, coiling about my calves and engulfing my knees. Stunned I watched as they continued to rise unabated, until it felt like a clamp, a biting restriction about my chest and throat. It was like jumping into an ice water filled swimming pool on a ninety-plus degree August afternoon. I finally caught my breath after several waves of intense shivering and turned to check on my cats, who quickly ran from me, their voices pained yowlings. Stunned by their fear, I saw them jump on to the back of the sofa and with a sprightly burst spring to the top of a bookcase, where they huddled together, dark dagger eyes fiery and wary.

[More unintelligible markings—MJ]

Flickering twice, the lights winked out again, before they settled on a dimmer candle power.

What the hell is going on, I thought. Sitting in the drafty room of shadows, I looked outside to the leaf heavy maples that line my driveway only to view stillness and calm. Announcing himself with a cough, I turned to find my visitor sitting in my favorite armchair.

"And so we meet," said the flat, cold voice, sounding a bit distorted and far distant.

"Who? You're—"

"Howard Phillips Lovecraft. Indeed I am."

"You're . . . dead," I said, turning to look at the empty Glenlivet bottle seemingly bolted to the desk beside my PC.

"Am I? Do you believe everything you read?"

"Christ, I'm having a conversation with . . ."

"A specter? Perhaps you've had too much to drink and I'm little more than a drunkard's wobbly imagining?"

If that bottle weren't empty I'd drink to that.

"My point exactly."

"Huh? Are you reading my mind?"

"Why not? I've read everything else you've written."

"That's impossible. You were dead almost forty years before I ever picked up a pen, and I doubt there's a library on the other side."

"What do you know of the other side? Your slothful mind is too limited to envision the beyond."

"I thought—"

"What? That you've taken my work to another level with your paltry tales."

"I've respectfully tried to build on what you wrote. I admire—"

"You admire nothing! In how many of your utterly tasteless stories have you painted me as a timid, emotionally ill-prepared man, afraid of the world and life—"

"That was just—"

"And have you not repeatedly suggested some deeply buried homosexual tendencies? You've slandered my father with talk of his succumbing to syphilis . . . [two more lines of unintelligible markings—MJ] *. . . of the filth-bearing ghetto dwellers. Without a care you've tarnished the name of my dear mother, rattling on about her mental state, how she supposedly spoiled and overprotected me, and those damnable curls . . . How many*

pages have you filled talking about her so-called attempts to feminize me. Misusing literary license, you've lied by placing me in dresses as a child. Then there's the mantle of bigotry you have saddled me with. Have you no pride in your lineage, Anderson?" The sharp words came out edged with venom. *"What do you know of my joys, my fears? You know nothing. You did not live my life. How can you, washed in moral decay and self-loathing, understand the soul of a nineteenth century gentleman?"*

And he was right, over the years I had often written about him and his travels beyond the wall of death. "Water Litanies," "Dunwich Beach," and "Whisper the Name Darkness" all featured his adventures as a disembodied soul, roving the cosmos as an observer of Cthulhuvian events. When I had talked about his life, and family, which was often ("One Thought Over the Edge" was brutally specific in describing his novelized travels from the sidewalks of Providence into Dreamland and Cthulhu Country), I had bent the truth and lavishly embellished upon the erroneous thinking harsh words don't offend the dead.

"Your vision is filled with burned-out futures of urban decay—cities crawling with dirty and diseased flesh. Cities seething with the hardened criminal packed tightly abreast to the petty and the violent, the deranged abiding with harlots in squalid housing, and every one of these demons sucking the marrow from this once great country. You see her withered and cracked. You have never seen her glory. Your world is little better than a pockmarked stage of angered, lusty vermin scurrying about pathetically trying to fulfill their insignificant desires . . . I am not a bigot. I am a pillar. And yet you talk of me as if—"

"Everyone has character flaws. I—"

"Yours could fill a weighty tome. The whoring, betraying far too trusting friends, your seemingly endless envies and petty jealousies, and what of your incalculable lies? How many have you wounded with that foul barbed tongue of black deceit? Look at you, stinking of smoke and alcohol. Can there be anything more disgusting than your base filthy habits? And what of those two innocent young women? Poor accepting and believing virgins you broke on the rack of failed marriage—both were completely your fault. You talk about my fears and failures . . . What are you hiding from?"

Many of the things you were, I think. "To be candid . . . failure."

"Enough of this. My time here is limited and there are a few things I must tell you before I continue my wanderings. No doubt you've questioned your sanity, or the effects your drinking may have produced, or perhaps you have decided that this is a real paranormal experience . . . Let me

assure you I am real. Although I lack a corporeal body, this," he said, making a sweeping motion akin to one you might see one of the hostesses on The Price Is Right make, *"is simply something I use for effect. On occasion, it serves a purpose."*

And indeed it did. Although I write tales set in imaginary places, involving the surreal and the supernatural, I have never placed any credence in metaphysics and the occult. What is real, is real—the rest is simply fodder for the pens and pocketbooks of hapless dreamers. Yet, this apparition, this angered specter, sitting a few feet from me in my armchair . . . By the power of heaven, and the might of hell, I believe!

"Now, I shall show you your damnation," he said, rising from the worn forest green chair.

Without further motion or comment from my angered visitor, the room again cooled as the walls began to undulate and then vaporize.

"Wait," I cried.

Up we rose as if we were unwanted meteors cast back into the sky, on some hell-ride through the stars we were bound; to where, I feared to fathom.

Across nebulae, traversed in fractions of seconds, flitting by clusters of bright blurred suns, spanning black abysses where greatly dimmed reddish suns peered out like demonic eyes touched by cataracts, we traveled. Beyond the galactic nucleus, past Cygnus; to a destination I was terrified of reaching.

Clangs, scrapes, and low frequency vibrations (Primal, unmetered flutters of pressure. Could they be the mind-numbing heartbeat of some cosmic abhorrence?) assaulted my ears and stirred dark imaginings within me. Riding atop waves of tumultuous drones, this symphonic nightmare—what else could I call this chaotic tangle of noise?—made me long, no beg, for the more humane litanies of hell. Above that lantern jaw I saw Lovecraft smile in reply to the fear that played upon my face.

In the tableau above us ochre storms mixed with pale green and violet kaleidoscopic effects. Set against the torn, pieced together backdrop of swirling black tentacles lashing through spotted vistas of bluish tint, the cosmos raged.

Then we stopped. Standing at the craggy edge of a winding catwalk on illuminated bubbles which popped as they disengaged from the brown spongy mass below (could the throbbing ground be a living being?), facing a horribly veined horizon, he spoke, *"Here is the beginning. Here you will meet pain and fear. Not the lowly fears of failure and impotence, but the soul damning fear of utter madness."*

For a fraction of a second that seared itself to my mind as if it were a lifetime of primal nightmare, I stood before the seething mass of chaos, Azathoth, stupefied and blinded by terror, while my guide laughed.

Dear God, am I still in my own dimension? I, the unbelieving, morally weak asked, desperately pleading for divine intervention. My reply came in the form of fulminating flutelike pipings, mocking and squelching my hopeless inquiry.

As soon as I knew no god would save me, we were off. Moving again in an unnamable manner, without ambulatory motion, but not floating (at least not the Peter Pan vision of floating I once held)—perhaps, no definitely I was now certain, propelled by the desire of my cruel host toward a dirty, sickeningly yellowed orb, which must have towered eight or nine stories above me.

"Moments from now you shall see what I will bring down upon you. Eternal life, and immortal soul defiling pain you shall find in the bowels of Bug Shaggog," he said as we passed through a valley of steep, sheer walls. The sides of which resembled the inner lining of some beast's entrails.

Then we turned, left, I think, and were spun—upside-down or perhaps some variant of sideways that defied physical law, I could not tell which—to behold visions, or aspects of visions I almost thought I'd seen hinted at in the paintings of H. R. Giger, Thomas Brown, and Randall Marsden. What surreal damnation lay before me?

My question was answered by my guide's pleasure born, barked laugh. *"Mr. Anderson,"* he hissed. *"Meet your doom, Bug Shaggog."*

With a convulsive shudder and a silent scream I looked upon horror— a grotesque of proportions no sane mind should behold. God, if I could have sewn my eyes shut; erased its image from my thoughts. Such were the desires of this godless drunkard as I stood before the eyeless being of twisted limb and demented design with my jaw agape and both feet firmly in the grave of madness.

From the sides of the behemoth's oval thorax, rough edged, jagged surfaces (arms? possibly legs?) separated from the mass. Outstretched, they wildly jerked—groping, lewdly inviting me to some deadly dance. Before me, was its abdomen, a dirty yellowed mass, smeared with faded red stains and glistening black pocks. Torn open in places, the bloated mass revealed a core of cannibalistic, insanely mutated maggots, feeding on each other. As one would devour another, starting with its head, the prey would spew dozens of infants from its rear into the stewing mass. [Again another unintelligible section. Four lines in length—MJ]

Perhaps if I had the strength, I would have swallowed my tongue and saved myself. Although the desire was present, but I could not find the fortitude. Despair gripped my mind and my bowels. Enjoying my reaction, Lovecraft laughed as I soiled myself.

A lost sailor, soaked in terror and hopelessness, blown across cosmic seas by dark storms, pursued by black sails filled with hate, nightmare, and horror, knocked about by wave after wave of cursed visions beyond human ken, I prayed to be freed. Let me return to my cats and my home. Turning to my guide I begged, vowed, to repent my literary sins. I would tirelessly work to make the name Lovecraft a god.

My pleas and vows fell on closed ears, and with a simple gesture, the fingers of his right hand snapped, I was returned to my home.

For the merest second I dared to dream I had been granted that which I begged for—a reprieve—but just as I dared hope, dared think I had been lost in an alcohol induced vision, just as my thoughts reached for the bright carrot of hope, his voice returned.

"In two days, one day for each decade you have slandered me, HE shall arrive for you. A meager feast for Him you shall be, but a feast none the less. For your crimes against me, I sentence you to run on the eternal wheel of madness, with no destination before you and horror forever at your heels."

And the voice was gone.

As his words reverberated through the room I understood he'd been changed by his outré travels and the dark knowledge he'd acquired on his cosmic walks. Altered, the veneer of civilization stripped away, his virtuous merits were corrupted by decades spent roaming and plumbing unholy secrets garnered from the Old Ones. And now, the chosen had come for me. I had caught his attention and his anger—I was to face a horror no longer confined to the page. Soon Bug Shaggog, Lord of Ild-Ryn, installed by Azathoth himself as Lord Protector of the Chaos Stone, would come for me. Years of placing characters in this hopeless situation had turned the tables; my words had come to life.

Slumped across the sofa, I came to; apparently I'd passed out again. With a dry mouth, that tasted of ashes and a head impaled in the arms of an iron maiden cast of single malt scotch, I found the kitchen, aspirin, and OJ. After a quick shower I began to curse the fiddler and recall a strange dream—something about being visited by Lovecraft. Yeah, he'd been here and he was full of vengeful anger. That's a good one; a dead man mad about a couple of fictional tales that cast him in poor light. The shit a drunkard stumbles across still amazes me. No wonder the girls all seem prettier at closing time. Feeling beaten down by the shower and my drumming head, I went to my recliner to close my pained eyes.

I awoke the second time to the sound of the fan in my PC exhausting air. Damn. Why do I always leave things running? Reaching for the mouse, I received a shock. Hot needles ran the length of my arm as the screen saver (a revolving, forty-print pictorial gallery of the Cthulhuvian surrealism of Randall Marsden, who, I had read, was butchered by some animal last fall) blinked off revealing a handwritten note. After years of seeing, reading, and owning HPL's letters—twenty-seven handwritten pages to be exact—I instantly recognized his scrawl.

I guess the best way to describe my reaction to the image on my PC is to quote the utterance which escaped my lips. "What the hell!" I'm certain a bewildered stare was frozen on my face as I looked at the note which was surrounded by a broken ring of oddly shaped triangles, all of which bore three-dimensional runes. Above the runes was a clock. The brief note said: *Anderson, you have forty-eight hours to ponder your fate. H. P. L.*

What bizarre game had I concocted to play upon myself while I was half-smashed? And how did I get the computer to mix intricate three-dimensional drawings with a handwritten note, when my PC doesn't have the capability to produce either? Moreover, the runes floated three or four inches from the monitor! I could pass my fingers through them. Yes, I was sober! Suffering after effects certainly, but sober.

It was then that I noticed a heavy layer of gritty red dust covering the arms of my generously stuffed green chair, and the two slimy footprints in front of it. Momentarily, I thought my cats might have regurgitated the ochre material, yet, as I stared at the shiny glop, I realized the impossibility of that occurring; the glop contained tiny pieces of blue stone which resembled four-sided triangular role-playing dice.

Through my blurred, alcohol induced haze I quickly came to realize something was wrong. As I wondered about the slime soiling my almost new carpeting, the clock adorning my PC's monitor and struck the hour. The dull clanging drone sounded like someone had struck a deep iron bell. How in God's name can this be happening? My PC has no sound card or speakers—all it houses is a simple DOS based word processing program.

Then the voice, which I somehow knew to be Lovecraft's, said, *"You now have thirty-three hours left! Spend them considering your fate."*

All thoughts about being visited by Lovecraft in a drunken dream vanished.

With nerves etched by too much alcohol and dire apprehension I sat alone with my multi-legged fears scurrying for safety as the cold uncaring clock, with its badgering tick-tocks, walked off the first day. But with the chime announcing midnight, realization like a fatal decree made its presence known; there is no sanctuary for the condemned, no denying damnation—no eleventh hour reprieve. I have a little less than a day left.

Now, almost two full days since the specter departed, two days framed like stark claustrophobic nightmares in my thoughts, the undersides of the clouds are dyed black, youthful light has been summoned to bed by Mother Darkness—no violet tones or shards of crimson stencil the sky. Soon he, the executioner of Lovecraft's sentence, will arrive.

So I wait, and drink, and drink . . . and drink a bit more.

As if they are statuary carved from bereavement, my cats sit motionless, fearful and distant. Shortly I will free them in hopes they may escape my doom. Surely some neighbor will grant my dispossessed children solace. Surely Lovecraft will spare my cats.

With little time left I'll try to finish. Forgive me if I have not been clear, but between the taxing potency of drink and my ever-mounting fears, I find it hard to record my thoughts, sporadic as they are.

Some astronomers look to the heavens and see gaseous jewels of wonder, brilliantly burning diadems, and the resplendent tears of god painting the cosmos; Pre-Copernican fools! With their out-of-focus Hubble vision, they see nothing. The nature of the universe is a calculus problem set before a toddler who has yet to conquer its fingers and toes. Listen not to their Neanderthal mumblings.

Hear me, children of the race I cared little for. Seek contentment in television or sex. Yoke yourselves to the burden of economic struggle. Pursue the trivial and the mundane. But do not stir the simmering pot!

Artists, revelers—you who drink from passion's deep cups, you who have basked in the lush gardens of nameless Aphrodites and the restless dark waters of unanswered longings—beware! Beware what you write. I caution you to watch what you say. Guard your thoughts! Many are the things, within and without, that we do not understand—some will take us far, others, into the eternal peril of damnation. So I beg you, walk softly, tread cautiously, lest you, like this madness succumbing fool, raise a beast from its unaware hibernation.

For the thousandth time since sunset bled to death I watch the clock march forward by even measure. Ten minutes left. Once a child gazed skyward and toyed with bright dreams of space travel, now the man cringes at the stark cosmic truth. Two minutes. When does the mock NASA announcer begin his doomfaring chant?

What nightmarish power strips away the potency of the two-thirds a bottle of scotch I've soaked myself in? By the authority of what hellish tribunal am I forced to . . .

Is that?

Curse the blind fate of man . . . Curse these eyes that behold . . .

Across the distant fields to the southwest . . . He materializes . . .

There he sits—floats. Mocking me.

If I owned a pistol . . .

'. . . The fire is out, and spent the warmth thereof. This is the end of every song man sings . . .'

Harried, hammering heartbeats toll the century-long seconds. No music finds its way to my ears, no colors illuminate my soul; at the end, all I find are 'shadows of shadows, passing.'

In a moment I shall be a carcass, married to chaos and madness. Broken, I go to live in the catacombs of irrevocable damnation.

Midnight on a
Dead End Street in Noir City

Across the bridge the hourglass is empty. Autumn shadows embrace the fallen stars ... A haunted saxophone, slow as midnight on a dead end street. On wings of loss and guilt the melody soars low. Falters, cries ... If Tralk was the tenor player at The Zero ... A new bride in the tapestry.

Sure, I didn't intend it as such, but for this occasion I guess we'll call it a voice over. Sometimes a mood comes over me ... Just seemed to fit with the sax player's tenor.

No, Miss, I'm not Rod Serling. Rod was one of the good ones, he went Up. No, not a demon or an angel either. Call me Midnight.

Not Mister. I don't go in for formal. I mean, c'mon, look around. Anything here look Uptown?

How and why? Well, you've come off the lost highway and hit the streets of Noir City ... No umbrella and no gun, and by the look of it short on foldin' cash ... and no brain. If ya had one you wouldn't be here. Not tonight ... or any other night.

Say you were lookin' for spring skies up close—HERE? I don't know if you're fucking stupid or a lair ... Guess that'll come out. Everything does. But back to the reason I'm here. This is my street. I walk it every night. No, I don't sleep in a casket by day. The junkie with the tattoo over there calls me the Nightwolf, others here call me other things. Not to my face mind you. They're still holding out for hope. I'd laugh but we don't allow that here.

Which you ask. Hope, or laughing. Hope's a no-no. Maybe laughing, if it's the bent on the end of tears type you come upon in asylums or at the end of the line.

The reason you're here—that's not up to me. Somewhere you made a deal, or slipped up, and this is your lot.

Fate? Back there they've got a hundred names for it—they don't mean shit here. Skip the long face, you should have been a good girl and gone to church instead of sellin' your ass to every sleazebag with $25 and I should mention, drowning your infant daughter in the bathtub wasn't a real good idea.

Yeah-yeah, big-old meanass junkie-pimp you were shacked up with smacked the shit outta you every day and the kid wouldn't stop cryin'. Big fuckin' deal—you had options. But you choose not to exercise them. It's of no concern to me why you did it. You're here and here you'll stay. There's a few details we've got to work out, but I'll get to them. Just bear with me. I'm in one of my moods tonight and you'll just have to go along for the ride.

What do you think of the sax player? I enjoy him. As I recall he murdered his wife for cheating on him and was on the lamb. Thumbed a ride out on the Devil's Highway and got dropped off here . . . Tomorrow night there'll be a different soundtrack—I like to mix it up a little, depends on my mood. Not that it really ever changes . . . Might be a piano player or a guitarist. Sometimes it's a trio . . . Always something slow, autumn poetry floating on melancholy wings. Whatever fits the skyline. Or my mood . . .

My mood? It has everything to do with what goes on here. This is my street. My rules.

Game? Some of 'em think it's one when they first get dropped off, but it doesn't take long before it hits 'em. After that they just wear down . . . Might take an eternity, but it does happen. To everyone.

That guy? He's not a guy, not in the way you think. He's a demon. Talon to tail, a stone cold butcher of infamy. Just promoted and this is his beat. Lemme give a tip. He's a F.N.G., so he's plenty hungry. Lookin' to up his juice with the Slaughterer of Souls.

That's his boss, not mine. I don't have one.

Yeah. That's part of the deal here. You fuck up, he crosses the street and you're on yer way Down. Express elevator. Tahell on a wormhole rocket-shot . . .

No it's not purgatory. You're here Forever, unless he takes you. So watch your P's & Q's, he's a real bastard that one. And I *never* step in. Let me repeat that—N. E. V. E. R. If yer goin' bye-bye, bye-bye—if I even notice. You check out, there'll be another one come along in a bit. Tellya the truth, I don't mind some new blood every once and again. Keeps me amused.

Over-fucking-crowded? Are you nuts? It may look like it's a only a block or two long but wait 'til you start hoofing this baby . . . The street goes on and on and on. And no, there's no new just down the way. It's same old after same old. The next block is a minor variant of this one and same for the next. Same stage, same music . . . Only the players change.

Maybe I'm in the market for something new? You must be tryin' to make me laugh. You can offer, but I'm not buyin'. And as I'm feeling generous tonight, here's a tip. If he comes over here to collect you, he won't be interested either. Might let ya do him just for the hell of it, but after he fills you with a burst of lava or venom—I really don't know what he's packin', yer on yer way Down.

Like I said, you fuck up and yer gone. Plain as that.

Now we need to you slot you in somewhere . . . We've got six groups here. I'll let you pick which pack you run with.

This side of the street is Group 1—pessimistic, morally corrupt, truly evil, guilty, just plain paranoid, marinated in melancholy, cruel, alienated, bleak, busted, sullen, disillusioned, disenchanted, desperate, forlorn, brutal, unhealthy, seamy and a few others things. This bunch is the oldest of the old-timers.

Or on that side of my boulevard of broken dreams there's Group 2—choking on melancholy, alienated, bleak, disillusioned, guilty, desperate, dried-up, cruel, backstabbers, swindlers, blackmailers, brutal, unhealthy, fragile, seamy, disenchanted, pessimistic, disgraced, gross, busted, morally corrupt, or just flat-out paranoid. Pretty much the same crowd as that side, but I've got put them somewhere. My system's pretty simple, they show up I've got to assign them, so I point and off they go. Sometimes I'm of a generous mind and let 'em pick.

Group 3 is for those who think there's safety in crowds—obsessive, brooding, menacing, sinister, sardonic, disillusioned, drunks, the existentially bent, dour, timid, fearful, lowlifes, oblivion seekers, cruel, violent, sexually burned-out, troubled, hot-tempered, psychotic, torn, scared witless. You're probably wondering how I tell them apart from the other two groups. I don't. They're the pack of gloomy Sundays and yesterdays in Group 3. That's that. To me, every player here is just like the other.

Now number 4 is your basic loner—lowlifes, violent, corrupt, sexually obsessive, brooding, menacing, disillusioned, burned-out, screwed-up, cruel, dangerous, hot-tempered, psychotic, torn, scared shitless, sinister, sardonic, savage, lone wolves, mad, his or her way or no way, and a few with their hand under existential's skirt. A motley crew of assbags if I ever saw one.

Five is the barflies—doomed, mysterious, double-crossing, gorgeous, jealous, suspicious, predatory, tough, unreliable as old ammunition, irresponsible, scummy, steamy, cruel, fatalistic, treacherous, venomous, larcenous, garish, kinky, resourceful, seductive, greedy, gin-soaked, driven, manipulative—no, I didn't say bitch, but I've seen my share, desperate. Why they're my barflies speaks for itself.

The bedroom types usually wind up in Group 6—gorgeous, aspiring, submissive, jealous, suspicious, vamps, murderous, irresponsible, seductive, doomed, cruel, femme fatales, larcenous, mysterious, blackmailers, bombshells, for hire if you've got the stomach, double-crossing climbers, predatory climbers, tough, kinky, greedy, driven, steamy and cold as diamonds, fatalistic, treacherous, shapeshifters, manipulative climbers. Outside they're all top-shelf lookers . . . You'd fit right in.

Very good my dear, just like Dorian Gray, all the ugliness is on the inside. That's what matters on this street . . . See I enjoy a little scenery, so I leave the ugly on the outside to my brother.

Did you think there was only one street like this? Lady, this is Noir City. Every street is a variant of this one. Over on The Crooked Mile it's always high noon and on Desolation Row it's always twilight. My cousin Nick runs his street from a narrow barroom he calls The Skyline and my aunt sits under a broken streetlight on Singapore Wharf. Wish you could see it, it's straight outta a grainy old Saturday night late late flicker. There's a conniving old hag on the East side of town, Abraxas Trot—got about a hundred cats living in her apartment—she's got a major league jones for rain. On her street the rain never let's up. And she's got this loudspeaker system rigged up to play "Singin' In The Rain" non-stop—*Fuckin' Gene*

Kelly, don't that beat all . . . . My thing's midnight. Always midnight. Dry. No breeze, moon just so. Always midnight . . .

Time doesn't work here the way you understand it. It's all a loop, sort of. You go about your business for a time then you blink and everything has reset.

I'm a people watcher, always have been . . .

Huh? No I did not sit down with a pencil and paper and figure out the groupings. Just an off the cuff thing that came to me . . . Kinda like shuffling a deck of cards. Things wind up where they are and that's that. Your last round was like that. Kinda, *there but for fortune.* If you'd worked at it you could have moved, changed stations. Might have even redeemed yourself with a little elbow grease. But you didn't. So get over it.

I see what yer thinkin'. There's no escape. And few rules and regs. Your inside and invocations and lamentations ain't worth a shit. So grin and bear it . . . You were pretty good at that.

Why? Always they ask why. There's no why. Like I said, somewhere, sometime you made a deal, or fucked up, and this is where you wound up.

Yeah, simple as that.

Damn that boy can sure blow. The guilt pourin' outta the bell of his horn just reaches up and cries like dead moths on a dead end street. You wouldn't think something so slow could hold the melody so well . . . You see that redhead on the bench? She's suckin' it in like it's heroin. Look at her hold it in . . . That's what this is all about.

Well, darlin', time for my boot heels to be movin' along, so pick your cellmates.

Sure, you might see me from time to time. Depends on how things play out for you. But I got you figured for a Downer—Black City gang bangee all the way. An hour from now you'll be on your knees and a day from now, hell, maybe you'll make it three or four, you'll be in the check out line. See the look on his face, he's in agreement. And believe you me we don't agree on much. Hey, maybe when you get down there you and Tra-

lala can have a championship fuck off. I think there was some movie—
Never mind, you'll know what I'm talking about when the time comes.

One thing. Try not to muck it up too much, or at least make it interesting for me before you leave. And please remember, I've seen it all. Over
and over and over. If you feel the need to dabble in a little intrigue, don't
waste my time with anything less than an Oscar-winning performance. Ya
clear on that sweetheart?

Good. You forget that, every ghost round here will whisper funeral
and there will not be a so sad uttered.

What'll it be? Number 6? You've got the ass and the experience.

Number 5. Interesting group you've picked. I would have figured you
for a 6. We'll see if it works out for you. Point of fact, if you think the
booze is going to make it all go away, or take the edge off, it ain't. Like I
said, no escape.

Yes, I know your name and I haven't used it because on this street
you're all just moving props to help me pass time. If you stick around and
it amuses me, I might drop a tag on you. Until then, you're just something
I may or may not pay attention to. There's only two people on this street I
give a rat's ass about, that's me and the sax player.

I doubt you'll be number three . . .

Skip the tears, honey. They won't make you any points.

One last thing. *Stay away from my sax player.* I don't want anyone
fuckin' with his tone. You get within ten feet of him and I snap my fingers
and the Slaughterer of Souls' deathstalker there takes you.

So take a minute, look around. If you last, maybe see ya around . . .

(after Bohren & der Club of Gore's *Sunset Mission*)

The Master and Margeritha

Beyond her window the cluttered city, the wind rubbing across the buildings—outside every door, every window, in every cabinet, every howling
heart and assaulted eye, all the goddamn emptiness of everythingatonce—
and movements: religion incorporating cultures; hasty politics outlawing be-
lief; reality decomposing morals; the special illuminations of beerlight window lanterns summoning—*with their curved electric blues and yellows and
reds*—the ashen-faced, those now robbed of even false secrets, to the courtyards of ruin; the innocent, trying to sidestep every spill of dead-calm, while
trafficking with the hook-taloned complexities of the disturbing; scumbag
grease cruisin' the doomed; grunts inscribed with fear; all the hearts that
won't live to tell— Those (never-brides just holding on, mirror images of
solitary rainy afternoons and sleepless nights) held in the windows of lonely
houses, now lost to How It Was Then and the bitter kisses of Nothing Lasts
Forever; self-pity(ranting through its gag); color blinded, SPLASHED to
nothing; infiltrating demands dissecting; chewing out loud
    & krazy klick-klacks & ***KLAAAAAANGS*** & knock/knock/
KNOCKS3times-i-n-a-row-*superquik*; flex and reason, drying up or shifting . . . Before their appointments to weep, bottle-blondes in furs in high-rise
apartments, and disillusioned brunettes too tired to walk properly, scraping
wretchedness from the streets, offering skin for pennies per square inch;
moist red lips and drug-dead eyes; views not equipped for insight; miscalculations and criticism; MACHINES and squatting edifices; tears hiding under umbrellas; the fatigued train of awkward ghosts, pockets saturated with
nervous, tumbling, as the day flickers before it falls into the tunnel—
    Rain upon the city at night; notions of *other forms* in the city. A
woman in a room, dreaming. Her loneliness a shape to spend the hours
with. Yesterday. Today and tomorrow. Her eyes and soul fixed upon the
province of the luminous—Ascension.
    "The Master," she whispered.
    The rain [no friend] and the night [a public bathroom, not a chapel]
pass. Another day dawns with dark clouds billowing. The weather report
poisoned with grim, "More tears, arriving."

Most marionettes never rage against their webbed tethers. Some, the very few, the spiritually driven, strain, extending on tippy-toe to reach that just beyond their grasp.

Lunch break came and she watched the automatons—a human assembly line of streaming numbers adding up to nothing—file out . . . . >
Some hours later the herd repeated its formulaic exodus . . . . >
Home to sleep and eat and shop and chatter and clean, but never—Never!—never to question, or dream.

"The Master," she whispered to the *spectral* dawn of twilight.

And after dark, the dungeon-skirt of night again draped over the abyssal maze outside, she stood alone and desolate; a portrait of silence, clothing her yearnings in thin costumes woven of misery-summoned imaginings.

Perhaps?—Possibly?—past the grime-skinned casement, over the rainbow, beyond the choked urban sky, starless and bible black—There! To the left of Cassiopeia—lay worlds inhabited by races with vision and the strength to live their dreams. ("Yes. Out-there . . . Somewhere beyond sorrow's quotations." *Sotto voce,* as all her words to herself were.) Out of *This*world, beyond the invisible walls barring her from the ever-sparking festivals of love and the advent of passion, beyond the handful of hopeful journeys now departed (without fond farewells) to some time ago, was some*where* she could call, "Home."

She closed her eyes, as if to pray. "The Master," she whispered.

✤

She liked Tuesday best; *They* never came out on Tuesday nights. The simple restaurant was always quiet, and after, the library, quieter still. Among the mountainous stacks, those bold sentinels of knowledge, she searched for inspiration in the resplendent dreams of others—tearing at their bounty like an empty-bellied animal. Tonight their impassioned tales of triumph and misadventure did not touch her.

She returned to her apartment—a tight sanctuary, but a sanctuary nonetheless—leaving her shoes by the door; careful not to allow the dull dandruff of urban squalor to invade.

The teapot whistled. She opened the window, praying for a breeze. A fresh breeze. Like the vapors from her tea cup she rose aimlessly, perhaps drawn by unseen forces. She thought about putting on a symphony—Mahler? Schoenberg? Perhaps her beloved Berlioz—to freely revel in the buoyant waltz. She almost settled on Satie's *Gnossiennes,* but turned away.

She found herself again at the window, wanting to push its confining edges outward. Her gaze directed at the heavens. Beyond the weight of this atmosphere there would be a song so pure, so harmoniously resonant, the stars themselves would shine bright smiles. She closed her eyes so she might hear better.

The clock marched forward. She did not. Lost to the night, the softly-calling stars that shone a vibrancy denied and the promise of freedom, she was like a mirror filled with statues; each dust-weathered carving, reflecting the submerged inklings of the others. After a time the veneer of motionlessness cracked—

There was the scent of stars, and in the wildfire of Beholding, a book, aeons old— *The Book of the Dominion of Mysteries;* the words of the Master—appeared before her. Her hand, welcoming, wanting, lifting itself lightly, reached beyond the fixed borders of the window casement. Swimming through the churning embroidery of blackness, her alabaster fingers found the spine; like doves returned to the eaves of a church, they caressed it.

She did not open the book for each phrase was forever inscribed upon her heart.

> '*I am a chalice,*
> *and a bed,*
> *and a sweet night never-ending.*
> *I am the luminous stars blooming.*
> *I am the lover's song.*
>
> *I wait . . .*'

"The Master," she whispered, her inner-eye caressing the ivy flow of each declaration.

Like water filled with sunlight or a mirror holding Spring's first bright blooms she reflected the gift. She brought her fingers—each heavy with the fragrance of tranquility—to her lips, as if to kiss each word. When she opened her eyes the book was gone.

Uncaring, the clock continued unnoticed.

She longed to embrace sleep again. In its arms she would travel, a star embroiled in the romances of Morpheus. Relentlessly—night after night—beyond. Unlimited.

Her bare feet padded the worn trail to her bed.

She closed her eyes and slowed her breathing; not counting sheep, but letting her thoughts bubble and rise as she found her deep center and fixed on a single word, her personal mantra: *Becoming.*

Soft and slow into light misty sleep. Then, quietly, into deeper slumber. Further. Toward *Becoming* . . . Toward the different form, incomprehensible to the mundane.

"The Master." A whispered sigh of love.

Sleep took her even breathing. Her feet left faintly heated imprints on the descending stairs. Beyond the liquid brambles of Today's shadows, an expression of light on the Pilgrim's Way, watching all she knows, the traces of yesterday—yearning, illusion, the breeze so like a child's easy song slowly circling a mystery—change seasons.

In and through the shaded places of the Cavern of the Three Kings. Afterthought and speculation falling away like autumnal molting. Down the tight snake-coil of the seven-hundred steps she traveled. Down and down and down . . .

through the burned avenues of a many-columned corridor, its linear corners hiding assassins, by sublime trees—limbs blended like flocks in flight, and shapes and sand-eroded spires as seen in fogs where demons traffic with wraiths or Chinese paintings filled with festivals of love and death and war, by ziggurats forgotten kings borrowed from Paradise . . . through twisted gorges, winds crying in their ruining bellies, and the courtyards of hunting birds and the paths left by scorpions with murderous appetites, and villages of insects leaking like pain onto the sands, and the stony hills that hold no blue pools . . . until she arrived.

Standing in a crimson glade—a heaven woven of gathered gentle gardens—she took the fragrance-heavy sweet air into her lungs.

Free! The thought sang.

Free to revel in the open after so many years imprisoned by unmoving gray behemoths with dull-eyed clockwork automatons filling their cold bellies.

Her first steps in this realm as a free woman were bold. The pangs enchanting her heart propelled her.

She cupped her hands and drank the nectar of a crystal spring. She placed a coral-colored berry on her tongue and let the wave of sweetness breathe upon her palette. Surely, life this paradisal was no dream.

Drawn to the song of the Master, unencumbered she walked her dream.

Up—the long slopes of gray mountainside.

Up—the cloud tendrils reaching down to caress, to purify.

Up—to the Master—to the *Becoming.* Her feet, rose-petal wings ascending, carrying her like alabaster doves to the threshold where no wounds may travel. One last step and into the Garden of Love.

He is there. And she, adoring, gazed upon him . . .

"My child."—His smile, the birth of a star— *"Welcome."*

Far above the ballets of lions-bloodied and dragons-bold and the wicked madrigals of preening ravens and the LongLonelyNight-stories of coyotes, and the sloping fields of snow, the Seventy-Six Winds of the Moon carol the Master and Margeritha's wedding hymn. The stars of the heavens, like proud loving eyes glowing, heating their festival of love.

"Beloved." His hand outstretched.

Beloved, the pledge rang, the siren song of promise. Truth and love stood revealed before her.

She steps forward—leaving murmuring melancholy to its mourning in shadows

—To join Him upon His mountain-cloud; to hear the singing winds adore Him. To see All as He sees it.

—To be more than an image covered in paint and cloth

—To be alive! Breathing, full of hungers, hot with their own lives.

—To take His hand, her breath ripe with hope, the new ether.

—To touch and be touched.

—To become His Beloved, His conception vessel.

—To be embraced: understood: assimilated—she in Him, He the flesh of her/*transfigured-full measure.*

—To be His bride; the pastoral heart of faith, stretching out in the wondrous.

—To wear His crown, to gaze upon forever-flaming

—To become one with God, *The Master.*

In the Becoming *that slow-motion arabesque of harmonious sensation—cherished and cherishing* her fingers find him, his find her. He smiles, as does she.

There is no separation in this nature, no speech. They are One— lovers; naked/pleasure-in-pleasure—beyond all low temptations, a flame of fidelity which illuminates but will not burn. They are perfect understanding-ceaseless. They are everything that shines.

In the Beginning there was One—a perfect angel in the hungry blackness—that could not die.

(after H. R. Giger's *Master and Margeritha* [1976])

Hello Is a Yellow Kiss

Dearly beloveds (some wounded by fake virgins and blackmailers, some by Daddy—or Mommy, some by farther down the line or God's will) outta spare dreams, sliding down Dead Street at closing time. That's the first thing you see . . .

The City—no vacancies, tons of bars and grills . . . Madmen boiling hot and paranoids . . . Laughing coldly, ladies in red—legs up to here—most from Hell. Tough guys and dangerous crossings, dangerously close . . . Incidents that weren't there . . . Prowlers hiding in hangovers. Hugs broken by a body of lies . . . The face behind the mask D.O.A.. Pretty young boys and once, pretty young girls who rubbed unavoidable night the wrong way and couldn't buy an ace. Desire . . . The trigger that stops the Hard Way dead in its tracks . . . And a lack of fresh air for those who's clock has punched out . . .

Carl Lee left Noir City with a hard case of the traveling blues . . . New York . . . Tennessee . . . Riverside . . . Rosedale . . . Walking, not riding. No one at his side. He left the last Rene?, or Lynn?, back in a ditch—no moving teeth and tongue. Just curves and layers and blood, and white glistening bone . . . Rambled on . . . No thought to her smooth young face, sideways and lifeless. Sixteen. No thought to her soft brown open eyes, open mouth frozen in a last kiss with nothingness . . . And he didn't give a fuck what her name had been. She lied . . . They all lied . . .

He never gave a fuck what any their names had been.

Walking. No home to hurry home to, but looking for something . . .

The road. Not a place for long engagements.

He stood on a ridge of rocks. Looked down into the distortion. The bleak sun burned everything . . .

West Texas. Headed for the open desert, birds slashing across the blue sky . . . The open desert, shimmering and painted with cactus and bugs and scorpions and mice and rattlesnakes . . . October in the desert, not much jumpin', no livin' easy. The lizards used the sun as armor. He tied one to a cactus. Looked at it like it was a picture over a mantle; the long line of the tail lingering in the open blue, the abstract flight of blood on the altar of green, the mouth sleeping on the faultless page of sun. Even dead its black eyes held heat. Carl Lee looked at the skin, looked at the muscles, remembered a deer when he was seven. A buck knife moved through the hide, the curve of muscle, white glistening bone. Blood.

Dust to dust . . .

Thoughts following a star down the line . . . west . . .

Dawn—a moment from too hot—at his back . . .

His thumb flashed. A two-toned pick up, white and rust, dark and light. A pale, skinny blonde. She smiled. He got in. A shabby little trailer on the outskirts of a forgotten little town kissed too many times by the wind and promises. A bottle of cheap whiskey. Watched her drink. Felt the burn . . . washed the blood from his knife. Washed his hands. Watched the diluted blood find its way down into darkness. He looked in the bathroom mirror and traced the scorpion-like tattoo on his chest with his finger.

"Cassilda," he howled silently.

A lost weekend with little sleep. Heartbreak hotel. Shooter's Saloon—just another cowboy Peyton Place, everybody trying to fuck another one before yesterday or tomorrow gets in the way. Cowboys, leather skin hard as the hardwood floor. A plaintive piano backing Willie's dream that didn't come true . . . Coarse-faced sons-of-bitches thinkin' they were fuckin' matador-heroes in white hats, livin' out oil-rich ecstasies in the eyes of the beautiful, good-hearted women swayin' in their arms. No big bright blue, only the sky opened by bottles of beer for the waltzing fools . . . out back of the bar. In the back of her car he tried to fuck her. Wound up using his knife after she told him in that blunt drawl, "Cassie isn't short for Cassilda, Dummy."

Mama called him dummy—once . . . *Scissors telling Mama the Truth . . .*

Dust to dust. . .

Walking. No home to hurry home to, but looking for something . . . Looking for someone . . .

The road. Not a place for long engagements . . .

Rambling on . . . west . . . Where the ghosts and the coyote and the canyons and restless oracles with distant eyes express echoes of the curse of luck still as the broken fences lining the dead roads . . . Where the wind cries in the wires . . .

Walking . . . dust to dust . . .

❉

Dr. Archer sat over the pages of the open book adjusting his unsightly horn-rimmed eyeglasses. The TV crew was in the other room waiting. This would be his fifth televised interview on The Carcosa Syndrome. He wondered if Carl Lee ever watched TV. He was certain Carl Lee was headed this way. His last three postcards were from Texas and Oklahoma and he'd been promising for over a year that *The Truth will come for you.*

Archer had finished his interview. He was on his third scotch. Carl Lee's postcards were spread across his desk. They all said the same thing.

You wanted to see the Truth, to understand it. Never fear, one day, the Truth will come for you. It will stand before you and reveal itself. Watch for it.

He had a truth for Carl Lee. She was sitting in the sun room. Sedated and strapped in her wheelchair. All he had to do is get his former patient in the room with her . . .

❊

Her wheelchair was parked between two clay containers, between two large friendship trees. She was looking out the wall of glass. The afternoon's heat played on the hills. Distortions. In the sand. In the air. Cactus, the scrub trees bent. The dust swirls.

A century in seclusion with the green birds . . . The humors of the lantern as sedatives . . . And she misses having shoes. . .

She wiggles her toes. Almost smiles.

"When will you come?" she whispers.

Her fingers tighten on the arms of the wheelchair.

The ring on her finger is so heavy . . .

"When will you come," she whispers from lips—tattered, dry garments, midnight tender, midnight cold.

❊

Carl Lee had been out in the badlands, came into Gallup because it was there, because he tired of his talks with the goblins that wandered down from the sandy hills and out of the lonely ravines of embedded fossils and petrified trees. For fourteen days he lived off snakes and a coyote for meat. He'd slept in a small fissure under a red and gray and tan formation which brought to mind the wrinkled wildfence skyline of Carcosa.

In a truck stop diner on the side of a dusty road he has bacon and eggs and white-bread toast and black coffee. The waitress is called Dolores. She has real short hair. He wonders if she remembers being young. Almost everyone speaks Spanish. There are saints by the cash register. Carl Lee sat in a booth near the counter, near the TV. From time to time he liked hearing the news, National, never Local—all those greedy brick-stupid, fucked up shithole-motherfuckers fuckin' up the world with this and that and every other stupid got-ta-have-it new thing that flashed down the speedway. Fuck, half of the shit was parked or dumped out in the desert and the other half sat in their yards, or basements. And oil and gas and money and land, they were killin' each other all over the fuckin' place to get more. Every one was in a hurry, even if it was to get their ugly face on TV for a whole two minutes. *Whole world's fucked up with their easy come, easy go. Goin' alright. Goin' ta Hell. Fuck, they're already there.*

George Strait singing "All My Ex's Live in Texas" on the jukebox. Carl Lee didn't have an ex, but had left girls in nearly thirty states. He couldn't remember if it was six or eight back in Texas. He remembered something about going to San Antone, he thought it was a Sunday and sunny, but he'd be fucked if he could remember any of their names. But he remembered what they looked like underneath the lies, curves and folds, white glistening bone, and blood. George Strait stopped singing and Carl Lee watched a heavily made-up bottle-blonde on CNN talking about some big fire in Atlanta and some congressman who raped some six-year-old girl. She said they'd be back with a report on a startling new psychiatric discovery on shared dementia and showed Dr. Archer's face. He stood by a fragile blonde woman in a wheelchair.

"Cassilda," he howled silently.

Face to face with Dr. Archer's moving teeth and tongue. Carl Lee sat rod straight—riveted. There was his tormenter.

And his dream.

She didn't move. Didn't say a word but Carl Lee heard her speak to him. "I'm waiting for you, Carl Lee. Come and free me. *Please.*"

Cassilda laughed. She had a Raymond Chandler evening laugh, autumnal. It hit Carl Lee right in the heart. He always counted on her coming as a wave of summer sunshine, but the quiet, autumn-light fireworks in her eyes suited her.

That fuck, Archer, had her. Had her tied in a chair, his jazzed-up needles filling her with poison, Carl Lee could tell by the glaze in her eyes. He'd been there. And the nightmare dealer had The Book in his fuckin' dirty hand. He was a virus full of spells, fuckin' evil spells—pourin' out his mouth and his cold ugly eyes and his goddamned needles. Pokin'. Night and day all the skinny-ass nurses in white dresses and white shoes and smellin' of too hospital clean to be healthy—comin' in to poke away with Archer's fuckin' poison needles. And all that fuckin' white light. Eatin' away at ya. Eatin' right through your skin . . . "He's a dead fuck."

"I'm hoping he'll be recaptured soon. The more we understand about *his* condition, the sooner I'll be able to cast a healing light on this poor woman's unfortunate condition."

Carl Lee almost threw his coffee cup at the TV. More abasements from his leather cunt-mouth of lies.

Dead! His fucking Light! I'll give him more light. *He'll burn in the desert of my hands. I'll cut out his fucking eyes. Let him see Truth's black flame.*

Curves and layers and blood, and white glistening bones . . . He wanted his knife in his hand. Wanted flesh torn from the hands of God and the basket of life, to feed, with both hands, to Death.

Carl Lee's boots were out the door. Back to his cheap room, grabbed his stuff. On the other side of the door to #9, another dead girl, soft brown eyes wide open, stuffed with nothingness.

Everything out of his mouth is a crime—a lie! Fuck him and his "mask of sanity" shit. Carl Lee had a good idea about what lay behind the doctor's mask. *Fuckin' Carcosa Syndrome! Lies. He's so full of fucked up bullshit-lies. Gonna show that evil fuck the Truth, then take Cassilda out there . . . After I cut out his lyin' tongue, I'm gonna paint those fuckin' white walls with his blood.*

His plan came quick. There was no time for sleep, no time for anything but to get to Cassilda, to free her from the death dealing hands of the monster. Carl Lee bought a conservative 500-dollar suit, a hair trimming kit and some hair dye. He also bought a briefcase (to conceal his knife) and a pair of clear glasses. He was going to walk right in Archer's asylum, cut out Archer's heart and free Cassilda.

And anyone who got in the way was fucked too.

In a public restroom he cropped his hair into a near skullcap and trimmed and dyed his beard and eyebrows. He looked into the mirror, suit and tie—colorful, but not too loud, just something to help divert eyes from his face—tortoise shell glasses, and a dark brown beard. He'd been clean shaven and had long sun-bleached blonde hair when he was a prisoner in the doctor's hellhole.

Carl Lee sees Archer in the mirror. Cold ugly eyes behind unsightly horn-rimmed eyeglasses, moving teeth and tongue . . .

"I will feed the tongue of Death your last words, Doctor. The worms can have the rest."

✹

A century in seclusion with the green birds . . . The humors of the lantern as sedatives . . . And she misses having shoes . . .

She walks the garden. Bare feet gently pushing aside the black, curling leaves of the Winter Tree . . .

"Will he never come?"

I've taken off my mask. Come to me and we will stand face to face . . . We will sit in the Room of Yellow Curtains before the fireplace and with the evening painted all around us we will read of the thirst in times past as the wings of black moths whisper their melodies to us . . . And we will play as angels and demons play . . . Come home from your star-chasing in dream-time. I offer you my hand . . .

"I grown so pale here."

She sits on a bench in the garden. Unbuttons the buttons of her blouse. Reaches under her skirt and slides her panties off. Her fingers, angels to her demon, stray . . .

✹

Fredric Galt stormed into Archer's office, shouting about deceit and treachery. His right hand a fist. His chauffeur/bodyguard harder at his right shoulder. Fredric's eyes the hardest thing in the room.

He walks to Archer's desk and picks up an ivory letter opener.

The doctor had seen the same murderous rage in Carl Lee's eyes. Knew the energized hand before him was, at this moment, no less deadly. Knew his next move in this game of chess with Death might be his last.

Cool bedside voice. "This is all a simple mistake of judgment. If you'll allow me, I can explain."

"Mistake? *The fuck it is!* When I'm done with you, you conniving fuck, you won't be able to clean shit-stalls in the poorest Third World country. I'll purchase this facility and have it torn down—*with you buried under it!* You're using my wife for some twisted experiment. This is the woman I love, she's not some aberration . . . You have to be out of your mind to fuck with me." Fredric thought about calling a former C.I.A. operative he knew and having Archer terminated, inch by slow inch. He looked at his bodyguard. *One word, doctor, and James will turn you into a welcome mat at the gates of Hell.*

"No one has ever fucked with me and continued breathing." Voice fast and hard from bared teeth. Cold. Deadly.

"Mr. Galt, please. You don't understand what's going on here."

"I understand fully well—"

"Please let me explain."

Galt's expression said talk fast.

"This former patient of mine is critical to understanding—curing, your poor wife's condition. With his help, *I can return Susan to you.* If you will just give me a few days."

Fredric listened. Archer diagramed and outlined his procedure.

"Tuesday. 10 A.M. If I see no improvement in Susan's condition your career is *over.* And if you stick one more goddamn needle in her arm, someone will show you what it means to truly be a pin cushion." Fredric said, turning to James.

"I hope I have made myself clear." He had. To both men.

James opened the door for Fredric. Before James left the room he turned, looked at Archer, looked down at his hand, made a terrible fist. It looked like it was forged to pulverize granite. With a smile, he returned his gaze to the doctor's whitening face. All phrases, all opportunities closed. No escape, target locked.

Behind the closed door of his office Archer sat. His shoulders slumped. He looked like an old mattress someone had taken a tire iron to.

Scotch, three fingers times two to sweep out the sharp chill of the predator.

Archer began Susan's hypnosis two hours after her husband left. *She'll be ready, appear to be better, but still require long-term care. He'll understand she will need to stay here . . . All I need is this one performance from her . . .*

Fearing Galt's temper and James's hard promise of aggression should Susan miss her cues, Archer went to his office closet and opened a fire safe. From it he took a Glock and a shoulder holster. He'd been threatened by madmen before.

❖

He couldn't pull up in a cheap Chevy or some dented pick up, so he'd stolen a black 550i sedan, thinking it would fit the illusion. Carl Lee drove passed the house of a kindly old woman he skinned almost two years ago while escaping the asylum, smiled. Carl Lee spent two days in the public library, online, researching Archer and his work and his new theory. He'd found his way in.

The 550i was a jackrabbit on its way to eat the coyote. Its race with the wind ate the miles of I-40 West.

He slowed his breathing. Just a few more miles.

To shake off the highway dust, he drove through an automated car wash for an "ultimate" wash and wax.

Appearances. Don't offer them reasons to think you're not what you look like. Stay firm and quiet. Solid. Scare them politely and this will work.

❋

"I represent Mr. Fredric Galt.

"Appointment? No. Mr. Galt instructed me to come here and check on Mrs. Galt's condition. If you'll call Dr. Archer, I believe you'll discover I do not need an appointment." Carl Lee took a cell phone he robbed out of his jacket pocket. "Perhaps you'd like me to call Mr. Galt and tell him I'll be unable to check on his wife as I have no appointment." Voice courteous and firm and not to be contradicted.

If I have to, I'll gut this stupid-ass bitch. And anyone else I have to, to get to Cassilda.

Privy to every eddy of the facility's whisper-stream, the receptionist had heard about Dr. Archer's encounter with Galt. She knew Archer had erred, many asserting to the point of professional suicide, and was terrified of Galt. She dialed Dr. Archer and spoke quickly.

Less than five minutes. Archer appeared. Walked right over. Extended his hand to Carl Lee. Carl Lee smiled, took Archer's hand and flatly stated the reason for his visit.

Jackpot. Those damned interviews worked better than I'd hoped.

"I'll be happy to take you to her, Mr. Walker. If you'll please come this way." *Stay calm. You can leave him with her and come back with attendants. He's here. He's come for his Cassilda. I can't believe this . . .*

No verbal exchange in the hallways of calming, fresh-as-the-morning paint. Each troubled by and suspicious of the other. Each weighing options of vision in the chess match . . . Each in his heart, knowing the other was truly mad.

The door to the stage. Commitment beyond.

Leaden, drug-frail. Pale. Strapped to her chair. Her wheelchair was parked between two large clay containers, between two friendship trees. She was looking out the wall of glass. The afternoon's heat played on the hills. Distortions in the shamanic sands, in the parched air. Cactus, the scrub trees bent and brown. The dust swirls.

Carl Lee boiled. Cassilda subjected to this. His hand hungry for his knife and Archer's blood.

"Susan, you have a visitor." Dr. Archer said. "Do you remember him? Perhaps he visited you . . . in Carcosa?"

Eyes wide with disbelief, Carl Lee spun into the slap of his failure. Archer stood there gun leveled.

Ugly, perverted. Firm as a solid door to a locked room. "Did you think I'm fool enough not to recognize my star patient, Carl Lee? How many times in our sessions did I tell you a person can change his or her mask, for it is merely an expression posed above the neckline, a script or color if you like, we change to suit the needs of the day, but our eyes never lie? You can change the flag, but you can not change what it stands for.'

"I can't tell you how delighted I am. I've looked forward to this day for some time now . . . I want you to know I'm very excited by the things we may uncover in our coming hours together." Cold hard smile under cold ugly eyes.

"Your room is ready. It's been ready since the day you left me.

"Have you no greeting for an old friend?

"I'm sure a few days in The Room will reawaken your memories." Archer's downturned mouth became a smile. Infected by Carl Lee's distress it darkened. He almost laughed.

Somehow ambushed. His part of the room nervous, weak, vulnerable. Dismay, question marks buzzing, climbing. Carl Lee's mouth tasted of ashes and dead moths. This close and his tormentor—captor, was gloating, about to cast him into Hell again. The doctor was over confident, the gun, harder than any security blanket or line of tanks, the distance between them.

Cut down. Facing the triumphant eyes of the rat.

Red—hot, pulling, bites, scrapes. His fingers are streets of shadows, ideas twisting, stretching for magic. Revved up, Carl Lee lunges.

A shot. Burning. Blood. The demoralizing flame of pain.

Carl Lee still came forward, full-on hate/rage/panic discharged. Took the doctor down with a knee to the balls. Clawing. Punches, the dance of blood, hammer blind. Ripped his horn-rimmed glasses from his face. Plunged the broken ear piece into his throat. Blood . . . Hands, fingers bent, on each other's throats. By furies possessed, brothers, in blood and hate . . . knotted. Grinding. Paper skin tearing . . . Wrestling with dreams each might never see.

Hand fumbling with the catch on the brief case. The Knife.
Cutting . . .

Desperation. Archer's hand stretching for the Glock two feet beyond
his clawing fingers. Helpless.

Hacking downwards with the side of his hand, Carl Lee chopped the
doctor's windpipe.

"I told you to watch, motherfucker. You watching? You wanted the
Truth. This is it."

The poet, writing in the anatomy, cutting, deeper, red and wet, uncov-
ering the plain white truth . . . Curves and layers. No breath. Heat reced-
ing . . . Pick's up the gun. Puts a round in Archer's left eye.

"When you get to Hell, study it well."

Returned from the red-fire cloud of rage and pain, Carl Lee looked at
his arm. The shot only a flesh wound. Finding the worse over, to her he
rushes.

"*Cassilda*. I have come for you. "

She looked at him. Thought it was Fredric . . . Struggling to find her
voice, any voice, in her dry-cotton throat. "I . . . Fredric? Seclusion with the
green birds . . . The lantern . . . in the Fourth Tower . . . Can't shake . . .
sedatives." Voice autumnal, haunted by the unspeakable.

"Couldn't call home . . . Get away . . . Have you seen my shoes,
Uoht?"

He looks at her bare feet and smiles. "It's OK, Sweet Princess. It's just
the monster's drugs. They wear off you'll be fine. I promise. You need
never worry about him again. He's in Hell.'

"When you're out of here you can have all the shoes you want."

Gun in his right hand, knife in his left. Standing there quietly shaking,
wondering what to do next . . . Cuts the restraints on her wrists.

She looks down, flexes her wrists, fingers. Sees lonely white angels.

"Free?"

"Yes, Cassilda, you're free."

Two days early, Fredric and James walked into the sunroom. Carl Lee
knew Galt from his photos in on the internet. A rapid not-so-quiet bark,
the discharge flexes through jacket and muscle. He struck down James
with a single round. Fredric's bodyguard's eyes roll to a place beyond human sight.

"I wouldn't move if I were you. I know who you are." Carl Lee said to
Fredric. He needed time to figure out what to do. What would Cassilda
think if he shot Galt in front of her?

Yer dead asshole. It's just a—

He's . . . And it hit him how much he looked like Galt. *We could be brothers.*

Two Fredrics? Blinking eyes. *One, a mirror? Of lies.* She's reaching through the cloud-haze. She looks at both. She'd lain with one, the other one . . . The bloody one wore no mask. He was here to bring her home.

Standing. Two steps. Cocks her head. Almost free of the drug-daze . . .

A soft pale hand on the wrist with the gun.

"Wait, Thale." She takes off Fredric's ring. Throws it at his feet.

"You locked me away with the green birds . . . Locked me out of the Fourth Tower. Took my shoes. *You took my shoes, Uoht* . . . I tried to love you."

"I love you. I've always loved you. Mother—"

"'Foul-spoken coward! that thunder'st with thy tongue'—Mother is DEAD. She didn't want you to marry me. She wanted you for herself . . . That's why she never remarried after she killed your father. She wanted you in her bed."

"Susan! Stop. Wake up—*think.* Look at me. It's Fredric."

"I know you, Uhot. You filled all the hours with those women. Fucking fresh skin, cunning doorways hidden behind masks, dragging me to another desolate tomorrow in tears . . . You insulted me, scarred me with every one you fucked. Your mother stood behind the curtains in her black grave-cloth and watched you fuck them like a ravenous tiger. Wanted you fucking her, not them. I saw her touching herself as you fucked them. I heard her moan."

She's touching herself. "Fucking—your lust was quicksilver— fucking. *Fucking.* She loved to watch your body strike your dainty does."

Her pale fingers tenderly stroke Carl Lee's cheek. She takes the knife from his hand.

"That raven-bitch had flint in her heart for me . . . 'But I digress too much.' My hand is no longer forlorn, fashioned tear for tear it is famished marble. 'Witness my knife's sharp point.'"

Sweat bonds her linen robe to her heaving breasts. Fredric lies at her feet, bleeding out. Her toes pressed to his unmoving lips, she pushes, turns his head aside. "That way lies fair Carcosa, where you shall never abide.'

Cassilda stands before Carl Lee. Her white linen gown, a wedding gown. His agony stops.

Face to face. Joining.

"Hello." Shy. Respectful. In awe. Autumn-hued romantic images dance drunkenly with curves of slow moving dream-flesh in his mind. The music of the stars is a gentle road.

"Hi." Muted. Just awakened from bereavement.

He drank the midnight hours vibrating in her eyes.

"Sweet Princess."

"'Nature puts me to a heavy task so I may live again."

"'O, take this warm kiss on thy cold pale lips.'"

She kissed Carl Lee. Slow. Her lips were sweet as lemonade, soft as velvet midnight. All his ghosts fell away.

"Sing me back home, Thale."

He was floating. Gleaming. His happiness sat on his shoulders and sang. He began to hum a gentle ballad cloaked in April awakenings . . .

"If madness has a color," she said as she slid his knife in his belly.

She stepped back. Looked into his blasted eyes. Her mask no longer hid the lie . . .

"Do you think it's yellow?"

Mild as sanctuary dust, her soft white hands no longer the subject of fire. No tears to wipe away. The spices of decay gone.

Mouth silent. Eyes straight—etched, staring at the still beast. All he saw was the spreading blackness.

✤

The yard was now, finally, full. The gates to Carcosa's phantom gardenvale open . . . Lonely birds smile on the shepherdess. The moons shine whitely and fall, gently, upon the lake . . . Through the gates, free of the labyrinth. She opens her parasol and walks in the garden. Bare feet gently pushing aside the black, curling leaves of the Winter Tree . . .

A line of questions comes. One by one they hand her their note—One line, one short question. She smiles and points . . .

Blue windows unfold. There is a pale figure with a great black mouth on the hill. It opens all the Mirrors of Truth and whispers, "Alone."

The next question appears. She changes her tongue and points . . .

(*again, for Susan McAdam*)

The Faces of She

Faces and windows attract me—some call it being nosy, I consider it simple curiosity—it's how I pass my time. Certainly other attractions occasionally whisper my name: a book or film, candid fits of debate between those in love enough to kill, and often, the non-facial features of a woman's anatomy pique my baser interests—I am not, after all, a monk cloistered by vows. But faces, they mask secrets, and thus command my deepest interest.

On a heavily overcast Friday afternoon where I was bound in boredom that seemed as heavy as a saturated winter overcoat, I looked out my rented-for-the-night second floor window, hoping some event or action would present distraction. Hell, I didn't care if it was a great pair of legs or an auto accident. No, I do not desire harm to come to others, but a minor fender-bender and its heated aftermath hath its charms. All I desired was that singular occurrence, the flash that would free me from the inexpensive-to-begin-with decor and stale air of this traveler's flop-house.

Caged in soiled and yellowed, yellowish wallpaper, perhaps caused by innumerable clouds of nicotine and certainly by age, and the salesman's blues (a combination of waiting, waiting, and a hellish amount of still more waiting, and the pressure of my supervisor's sales bonus; which is almost enough to set the steel wheels of madness in motion), I was about ready to begin praying for some event to commence. A crumpled paper being opened harshly in the brisk hands of the wind or a fly strafing the crumbs of my breakfast bagel. Hands affixed to the window ledge, as if I could control the image before me as if it were some Miller-Lite Etch-A-Sketch meets pinball machine ad, I scanned the uninspiring universe of motionlessness held within the glass canvas.

Below me was the face, under a tilted, threadbare hat, part of which was held in shadow by the oddly angled brim. It was a wide flattish face, with heavy lids, although I only viewed one eye, and a bent nose—imagine 40% boxer mixed with 60% witchlike crone.

From just inside the lip of the alley it peered to the right, down the gray on gray empty street, looking at, or for, something. What? I asked the desolate landscape. There was something in the expression, something in its uncommon demeanor, that suggested being ill at ease, or perhaps worse, hinted at dread. Whichever it was, it was unsettling, but all forms of voyeuristic activity are by nature a bit unsettling, it's part of the thrill.

Captured in the web of my always-at-the-ready and demonically overactive curiosity, and thankfully unnoticed, I observed the face, not so much look up as tilt back, as if suddenly magnetized by the gray-veiled heavens. Tipped back, just a bit, the eye closed, bringing to mind one of those dolls which when you lay it down the eyes close. Was the sentience behind the face divining the meteorological prophecies of the leaden-oppressed sky? As if in a stream of consciousness soliloquy or a poetic rhapsody to some cloud-obscured deity, the lips moved; hurriedly voicing words or sounds I could not hear behind the glass barrier of my perch. Was it praying? Perhaps it was desperately trying to recall details regarding some earlier, but now critical, missed appointment? Could it be orally filling in gaps in its memory.

Then, as if the doll had been suddenly righted, the eye opened and the face receded into the alley.

Who was that? And what had she been doing? Yes, I was now certain it had been a she, although her shabbily clad form revealed no tell-tale outward signs of femininity.

I would not find proof of my determination of her sex for many weeks, often during which her face would plague me. And how could it not plague me; with my hellishly bothersome curiosity now alerted I constantly searched for her—across lunch counters, on the edges of business districts, sometimes near soup kitchens.

Three weeks later I viewed another such face. Different city, but the same face, or at least the identical expression. I had been in town two, of my scheduled, four days when I encountered it. Again it was a she, perhaps her twin. Why did that bother me? Was it the fear that my personal symbol for love, both motherly and romantic, could be cast in the guise of a homeless, unwashed and unwanted, wanderer?

So I watched, no, stared, like a nervous scientist anticipating the results of a questionable experiment. Comfortably ensconced on a bar stool near the window of a darken pub, I took in every nuance. It was like viewing a small segment of a film you've already seen, and seen it I had; a hundred times, over and over, in my sometimes endlessly-looping thoughts.

If there was a difference I could not detect it. Yet, to be accurate there was one; this time I could see both eyes. I'm uncertain as to how long I watched her replay her twin's bothersome behavior, but it must have been at least a few minutes before she disappeared in the alley.

Leaving the change from my ten, I quickly exited the bar and crossed the near-empty street. Two steps from the alley I froze. What the hell was I doing? Suddenly disgusted with myself and my inane interest I turned to leave. Then while pausing to light a cigarette, I heard a soft, distorted moan. Was it a pained cry? No, it softly rang in my ears like the vocal emanations of sexual pleasure. Jerked into action and bearing a striking similarity to an actor in one of those stupid "B" movies, I turned again and walked into the dim alley only to face bricks and a dozen uneven piles of discarded and seemingly forgotten refuse. I thanked winter's cold hand for nullifying its stench.

Where could have she gone? There were no doors and no windows (none that any human without a grappling hook could access) that could have been used as exit points. Certain she was still somewhere in the cul-de-sac, I began tilling through the frozen mounds of garbage, but my search was an empty one. Had she fled the alley while my back was turned? Impossible. I would have seen her walking or running down the street when I turned toward her moans. And how could she have moaned inside the alley and be on the street at the same time? Yet she could not have just vanished like some misty apparition.

Thwarted from my investigative enterprise, although at the time I was not aware of precisely just what I was hoping to learn, I returned to my hotel room to analyze the event. Two separate sightings, in two cities nine hundred miles apart. How did the homeless old crone travel? And why here? This city was more firmly bound in the grasp of icy winter, than its southern counterpart. Perhaps fatigue was exercising some form of tomfoolery on my drab leisure time?

Later, after a fitful sleep brought on by three neat glasses of scotch, I decided to visit the alley my first she had disappeared into when I returned to —————— next month. Rising the following morning, I immediately made my reservations; luckily, I thought then, reserving the same room I had occupied on my previous visit.

My three-and-a-half-week wait did not pass uneventfully; around me spring erupted. Twice, mere days apart, I was certain I saw my she (in a third city no less), unfortunately on these occasions my time was not my own and I could not stop to investigate, although, both times I later managed to return and look into the alleys the shes had withdrawn into. Astoundingly, the pair of blind alleys resembled the original alley I had at length investigated; all seemed to be exact duplicates of one another.

What mania was attaching itself to me? And why? Surely the pressures of my work and my odd hours (split between my endless blur of daylight activities and my restless post-sunset, for-the-sake-of-my-sanity wanderings) must be exacting a toll on my mind. Luckily, or so it seemed once again, I had some vacation time coming soon. So, when my vacation, the normal two weeks in duration variety, presented itself, I vowed to forget this puzzlement and its quizzical participants, at least for the present, and engage myself in some relaxing diversion.

Hearing an old favorite of mine, Jack Bruce's "The Ministry of Bag," on the local college radio station, it hit me. Deciding to fill in a few holes in my record collection, I looked up the names and addresses of all the record shops in town, perhaps one of them might have a couple of pieces that had eluded me over the years. Armed with my list I began searching.

It was a lovely day for strolling the maple-shaded side streets of downtown, and the fourth shop rewarded me with an inexpensive and still sealed copy of Bennie Maupin's *The Jewel in the Lotus,* as well as a pristine copy of the Octafish Octet's *Cultivating Sunken Galleries.* As you might well imagine, I was quite ecstatic, Allan Grey's bass clarinet work is legendary and this recording, issued on the long defunct Red Circle label, is a true modern jazz rarity. With my new found treasures in hand I walked back to my car intending to head home and enjoy the remainder of the afternoon lazing in my armchair, a scotch on the end table and the LPs spinning on my turntable, but as I placed my key in the lock of my car I noticed a book in the window of the shop I had just left.

Two ninety-five for Julie Coryell's long-out-of-print *Jazz-Rock Fusion: The People, the Music,* I was quick to reenter the store and a place a five on the counter (I would have gladly paid ten or fifteen—Hell, if pushed, even gently, I would have quickly parted with a Jackson). Just about on cloud nine I left the store whistling, musical plans at the ready. And there she was; the face, the eyes—glazed, rapt, and staring. What mystical apparition did she receive? What siren called to her? What invisible overseer issued commands? I asked myself as I looked to see if I could ascertain the object that captivated her.

Shocked into action, I bolted across the near empty street calling to her. Reaching the far curb the clouds parted and I was momentarily blinded by the sun blazing in the shop window before me. Blinking and shaking its fiery image from my gaze I looked to find her gone again. Like a daring superhero boldly undertaking the chase, I rushed into the alley to only discover that which I had encountered on my previous investigations—the big fat goose egg.

There I stood in the empty pocket of a cul-de-sac. Dazed and confused I should have been, yet all I seem to recall is anger and bewilderment. "This enigma be damned!" I shouted, my cry merging with its own echo. Before row upon row of red brick that seemed to be an unsolvable giant crossword, and mocking elevated windows, empty of even curtains, I vowed to expose this illusory trick.

But how?

Like the narrator often says, start at the beginning.

So, the next morning found me up early and driving back to ——————, standing in the first alley, searching. Again no clue revealed itself. Utterly frustrated—if only there was one loose thread of this tapestry to yarn on—and almost broken by this unyielding riddle, I leaned against the wall underneath a darkened window. As I smoked a cigarette, attempting to vent my dismay along with the smoky stream of nicotine, a sound came to my ears; dim and very faint, but a sound nonetheless. Pressing my hands and later my ear to the wall, I heard as well as felt the baffled yet audible sound. Looking like a man groping the wall—heated lips whispering promises, fingers kneading mortar, palms pressed to brick—in some perversion of love making, even my loins were pressed to the barrier, I fought to break through.

Was she beyond this barrier, or was I merely entranced by the oddly toned whine of some invisible machinery? Desperate, I envisioned her alone and frightened, calling for help, praying for deliverance. Battering my will against the sandpaper finish of the wall I succeeded in little more than scratching my cheek on a jagged piece of mortar. Despite my minor abrasions, I thought I discerned a word. Sung, I was sure. Yes, a word—*Carcosa.*

Carcosa, it caressed my psyche like a protective familiar, yet there was an inner certainty I'd never heard the word before. With Herculean effort I quieted, stilling my quickened breath to perhaps hear another word, or perhaps an entire phrase, and my efforts were rewarded; there rang another.

"'The Hyades shall sing. Where flap the tatters of the King.'"

Legends to place upon the map of my obsessive curiosity, which had now ballooned into a commanding need. With this free-wheeling, self-absorbed need now fueled by oceans of adrenaline, I was ready to conquer the enigmatic beast, ready to pry the truth from this bewitching hag, but how to storm the fortified walls of this red brick keep. I slammed my fists upon the wall, and called to her, nay, begged for her to rush to me, as if she was my true and only love, but as if my cry had interrupted whispered secrets, all sound scurried from my ears.

I stood motionless, beaten—bitterly alone in the vicelike silence which hammered at my desperation as if it were mighty waves of mocking laughter. Denied. Scorned. Bitterly alone with less than a dozen meaningless words.

Yet I had something. More than I'd possessed hours earlier. Perhaps I could not find the door, but I now held a key, or at least its mold.

"Carcosa ... The Hyades shall sing. Where flap the tatters of the King."

Carcosa, the Hyades, and a tattered nameless King? King of what? I asked. The homeless? Do they possess a secret religion we fail to be aware of by retaining our lofty and self-concerned distance? Carcosa. How puzzling and beautiful; two vital elements of the perfect pursuit.

Somewhere in this city of enormous libraries and heavily attended universities, yes, more than likely, if not definitely, in the college district, where raven-eyed knowledge seekers pore over the words of others like answer-consumed mages desperate to miss nothing, somewhere in the dusty corners of a quaintly named used book shop lay the red-slippered answer that would deliver me home to my mundane sanity.

Plagued more surely than the set upon Egyptians, I walked the streets searching, my question leading me from doorstep to alcove to dusty aisle shelf. For four days my questions to librarians and bookshop keepers flowed like the night sands of the Sahara through my fingers leaving me with nothing. But on the fifth day, the sunshine of a positive response dissolved the gray shroud of my previous failures.

As I shambled, as aimlessly lost as my shes, by a ratty imitation of a used bookshop, I read the sign below its name. Horror, Fantasy, Sci-Fi, Mythology: We've got it all COVERED! Something turned me squarely to the gore-postered doorway of the small shop.

"Carcosa. Sure have. It, and your fragment, are part of 'Cassilda's Song' from *The King in Yellow*. ... No. It's not a recording. It's a play with a mythological setting. Some say it sparks madness in any who read it," said the anorexically thin shop clerk in the frightfully soiled Cannibalize Horror T-shirt. "Like in John Carpenter's film, *In the Mouth of Madness* ... Sure, I've got a copy ... for sale? Well. It's very, very rare. And certainly not cheap."

Answers seldom are.

I set the slim black volume with its scorpionlike yellow rune on the dining room table and stared at it. Just stared at it. Like a prurient adolescent transfixed by his first naked breast I relished just being in its presence. This close to conquering the mystery of my alluringly enigmatic she's lyrical excerpts—I was afraid to touch it! Like a stupefied fool I aimlessly rocked on the mental teeter-totter of indecision. Up! Afraid to release my enthralling obsession. Down! Afraid to open my personal Pandora's Box and find it empty. Up again! Plunging. Down.

Four double fingers of single-malt provide the energy to enliven my frozen hand.

And I read it. *All of it!* Heart, head, and hands all partaking of its revelries. It was like the effects of just enough alcohol mixed with the afterglow of the most heated primal rutting, or a sweet addicting narcotic, blissfully crippling and impossibly irresistible. The beauty of the words.

> '*Songs that the Hyades shall sing.*
> *Where flap the tatters of the King.*
> *Must die unheard in*
> *Dim Carcosa.*'

Again and again I read the passage, letting it coat me. I heard the homeless hag's voice sing as if in prayer. The sublime beauty and the unencumbered need of her lamentation filled me.

"Soul of my soul—"

Indeed! It was the song of my soul, echoing, like a harmonious twin, the souls of my lost shes. Truly struck, the golden cord within was lush and resonant—vibrant. All other song fled my memory, banished by this purity.

Sweetly consumed, my compulsion now surpassed all; food, drink, rest, they were paltry, insignificant requirements in this universe of necessity. Clad in the fortified armor of the knowing and charged zealot I followed my clutching imagination, back to the alley. Willing to wait, and pray if need be, for her return. But I had no need to wait. Turning the corner of ————— Street I saw her, barely half a block away just at the alley's lip.

Energized and truly thankful, I called to her. "Cassilda! Sister?" Why that name, that poetry of a name, etched forever in my heart and now on my tongue, ushered forth I knew not, I only know it felt right; it was as sublimely fitting as red on sunset. And I must have struck my mark truly, for she paused and turned to face me as I stopped to consider her. Then, there as an unseen spark of recognition flew between us, eye to eye, below the canvas of twilight, came a sonorous buzzing and she fled, as if suddenly called home to supper by her parents.

Reeling in my all-too-slow-to-respond wits, I quickly tried to follow, stumbling twice, once falling. Into that garbage-strew maw of an alley she vanished, as if she were a vaporous apparition sucked into the hungry blades of some giant fan. Gone again.

"Cassilda! Dearest sister, leave me not!" I pleaded with the blank walls. This time I would not be denied. I would search until I found her or expire trying. So close there could be no middle ground.

And I searched. In vain. But then I heard the sound, the sound of voices. Low, or perhaps veiled by a great distant, but I distinctly heard them nonetheless. Behind this damnable barrier that cursed me with its hard face. There must be a button, a switch, or spring that would reveal some aperture, I thought, running my hands along its uneven surface.

And I soon found it. The bricks slid to the right, and into the darkness I lunged. Following the sound of distant, massed voices joined as one, I descended, feeling my way through the night-colored intestines of the city.

Down and down. Determining my progress by the ever clearing, now louder voices. Whole words, and snippets of phrases, now reached my ravenous ears. Some mixed with unintelligible sounds.

Down and down and down. And there before me, a sliver of dim golden light.

I rushed headlong until I was among the collected throng. All were masked. No longer haggard and leathern, their faces were now covered by a smooth pallid mask which mirrored the lustrous continence of their god-king.

I was home. A right and proper member of his congregation, excepting my uncovered face. Filled with joy I stood among those, the knowing shes, who had read, and divined the essence of the King's play and heard the pure music of his words.

I listened. Only understanding some, certain the rest would come as my adrenaline-enflamed excitement quieted and I could concentrate and absorb the purity of his words.

And the song, resplendent in its golden beauty, reverberated within every corporeal and spiritual cavity of my being. Truly the faithful hear the voice of god. Lost to the consuming bliss of my epiphany, I felt more than heard the near-silent hum—the om—fill each member of this holy conclave. As my eyes refocused to accommodate the brilliant lighting within the sweeping cavern, I beheld the twisting movements of a floating, shimmering translucence.

From under the tattered reignments of the King the serpentine form flowed. Dancing above his enraptured daughters, its fine yellow tendrils, thin as strands of silken hair, caressed their raised foreheads, pausing to anoint each, before traveling on to grace the next. Although their faces were pained, their eyes were filled with rhapsodic adoration. They were in love.

Jealous of the blessing the King bestowed upon them, lost in a needful want, I watched a few strands move toward me. I prayed he heard my prayer. Then, as if my desire had magnetized them, the delicate fingers of the King were before me. With the supple grace of a feather arcing on a gentle, buoyant breeze, one tendril touched my brow. What peace filled me I cannot describe, but fill me it did, entering a pore on my forehead, as it had done to the others, winding its way through my skin, around bones, and inside my veins, finding my heart and my brain. Joy, bliss, Nirvana—a complete glowing sensation encapsulated me. It washed over me, this glowing song—vibrating within my flesh. I understood, that truly, these, the faithful, receive the living word of god.

How long the finger of the King bestowed its gift upon me I cannot say, but my rapture, at once and repeatedly, drained and filled me. It gave and it took. Then it was gone.

I was lost, frightened. More alone that I'd ever been. I wanted to scream, to cry out for the aid of my new god, but my voice had no power. Physically I was as spent as I was spiritually drained.

Then from some hell below came a sonorous drone, a subharmonic vibration—its geological voice the most threatening of beasts. It threaten death just as I had discovered god. Reawaken, my long-standing and insurmountable terror of earthquakes spurred my feet into action. I was involuntarily running for the tunnel's opening before I could stop myself. As I entered the orifice my ears caught his holy command, "Unmask!"

I heard them voice their response. "Unmask!" But there came a great rumbling and sighing of the earth, where dust clouded the air as if it were the fogs of nightmare, and my feet, closely followed if not propelled by my timid soul, took to the tunnel in desperate fear. I did not turn, and thus did not see, the ceremonial unmasking. Oh, to have seen my dear sweet sisters expose their what must be truly beautiful faces to the King. To have been granted the blessing of seeing him remove his pallid mask.

❋

Now that the tunnel in ——————— is forever sealed—a bank of all things now covers it—I have returned to ———————, only to find the block on which her alley stood leveled for some new cement and steel behemoth. Denied the presence of god for office space! By the powers of chaos, one thousand earthquakes I curse the infidels with.

So, I now haunt the streets near the alley of the third city I saw her in. Never far from its entrance, often looking skyward toward the place where the black stars hang, toward Aldebaran. I see the twin suns, the Lake of Hali. I see Carcosa—its jet towers like crooked-peaked witches' hats. How I long to mirror the face of god, and to wear the pallid mask. And my sisters, I must see my beloved sisters unmask! I must look upon the naked countenance of my King. Somehow I must find my way back and join their harmonious worship.

Protectively shielded in my resplendent robe, woven of faith and prayer, I battle the inexorable advance of the clock. I am immortal now. I can endure the King's test, for only in harmony with his holy choir can the rapture of the King be eternally experienced.

"Good-bye, day." I gladly remark to the sun that again bleeds to death in the arms of the horizon. Fully transformed, resembling those I often, if not always, avoided—if I noticed them at all—I await her. I probe the heavens for a sign, and repeatedly reexamine every reachable surface of the alley, unable to discern catch or spring, desperately hoping, while continually praying to hear Cassilda's rapt song perfume the night.

Good Night and Good Luck

Why? Because it's this or the bottle . . . or a bullet.

I was married. *Maggie.* She was a designer, loved clothes. When she was a kid she admired Emma Peel, the clothes, the attitude. Kinda looked like her too. That's where it started. When we were in college she used say if John Stead dressed like Oscar Madison . . . Well, that was me. I loved it when her clothes were off. Don't get me wrong, she looked fantastic in just about anything, but seeing her in nothing but her birthday suit was the best birthday present I ever got.

One night nearly ten years ago she got a flat on the way home from a fashion shoot for her new line and was attacked. Gang-raped and murdered.

Yeah, some of these pieces of shit have sex. Killed a few I caught in the act.

Her wake and funeral was a closed coffin affair . . . I buried her with her wedding ring and a cheap zirconium necklace I won for her on our second date . . . We went to the carnival and got stuck in a minor power outage on top of the Ferris wheel for twenty minutes. She held my hand and told me it was going to be all right. I'm afraid of heights. I think that's when I fell for her.

Viewing her body, that was . . . Her head had been severed to get at the brain and a good part of her torso had been eaten. Every time I close my eyes that's what I see . . .

Now I live in the hills above the city. I stand out in the backyard and look down. It's a view of Hell, but for what I do it works well.

City's changed. Back when Maggie and I were kids, eighteen, nineteen, it was a playground. Everyone was shining, filled with we can change the world dreams. We laughed, smoked a little weed, went to half or our classes on campus and didn't worry about traffic patterns or the stain that was about to bloom.

Now you have vacant houses and buildings all over the place and the denizens of Nightmare come out to prey every night . . .

Every fuckin' night.

I watch the sunset, not in that old life, romantic sense, drink some OJ while cleaning and loading my guns. All the horror stories and fantasy novels I loved reading way back when, that's all bullshit—crosses don't do a damned thing, because if there ever was a God, he's dead, or gone off to the rest home where all the European gods of old are whitening peaceably.

You don't want to believe me, then why do a lot of these monsters live in closed down churches and wear crosses? They ain't scared of God. Garlic ain't worth shit and silver bullets work because they're bullets. The one lesson I learned is you put a hollow point or six between the eyes of any of these aberrations and they go down. When they're down, you burn 'em. The cinders don't magically reform and there ain't no movie PTOOF where they come back and rip out yer throat.

A knife or a spear will work too. A two foot pice of rebar to the back of the head worked on a she-cannibal busy munchin' away on a young boy once. Anything that puts a man or a woman down will stop theses things. I've never tried poison and the like, on the streets I hunt, everything comes at you quick. You've got seconds to take it down.

Like I said, the stuff in the stories and movies doesn't work. Early on I threw holy water on one and the fucking thing laughed, then got really pissed over the fact he was going to have to spend the night in a wet shirt. Christ, it lectured me about man and God, asked if I'd ever heard of Nietzsche or Kierkegaard. Fuckin' godless-monster lecturin' me—shit, I would have laughed myself if I wasn't so scared shitless. I took his head off with a shotgun blast—that worked. About a month after that I tried garlic and the thing threw the garlic at me and said, "When I ate *food,* I loved garlic. These days I don't like to taint my meat with unnatural flavorings." It smiled—*fucking smiled*—and I went into full-panic mode. Started shooting and the thing went down. And after empting a clip in its face it stayed down.

That's life. Sometimes you learn the hard way. I got lucky and learned early to skip all the superstitious bullshit . . . ten years doing this I've learned to keep it simple. Shoot 'em and burn 'em. Then move on to the next.

So here we are on this battlefield, knee deep in monster carcasses and you're proposin' I take you on as a partner. Sorry, but I can't help you.

The why is easy. I might get to like you, or feel protective and that would slow me down . . . You'd be in some shadow, or just out of sight, and I'd hear a sound and wonder if you were about to get zapped. When I turn to check on you, out pops my demise and I'm too busy worrying about you to notice. I can't afford to empathize with anyone—it would only end in trouble.

I'm in this for blood. Pure and simple. They took from me. *I take back*. I sleep and eat only because I have to. Every other waking minute is the hunt.

Where do I get the money to live. Look, they go down, you go through their pockets. They may eat us, but they take things too. Watches, which you can pawn. Money. I have no friggin' idea why, but they always have money. And they love jewelry. Some of the fucks even carry guns. I've never seen one try to use one, but some just like the feel I guess. Maybe it's something about the look? Some attitude?

Look, mentally they're just like people. Fucked-up, but people. And there's one great truth about people, they want THINGS.

Maybe it's a way for these things to stay connected to their old lives. I could give a rat's ass.

Every once and again you'll come across a nest—vampires, ghouls, zombies, *other things*—like that thing there, part wolf, part who fuckin' knows. Sometimes you'd find a pair living like they're married. Some of these warrens are real treasure troves. I've found art and rare books. And if times are tight, you can steal. I do it from time to time. Look, I'm providing a service to the living, so a freebie or two ain't really hurting anything. I've got to eat. And I need ammo.

Plain and simple. Take what you need to keep hunting—Don't look back.

You say you want to learn. That I understand. They ripped up your life and you want revenge—been there, done that. In spades.

Already told ya, I don't do partners, too much baggage. And even though you're in great shape, I'd pick a man over a woman. You're too emotional and that will get you killed. Besides you look great ... And distractions, well, they're a sure killer. I may be full of hate, but I'm still a man. One's who's never been a monk ... Boils down to some where down the road I'd look at you and for a second or a minute I'd get lost in a thought—you can guess what kind, that's when my head would come off.

The only way to stay alive out here is to stay frosty. Lock down all that shit before you step out into the night. You bring it with you, you go down.

What I do is not emotional. It payback, cold and calculated. I know what I'm looking for and I've got a good idea where to find. When I see it, I kill it. No questions. And no hesitation. I'm out here for the body count. If that's the way you play it, you might—*might* get lucky and keep on living.

But it's a just matter of time. For me, for you—can't win every time. I understand that and I'm fine with it. One day I'll be lunch. Blood or meat, depends on how the thing's wired. Just hope it's fast and I don't see it coming.

Fuck they useta be people. They're bugs. Step on 'em, walk right by—this ain't no waltz. You get lucky another comes. You terminate enough of them and some poor soul out there get to stay alive. *Somewhere out there is another Maggie. Maybe she gets home safe.*

This is a war, cold and mean. A war you can't win, but don't you ever forget there's only one thing to do to evil, *you kill it.* If you miss your old life, you're fucked. If you pause, or remember you pastor talking about mercy, if you blink, if you do anything but kill you go down. You shoot and never ask *fucking* questions. Especially of yourself. Goddamnit-lookatme. Nod if you understand . . .

Good.

You were a help here and you've got my thanks for that. I owe you, so I figured I'd pay you back the only way I know how.

I've covered the basics. Now please get out of here. I've got work to do.

Do I believe in anything? *This gun.* If I believed a God or miracles, then I buy into a hereafter and if I believed in that I'd eat a bullet to be with Maggie.

Good luck.

My name? I don't have one anymore. I'm just a finger on a trigger.

You look shocked. Don't be, your new role in The Shit just started. You're not alive anymore, yer just a finger on a trigger. If yer smart, that's what you'll put your head around. Do that and you'll get a little back. But it will never be enough to fill that hole in your heart. The only way to stop the acid behind your eyes is a bullet and you're not ready to take that way. You're way too hungry. Like I said, been there, done that.

So good night. And good luck.

One last piece of advice. Two guns won't cut it. You turn a corner some night and there's a crowd of 'em yer gone. Carry five—at least two autos. And a shotgun—stopping power equals body count.

Night . . .

Goddamn-stupidfuckin'-beautiful-kids. At least they're tryin'.

Patti Smith, Lovecraft, & I

for our dear messenger of Innocence & Experience, Patti Smith

I sat on the other side of reality. I was using a threadbare page taken from the Book of Chaos as a carpet. I was smoking, measuring eternity with colors I had borrowed from a hummingbird. Two innocent souls sat with me. Patti Smith, the oracle, and H. P. Lovecraft, his shadow confusing the emptiness with its woven dreamlight. Patti—aroused by the infernos set by Whitman and Blake and Rimbaud, spoke of a sky with names and magic sand. Howard's hands were a festival of knowledge. I sipped my tea and blew smoke rings. Playfully, they haloed the dimmed constellations.

On our carpet, woven of language, suspended o'er ruin we had come to bring the balance back. Patti, shining—*O those beautiful, glory-filled eyes,* opened a river and gave a necklace of Spring as ransom. Howard, always the first to share his basket of kindness, clapped and birds of balm arose, their mouths of Summer singing luxuriant kite stories to soothe the hollow nothingness. I, with laughing eyes, whispered, "Let there be light." . . . And Howard added, "And more light."

And from the inmost deeps of our struggling souls the light of the ages, pure and fair and hopeful, flared. And the blackness pulled back, releasing the balance.

As one we three turned and the one tree, its roots deep in the bed of sun, appeared.

Howard smiled on what we had lifted from the forge and said, "The poets of old and all the sweet, innocent souls yet to be born are pleased."

The Collector and the Hand Puppet

I was a still life in a holding pattern. Then I was Lydia's hand puppet—a dial she'd turn with a laugh. Gravity came, she'd open the blank pages of the book and write . . . Her dark life crazed this way, and b~o~i~n~g, there I went . . . Every morning—I'd lean in close and say, I'll do anything you want—until the last . . .

❀

The backside of 2 A.M.

A laugh knitted in shame this moon with its shocked, sad face hand-cuffed to the church tower. Ghosts and angels kneeling in punishment, as if prayers and the gallows weren't enough . . .

Sin. Mayhem. And sin.

Jaws with quick teeth torment ears with flapping tales. Eyes fall under the grave chill in the slaughter of pox. Gaunt portraits of hangovers and the undertow litter the shadows . . .

Fucked up.

Let down.

Big plans.

Yearning.

A one way ticket kissed with blood. Empty games, chasing saints with clocks to change. Cruel ties down blue eyes. A train of smoke disappears with another day . . .

Harm in a starring role in All-Night windows . . .

I light a cigarette and watch. My time will come. I can wait. I'm blessed with cold steel that knows its master will feed it . . . When the time comes.

A girl with fiery hair and lips touched by evil passes. Some other night she might entertain me.

I mark her path . . .

Out of confessions and hopes of April in short sleeves, some of the dead are out too. Until they get slapped by the sun and collapse . . . Others pass. Johnnies in love with Lost and sinful Suzies full of tricks and c'mon baby and hot tips . . . then they're gone.

I am left to Now and the slow, ragged dynamics of night's shadow chamber. On this beach where terrified ended up bruised by the criminal, the wind, its belly full of unforgiven whispers, its breath a funeral of Greyhound baggage, plays like a haunted tone poem.

I can wait . . .

Outside a bar a large, brutish man backhands a slight of a woman. Breathing hard, a crowd gathers *to watch*. A second slap to prove he's still on top. Fuck you with a splash of blood. A split lip and a broken nose. Love is gone. She runs, stumbling over tears. He walks away in the opposite direction with a half drunk blonde. A dozen faces look this way and that. Words fall off the face of the crowd. I bend to pick them up. They won't be needing them any more tonight.

I've got time to kill. I wait. Watch a pair of rats—city living fat—on their way to a late dinner. Someone's trash with chunks of Chinese take out, or a dead baby in a garbage bag? Here where you can get the $29 skullfuck special to show you just about everything with urgency on top, I'm betting on the baby in the bag. I don't know why your shocked, in Mississippi they've got swamps and gators to dispose of their unwanted items. Here they let The City take out the trash. That's what your taxes are for.

Lydia turns the corner. Pure control, a full deck of secrets and thunder, a mechanism of gluttony, all behind that hint of excited in her eyes. On her way to Funtime. Cat and mouse slaughter with some nasty little, wicked fuck-friend she can conduct. Another slave to bend to the hard soft thing. She might be the loveliest woman in the world dressed like that, but she's bad. Eyes of cream and sugar, voice blossoming with intimate dimensions granted—martyr-fool she'll take you to the bedroom and whisper, "*You* . . ." Hell, she'd take the Devil on a white knuckle ride.

I pull her into the alley . . .

"You?"

Smiling. "Me." I wink. This time I'm the vampire, she the impotent scream, to dry to be soothed.

"But—"

"Dead? You certainly left me that way, but I chose not to be minus. My love for you, my need, would not let me leave."

Her face is saturated in facts and memories. "Undead? Like in ghost?"

"Something like that. You'll understand shortly."

Blinking. Eyes wide with understanding. The details will dizzy her with bitter in a moment. But she got you only die on the outside.

Almost pleading. "You don't want to do this." Almost. Desperate . . . almost.

It's something I've never seen.

I cock my head and smile.

Gone the rich girl sex voice. "I was drunk—stupid. I didn't mean to— I was so ugly then. I was lashing out, *not at you*. You know how fucked up I was. You were just there . . . The gun just went off." Out of fire. And searching for the next word.

"And your giggling as I lie there? I heard you. You whispered, 'Worthless, Fuck.'"

"Fear. Blind fear."

"Of being caught perhaps. But that didn't happen. You cleaned up so well. Lied to the cop and fucked him to keep him looking in other places. Bet the handcuffs really turned you into a savage."

"I was so scared. I didn't know what I was doing."

"Show me scared."

She might want to, but it's really not in her. Too many years as the alpha striking what she subdued. And getting off on it.

"This time you pony up. Stark power-bitch who never had to struggle, or frightened by the ambush little angel. Pick one."

No contemplation. Teeth out, shooting. "Go fuck yourself." The rich girl sex voice back in full force. Lydia turns to leave, to dismiss me again.

Reckless scarlet. One last gasp. Her shell will begin cooling soon.

Lydia always told me she was a doll. Perfection, the legs (in high heels and stockings, men couldn't catch their breath), the curves, eyes, hair— wild, suggestive, and just so. Perfection. She was—well, almost . . . She is softness now. Perfect.

Lydia loved these streets, knew them well. Played the players and poured the weak down the drain. Never looked over her shoulder. Never . . .

In her torn black dress, Lydia looks like a sleek black cat, she does not speak (her defiance and her hunger still cling to the now blind flesh, wet with bitter tears we left a few blocks back in an alley).

We walk, I leading my puppet . . .

Her eyes are softer now.

"Who's The Collector now?" I ask, snapping my fingers and pointing to the empty spot on the pavement beside me.

Harm fluctuates on widows. Crippled by the thick shifts of crawling gloom, the attempt of street lamps, not strong enough to puncture the poison glow of Last Ride black, fails to be anything other than limp. We move along the street of wounded zombies in old shoes where woe and crime broke in.

Cigarette butts and condoms deserted before dessert.

Beautiful women—traumas seeking alternate realities, who will let your sharp desire between their passion for a few shots of Jack and a bottle of aspirin, if you're out of Oxycontin . . .

Sin. Mayhem. And sin.

Side doors where you can get a pizza

or a gun,

or naked waiting on a ratty couch, beautiful and undocumented and she'll say, "Now, Mr. Faust, let's wash up before our trip." . . .

Drunks dreaming grainy 8MM dreams. Drunks dreaming about dreams infected with one false move too many . . .

Fucked up.

Let down.

Big plans.

Yearning.

Blood.

And alcohol . . .

I smile and look in a window at love. He's scratching his balls, yawning at the football game. His wife/girlfriend/chattel, stands at his side. I hear her whisper, "I'll do anything."

Night burns here . . . even in the rain. Nothing is hidden away here for long. Here even exhausted lips are loud.

It a hot night. They're about to close the bars . . . and the crackwhores and heroin hookers and the pimps have their attack glances sharpened and their claws out . . . some want gold, others will settle for a few short breaths of amnesia . . .

I smile and tug on the collar leash.

I imagine Ken Nordine supplying the lonesome noir-jungle voiceover, "*Close the curtains . . . The neighbors are trying to watch TV.*"

I walk a little faster. Lydia scurries to keep pace.

These are my streets now.

The Only Thing We Have to Fear . . .

One room, 22 by 24; bed/sofa unit, chair, metal desk (centered my Kobo Ex-72653 mobile terminal clawing the Data-verse), the Music Cube that passes for a stereo, bookcases—dusty yes, but so are many of the bruised corners of my heart, recycled wooden table with two hardback chairs of bio-D Plaz-stock, other assorted stuff (one tight bathroom, one closet) . . . with the TRU-Definition TV monitor on and the coffee pot keeping things hot it's rush hour.

Third floor over the main entrance, a fire house half a block away, somebody's always goin' somewhere. Didn't leave me much time to dream. And I didn't get much sleep either.

Funny how a high plains kid who spent his summers running under a vast open blue found himself living here. And liking it.

Back there, then, the clouds were dreams and I was tethered to them. They rode the wind for glory and I tagged along. Not as fast mind you, but fast enough to get from there to here.

Maybe too fast. Depends on who you ask.

Don't ask Sparks. She lied.

The only time she told the truth was the day she shot me.

With my own gun.

Long black hair, Betty Page bangs, deep black eyes, warm hands, cleavage soft and deep as my starry-starry night dreams. And that comforting alto always whispering or singing of long ago and far, far away. It was all black with her, never a blue dress, never white or green. Black. Always black. Except for the two silver skull rings. One on each black-lacquered pointer finger.

How I miss those hands. And her eyes . . .

I think there was some old movie where they said lovers are not truly separated by death. I always thought that was funny . . . But no more.

I'm back and as soon as I find her we'll never be parted again.

I met Sparks in a deserted warehouse turned make-shift club down in the Shiki District. The Mars-by-way-of-LSD lights were from some 23rd century sci-fi lazers-gone-wild film and the b.p.m-riddled thump straight out of a Japanese anime meets techno acidblast of Godzilla out remodeling the dance floor, tail batterin' away to the no-frills-fingerlickin'-acidpussy-scherzo of the lick-my-ass-brutal-world lightning stomp. Some S&M she-ghoul in latex ready-to-wear handed me a fluted glass of Clear Blue. Tagged, I just stood there in the whirling electric eye. The crowd parted and she was there. The napalm-blurred blast of stomp-beat ceased and a frenzied ode to oblivion spread out like liquid tentacles of electronic lust. Arm in arm with two silicone job "get-dirty" blondes in snakeskin and black lace straight out of darkness and into a I Wanna Sit On Dracula's Face porno she walked toward me. Slipped out of their arms and kissed me. No Hi, no smile, just kissed me with that full court press. Talk about gates opening.

They say a kiss can be heaven or it can be deadly, hers was both. With hexes, medication, and utopia on top.

Wall to vibrating wall. Flesh, every glistening inch of eat me-beat me, dancing in the chemical playschool. Cranium acceleration set to Last Exit: Severe trauma roared and there I was, at Ground Zero with Sparks. Black dress, black nails, cigarette. Hot lips, cold jewels—at least 20 grand worth by my appraisal, drop dead intoxicating eyes. The sub-lightspeed Hell-stomp filling the air couldn't hold a candle to my pounding blood pressure.

She was the Queen in this court, and many others as I would later learn.

We didn't dance, didn't talk, just that click—eye to eye. Like lightning we were outta there. No words. She just took my hand pulled and I followed.

Down the hole right into Wonderland. Clubs at night, most nights—the others were galleries and readings tucked in small bookshops housing the tomes of madmen, kitchen table in sweats with toasted bagels in the morning. Afternoons we met life in a hundred landscapes—the common, the idyllic, and playschools fueled by chemical desires. We danced on cobwebs, rolled in sediment drifted down from the summit, collected shells and small animal bones, or sat in armchairs and read to each other. Anything, mortal or divine, for passion. She lead, I followed.

For three months and seventeen days.

Hell, one night we got lightning tattoos on the side of our pointer fingers. Had this ritual where we'd point at each other, touched fingertips—lightning. Zap—POW! Everytime! We be curled up—loved! Adored that universe of hearts burst open, the fireball—and we achieved The Unlimited, we'd laugh about it.

She dressed as Elvira, as Vampirella, as nameless dead queens, or the King of Elfland's majestic daughter. She fed off me. And I gave.

She was gravity and I was drawn to every riff and nuance of her cosmos. Pinned to the melody of her every, "I've got you forever,"

But a darkness, one slender finger of dark design, stirred in a corner. There was a shift, the creation of distance. A whispering snake in our garden . . .

True, I was a seeker, a dreamer, but I had always feared perfection— in this cluttered world of fragments overcome and teeth pronouncing never enough, the taxes of the crow always come. Figured somehow, someway, one day there would be black wings over the candle and a demanding bark would shake the joyous smile of love's pavilion from my sight. And I began to fear, perhaps, one night as I lay asleep, a worm of doubt or loss would slip in and fuse with my joy and in the rooting I might stumble and ruin the horizon.

Fearing that with the slightest false step I might drop the egg, I held back. Tentative here, hesitant there. Love unguarded vanished and she knew it. Wouldn't accept mud in our summer garden, on our sheets.

We didn't fight, but we took to our bed less often. Signs of disappointment and failure and hurt began to cloud the plans in her eyes.

And there was the afternoon of the push. After a bottle of wine and a joint, over something as simple as soup and bread, I struggled with a question and she knew we had become separate countries. Sparks was up, walking around the room. For the first time she looked helpless. And an offending cloud of rage took her.

Her mouth opened, no request, it closed, no attack came from it. And I stood without words to resolve The Ending that had entered our sky.

She only whispered, "No."

Honesty had been cast aside. There was my gun in her hand.

She was an angel with a bullet. Hit me with a hat-trick. Three right to the heart. Tightly grouped. Closed my eyes. Exit light. Exit moon. Exit this life . . .

Matinee ended. The virtuoso has left the stage. The music silenced. Darkness drones . . . And I was drifting. The nebula of my hunger wanting rebirth, demanding return.

On a finger of cosmic gestures, under a ribbon of celestial serpent limbs danced a being. Stars in his hair, in his eyes. He created novas with his alchemical breath, his fingers a forge writing with light. His eyes locked on me and laughed, cold and sad. Accused me, chattering in a crystalline voice half full of secret noise, of desertion. I had abandoned All Things Possible, visited moments of quicksand. Left the billows of Lovely for the camp of shut fast.

"Pleasure for pain. Fool, caught on I and if. I remembered all the times when unfinished fell and I tired of cold endgames. I cried at the loss and in an act of divine love opened the door for you and you filled it with bricks of plague, choked it on facts. You allowed the worm of nervousness to flutter in the sky."

His head bent down. His expression said it measured my sin of fear. "You will forget question marks." He opened a valise, out poured fragrant moonlight. Each sprout of wondrous other ignited around me.

"I cast aide winter and give you another spoon. Dreams hatch. Return and feed on the kiss of brightness. Never again window shop in the dirty mirrors of fear, I give you moments of gold."

Pure laughter stamped me.

Returned to the landscape of real. Flesh and blood on the platter, air wild with lightning carries whispers of industrial noise. Plaz-stock chairs and newspapers. Outside the window color, the living flow of motion—programmed municipal auto-carriers whooshing along their mechanized tracks, people in their uni-fashions of citizenship.

Home. No scars upon the flesh over my heart and no doubts within it. Whole.

I have spent six nights searching. No glance or conversation reveals hints of her passing. Tonight I will again take up the search. No drama will keep me from her. Sparks will see my smile, see disappointment and mistakes can find no harbor within me. I am the smithy who fills the air with summer flowers. My eyes billow with all the enchantments I shall paint her in. Forever.

The Corridor

The Corridor—not to Hell-proper, but to someplace *very* close . . . The place reeks of foul, damp ass and burned flesh . . .

Crowley turned and smiled at his demon-guide. "*This* is the site?" The Beast 666 asked, wondering if this assembly was the line awaiting admittance . . .

Standing on the hilt of what some might call a horn, projecting from the wall some fifteen feet high, a boy—drowned in a bathtub by his own mother—was pissing on the crowd; a woman, waving desperately, tongue laving her lips, was screaming, "It's fucking hot down here. What about a drink for me?" . . . Some woman 700 years old was fucking some kind of half-lizard man. There were three-legged things in silk stockings and pierced tongues peering from assholes and horns surgically implanted on foreheads and contaminated lace and tattoos and scars and demon-things of every stripe. This was Asylum-anything, provided warped-with-the-lid-off and entombed in inferno was strictly adhered to. Crowley could have been in some neo-Goth nocturne of noir turned S&M screamfest or in the mind of some painter, bent by dark magic and fractured emotions. But this was Hell, the screams and laughter and cries of the damned souls all attested to the not so plain fact.

"This is a gallery . . . Answer *The Question*—Hardly an inconvenience for a genius like you—and you'll get to the Carnival. Answer not, or falsely"—a big smile—"and you'll receive something *somewhat* different." A bigger smile. "And by the way, the old devil-devil won't work here."

Crowley, like every demanding intelligence who came seeking admission to the Carnival, wondered what would.

The mage's escort laughed a slight, dry laugh. Crowley's disdain roared quietly.

"Of course, if you're not up to the task, there's always the gauntlet."

Crowley waved Forneus's comment off and began walking . . .

Despair sat on a hard back chair, tapping a red ball back and forth between his feet. *Just another Time-killer,* thought Crowley, turning his raven gaze.

"Bet you'd like to fuck her in the ass," Crowley's demon-guide said, pointing to a woman-thing who called herself The Black Pearl.

The Black Pearl licked her robust lips as her vassal, Ickx, continued servicing her. Hunched and pocked, the pus-filled pimples and growths surrounding his nether region popped with each thrust.

"I like mine somewhat . . . cleaner. In this place, or the one we left, a diseased whore is a diseased whore."

"It would be such a shame if you failed and wound up in The Cottage of Pain. Maybe he might assist you?" Forneus said, pointing out the pornographer, Jacob Kite (impresario of anal-this and cum-that and Young/Hungry/Willing-TEEN-everything, Right Here! Right NOW! FREE!), who whilst juggling his spherical fantasies, hurled a childish obscenity at a woman who was suckling a very plump black rat. Forneus smiled and adjusted his crown.

"I rather doubt he's up to counting his fingers and toes."

"But there is always the slim chance, from the mouths of babes, or royally fucked-up idiots, one may discern some inkling."

"Next, I suspect, you'll tell me, Wendy's leaving Pan and coming over to give me a blow job."

"Stranger things have happened. She sure seemed to enjoy that week sailing on Hook's dildo attachment." Forneus laughed.

Crowley almost laughed at the thought of purity finally getting its ass in gear.

"Well, Little Alick, how about asking that one?"

Crowley looked at the thing framed against wallpaper made of insects. Claes, the Bishop of Flesh, rolled his eyes, picked several fat bugs from the wall, quickly popping them in his mouth, and returned to picking lice from his overly large and deformed genitals.

"I might get somewhere if I had a pony, but that pig couldn't find dinner on the end of his spoon."

"We do have timetables here, Little Alick. I'd pick someone to ask."

"Who?" Crowley inquired aloud, while viewing the grotesque throng.

"Ahh . . . Yes, there are so many. Aren't there? Well, which one is the right the one, is the prelude . . . Pick wisely. One chance. Heaven or Hell—haha*haha*hahahahaAHA*HA*HAHAhaha*ha*HA*HA*HAHAHAHAHa . . ."

Crowley picked an expression from the sixteen gathered, gave ear to its question, and dismissed it. He turned to the next, more hallucinatory drivel. After three blistering tears of gibberish, one disdainful glare, five (nearly-comedic) obscenities, three blunt enticements to copulate or use his quick-tongue for something more than an exhibition of *true will,* three invitations to join them for lunch (a raw morsel which yesterday walked on two legs and enjoyed beating his wife on drunken Saturday nights, or whenever the urge itched like a bad burn), and a query from a mummified child who asked if he was his Daddy and why had he deserted him, he paused to ask a question of the questioner.

"Which, personage, would you select to query?" He asked his guide.

"None of course. I'll simply walk the gauntlet." Talons, looking like they belonged on a piece of farm machinery designed for reaping, flexed, as if being readied. "A little blood, sweat, and a scream would attune one rather nicely to the Carnival's festivities I should think," Forneus said.

Crowley turned to the Bishop of Flesh. With the disgusted eye of an artist, he surveyed the man. Crowley had never seen a man, or woman for that matter, so obese. Only the eyes and nose and lips, and the short, womanly fingers, bore a resemblance to human—the rest was a nightmare he'd had as a child after eating a greasy stew. "And you, sir? Have you advice for the skeptic seeking the Next Step?"

"Power . . . It pecks viciously at one, doesn't it? I myself, regard that quest as a thoroughly useless disbursement of one's verve."

"Yes, thank you. And fuck you and the horse you rode in on!"

Crowley comes upon a minstrel, who in a former sphere pulled magic from the Current, the notes of his golden lute gentle as reverent Tibetan candlelight.

"And if I asked you The Question, would you speak of the Inmost Light, or . . . the sadness of things?'

The minstrel strikes a different chord. *"Dead! Dead! Dead! Dead! Dead! Dead! Dead! Dead! Dead!"*

"Yes, you've a point there. All here are, most certainly, dead. For some time, by the look of it."

Forneus laughed so hard he shed a blood tear.

"The clock is ticking, Little Alick. I've other guests who require my attention."

"I've walked through fire before. Where is this gauntlet?"

"Right over there."

"In the Freak Show?"

"We call it the Funhouse here."

"Of course you do."

✸

Under a fiery sky. Under the burning sign:

One free spin of

THE WHEEL OF POWER

Other Games of Chance
(*3 shots a soul*)

stands a certain Caligari, first among Satan's children of Sin and Death, here in this incarnation, the Ringmaster, his tails pointing and lashing. Round and round he waves his top hat cowboy-style. The top two buttons of his bloody, once white, lab coat, pop off.

"Gather round! Gather round! Quiver and Quim, Fine Fryer and Bun Duster! Step right up! . . . Tattlers, cheats, gluttons, sloths, and dog-bones, and those of you didn't give a shit about honesty and jumped head first to err on the side of wickedness, gather round. Gather round! Watch the buffoons BURN! See the Bone Machine tickle the ivories!'

"You dear lady." She looks up. Newly descended and assimilated into this twitching, smoldering mesh of sodomy and unrepentant desolation, she wonders why she's here. "Couldn't get old, Saintly Michael, to give you a good tickle and poke? Fear not, Madame, even the ugly ones can jiggle their wrinkly, fat asses in the party line here—It's a hot one! And I guarantee you'll find lots of comers . . . What's that, Deary? No—no refunds. You've played, now it's *pay* time!"

Caligari stands on the lip of dry, weathered boards, warped, perhaps cast off from some greasy river, and leans down over a tall cadaver.

"And you, sir—I saw your immigration forms, Mr. Igor Maggot, isn't it? Got a small dick? We've a cure for that. Right this way! Oh, no need to feel so shy about it. One of our midgets will think you're hung like an ox. Yes, yes. We've plenty of boys.'

"Step right up! Step right up for *spectacular* thrills! We've Feasts of fire! Feasts of Water! And for those with a sweet tooth, we've Feasts of re-Death—You get to pick how they die the second time!'

"Come one, come all! To the show that *never* ENDS!"

His gloved hand, hiding the cysts of sin, dives into a black moth-wing bag and pulls out fistfuls of pills—reds and yellows and little black ones that will choke you on eXtascy. They rain, along with sweetmeat maggots for the kiddies and redi-packed—with the sharpest poisons—hypodermics for all attending hopeheads. Greedy hands leap. And the master of ceremonies dashes across the stage to pass along some treats of enticement to the hungry, waylaid dogs in the other waiting pen.

"Don't miss out, My Pretties!'

"Come see the Eel-boy wiggle and sizzle in the frying pan! And a Laughing Ass—yes, Hun, it's a big one. No, there's no pinching allowed. If you're really into asses that much, you can kiss the anus of the black goat.'

A diseased crocodile, blinding the hearts and eyes of the dazzled onlookers, Caligari devours the pain leaking from every fettered mouth.

"Or those whose brains dance in the light madness of the lascivious, for you, we have Sweet Young Alice's 21-shows-a-day tea party. See her take on the Caterpillar, The Mad Hatter, the March Hare, The White Rabbit, the Lobster, the Mock Turtle, and each and every Card Guard— You want to see plowed? Well, the Spades know how to dig a furrow." Caligari leans over, hand cupped to the side of his predatory iron lips, and to a trio of bound, cadaverous puss-bags, whispers, "And she might even indulge in a little audience lend-a-hand.'

"Cost, you ask, Sir. The cost? It's merely the two pennies from your eyes.'

"Roll up, Ladies!—You too, you old bag! Roll up! Roll up! Gents, ready your throbbing little weenies! And ready your eyes! Roll up! The show's about to start."

❦

Crowley shook his head and slid his hand in his pocket for the coins.

"No need for that. You may enter for free, Alick."

"And the reason for that is?"

Forneus smiled the blackest smile. "They pay to see The Show. Your gauntlet is today's main attraction. And it just wouldn't be right to charge the performer for his participation, now would it?"

Forneus held the blood-red, tattered tent flap open for Crowley.

And Crowley passed through.

Heat. Raw bleaching heat. The walls of the tent boiled with it.

"It's just through here, Little Alick."

Ever the soul on a mission, Crowley followed Forneus out an opening in the back.

There were bleachers to his left where a crowd was just seating themselves. Women fanned themselves with severed hands. Children found shade under women's skirts or in the shadows of tall men. The men just bitched about the steaming temperature of the sewermaggot Armageddontrashslop they were told was beer.

There was an X of bones on the ground.

"You'll start here," Forneus told Crowley.

"I see no gauntlet to run."

"Walk," Forneus corrected. "Calm you frets. The Boys will be here momentarily. They never miss a performance."

And they came. Werewolves, who rose up on their hind legs to rape history with their unclothed impulses. Werewolves who warmed themselves on cries of pain and drank every shadow and tremor of blood. The Harvesters, here to stricken again with their sticks . . . And their questions.

"Are there rules?" Crowley asked, taking of his shirt.

"One step. One question. Simple as that. Wrong answer you get a whack."

"And on the Other Side?"

"The whole of this carnival-eternal for your pleasure."

Crowley looks into the bitter eyes of his first assailant, takes a step. Face to face.

Judas, dagger tongue glowing: "Jesus or Mary?"

"What?"

"Jesus or Mary?"

Crowley turned, looked to Forneus. Forneus shrugged. Then laughed.

"They ask, you answer. No help-lines here."

"Jesus or Mary?"

"Mary, of course."

Judas stepped back and a fat little demonite did an off with his head.

Crowley booted it aside with his second step.

Hitler: "Jew or Russian?"

"Russian."

The crowd booed and threw oily slimeballs packed with nails and lice at Hitler. Hitler stepped back. Threw his stick to the ground as another fat little demonite swung his machete. His head hit with a dull, wet splat and rolled unevenly.

Rasputin: "Is the cunt of a nun sweeter than an angel's?"

"Yes."

The crowd hisses, calling for his head.

Rasputin steps back. Right into the singing arc of a demonette's axe.

Now there were three pretty, bloody heads in a row.

Crowley sailed through the next five rounds and the next five heads sailed from their shoulders. The audience, thinking Crowley would have been beheaded by the second round, loved it. They clapped, they cheered . . . The more beheadings the merrier.

Forneus' great gray wings shutter with angry disappointment. Feathers, like blighted dandruff, softly sway downward and settle to the ground.

As if someone had rang the dinner bell, singed and pocked rats were pushing and shoving and biting each other in the ass to get one of the heads.

A street junkie, spike still in his arm, a tattoo *Fuck Despair Before IT Fucks You* over his heart: "Is Yes a pleasant country?"

"The poisoner of the common man is Possible."

Answered, abyss traversed. In and through the black gates. And the hungry watchers were retched back to their cramped slats and cubby-holes and burrows. Hisses of disgust ringing like a carrion stench. Crowley smiled triumphantly—and was quick to step lively along the dark path.

"I'll have my pleasures now, thank you."

"Not quite yet, Little Alick. There's one more *little* something to tend to," Forneus said gleefully.

Having forgotten to open his invitation upon passing, Crowley had been wandering the Great Beyond for so long he forgot about the Blood Signing . . . There was one more encounter to come. Crowley thought he was about to face the Lustrous Angel, Satan himself.

Forneus pointed, Crowley turned to face. . .

Stars . . . bright as distant diadems. Gentle twinkling things . . . and approaching, a hand . . . smooth and tender . . .

GROWING . . .

Coming closer . . .

Crowley, stunned, turns to Forneus. From his wet leather cunt of a mouth, Forneus laughs.

There sat the angelic star-child. An infant of pure, untainted skin and eyes wide with tales to astonish. Clear blue eyes, eyes full of wonderment. Countless, golden stars streak his haloed locks. A naked infant, larger than any sun or solar system. And he holds The World on a golden chain, shaking dreams from it.

The Answer born as a vision of the purest innocence . . . The secret to all the gates . . . This child? Here? Crowley wonders.

His mouth is open and desert dry. His thoughts fire, meteors spinning . . . He finds his voice and asks him The Question. "Why are we here?"

The Boy, full of whims, as all children are, hateful of can'ts and damning NO!, smiles a cold smile.

Fangs. Bloody fangs, wet with ghosts and vanished halos. His eyes grow cold, go black.

Crowley shrinks in his skin. Fears The Dream—*all dreams,* are merely This Child's whim.

"All fall down," the infant breathes.

The signs in the stars go silent. Nothing . . . All light, all life, is extinguished.

The boy yawns and puts his thumb in his mouth. He hears the great, soft paradise teat, full of sweet warm milk, coming. His lips are wet with his smile. Hopes the loving hand will clean his burning, itching bottom . . .

Perhaps after his nap he'll play again . . .

(After H. R. Giger's No. 274, *A. Crowley* (The Beast 666), The Moody Blues *every good boy deserves favor,* Emerson, Lake & Palmer's "Karn Evil 9," and Kubrick's *2001: A Space Odyssey*)

Stone Cold Fever

I live just under the radar. I hunt [mostly for money, *but . . .*]. Rats. They run. I don't blink. You hurt a woman or a child, I'm the sharp decree coming to cut off the flow of air that keeps you ticking. You get caught you'll never see your bed again. . . . Hope you've got a taste for worms.

◆

Paulie let me in the Bamboo Club. Lights, NO CAMERAS, smoke. Girls and a brass pole. No clock. Not many words. Plenty of dollar bills. I sat at the end of the bar with a cup of coffee. No milk. No sugar. I was searching for a match when Toni came over and sat down.

"Hi, Handsome." Full moon smile. And that wink. Even yer knees stop breathing. Antonia Zanta; tall, leggy, and curves a snake would die for. And smart. Blond—an Aryan had played backdoor man with one of her ancestors. "You heard about the missing boy on Channel 6?"

"No. I've been parked on a ridge in the woods, watching a meth-shack."

"Katy Cappiello's fourteen-year-old son is missing. Two days ago."

My eyes didn't stop, they went right to, "Do or die!"

Kathy Cappiello.

The name cut fifteen years off my life. I was twenty-two, swinging, mostly with my right. Bleeding. And there were two dead assholes on the floor. In an hour I'd be in Ellis Hospital for a two week stay. The first of many conversations with the cops would happen there too. I don't think I'd been awake for an hour the first time they started asking me questions I've now heard over and over and over. I'm not sayin' the cops are bad—hell, they try, but they're limited.

We had a band in high school. The Blind Lovers Blues Band; our logo was a bleeding heart with an eye patch over the spot where the heart would be if the heart had a heart. We played in basements and at the high school three times. Hans played guitar. Paul played organ. Mike pounded on the drums and Dom played bass. I sang; I wasn't good, but a few girls smiled at me. You take what you can get.

Kathy was at every show. And she smiled. But she was too young and her older sister, Pam, made sure I knew it.

Eight months after we formed, Hans and Dom went off to college, Mike got a welding job and a baby, and Paul headed to California. I went on a tour with a bunch of we-know-nuthin' kids in Southeast Asia. We learned a lot. Don't believe me, read Marc Baker's book, he laid it out straight in 'NAM. Yeah, we learned a lot. Some of us even came home.

Hard. Lean. Gritty and sacred, I came back to the World at twenty-two. [They said The War was over, you can lie down now—I told them to kiss my ass.] Drank some beer. Got a job to pay for the one room dump my landlord called an apartment and my bar tab. Four months later I got some new friends. I still have them.

One night I walked by a boarded-up, abandoned two-family that was on the city blocks for back taxes and heard a girl scream. I've got a very hard, very mean Thing when it comes to hurting girls. I was in the building pulling five Nazi creeps off Kathy's older sister. There was beer and smoke. There was a radio (to this I hear "30 Days in the Hole" and the world goes red), and feverish evil. There was a lot of blood. Learned my lessons well In Country. And I've got the scars—and a Purple Heart—to prove it.

Pam didn't get out of there alive. She's still breathing, but hiding in a dark corner in a sanitarium for the last fifteen years. That ain't being alive. If you think so, go fuck yourself. Kathy was there too. Locked in a closet; she was to be dessert or the finale. They never got a hand on her. I saw to that. But she's got scars. You don't walk through the fields where the plague burns and walk out without dripping with New Truth. You didn't then, you don't now.

Kathy and I went out once, but the screams got in the way . . . She got married and had two sons. Her baby was missing . . .

Two days and all the cops had was his bike. You hurt a woman or a child . . .

"You're her, Lancelot. Unrequited perhaps, but you've always been her savior."

I put my cigarette out in my coffee. "Call, Shade. Tell him to bring, Shadow."

Toni smiled. We were going hunting.

❖

"Ain't been strapped all week." He touched the .38. Touched like it was his girlfriend. "Startin' ta feel like myself again. Who and What?" Shade asked.

I told him about the boy. And if there was a Who, well, he knew The What.

"Got pictures of the boy, Boss?" Shadow asked.

Toni handed the boys three new pictures of Kathy's son, Frankie. Shadow, put his finger on the boy's cheek. Stroked it. I watched his eyes narrow. He'd walked the dark road. We never talked about it, but I knew; Toni knew somebody who knew something and what Toni knows, I know. With Shadow, you touch a child, you paid—full up. Shade leaned the three pictures of Frankie against the cups and glasses sitting on the bar, so the light washed on him like he was an angel. Ever the poet at heart, Our Shade.

"Gone two days. Not good." His eyes said the same thing. And more . . . Shade was pissy when he was working. Anything that pulled him away from his headphones—always filled with Satie or Eno or spatial drifts of quietude—pissed him off.

I laid out the plan. We parted. Left our coffee to grow cold. Gathering before the hunt. Shadow on the phone to his connection at the police department. Toni over to Kathy's in search of anything. Shade was on the other phone, calling in favors. The curtains to the underground were open. And we weren't waiting in any line with forms in our hands . . .

Me. I hit the Street. A thousand eyes. A thousand ears. And many of them know me, owe me. And those that don't have heard the whisper stream in certain bars. In an hour, they'd know this one was personal and I was doing hard time. The cops—hell, they try, but they're limited.

❂

Frankie had just gotten into gaming and had a new set of friends. His game of choice, Call of Cthulhu. I hit The Wizard's Keep in the strip mall on Union Ave. Showed the pictures. Got "Yes, sirs" and "Not this week." Got a book on the game. Left my number. Called Toni. "Bring the boys home."

Thirty minutes later we were the back alleys and starlit chambers of la-la-land gone tomb black and dangerous. In a room over the MEN's restroom of the Bamboo Club we read. Of Those Who Dwell and The Chaos That Crawls. Of Unholy Dimensions and Bitter Black Pits Opened. It looked like young Frankie had left baseball and cartoons behind to go walking in the dark realms of oblivion. We hammered the phones. Coffee and cigarettes were served.

Day 2 of nuthin'. The phone rang. Some of the kids hung around a rotting old bungalow near the old Maqua Company. Might be a kiddie-raper? The kids say no, but . . . he gives them pot and beer. Some kind of Satanist or something . . .

Shadow checked him out with his police connection. Not on the sex offender list. No record. Seems clean. "Fuck that." I heard him whisper. He could smell corruption two galaxies away. "All fuckin' fits." Had his jacket on and his hand on the doorknob before we were out of ours chairs.

Ten-minute drive. Around the block three times. Shade was out of the car and walking by the house. His inner mystic eye was wide open, his antennae up. Half a block down he hit the bushes and skipped out back fer the looky-see. We parked in a convenience store lot two blocks away. Shade went in and bought smokes, a candy bar, and a map. As long as the illusion makes sense it works. Safe for maybe twenty minutes.

"I'd feel a hell of a lot safer in the dark," Shade said. "I've got this deal with darkness." His smile was thin. "Three open windows. Just cracked for air. Dark curtains. Hard to tell what lies on the inside. Good news is the locks are old junk," he said, throwing his binoculars to Shadow. "If there's no bar on the door in in ten seconds tops. A TV's on—all news by the sound of it."

Toni skipped the round of hard question we were about to throw around and got out of the car and dialed the number Shade had. "A man answered, said there's no Helen here. We know he's home."

"Fuckin' all rumor and hearsay. Could just be a weirdo—fuckin' Michael Jackson complex, or something."

"Fuck that! This one's right. Maybe the kid's not in there, but this assbag ain't right. Smells like a tuna boat loaded to the gills and parked in the middle of the Sahara."

I looked in those eyes that never laid down for any savage and knew he was right on this. He was comin' at it straight on righteous.

Shade, you play backdoor man. Shadow, the window by the bushes on the right. I'll ring the bell. When I'm in, you come. Not before."

Toni eyes said fuck.

"Not this time, darlin'. Someone has to be clean on this. If he's the monster we think he is and we can't get out clean, we're gonna need cash and lawyers. You're the brains, you save our asses if we get bogged down."

She blew me a kiss. We'd never, but it was there between us. "If you don't come home, you're in the deepest shit you've ever seen. Understand?"

"Yes, ma'am." I knew she meant it. Just for a second the word home put it arms around me . . . After all these years? Maybe . . . but not now.

She was gone and we were moving. The boys are lean and fast. At any speed they move like the sound of dust. Even that guy on the Rainbow Bridge who can hear the grass grow wouldn't hear 'em coming. They were gone before my hand was on the rusting chain-link fence. I was dressed causal, black slacks, black shoes, turtleneck and jacket, so I could play salesman. It was dark, but not too late for sales types to ring doorbells. Odds were he'd open the door. I was glad I'd shaved this morning.

I put my friendly face on. Adjusted it. Moved Toni's black portfolio to my left hand. Shoulder hostler unsnapped. Safety off. Ready. Willing. And Able. If this fuck was wrong, he could bet the farm and everything on this side of Hell on Willing and Able.

I hit the porch slow and even. Dim lights on inside. Candles? No shapes in the windows. But there was flickering. The TV? A bit of color, it seemed right. I pushed the doorbell. Waited. Forty seconds. Reasonable. I pushed it again. On the phone? On the shitter? Just not going to answer? 35 . . . 36 . . . 37 . . . The door didn't open. Sometimes when you're doing hard time you do it the hard way. I kicked it in. I could apologize and throw some cash around later if need pressed me.

All the trappings of the Call of Cthulhu game we'd run through earlier hit me. The place was a cavern of dead souls, of life unmade. Not being a big fan of any kind of horror, I didn't have the words or the experience to translate all the shit that boiled in this unholy mindfuck ripping at my eyes. Demon faces—masks?—on the walls. And what looked really human skulls. Posters and diagrams printed in the depths of Hell. There was a stone with a painted goat's skull on it . . .

Four lightning steps in and I saw him in the dining area that opened on what should be, in any normal house, the living room. He turned—whipped around. Black robes with weird markings, like some haywire wizard from an old horror film. A bloody knife in his hand. A dead boy. Frankie. The boy I was here to save. A dead boy on an old door on two sawhorses. Less than twenty feet from the carnage I could see the child's torso was ripped wide open. There was a fucking candle burning in his belly were his guts should be.

"What?" Was all the monster got out.

I put the first hollow point in his gut to take him down. He was on his knees. He'd dropped the knife. Six steps. Quick. I was too hot to wait for the kill. I pressed the Glock to his forehead. "Think yer goin' to some kind of heaven you rotten fuck. Think again, 'cause this is where you get flushed." And right there he knew it. I doubt his mother had ever told him anything plainer. His lips parted. "Fuck you, Asshole." Before he could beg, or pray.

Shade was coming out of the kitchen. Shadow out if a bedroom. But it was over. Over. Bloody. Their eyes said it all.

I've got a fuckin' $750 watch and I was late again. All these years later and I was going to see another innocent boy go into a bag. If you think The War's over, then go fuck yourself! Until we stop putting kids in bags, nothing's over. Not even close!

✹

We dealt with the cops and the prosecutor. We went in on a hunch and things got messy. Got slapped around. Threatened and bruised. But the Assistant D.A. knew where public opinion would drop once word of the horror scene got around (People may be fucked up these days, but when it came to psycho-fuck cannibals ripping the guts out of babies they probably just defiled, well, give 'em what they gave and then some!)—and there were only two shots—mine—and he had a knife; self defense pure and simple. And the Assistant D.A. knew my best friend was Toni and her sister was the State Attorney General's wife. In the end they didn't even put out a hit out on my P.I. license.

✹

Ten steps up to that door. That sad door. Shade and Shadow stood by the car smoking. They had no words. Feelings, but no words. Toni had her arm in mine. I rang the doorbell and tried to breathe . . .

Her face was older, strained. Eyes red, stained by the smoke and searing heat of the fires of Hell. But it was the same eyes and the same face from all those years ago. And between us . . . there were the screams.

I hugged Kathy. She hugged me back as she cried. This was the second time I failed her. More screams between us. Her tears burned my heart. I hadn't recovered from the tears she shed for her sister yet and . . . That piece of shit was dead, but that wasn't good enough. Not even close! Anytime The Devil wants me to sign, I won't even stop to blink.

There weren't a lot of words. No need for 'em when you share that pain. Brothers, or families, in arms, in ruin, in tragedy, when Truth comes in in its black boots and kicks you awake, means you all carry the load. And it hurts. Deep as any hell.

❋

Toni summed it up for a reporter after it was over. Some horror writer named Lovecraft, sixty years ago, made up this fictional mythology about terrible monster-gods who were waiting to come back from some unnamed hell and clear the Earth. This Lovecraft had a black bible of poisonous sex magic and blood called the *Necronomicon*. It in lay the directions to set them free. And this wacko-fuck had taken it to heart and was planning to free them to ravage and ruin. Not in My Town, motherfucker! See this Glock? It knows where you live!

Your wanderings lead you to hurt a woman or a child. I don't blink.

(this one's for Stan & Jack & the FF! Make Mine MARVEL!!)

my THANKS*! !!* to:

beelzeBOB Price for about 10,000,000 things! !!
ST.anley C. Sargent who kept at me the way gOOd friends will!
Victoria Price who made me "bloom" again.
Tom Brown who always BELIEVED. And da COVER! !!
Ankh [Ann K.] Schwader for her friendship! and helpful comments! !
a certain *Mr. Wilum Hopfrog Pugmire, Esq.* who helped get me out
    West.
Jarred Wallace who had his talons in my journey West.
Sarah Gerhardt for being the bEst nursemaid.
Alanna, Mistress of the Yellow Chamber, for being such a charming
    deadgirl.
Brian Lumley for his kindness!
Jeffery Thomas who liked my stuFF right out of the box.
Michael Cisco who pushed me to other districts.
Peter Worthy who was supportive when others were not.
Susan McAdam for the talks, many an inspiration, and never laughing.
Leslie Joshi for the event without knives or rope that rescued "AEWKOR"
    from the deleted bin.
Derrick Hussey for going along w/ S. T.'s idea & a wonderful day in NYC.
S. T. Joshi for asking & editing & the intro.

And always, with LOVE, to J, who never laughs too loud.

And to Stan Lee & Jack Kirby, Steve "Dr. Strange" Ditko, Philip Laman-
tia, Robert Bloch! !!, *Robert W. Chambers*!! ! ! !!, the Brothers Quay, Al-
fred Hitchcock, Clark Howard, Lester Dent, Hammett & Spillane, Henri
Michaux, LIN CARTER, Harlan Ellison, Frank Zappa, Bob Dylan,
Weather Report, and Brian Eno, my undying thanks for the many things
you poured into this cauldron I call a brain! !!

                                            With admiration & respect
                                                    & love,
                                                        a bEast

As I am uncomfortable with this bio thing, I'll let an old bio Bob Price was kind enough to pen speak for me. It's not completely up to date, but I guess it covers the basics well enough . . .

"Joseph S. Pulver, Sr., a life-long fan of pulp horror, fantasy, and science fiction, found himself exiled from a happy anonymity as of 1999 when Chaosium, Inc. published his highly acclaimed Cthulhu Mythos novel *Nightmare's Disciple*. Though these days he writes mostly Surrealist poetry, his effectively chilling fiction and verse has appeared in collections including *The Book of Eibon, Nameless Cults, Lin Carter's Anton Zarnak, Occult Detective, Rehearsals for Oblivion,* and many others. He has received several honorable mentions in Ellen Datlow's *Year's Best Fantasy & Horror.* Joe also edited Ann K. Schwader's verse collection *The Worms Remember* (2001)."

—*Robert M. Price, 9/07*